"As a native of the Deep South, I found *Folly* to be a true delight. The character of Simp Magee is dead-on, especially for anyone who ever listened to a family member ranting about squirrels in the pecan trees, in the fig trees, or in the attic. Simp's political leanings, how he acquired them and how he embraces them with his entire being, made the character even more vivid. Peripheral characters all have motivations that ring true and the writing style evokes Grisham, with a dash of Clyde Edgerton. An excellent read and a genuinely entertaining debut."

—Rysa Walker, author of
the CHRONOS Files series
and the Delphi Trilogy

FOLLY

Daniel Holliday
FOLLY

BELLE ISLE BOOKS
www.belleislebooks.com

Copyright © 2022 by Daniel Holliday

No part of this book may be reproduced in any form or by any electronic or mechanical means, or the facilitation thereof, including information storage and retrieval systems, without permission in writing from the publisher, except in the case of brief quotations published in articles and reviews. Any educational institution wishing to photocopy part or all of the work for classroom use, or individual researchers who would like to obtain permission to reprint the work for educational purposes, should contact the publisher.

ISBN: 978-1-953021-94-6
LCCN: 2022910144

Project managed by Mary-Peyton Crook

Printed in the United States of America

Published by
Belle Isle Books (an imprint of Brandylane Publishers, Inc.)
5 S. 1st Street
Richmond, Virginia 23219

BELLE ISLE BOOKS
www.belleislebooks.com

belleislebooks.com | brandylanepublishers.com

*For the Hollidays—Miriam, Josephine, and Shirley—
whose smiles and laughter make life a special treat.*

And for our editors: Laura Markowitz, a vivacious yet patient talent who has a muse of her own; Matthew Miller, who helped us rediscover the original structure of the narrative; and Mary Crook, who led us the rest of the way through the wilderness.

Thanks to the entire Holliday clan, and a thousand thank-yous to all our many teachers and friends for your kindness and inspiration. A special thanks to our early readers and supporters: Robert and Anne McElvaine, Todd Neumann, Lecia Mauer, Denise White; and to Robert Barth for his encouragement.

CHAPTER 1

Ezra Magee had a sudden premonition that he was about to break his neck. Standing at the top of the stairs, he became queasy as he watched the once-fixed staircase begin to move and twist in menacing undulations. Not once in ten years had his staircase—or any other, for that matter—moved with such murderous intent, but then there was a first time for everything. He considered going back to bed, but the bourbon was in the kitchen, and he desperately needed another shot to steady himself, the hair of the dog to right how wrong he felt.

He gripped the banister and took the first step, landing heavily. The floorboard creaked, and Ezra froze, one foot suspended in midair. It wasn't that the sound itself was unusually loud. What made the creak so jarring was the absence of any other sound in the house: the clink of spoon on cereal bowl, the easy murmur of mother and child, the scramble of dog paws across hardwood floors. Ezra chose not to stand there contemplating the silence. He walked down the stairs, step by careful step, choosing instead to focus on the rhythm that pounded in his head.

Once in the living room, Ezra sagged against the front door. Squinting through the sidelight, he saw a heap of newspapers on the porch. The one on top was fatter than usual. *It must be Sunday*, he thought. Where the hell had the week gone? The booze made his fingers unreliable, but he fumbled with the lock until it clicked, then opened the door and breathed in the muggy West Virginia perfume of hay and mildew with overtones of pine. The summer air made him crave a cigarette.

His front lawn featured a variety of knee-high plant life, more weeds than grass. The soldierly row of pink, orange, and white impatiens that lined the front walk had browned and withered. The planters by the mailbox were filled with the petunias Celia usually kept blooming well into autumn—petunias that were now dead before the Fourth of July.

After Ezra stepped out onto the front porch and closed the door behind him, he saw the green minivan backing out of the driveway across the street. The McCarthy family was heading to church. Hoping they hadn't spotted him, Ezra frantically searched for the untied belt of his bathrobe and, failing to find it, clutched the robe closed in front with one hand. He combed his free hand through his unruly mop of brown hair. The last thing he wanted right now was to engage in neighborly small talk with Chip McCarthy or—even worse—his wife, Sally, who was a close acquaintance of Celia's.

Lucky for him, they were in a hurry and only tooted the horn and waved. When they turned the corner, Ezra let go of his bathrobe and bent over to pick up the newspapers. The swift movement flipped Ezra's stomach, and he opened his mouth and unleashed most of the previous night's alcohol onto the welcome mat. Head spinning, he braced himself on the handrail and wondered how he'd managed to sink so low.

Until a few months ago, Ezra had only experienced two memorable hangovers in his forty years: the first one during his senior year of college—he could no longer remember what had motivated him to drink an entire bottle of Jack Daniels—and the second one the morning after his bachelor party.

A water hose was coiled around a bracket on the west side of the house. Still weak and lightheaded, Ezra stumbled slowly toward it, grabbed the nozzle, and turned on the aggressive spray to wash the stink off the front porch. As soon as he reached the front steps again, dizziness overtook him, and he dropped to his knees and released the hose, which began spraying water wildly across the front steps. He put his head in his hands and moaned. Could he be any more pathetic?

If recent history was any indication, the answer, depressingly, was yes.

Soon after he had first been hired to teach history at Cunningham College, Ezra had attended the dean's annual start-of-the-semester faculty party. Toward the end of the evening, the chair of the Sociology Department, well into his cups, had climbed onto the living room coffee table and proclaimed his loathing for everyone in the room. The sociologist had then unzipped his pants and proceeded to piss on a potted palm. The dean had remained remarkably composed throughout the incident, but Ezra heard her say to the provost, "Let's hope we have just witnessed Dr. Foster hitting bottom, because if he goes any lower, I will have to take a swing at him."

Ezra had prayed he would never sink to such drunken misbehavior, but slumped over on his porch, face-to-face with his befouled welcome mat, he knew it was too late.

He stayed on his knees and barely managed to hold the hose as he rinsed most of the vomit off. Then he walked very slowly to turn the hose back off. He couldn't stomach the thought of a neighbor finding him in this condition, so he stumbled back inside and gently shut the door. He walked through the formal dining room, which was rarely used, and into the kitchen. He needed to rinse out his mouth, but he also needed a shot of bourbon—especially once he saw the man sitting at his table.

Ezra froze, rubbing his bloodshot eyes. He turned away, took a deep breath, counted to three, and looked back. Sitting at the kitchen table, staring out the window, was a balding man in his sixties or seventies. He wore a rumpled blue serge suit, and although Ezra couldn't immediately place the man, he looked vaguely familiar. Ezra walked to the faucet, turned on the cold water, and splashed his face. He cupped his hand, filled it with water, and rinsed out his sour mouth. He turned slowly back toward the table. The man was still there, now leaning back with his hands folded comfortably on his paunch. Ezra homed in on the man's wide tie, a chaos of stripes and plaids in painful dissonance.

In a flash, the man's name tumbled down the long tunnel of Ezra's memory, and before he had a chance to collect his twisted thoughts, he blurted out, "Jesus Christ. Reverend Johnson, is that really you?"

Ezra suddenly remembered he was standing before a man of the cloth, but it was too late to rescind taking the Lord's name in vain.

"Mornin', Ezra," Reverend Johnson said. He spoke with a calm, neighborly casualness, as if it were the most natural thing in the world to be sitting, uninvited, at someone's kitchen table. "How 'bout some coffee?"

"Uh, okay. Sure." Ezra's confusion propelled him to do as he was asked, so he filled the kettle and set it on the stove, then rummaged around the cupboard for a jar of instant coffee.

Ezra tried some arithmetic—how old was the reverend? His brain refused to work out the math. What was the reverend doing in West Virginia? Seeing the preacher made Ezra think of his father; not a memory (he didn't have many of those) but a feeling. Had his dad and the reverend been friends? Was the old guy even real? How did Ezra even remember his name?

"What brings you by this morning, Reverend?" Ezra asked as he grabbed a crumbled piece of paper off the counter and shoved it into an open drawer.

"You plan on readin' that?" Reverend Johnson gestured to the drawer.

Ezra blushed but chose not to respond. He didn't want to talk about the contents of the sheet of paper, and since Reverend Johnson had not answered his question, Ezra felt they were on equal footing. He waited in silence for the water to boil, rinsing out two mugs from the sink stacked full of dirty dishes. Ezra still believed Reverend

Johnson might simply disappear, but he was nonetheless self-conscious about the mess and began to load the dishwasher. Once it was full, he put in some soap and pressed the "on" button to start the load. The dishwasher's cat-like purr added a pleasant normality to an unpleasant, abnormal morning. And, odd as it was to have Reverend Johnson in his house, Ezra was glad for the company. He had a sense that he'd once been fond of the man, but he couldn't recall why.

"I hope you take it black," Ezra said, pouring the hot water over the coffee crystals. The quart of milk had gone sour ten days ago, and Ezra still hadn't found the time or energy to shop for groceries. Reverend Johnson didn't answer, so Ezra put the cup of steaming coffee down on the table in front of him and searched for Celia's sugar bowl in the kitchen cabinets. It was there, but it was empty. He wondered if he should offer Reverend Johnson a shot of bourbon in his brew. Ezra craved one himself, but he wasn't comfortable reaching for the bottle while Reverend Johnson was watching.

The reverend nodded his head toward the cigarette butts spilling out of a saucer and onto the kitchen table, and Ezra could have sworn that the saucer moved. "Does Celia know you're smokin' again?"

As the reverend spoke, Ezra noticed an almost iridescent glow emanating from behind the old man's head. But that glow was less surprising than hearing him speak Ezra's wife's name aloud, as if he knew a damned thing about her. Reverend Johnson had never been in their home. In fact, Ezra couldn't remember the last time he'd seen the old man.

Ezra peered closely at the reverend's face. A stubby bristle glistened over his chin and jaws. A prominent mole with hairs emerging graced his right cheek.

"You gonna read it?" Reverend Johnson asked again, pointing to the drawer. The dome of his bald head glistened in the invading sunlight.

Ezra took a sip of the fresh coffee and burned his tongue. He had read the note nearly two weeks ago. He didn't need to read it again.

The words were etched into his memory with the acid of regret. Even with the note tucked inside a drawer, he could picture Celia's penmanship, as precise as the handiwork of a medieval monk laboring over vellum manuscripts in a dim monastery scriptorium.

"Ezra? You're avoidin', boy. Go on and read it."

It was obvious that Reverend Johnson wasn't going to stop pestering him about the note. Ezra set down his coffee cup and took the note from the drawer, smoothing out the wrinkled ball into its original form. Without being asked, he knew Reverend Johnson wanted him to read the note aloud, and Ezra didn't see a point to arguing with what just might be a figment of his own imagination.

"'Ezra,'" he read, "'we're going to stay with Mother. Your drunkenness is intolerable, as is your refusal to talk about the changes that have come over you these last few months. I don't want Dillon around you when you're like this. He doesn't need any more stress just now and neither do I. I am at the end of my rope. I will not stay here and watch you destroy yourself. Your behavior is selfish and immature. Your son needs you and so do I. But unless you stop drinking, don't contact us. Celia.'"

The first time he'd read the note, and the hundreds of times he'd read it since, Celia's words were a knife constructed of his own guilt and grief, stabbing him repeatedly and endlessly. The note hadn't improved with age. He crumpled it up again and tossed it on the counter.

"There you go, old man. Satisfied?" Ezra rubbed the stubble on his chin and took another sip of coffee.

"Hmmm," Reverend Johnson said, scrutinizing him. "Celia's gone to stay with her mother. Took Dillon with her. Left you to ol' John Barleycorn."

John Barleycorn? Ezra hadn't heard that term for alcohol since he'd read Jack London's autobiography as a teenager.

"You got a problem with the drink, son," Reverend Johnson continued, nodding. "I oughta know."

There it was again, a hazy remembrance from his lost childhood: Reverend Johnson had been a well-known binge drinker. It had been the local church congregation's worst-kept secret. It was an impossible memory. Was it even real? Ezra shook his head, as if a door to the past was opening in his mind and he was trying to shake more of it out.

Ezra surveyed the preacher. Binge-drinker or not, the good reverend looked stone-cold sober.

"Admitting you have a problem is the first step."

Ezra's irritation reached a boiling point, but he still couldn't bring himself to yell "fuck off" at his childhood reverend, whether or not the man was real. "It wasn't just the drinking," said Ezra, with some hesitation. "We were having problems."

"Problems?"

"With Dillon. He's going through a hard time right now."

"Looks like you are too." Reverend Johnson gestured toward the collection of empty beer and bourbon bottles on the counter.

Ezra pulled a cigarette from his robe pocket, walked over to the stove, and lit it on the gas range's pilot light. His hands shook as he quietly pulled the smoke into his lungs. Until Celia had left him, he'd never smoked in the house, but now he couldn't see why the hell he shouldn't. He could do whatever he damn well pleased. Hell, if he wanted to, he could lie in bed smoking every night. He could drink and smoke and fall asleep with the ashes still red and dripping from the butt of his cigarette. *I could even burn the damned house down*, he thought in a surge of anger before settling into a flush of shame.

Ezra leaned with his back against the counter and stared at the refrigerator. On its front was a photo of Celia, Dillon, and himself from last year's summer vacation at Aunt Lenore's cabin. The three of them were a step away from jumping off the dock and splashing into the lake. Ezra studied the figures in the photo. They were smiling and holding hands. The guy wearing his face looked happy.

"So, what happened to him?" asked Reverend Johnson.

☙

It had started with a nightmare. Five months before Reverend Johnson came to visit, Ezra had awoken to the sound of his son moaning in terror. The bedside clock read 2:11 a.m. Celia was going through one of her bouts of insomnia that week, so she'd taken a sleeping pill before bed. Ezra was on kid duty. He eased quietly out of bed and went to investigate.

The hallway's dim light cast a soft glow into Dillon's room. The eleven-year-old lay stiffly on his back, blankets and pillows kicked to the floor. The boy's eyes were wide open, staring unseeing at the ceiling. Ezra could tell Dillon was struggling to wake from a nightmare. His small hands were clenched into fists at his sides. He whimpered and cried out in a strangled voice as the invisible terrors pursued him. Ezra rushed to his side and crouched beside the bed.

"It's okay. I'm right here," Ezra whispered. He picked up one of Dillon's pillows from the floor, then lifted the boy's head and put it back down on the soft rectangle. He re-tucked the blanket around his son. Carefully, he wiped the tears off Dillon's cheeks with the edge of the sheet. "You can wake up now, son," Ezra murmured in the soft Southern accent that had stayed with him from his Alabama youth. "It's okay to wake up now, champ."

Dillon didn't respond. Ezra swept the boy's dark brown hair from his sweaty forehead. The hair usually contrasted beautifully with the bright green eyes he'd inherited from his mother, but tonight they made his skin look ghostly.

"Hey, buddy! Wake up!"

Dillon's breathing became increasingly panicked as his glazed eyes continued to stare at the ceiling. "It's okay," Ezra said, exchanging his harsh tone for a soothing one. "Take your time. Come back when you can. I'm waiting for you right here, and so is Bananas." Dillon's eyes closed. Ezra looked at Bananas, Dillon's favorite stuffed animal, a raggedy monkey that sat on the windowsill. The boy placed him there each night before bed to stand watch and keep him safe from the bad things that lurked outside his window.

"Bananas is wonderin' when you plan on taking him down to see his family in the jungles of Costa Rica." Ezra was talking just to talk, to give Dillon something to grab on to, to reel him back from the nightmare. He continued to stroke his son's hair. "Don't worry. Everything is okay."

It felt like an eternity before Dillon finally relaxed and resumed the slow, steady breathing of deep sleep. Ezra checked the bedside clock: 2:45 a.m.

He sat quietly on the edge of the boy's bed. He wasn't ready to leave him, in case the dream started up again. The soaring pine tree outside Dillon's window rustled in the February breeze, and one of the needle clusters raked against a windowpane. Ezra relaxed, the peaceful sound and the cozy mess of his child's room soothing his nerves. Celia made Dillon pick up his clothes every night, but a stack of comic books remained by the bed, topped with his favorite book about astronomy.

Dillon had inherited his affinity for the sky from Ezra. A mobile of rocket ships hung in the corner of the boy's room, and Ezra watched the paper ships turning slowly in the soft breeze from the air vent above it. The Bell X-1 was Dillon's favorite. A few nights ago, he'd recited the story to Ezra of how West Virginia pilot Captain Chuck Yeager, who was first to break the sound barrier in flight, flew a Bell X-1 he had named "Glamorous Glinnis" after his wife. Dillon loved to brag to his best friend that his dad had a pilot's license, and that one day Dillon was going to learn how to fly just like Ezra.

Dillon always kept one eye up, hoping to catch a glimpse of something magnificent in the air. Getting the boy to bed in summer was a constant battle. Night after night, he begged for five more minutes to lie on the lawn and stargaze. There was an eight-inch Dobsonian telescope wrapped up and hidden away in the garage, ready for Dillon's birthday the following week.

Ezra looked back down at his son's pale face and felt the cold grip of dread settle in his gut. That nightmare wasn't normal, but it also wasn't unfamiliar. When he was Dillon's age, his own night terrors had haunted him with dreams so intense that he'd often been afraid to go to sleep.

At that point, Ezra didn't know what he thought about God, but he offered up a silent prayer to the night, asking God to spare his son the hell that was consuming him.

Dillon seemed tired the next day, but he was otherwise normal. Ezra didn't ask him about the nightmare, and neither one of them mentioned it to Celia. After school, Dillon kicked a soccer ball around the yard with his best friend, Wiley, and after dinner complained about having too many math problems for homework. Ezra was relieved that his son seemed fine, but he slept lightly that night, listening for Dillon's cry. None came. After a few nights, Ezra relaxed and allowed himself to sleep deeply again.

A week later, Dillon changed his mind about going to the movies for his birthday. He had lobbied hard all week for permission to see a PG-rated movie with Wiley, and after days of listening to his begging, Celia had finally relented. His sudden change of heart on the morning of his birthday confused and concerned her.

"Why don't you want to go?" Celia asked.

"Leave me alone!" Dillon shouted as he ran up the stairs and into his room. He had been moody all day, had barely looked at his new telescope, and didn't want Wiley to come over for cake. Celia was baffled.

"What has gotten into him?" she asked Ezra, who just shrugged. In the pit of his stomach, Ezra knew it had something to do with the nightmare, and his body filled with dread.

The next week, Dillon didn't want to sleep over at Wiley's,

something the boys had done frequently since kindergarten. Celia wondered aloud to Ezra if Dillon might be outgrowing Wiley, but then Dillon said he didn't want to go out for Friday night pizza, which was always a high point of his week. He gave no explanation and offered only a shrug when Celia asked why. A few days later, when Celia reminded him to bring home the spring soccer sign-up form, he told her he wasn't going to play.

In what seemed like an instant, Dillon's eager, happy expression had become anxious and wary. Celia sat him down one day after school and asked him if anyone had done something or said anything to upset him. Dillon's face turned red as he clenched his fists and yelled at his mother that the only thing wrong in his life was her unwillingness to leave him alone. Then, as quickly as his rage arrived, it dissipated. Dillon burst into tears and ran to his room. It was as if someone had opened a window inside his body to let the rage escape, to make room for the real Dillon to return. He was contrite for a few days after that, but the same anger returned when she asked him why he'd given up his audition slot for the role of swordfighter in the school play.

"Leave me alone!" became his standard answer to his parents' questions. Celia took it hard. He'd always been a sweet boy, but he was changing. She sent him to his room and took away his television and video game privileges for a week.

On the third day of his punishment, Dillon came down to breakfast, arranged himself in his seat as noisily as possible, and established a hard glare at his mother. Ezra hid behind his newspaper and watched his son and his wife give each other a wide berth. Ezra reached over and poured Cheerios into Dillon's bowl.

"Eat up, son. You're running late."

Dillon tapped three fingers from his right hand on his right cheek and counted to nine under his breath. Then he repeated the gesture with his left hand on the left side of his face. Most days it would have simply annoyed Ezra, a childish delay tactic at the breakfast table, but the icy coolness and methodical way Dillon repeated the tapping scared him.

"Dillon, quit fooling around and eat your cereal," Celia said.

It was the wrong thing to say. Dillon jumped out of his chair and ran upstairs. Ezra could almost feel the boy's bedroom door slam seconds before it echoed through the house. Celia pushed up from the table and ran upstairs after him. Following a few minutes of muffled shouting, the two came back down looking no less tense or angry.

Dillon sat down again and repeated the tapping, this time counting to twelve. Then he picked up the spoon and shoveled cereal into his mouth. Ezra stared at Dillon, who was moving his head from side to side, but he refused to meet his father's eye.

"Dillon, I'm warming up the car," Celia said. "Get your shoes on and let's go. No dawdling!" She walked out the back door and let it slam behind her.

Dillon swallowed the spoonful of cereal in his hand, then shoved his homework into his backpack. He stomped to the foyer, grabbed his sneakers, and jammed his feet into them without untying the laces.

"Bye, champ!" Ezra said. "Learn something gross today and tell us all about it at supper tonight, okay?"

Dillon didn't answer. He'd frozen in place at the back door, the same way he did the first time he'd walked to the ledge of the high dive at the swimming pool. He reached up and tapped the left side of the doorframe with his right hand six times in succession, then six times with his left hand on the right side of the doorframe. Then he shuffled his feet in an odd dance and counted to thirty-three by threes.

"Come on!" Celia yelled as she honked the horn. "We haven't got time for your games. We're late!"

Dillon lost count, and his frustration and embarrassment shone in the deep red flush in his cheeks. Tears filled his eyes, and he started the whole sequence from the beginning.

Ezra gripped the edge of the table. This new tick seemed to have developed overnight. It was as if something had been unlocked inside of his son during sleep, something that had forcefully integrated itself into Dillon's routines. It turned Ezra's stomach. He wanted to believe Dillon was just going through a phase; that his odd behavior didn't mean anything. But he couldn't. Ezra knew exactly what it meant, because it had meant the same thing to him when he was a child.

But when Celia asked him what he thought was going on with their son, Ezra was too afraid to speak the truth out loud. All he could say was, "I don't know."

For the next few days, Dillon was quiet. Celia was careful not to ask him questions. They did their best to walk through their usual steps. Ezra brought pizza home on Friday night, and the family played a miserable game of *Monopoly*. On Saturday, however, Dillon barricaded himself in his room after breakfast.

"What's going on?" Ezra asked, coming back from a run and finding Celia waiting for him on the back porch. Her face looked somehow older, more tired, as if the stress of Dillon's newfound defiance had finally pushed her into middle age.

"Last month, Dillon said he'd go to a Mountaineers game with Wiley," Celia explained. "They bought him a ticket, but now he refuses to go. Wiley is devastated! And Dillon refuses talk about why he won't go. Would you please talk to him?"

Ezra didn't want to talk about it, not with his wife nor his son. But he nodded and quickly climbed the stairs, his heart rate spiking as he knocked on Dillon's door.

"Go away!"

"You love basketball!" Ezra said through the closed door. He tried the handle and found that Dillon had locked it. Ezra's head pressed into the hard wood barrier between him and his son.

"I'm not going!" Dillon shouted. Something hit the door with a bang, something hard enough and big enough that it made Ezra jerk back with an audible gasp.

"Dillon, open that door at once, young man!" Celia yelled from the bottom of the stairs.

Silence. Ezra stared at the door.

"I mean it!" Celia called again as she began climbing the stairs. "Open it now or you're in deep trouble."

Silence, again.

The silence broke Ezra. He stormed down the stairs, grabbed his toolbox, and ran back up the stairs. It took only a few minutes to remove the hinges from the door, but by the time they finally gained entry, Ezra was nearly as steamed as Celia. But when he saw the shape of his son huddled in bed with the blanket pulled over his head, Ezra's anger dissolved in an instant, leaving behind only sadness and fear. He waved Celia away. He needed a minute alone with Dillon. She shook her head no, but Ezra folded his hands into a begging posture, mouthing, "Please," until she finally exited the room.

Ezra sat down on his son's bed for the second time in recent memory. He wasn't a comforting person by nature, but he once again stroked the miserable eleven-year-old's dark brown hair. "Hey man, look," Ezra began. "It's never okay to lock us out; this is our house. But you don't have to go to the game if you don't want."

Dillon sniffled under the shaking blanket.

"You really ticked off your mom. And me."

"I know." Even through the muffled blankets, his voice was remorseful. Ezra almost smiled out of happiness and relief. His son was still in there somewhere.

"I have to put the door back on now. You'll have to help me hold it."

Dillon obediently got out of bed. He wouldn't look at Ezra, but he stood in the doorway of his room and held the door in alignment with the screw holes while Ezra re-installed it. When Ezra asked him to move into the hallway and hold it from a different angle, Dillon hesitated. Their eyes finally met, and Dillon blushed.

"It's okay," Ezra whispered. "Do what you have to do."

Dillon tapped three times on each doorpost and did a shuffling dance while he counted by threes to thirty-three. Then he stepped into the hallway and held the door for his dad. They didn't say anything, but when the door was back on, Ezra stuck out his hand, and Dillon shook it.

"All right then. Since you're staying home, let's make popcorn and watch something bad on television." He put his arm around Dillon's shoulder and led him downstairs to the den.

"It's just a phase," Ezra said to Celia that night, once again lying to his wife because he didn't know what else to say.

Celia seized on the explanation. "I keep forgetting he's nearly a teenager."

The weeks passed, and Dillon's ritual behaviors became more pronounced. The night terrors came two or three times a week, and Ezra's sense of helplessness grew in lock-step with his son's eccentricities. Ezra barely slept, waiting for the sounds of moaning to reach him from his son's bedroom. Celia's insomnia continued to plague her nocturnal activity, but the pills kept her zonked out. Every night, after coaxing Dillon back to sleep, Ezra would sit on the edge of his son's bed, wide awake and wracked with anxiety and guilt.

Then he'd leave Dillon's room and close the door to shut out the creak of the stairs as he walked down to the kitchen for a pull of bourbon. Bourbon was quickly becoming his comfort, his sleeping pill, and it never failed to help him find the rest he desperately needed. After a week, one slug turned into three, sometimes four.

Ezra liked the taste of bourbon, although he rarely drank to excess. It wasn't only that it was the right medicine to get him back to sleep; it numbed the dread that knotted his stomach. He started sleeping down in the den, on the recliner. When the bourbon was gone, he went to the liquor store for another bottle and a pack of Marlboros. He hadn't smoked in twelve years—not since Celia was pregnant with Dillon. But the jolt of nicotine steadied his nerves. He had to sneak his smokes out on the back porch, but after a couple of deep slugs from the bottle, he didn't even feel the cold. Before settling back down into the recliner, Ezra gargled a swig of Listerine from the downstairs bathroom and changed into a shirt he grabbed from atop the dryer. He didn't want Celia to smell the cigarettes or the bourbon in the morning.

His life had shifted into a new pattern: Drive to the college to teach his American history courses. Attend faculty meetings, reply to emails, and try to focus on his students and his research during office hours. Come home and nod while pretending to listen to Celia's worried whispers about Dillon. Eat dinner without tasting it, watch television with his son, and try to believe everything is normal. Wake up in the middle of the night to his son's miserable whimpers. Numb his guilt with bourbon and cigarettes on the back porch.

Ezra Magee's happy life, the joyful rhythm his family had danced to for years, was slipping away. He didn't blame Dillon or Celia or even the booze. This was all his own damned fault.

☙

Reverend Johnson's coffee was now cold. He hadn't touched it. "But Celia musta figured out what was happening to the boy," the reverend said. "You told her 'bout the Magee curse, right?"

CHAPTER 2

The bow of the canoe poked out over the hood, partially blocking the view through the windshield, but Simpellion Magee sped on quite happily through the verdant countryside. He felt like a man who'd been sprung from prison that very day. Simp was taking his boy fishing. There was nothing more perfect than a man and his boy in a canoe at a fishin' hole. All was right with the world—Cold War, nuclear superpowers, and thieving Republicans be damned!

The idea for the fishing trip had arisen spontaneously during the final hour of his vigil in front of the television. He'd watched faithfully all four days of the 1972 Democratic National Convention. When George McGovern's nomination was announced, Simp had spoken to his empty living room (his wife, Trudy, had no interest in watching the political convention on television with her husband, and his son, Ezra, was already in bed) and declared: "Our man George is the newly anointed Richard-killer! Hand him the sword, lads! Get him a steed and get his ass over to that White House!"

It had been a lively four days in the Magee household. As events unfolded at the Miami Beach Convention Center, Simp had talked back to the politicians and pundits, cheered at the good parts of their speeches, and jeered at the milling politicos who waved banners and placards in the arena. He had experienced the conflicting sentiments of pride and disgust as he watched the quadrennial political drama unfold. But he'd also felt the tingling impulse of the true patriot, especially when the Pledge of Allegiance was recited or the national anthem sung, as he sat in his metal folding chair pulled right up to the old black-and-white television set in the living room.

As eleven-year-old Ezra Magee flew past him on his way to or from his room and his tree house out back, Simp would call out, "Damn flunkies. I hate those flunkies! You hear me, Ezra? Promise me you'll never be one of them pandering, pompous asses. You promise me, son!"

When Killian Cagle had stopped by to borrow a hand saw and drop off the mail, Simp had waved his arms and increased the volume of his personal commentary but failed to entice his best friend to join him. Because of Lyndon Johnson, Martin Luther King, Jr., the civil rights movement, and feminism, Alabama was rapidly changing from yellow dog Democrat to Republican—a party that Simp abhorred. Few in the little town of Folly cared about the fate of the Democrats, or about the victorious senator from South Dakota, but Simpellion T. Dillon Magee cared passionately. "Someone has to get those lyin' Republican bastards outta the White House!"

Killian had allowed to Simp, as he had dozens of times, that it didn't much matter who won the presidential race, because the same rich and powerful people would rule no matter who sat in the big house. Simp had taken the bait, as usual, and called Killian "a goddamn libertine nihilist."

"You callin' me French?" Killian had asked, straight-faced.

"You're a curmudgeon," Trudy told Simp later that night. "It's a wonder Killian puts up with you!"

Simp had laughed and grabbed Trudy in a tight embrace and nuzzled her neck with his bristly cheek. She shrieked loudly and batted him with a rolled-up magazine, and soon they were smooching. Ezra fled the room every time the two shared affection, which made Simp and Trudy laugh even more. Damnation, Simp Magee loved his wife!

When the convention had ended, the transmission was cut and

the little television screen was filled with electronic snow, which had reminded Simp of sunlight glinting off the river. Suddenly, he'd become aware of feeling stale from spending four days indoors yelling at the box. What he yearned for, he'd realized with sudden, ferocious clarity, was a fishing trip. That was just the thing to clear the cobwebs from his brain after the circus of stupidity, half-truths, and empty promises to which he had just borne witness.

Stuffed in the back seat, next to the beat-up cooler and a bag of sandwiches, Ezra watched the back of his father's head moving from side to side in time to Bob Dylan's "The Times, They Are A-Changing." Simp had it at near-top volume on the eight-track cassette player, which he'd pieced together from parts purchased at the flea market the week before. Simp was as surprised as Ezra that it actually worked (although he would never admit it). The problem was they only had the one tape, and they'd listened to it so many times that even Dylan's unconventional croon and poetic lyrics were starting to get on the edge of a nerve.

Ezra was happy to be going fishing. His dad was finally willing to leave the house after exhausting himself and Ezra and everyone else with nonstop political commentary for the past few days. Besides, Ezra needed to get out of the house himself. He didn't like the feeling that had started creeping over him of late. He couldn't put a finger on what it was, or what was different about how he felt; he just knew he didn't like the way the world looked when the feeling came on or the foreboding that accompanied it. Common things, such as doorways or steps, suddenly presented as impediments. And he couldn't tell anybody, because there were no words in his eleven-year-old vocabulary to describe the feeling.

"Nixon's gonna win," Killian said by way of greeting when they pulled up in front of his house not five minutes later. Killian lived in a cabin he'd inherited from his mother on Bald Knob, a modest inclination on an otherwise mostly level landscape. Simp hopped out to pop the trunk so Killian could load his gear.

After tying the cane poles onto the canoe, Killian crawled into the passenger seat and looked back at Ezra. The boy's bowl-cut hairdo was Trudy's bimonthly gift to her son. The freckles on his nose were becoming more prominent, and Killian could see the beginnings of the strong chin that Simp had given him.

"Hello, old chap," Killian said to Ezra, and patted the boy on his knee.

"That tricky bastard's a Quaker," Simp said disgustedly, speaking of Nixon. "They're supposed to be pacifists, but he's killed more people than God himself."

Ezra was glad Killian was going with them. Killian was like an uncle, although no one would normally mistake him for a Magee because Killian's mom had Cherokee blood, which was evident in his dark hair and prominent cheekbones. Ezra didn't know who Killian's dad was—someone presumably named Cagle—but he already knew it was rude to ask about a man's daddy. But staring at Killian's profile while the car bounced along down the road, Ezra thought he maybe resembled Simp just a little. Maybe all grown men looked alike, and he'd never noticed it before. It was something to do with the slope of their foreheads and squint of their eyes.

Ezra looked at his dad's reflection in the rearview mirror. As usual, there was unshaved stubble on his cheeks, and his sideburns came down below his ears. He had a rather large head with ears that matched. Simp's mother, a dyed-in-the-wool Democrat like her son, had named her dog LBJ in honor of Lyndon Baines Johnson, the thirty-sixth president. Killian often teased Simp that his ears looked like LBJ's, but never specified whether he meant the president's or the dog's.

The car swerved suddenly, and Ezra looked up to see his father staring out of the open window. "Look at that!" Simp yelled. "Where the hell's my gun?" A gray squirrel jumped across a ditch and scrambled up a tree. "The bastards are everywhere," Simp glowered. "Damn pests!"

"So how long you think it'll take us to get there in this wreck?" Killian asked. He had a unique way of calming Simp with a simple turn of the conversation, and that gift made Ezra even more thankful that he had joined them for the trip.

"That reminds me of something," Simp said, grinning suddenly. "See, there's this rich ol' rancher from Texas, and he meets a dirt-poor farmer from Alabama in a bar. The Texan buys the farmer a drink, 'cause he plans on having some fun with him. The rich guy brags, 'I can git in my truck at sun-up, drive all day, and when the sun sets, I'm still on my land.' And he takes a big gulp of whiskey. And after a while the poor farmer looks at the Texan and says, 'Yup. I had a truck like that once.'"

They all had a good laugh, and Ezra relaxed. His father was in a fine mood now.

"Didja know how Folly got its name?" Simp asked. It wasn't really a question. Ezra had heard his father tell the story so often he could repeat it by heart.

"It was named," Simp began, without waiting for an answer, "for Confederate Colonel Coventry Aloicious Folle. Spelled F-O-L-L-E. Funny name, that." Killian glanced back at Ezra and winked, and Ezra smiled because he knew they were both thinking that a man named Simpellion had no business making judgments on another man's name. "Folle made lots of money off the slave trade after it was made illegal. He brought them through the port at Mobile and sold them on the quiet to farms all over the South. Greased a lot of dirty politicians' palms, did enterprising Aloicious. He was an excellent capitalist and a terrible human being. And despite the fancy rank and uniform he wore, he had no military talent or training. What the man had was money. Old Jeff Davis and his boys hated Folle, but wars cost money. So, they sold him a military commission. He paid enough to be made a colonel."

Simp looked out the window for a moment, and Ezra tensed up, wondering if his dad had spotted another squirrel. But Simp continued: "Another thing you need to know about Folle: he was so fat he could hardly sit a horse. And sorry was the horse that carried the honor of the colonel's big fat ass. But Folle insisted on having his chance at glory and got himself assigned to General Albert Johnston's command. At the battle of Shiloh, General Johnston ordered Folle to report on the progress of one of his units then engaged in combat in a particular area. General Johnston either despised the man and therefore had no compunctions about sending him on a suicide mission, or Folle was fool enough to volunteer. We'll never know.

"Actually, the Confederates coulda won that battle. They caught Billy Yank by surprise and beat the hell out of him for a while until the Union's General Benjamin Prentiss got his farm boys down in the sunken road and stopped the Confederate advance. They said the bullets were whizzing overhead like a mad hornet's nest. That's why they named that particular part of the battle the 'hornet's nest.'" Simp was quiet for a moment, then continued. "Well, anyhow, Folle comes a'ridin' over a rise on his poor horse and sees that things are too hot for a fat man, so he turns tail and heads back away from the fighting. But just then, some Billy Yank draws down on him and puts a punkin' ball in Folle's ass. He bled to death before he got back to tell the general the Confederates were getting their butts kicked. But maybe it wouldn't have mattered anyhow, because General Johnston got shot during the battle and bled to death himself." For some reason, whenever his dad got to this part of the story, Ezra always wondered what happened to Folle's horse.

"So, how did the name of our fair hamlet come to be F-O-L-L-Y, not F-O-L-L-E?" Simp asked his captive audience rhetorically. "Well, it turned out that the dead colonel's kinfolk decided that Colonel Folle was a war hero, and they talked some politician into naming our stretch of earth after their fat-ass relative. But the fellow over at the county's Department of Records knew the real story—that Folle was a joke. So, when he recorded the name in the official charter, he spelled it F-O-L-L-Y."

Simp finished the story as he pulled into a gas station. Killian went in to pay for a few gallons and a couple of cold sodas while Simp pumped the gas. Ezra crawled out of the back seat and stretched. He looked around curiously. The house attached to the station had a front porch that needed painting with a mean-looking dog chained to it.

Simp put the gas cap back on and glared at the store. When Killian came out, Simp growled, "You ready?"

"I was born ready," Killian retorted as he limped back to the car, favoring his left knee. Ezra often wondered what had caused the injury that made Killian walk with a limp. "Had an accident a long time ago," was all Killian had said the one time Ezra asked.

Killian pulled a pack of Bazooka bubble gum out of his overalls pocket and flipped it to Ezra with a wink. The man always wore overalls. It was something else Ezra liked about him—that and the mystery surrounding him. Killian's demeanor reminded Ezra of one of the heroes in his comic books: the quiet strength that emanated from the hero's persona.

After they got back on the road, Ezra dozed off and slept until they arrived at their destination. He felt sticky and thirsty and a bit disoriented from having fallen asleep in one place and waking up somewhere new. Ezra grabbed a cold soda from the cooler and surveyed his surroundings. They were parked at the end of a rutted dirt road in the middle of nowhere, but in front of them rolled the brown-tinged waters of the Tennessee River.

"Looks like a good day for fishing," Killian observed as he and Simp began to work the knots loose to free the canoe. They stood for a few moments and gazed out as a tugboat pushed a line of barges upriver before Killian and Simp carried the canoe on their shoulders down to the water and Ezra followed.

Simp nodded toward the shoreline. "River's up," he said. "Fish'll be hungry."

"All that rain last week," Killian agreed.

"And now for the local news," Ezra chimed in, and was gratified when the men laughed.

They fished a slough a hundred yards from where they put in and caught a few crappies and bluegills, but Ezra was irritated by the bouncing motion of the canoe. When Simp was deep in concentration on something, his left knee would bounce up and down in a staccato rhythm. Ezra had seen him do it when his dad was composing a letter at his typewriter or sitting in his old cane-bottom chair on the porch, reading. Ezra privately called it the Sand Mountain two-step.

"It's the Irish jig," his mother told him once, "and he does the same thing in his sleep. It used to nearly drive me crazy, but it's a wonder what you can get used to after a while. I hardly notice anymore."

A jerking left knee was only one of Simp Magee's many "eccentricities." Ezra had learned that word early in life, since it was often used when people described his father. It wasn't just the jerky way he moved, his loud voice, and his quick-shifting moods. Simp Magee was an extraordinarily opinionated fellow and would take on anyone willing to voice a contrary opinion, often with colorful and salty language. He regularly wrote bombastic letters to the editor of the *Sand Mountain Sentinel* decrying government, religion, and the automobile industry's refusal to make cars out of recycled tin cans.

Simp believed a number of his fellow citizens secretly agreed with his libertarian socialist views. While few of his manifestos ever got printed in the newspaper, copies of the letters were often tacked up in public places. No one claimed responsibility for it, but Ezra thought it was probably Simp himself who did it. Although he didn't understand a lot of what his father wrote about, he knew it either made people mad as hell or made them laugh at Simp Magee, and that made Ezra hate those letters. Sometimes, he wished the typewriter would jam so badly that his father would be forced to give up his letter-writing for good.

After Killian caught a large catfish, they settled in for some serious fishing, and all conversation ceased as they stared intently at their bobbers. Nobody noticed as the canoe edged into stronger river current that was carrying them farther from shore.

Killian was the first to realize that the canoe had drifted fifty yards out from the shore, so he reeled in his line and began hurriedly paddling back toward the shoreline. A moment later, through the haze and the gentle lapping of water against the sides of the canoe, the sound of an outboard engine filtered over the water. The three of them looked toward the sound of the engine and saw a large white bass boat heading swiftly in their direction.

"Hey! Slow down!" Killian waved his arms frantically, thinking maybe the boat captain couldn't see them. A small figure at the helm waved back and pulled his boat slightly to the left to avoid broadsiding the canoe. Ezra admired the jaunty rooster-tail wake left by the motorboat.

"Jesus Christ!" Simp yelled. He and Killian grabbed paddles and frantically dug in the water. Ezra didn't understand why until he saw the wake rise up into a wave. It swelled higher and higher, heading straight toward the canoe. Before Ezra could let out the scream that was building in his chest, the water lifted their canoe and flipped it over.

As much as he liked fishing and splashing around in the shallows of the river, Ezra couldn't swim. He was afraid of deep water. Even wading up to his knees with his cousins in the summer made him nervous. He never let on because he knew that if the other boys found out, they would dunk him for sure.

As the river was about to close over his head, Ezra was gripped in the worst panic of his life. He could hear his father spluttering and then shouting his name. Ezra thrashed his arms and legs furiously, but he slowly slipped under the water.

Ezra tasted the river in his mouth, and his lungs felt as if they were going to burst. *I'm drowning!* he thought. *I'm gonna die! Jesus*

Christ, I'm gonna die! Looking up toward the surface, he saw a faint corona of light around the brighter dot of the sun, and in a moment of sudden awareness he heard the vibrating thrum of the motorboat engine as it sped upriver. A shadow moved across the brilliance of the sun.

Please, God, Ezra prayed. He couldn't hold on any longer. He reached up toward the shadow, and a hand reached down and pulled him to the surface.

CHAPTER 3

Ezra swallowed four aspirins and glared at his visitor. His bourbon headache had reached epic proportions.

"To what do I owe the pleasure of this unexpected visit, Reverend Johnson?" Ezra asked.

"A mite touchy, ain't we? I'm here for *you*, Ezra. Why else would I be here?" The reverend shrugged his sloping shoulders. "And seein' as how you're all growed up now, you can go ahead and call me Hiram."

Hiram Johnson. "Jesus Christ Johnson." The name slipped smoothly into his head, another fragment from childhood.

"You did tell Celia, didn't you? About the Magee curse?"

"Not exactly," Ezra admitted, his words coming out more gruffly than intended.

Hiram Johnson shook his head sadly. "'Who can find a virtuous woman? For her price is far above rubies,'" he intoned.

Was the man really sitting in Ezra's kitchen, quoting scripture? *Well then, to hell with it.* Ezra opened a new fifth of bourbon and took a slug straight from the bottle's mouth.

By the time Ezra turned back toward the table, Hiram Johnson had gotten up and was now standing at the window looking out over the back yard. "'The Son of Man came eating and drinking,'" the reverend quoted again, "'and they said, *Here is a glutton and a drunkard, a friend of tax collectors and sinners.*'"

"You want some?" Ezra held out the bottle, but Hiram Johnson ignored it.

"'Cast thy burden upon the Lord, and He shall sustain thee.'"

Ezra left the bottle on the table in case Hiram changed his mind. He wandered into the living room and lay down on the couch. He closed his eyes to the world, but he had no peace. He tried to rest, but instead he saw himself and Celia on this very couch, having the first of many fights about their son.

※

"Dillon needs help."

"Mhm." Ezra flipped through the TV channels for something to watch. Celia curled up next to him on the couch. She tucked her head under his stubble-covered chin and grabbed the remote from his hand, holding it away from him, semi-playfully. He didn't even try to play along or take back the remote. Instead, he reached in front of her for a slice of leftover birthday cake that had been sitting on the coffee table all afternoon and stuffed a generous forkful into his mouth.

"He wasn't even excited about the telescope! Something is wrong, Ezra, and I have no idea how to help him. He won't talk to me." Celia's eyes filled with tears.

"Uh-huh." Ezra stared straight ahead and ate more cake. He tried to avoid direct eye contact in their discussions about Dillon. Her pain mixed with his own was more than he could handle.

"He talks to you." She sounded resentful, and Ezra knew she had every right to be. Secrets have a way of doing that. "Maybe you can spend more time with him, find out what's going on."

"I spend plenty of time with Dillon," he muttered, thinking of the past nights he'd spent sitting up with his son, holding his hand, talking out loud to no one in hopes that the sound of his voice might pull his child back from the abyss. He knew it wasn't fair to be angry with Celia. She still didn't know about the night terrors. Neither Ezra nor Dillon wanted her to know, and the secret had introduced a tension between them.

"I'm just saying—"

Ezra stood up and walked into the kitchen. He pretended to rummage around the refrigerator, hiding behind the condiment-filled door while he calmed himself. Once he had regained his composure, the cool air smacking him back to his senses, he took out a Sam Adams Pale Ale, popped it open, and walked out to the back porch.

"Ezra?" Celia stood in the doorway, her hands on her hips. "What the hell was that about? I was talking to you!"

He needed air. He needed deep breaths, his lungs full of the chilly March night. He longed for a cigarette to go with his beer, but his smoking was another secret he was keeping to himself.

"Ezra? Are you mad at me?"

Ezra stayed silent. For the first time in their fourteen-year marriage, he simply ignored his wife, hoping she would go away and leave him in peace.

"Honey, I didn't mean to blame you for what Dillon's going through. I know it's not your fault."

It was too much for Ezra to hear, Celia apologizing to him when in truth it *was* his fault. "Just stop," was all he could say. "I don't want to talk about it."

"Okay," she whispered. He didn't need to look at her to know she was hurt to the core. When she finally walked back inside, slamming the door behind her, Ezra's eyes filled with tears.

He almost called her to come back. He wanted to tell her the truth that was eating him up inside: that along with the gene for his freckles and curly brown hair, Ezra Magee had given his beloved son obsessive-compulsive disorder.

They had been together for a decade and a half, and in all that time he had never told Celia he'd once suffered from OCD. He didn't mean to keep it a secret; he just didn't want to think about it again. If Ezra was being honest, in the beginning of their relationship, he didn't want her to think of him as a mental case. But now he realized he'd made an enormous mistake. She would never forgive him for that omission, because now her son had inherited the disease.

When Ezra was twelve—maybe younger, but he had no real memories before then—he had developed the same symptoms Dillon was showing. Ezra had suffered from OCD and panic attacks until his senior year of high school. It was agonizing, the repetitive behavior and constant need for order. And then, over time, with the help of medication and therapy, it had stopped. He had gone off to college and was more than happy to forget the past and never speak of OCD again. His Aunt Lenore, who'd raised him from age twelve, never mentioned it again either. Ezra had failed to warn his future wife that he might pass on this curse to their children. And now the horse was out of the barn. Dillon had it.

He knew Celia would be furious with him for many reasons. She frequently complained that he never talked about his childhood, but he couldn't help that. He didn't remember his childhood. And as for the years he *did* remember, living in West Virginia with his Aunt Lenore, he didn't want to talk about the therapy or the medications and their side effects. By the time Lenore had found the right doctor who had prescribed the right combination of medicines that allowed him to live a normal life, Ezra had already been branded a freak by his classmates. Cross-country running and schoolwork were the only things that had made him feel normal—the only things that brought him satisfaction in an otherwise unsatisfying existence. He'd been a loser, a social pariah among his classmates, and the pain and embarrassment had nearly drowned him. Why would he want his wife to know that? Yes, he'd had obsessive-compulsive disorder. But he'd gotten over it and moved on. He'd reinvented himself in college, where no one knew him. Celia had met him in graduate school, when he was secure in his new identity as a confident and normal (if somewhat quiet) man.

☙

In the week after his fight with Celia, Ezra had taken to sitting on the back porch with his bottle of bourbon after dinner. He no longer had the energy to hide his drinking from his family. A week into this pattern, Celia came outside to join him, bundled up in a puffy jacket and gloves. Ezra was in his T-shirt and jeans, too full of liquor to feel the cold.

"What the hell is going on with you?"

"Nothin'."

"Nothing," she repeated, her voice thick with doubt.

"What do you want me to say?"

"I want you to tell me why you're drinking so much and refusing to talk to me."

He shrugged, swirled the bourbon around the half-empty bottle, and took another swallow.

"Unacceptable. That's not an answer."

Ezra shrugged again.

Celia knew from experience she'd get no further information once her husband began shrugging in response, so she simply twirled in a half circle and stomped back inside. Ezra leaned back in his chair and looked at the dark shapes of the trees behind his house. In a few weeks, the branches would fill with buds. The new beech and oak leaves would look just like the beech and oak leaves that had graced the trees last spring. Nature was dependable in its patterns and replications. Just like his son carried on his genes and Celia's. It was just dumb luck that Dillon had gotten Ezra's gene for OCD. It was random fucking bad luck.

Ezra finished off the bottle with a final gulp, then slipped into the kitchen and poured himself four fingers of Wild Turkey from a new bottle. Celia had turned off the downstairs lights, purposefully leaving him in the dark. He retreated back to the porch, sipping the amber liquid, letting the numbness dull his self-loathing.

"Happy belated birthday, son," he said aloud to the trees in the backyard, remembering Dillon's birthday two weeks before. "I gave you my fucked-up genes with that special twist called OCD. I'm such a great, goddamned dad."

Ezra slipped his hand under the chair and pulled out his cigarettes and lighter. The first drag burned his throat. The second gave him a rush of calm.

Once his glass was empty and his cigarette had burned down to the filter, he poured another and lit another. After four cycles of drinking, smoking, pouring, and lighting, he went inside and crept upstairs. He brushed his teeth longer than normal, scrubbing hard against his gums and tongue. When Dillon inevitably awoke and Ezra returned to his bedside, he didn't want the smell of booze or cigarettes on his breath. Ezra rinsed with mouthwash just to be safe and then walked into the den and crawled into the recliner. He slept fully clothed and waited for his son to cry out.

☙

"Can anyone join this pity party?"

Ezra looked up from the couch to see Hiram Johnson leaning against the bookshelf in the corner of the living room.

"Your own damn fault for choosing to crash it," Ezra said.

"What about Celia? She get tired of waitin' on you to fess up?" Hiram moved away from the bookcase with his weathered hands clasped at his waist, his posture rigidly proper. "She's gone, and it's your own fault," Hiram continued. "You really made a mess of it, boy. You know it, I know it, and Celia knows it. But does Dillon know it?"

Anger painted Ezra's face with a red flush. He closed his eyes and Hiram melted into the background.

Ezra knew Hiram Johnson was right. Perhaps Dillon blamed himself for Ezra's recent deterioration. Yes, that was his fault too.

"Did you really think Celia'd blame you for passing on the Magee curse?"

"Goddammit, Hiram!" Ezra's eyes shot open, jarred by the full-throated boom of his own outburst.

The preacher put his hands up as if warding off a blow. "'And you shall know the truth. And the truth shall set you free.'"

"Oh, stuff it already. I'm a goddamned atheist."

☙

Ezra and Celia had the normal couples' arguments when they were first married. The longer they were together, the longer some of the bouts. But it was an unspoken code of their relationship that no matter how angry they were with each other, they wouldn't let it affect their work lives.

One morning, however, Ezra woke up in the recliner, the sun too bright to be early morning, and he checked the clock. Ten in the morning. "Shit," he mumbled, running a hand across his stubbly cheeks. She'd let him oversleep, no doubt on purpose, and he'd missed his first class.

He called the history department chairman, fed him some bullshit about a flat tire, and then rushed through his morning routine, pissed off at his wife and himself and the world. Ezra had half a mind to call her and yell at her while she sat at her desk, to make her feel as awful as he felt. But Ezra knew her anger was his fault, just another thing to add to the list of failures. He decided he would apologize that night.

But that night he walked through the door, sat through dinner, TV, and their nightly pre-bed routine, and didn't apologize. He didn't apologize the next night either. Or the next. When Celia finally broke down the following night, falling onto his chest while they sat in bed, with tears pouring from her eyes, she begged to know what was wrong. "I can take it!" she yelled. "Just don't keep me in the fucking dark! I feel like I'm losing you every damned day." By this point, after weeks of lying, shrugging, and avoidance, her pain barely moved him. He kissed her forehead, pushed her head from his chest, and stood up, walking out of the room to the sound of her heaving sobs.

Ezra wanted, even *needed*, her anger. He knew it was perverse, but he knew he deserved it. He hated himself for doing it, but the alternative—talking to her about his past, living with the betrayal on her face—somehow seemed infinitely worse. He hated processing his emotions, or whatever it was Celia called those conversations when he was pressed to say how he felt. It was the hardest part of marriage. She could talk a thing to death. She was nothing like his Aunt Lenore. You couldn't pry an emotional statement out of Lenore if your life depended on it. There was something comfortable about being around his aunt. They could talk about all kinds of things—the Pittsburgh Steelers, Watergate, bark beetles—but feelings seldom found their way into their conversations.

The tension was hard on Dillon. He spent more and more time in his room, and when his parents fought, he covered his ears with his hands until he could put on his headphones to drown out their bickering. Ezra tried to make it up to him by buying him comic books and Pokémon cards. He spent more time playing video games with him. He spent a weekend helping Dillon research and write a science report on the solar system. Celia came in once with a snack for the two of them. She had brought Ezra a mix of Goldfish crackers and salted peanuts—his favorite. Ezra forced himself to be civil, thanking her and giving her a peck on the cheek.

When Dillon was in bed, Ezra started grading the stack of term papers that he usually didn't get around to reading until after spring break. He even took a stab at a first draft of a journal article on Abraham Lincoln's early ideas about emancipation. For every bottle of Wild Turkey he finished off, he brought home another. He paid for his nightly binges in the mornings, waking up to hammers in his skull and a sour taste that stayed with him all day. He was too tired for his morning runs, and his pants began to tighten around the waist.

Celia went from angry to hurt and bewildered. He saw it daily, and it pained him, but he let it happen. It was as if there were two Ezras: an unfeeling Ezra who controlled his behaviors while a mournful Ezra was trapped behind some sort of glass partition, forced to watch as his doppelgänger destroyed his marriage. He knew he was crazy for letting it get this bad, but every day he continued to walk the same tense path.

He began talking to himself out loud. "You stupid sonofabitch" was the most common phrase he uttered. The hardened version of Ezra told him to face facts: he'd screwed up Celia's life. He'd screwed up Dillon's life. He'd screwed up his own life. When his wife found out what he'd kept from her (and it was only a matter of time before she did), she would see it that way too. By then, the marriage would be too far down the tubes to pull back to normal, and he knew, in his heart, she'd feel no regrets about tossing him out.

∞

"So, you planned all this, then," Hiram Johnson said, opening his arms slowly, urging Ezra to take in the empty house, to look in the mirror of his mind and take in the image of his lonely, hungover self, sitting on the couch.

"So, I'm an asshole. Nobody asked for your commentary. Why exactly are you here, anyway?"

"I remember having marital troubles once, a long time ago. There was another woman. It was a sorry mess." The preacher abruptly changed the subject. "Have you seen Sissy lately?"

The name blew a hole in Ezra's memory and his eyes flew open.

"What did you say?"

"Have you seen Sissy Namey?"

Ezra fled to the kitchen for a drink of bourbon, his heart pounding with fear. He remembered Sissy. If she was back, it could only mean one thing.

CHAPTER 4

Ezra's heart crashed in his chest as the wave came for him. He could see his dad and Killian, but it was the wave, rising higher and higher, blotting out the sky, that commanded his attention. He tried to run, but his legs were heavy, as if he were running in a field of sticky mud. He tried to wake up, but the wall of water kept coming. He opened his mouth to scream and heard the bleat of a goat.

A goat?

Eleven-year-old Ezra jerked awake and sat up, panting. "It was just a stupid dream," he told himself. He could still feel the adrenaline of panic in his limbs, and the sense of disquiet and anxiety that underlay the panic. He took a few shaky breaths to loosen the tightness in his chest, and when he felt steadier, he dragged himself to the window and pulled the curtain aside to look out on the reassuringly landlocked backyard, golden in the early morning light of summer.

The goat bleated again. Ezra spotted Mabel tethered to a stake under the sycamore tree. Squatting down beside her, Ezra's father was glaring at the goat with an extremely vexed expression on his face. Ezra cracked open the window to hear what was going on.

"Faint, damn you," Simp grumbled, and then he fell to the ground as if to demonstrate while the goat ignored him and placidly chewed a blade of grass. Simp hopped back up and loudly clapped his hands. "Faint, you miserable fucking goat! Faint, you horned devil!"

His father had been cajoling, threatening, and swearing at the goat for two days running, but nothing had yet induced the glossy black goat to faint.

Ezra sighed and moved away from the window. These were what his mother called Simp's "eccentric moments." Ezra didn't mind, as long as no one else was around to see it (and tease him about it later). What bugged him was that his father didn't seem to notice or care that his son was still suffering from the trauma of almost drowning three days before. Ezra couldn't stop obsessing about how he'd sunk helplessly down into the river, how his lungs had burned, how his arms and legs had seemed useless in the slithery water.

When they'd returned home that day, Ezra had gone right to bed. His mother had woken him from a nightmare hours later, cradling him in her arms as he shook so hard with terror that his teeth chattered. He had been grateful for her comfort, but when the nightmare came again the second night, and she woke him up and held him, he'd felt ashamed for crying.

"Are you all right, honey? You're shaking like a leaf! What in the world are you dreaming about?"

He didn't answer. How could he explain the dream without looking like a baby?

"Nothing. I can't remember," he had lied. He'd taken the glass of water from his mother's outstretched hand and gulped it down.

After she had tucked him in again, he lay in bed, eyes wide, too afraid to fall back asleep. He'd forced himself to remember that golden moment when Killian had pulled him back to the world of light and air. He'd remembered that first breath, the feeling of relief when he realized he was not going to die that day. He'd also remembered the silent ride home, his father glancing at him, the man's worried brow visible in the rearview mirror. And eventually he'd fallen back to sleep.

"Ezra? Breakfast, lazybones! Come on down!" His mother's cheery voice cut through his ruminations. Ezra threw on a pair of shorts and yesterday's grubby T-shirt and went downstairs.

Trudy handed him a glass of juice and a piece of toast and, with a mischievous smile, beckoned him to follow her. They went out to the front porch just in time to see Simp and Mabel locked in a staring contest. Ezra casually leaned against his mother, and she put her arm around him.

"My money's on Mabel," she said loudly. "Go on, girl! You can take him any day of the week!"

The goat did, indeed, look to be winning. Simp's face was blotched red with frustration and contorted with concentration, while Mabel chewed contentedly on some grass and fixed him with a sardonic stare.

"Faint, you good-for-nothing . . . " Simp began, and Trudy covered Ezra's ears to blot out the obscenities that rolled out of Simp's mouth.

"Simp Magee," Trudy said with some heat, "watch that mouth of yours!"

Simp ignored his wife and continued to swear and stare at Mabel. Ezra heard a rude snort coming from the road and immediately pulled away from his mom and folded his arms in a manly way. A group of spectators was heading toward the house. Two of them were his cousins (several times removed), Boyd and Floyd Dillard. They pulled a face at him that was clearly meant to imitate Simp, which made Ezra want to punch each one squarely in the nose. But there was Killian, too, who stopped near an oak tree and leaned against the trunk with his hands in his pockets and a wry smile on his face. Ezra was also surprised to see Hiram Johnson. Hiram looked sober enough as he made a beeline for the porch.

"Trudy. Ezra. Pleasant day we're having." Hiram took off his hat and shook Trudy's hand politely, readily accepting her offer of coffee. Ezra dodged out of the way before the man could ruffle his hair. Hiram sat down on the top step, his bald pate white and glistening in the sun, and chuckled at Simp's antics.

Now that he had an audience, Simpellion Magee was working

overtime to get Mabel to faint, but his threats were going nowhere with the goat.

"Give it up, Simp!" Ezra's Uncle Auggie strolled into the yard and hawked a glob of tobacco spit onto their hydrangea bush. "Boy, you look like a hippie, talkin' to a goat. Is this what you commie lovers do for fun?" Auggie needled his brother with a humiliating contempt bred of love, familiarity, and shame. Floyd and Boyd acted like that was the funniest thing they'd ever heard, cracking up and rolling on the ground. Ezra thought about going inside, but there was Killian calmly ignoring them, so Ezra stuck his hands in his pockets, leaned up against the railing, and set about ignoring them too.

"I'd be much obliged if someone would let me in on the joke." Hiram Johnson used his reverend's voice, which momentarily shut Floyd and Boyd up.

Trudy handed Reverend a mug of hot black coffee. "I blame Killian," she said, but with a smile. "I trusted him to keep an eye on my husband when they went to the cattle sale in Buford two months back. Simp was going to buy us a milk cow—something he's been meaning to do for some time. But instead of bringing home a cow . . ." She gestured toward Mabel.

☙

When Killian and Simp had pulled into the parking lot of the cattle sale barn, most everyone was already inside, waiting for the auction to begin. One of the stragglers included a burly, bearded, shaggy-haired man in a hunting vest. He was leading a black goat behind him, and he hustled over as they got out of Killian's truck.

"Hey fellers! Wait up!" he shouted. Simp and Killian obliged. "Look what I got'chere."

The man nodded toward the goat. Killian just shrugged and walked toward the barn, but Simp stayed and looked at the man and the little animal. "It'd be obvious to anyone but a blind man that what you have there is a nanny goat," Simp said.

"Right you are," the man replied, "but this ain't no reg'lar goat." This goat, the man explained, his voice lowered to a conspiratorial register, was a descendant of John Tinsley's original fainting goats. Simp brightened up. He loved a good story, and the man was clearly looking to tell him one.

Round about 1880, John Tinsley had shown up one day on a farm in Marshall County, Tennessee. Tinsley, who had looked out of place and very much like a foreigner in his tweed jacket, spoke with what the farmer thought was the flavor of Scotland. Tinsley introduced himself and explained that the four goats he was traveling with, who were grazing on clumps of grass, were unique in all the world because of a peculiar trait they shared. Naturally, the farmer wanted to know what that trait was. Instead of telling him, Tinsley clapped his hands loudly. To the farmer's surprise, the quartet of goats immediately fell over, every one of them, onto their sides. A moment later, they scrambled to their feet and went back to grazing.

According to Tinsley, the goats were born with a condition that caused their muscles to become stiff and lock up when they were startled, making them appear to faint.

"It's called *myotonia congenita*," the man told Simp.

Killian, who had come back to get Simp, caught the end of the story. He noticed that the seemingly backwoods goat owner had had no trouble with the words *myotonia congenita*. Killian sized him up as a snake oil salesman and suggested to Simp that they go inside before they missed their chance to purchase a cow. Unfortunately, Simp was already enchanted at the thought of owning his very own fainting goat, and his enthusiasm for acquiring a cow had waned.

"That's a fine story," Killian said to the man, "but what about giving us a demonstration?"

The man demurred. "I can't do it here. Folks'll think there's a gun gone off. 'Sides, it might scare the cattle."

Killian suggested walking into a nearby field. "This here goat, Mabel, she's still too young," the man said sadly. "She's only four months old. She's got to be at least six months old before the trait kicks in."

Simp was a goner. In no time at all, his money was in the man's pocket, and he and Killian were leading the little black goat over to the truck.

                        *

Hiram Johnson sipped his coffee and nodded sagely at Trudy. "Might we assume that Mabel has recently turned six months old?" The reverend's bushy eyebrows converged toward his nose to accentuate the question.

Mabel, who was unremarkable in every way except for her alleged genetic heritage, was indeed of an age where the trait was supposed to have manifested, yet there she stood, staring at Simp's cursing, gesticulations, and loud clapping, refusing to faint. Simp was convinced that Mabel refused to faint out of sheer, goat-headed stubbornness.

When it was clear to the crowd watching that the goat was turning out to be more stubborn than Simpellion Magee, they drifted away until only Ezra, Simp, Killian, and the goat were left standing in the yard. Mabel noticed the hydrangeas and happily munched on the blue flowers.

"Trudy's not gonna like this," Killian observed.

Simp only growled and stomped off, saying, "Never mind that goat. Where's my shotgun? There's a squirrel up that oak!"

                        *

Ezra was convinced he was going crazy. Eleven years old and treading toward the loony bin. People used the word "crazy" all the time, but Ezra had only ever known one certifiably crazy person, and that person was Sissy Namey. She was somewhere between twenty and thirty years of age when Ezra knew her; she'd lived with her widowed mother, Cora, a few houses down the road from Ezra's family. When Cora Namey died, there was talk among folks about what would become of Sissy, who everyone knew was as crazy as a bessie bug. Ezra had stood and watched with the rest of the neighborhood the day that folks from the state mental hospital had come to take her away to the asylum in Tuscaloosa. Two men wrapped her up tight in a straitjacket and carried her out of the house. She'd bucked and twisted in that white fabric like a butterfly trapped in its cocoon, her eyes big and wild, blue like the sea after a storm.

Before that, when he'd had cause to see her, Ezra was both repelled and fascinated by Sissy Namey. She would stand around in her front yard, staring vacantly into the distance as if there were important matters going on in some mystic realm that only she could perceive. When she spoke, the words were gibberish, but she delivered them with conviction. At times, something invisible would cause her to become overexcited, and her arms and legs would jerk wildly for several minutes. Her visage was that of a wild creature; every day she sported the same unkempt hair, the same crazed look in her eyes, and always a mishmash of clothing and coverings.

Ezra had never spoken to Sissy Namey, but in the weeks after his near-drowning, he thought about her a lot: was she born that way, or did something happen to cause her to become loony? Could you be normal one day, and then wake up the next day a tiny bit crazy? And would you lose an inch of your sanity every day until finally they put you in a straitjacket and drove you away to the nuthouse?

He went into the bathroom and stared in the mirror. Except for red eyes from lack of sleep, there was nothing Ezra could see that was physically different about his face. But inside his head it was different. He had that nagging sense that something was off-kilter. He suspected he was going crazy, inch by miserable inch. It was the only explanation for his night terrors, and other things—the panicky feeling he was getting at the strangest times, like when he got out of bed in the morning, or when he crossed from one room into another. That was crazy, right?

"Ezra!" his mother's voice floated up to him again from the porch. "Chore time! The weeds are taking over my sweet peas."

They worked in the sun for an hour. Ezra brooded as he pulled up spears of nut grass, clods of crab grass, and Johnson grass rhizomes. His mother tried to engage him in conversation, but he answered in monosyllables.

Finally, she stopped and looked at him. "Who are you," she demanded, "and what have you done with my son?"

"Huh?"

"I just offered to get us some ice cream, and you didn't say a word."

"Oh. Sorry." He gripped the next weed and yanked.

"Honey, those nightmares you're having—can you recall what they're about?"

He shook his head and closed his eyes, wishing she would leave it alone. The more he talked about it, the more real it felt.

"Are you ever going to tell me what happened on that fishing trip?"

Ezra shrugged.

"Look at me, sweetheart." The kindness in her voice undid him. "You tell me now, Ezra Magee. What happened on that fishing trip?"

"The canoe . . . we . . . in the water . . . I was gonna drown." A sob escaped, and hot tears streamed down his face.

"My poor baby!" Trudy gathered her son in her arms. "Shhh. Shhh. You poor thing."

Ezra pulled away and self-consciously wiped his nose on his arm. "I'm eleven years old! I'm not a baby."

Trudy sighed, pulling her son back into her arms. "You'll always be my baby, no matter how old you are. Why didn't you tell me you almost drowned?"

Ezra said nothing, but the shame on his face made it clear.

"Your father should have told me." There was sadness in her voice. "Your daddy does things his way, but we all have choices, Ezra. You can choose to talk about what bothers you. Do you understand?"

He almost told her right then about how he was turning into Sissy Namey. But they heard a shotgun blast, and his father yelled, "Goddamn squirrel!"

He and his mother ran into the house to take cover. When Simp was hunting squirrels, it was safer to be inside.

☙

Ezra and his parents went to Granmaude Magee's house every week for the Sunday gathering of relatives at the communal dinner. Simp's mother, Maude Magee, had received the nickname "Granmaude" from her grandchildren, and eventually became Granmaude to everyone she knew. On warm summer Sunday nights, the family spilled out of Granmaude's house and onto the porch. While the adults talked, the children ran up and down the steep hill beside the house playing freeze tag. Normally an only child, Ezra enjoyed being part of a wild pack of kids every weekend.

The Sunday after the fishing trip, as he and his parents walked up the front steps into Granmaude's house, Ezra suddenly felt a knot pulling at his stomach and a tightness in his forehead. Instead of the strange sensations he'd been having lately—like an uneasy prickling of the skin or an itch that couldn't be scratched—he was hit by a sense of doom. Ezra thought of his father's penchant for swearing when he was irritated and internally called up a few of Simp's favorite epithets. It did nothing to allay the hollowness in his chest.

At the top of the front porch steps, he stopped to tie his shoe while his mother and father went inside the house and called out their greetings. When they were inside, Ezra stood at the threshold and tapped the left side and then right side of the door frame, three times each, with the forefingers of each hand. Calm washed over him as he then stepped through the doorway and into the front hallway. The tapping warded off bad things. He didn't know *how* he knew this—he'd never done this before—but he knew it, plain as day. A pleasant feeling rose in his chest: he was in control. It was the first time since almost drowning that he felt calm.

Too late, he noticed Granmaude standing in the kitchen doorway, watching him. Ezra turned bright red with embarrassment and thought of Sissy Namey. *Is this the way people had looked at Sissy when she started to turn loony?* Granmaude didn't say a word—just gave him a nod and went back to the kitchen.

Dinner was ready, and after washing his hands, Ezra squeezed in between his cousins in the middle of the table. The chatter died down as everyone waited for Granmaude to say grace before they could fill their plates with fried chicken, corn on the cob, fried squash, and potato salad. Ezra had Boyd on one side and Floyd on the other, which guaranteed that he'd never get to eat his own ear of corn. His cousins would wait for him to butter it just right, then they'd ask him to pass something. When his hands were busy, one of them would swipe his ear of corn and eat it.

As soon as a loud "Amen" lifted from their bowed heads, the family set to piling their plates high. Granmaude was the only one who waited. "Simpellion," (Granmaude's voice had a slightly singsong quality that Ezra liked) "yestiddy, I could hear you yellin' all the way down to my house." Granmaude shook her head, and her low bun of dark gray hair bobbed from side to side. Ezra had never seen her wear her hair any other way, and he wondered idly how long it was.

"Sorry if I woke you up, Mama," Simp said.

"You didn't wake me up, son, but you coulda woke the dead

down in the cemetery." A note of humor crept into her voice. "It's that fool goat, isn't it? Hasn't fainted yet?"

Ezra wished someone would change the subject. Luckily, his rowdy cousins were too busy stuffing their faces with food to interrupt and do their imitation of the goat and Simp in a staring contest.

Later, the older cousins organized a game of Capture the Flag, and Ezra ran around shouting insults and laughing with the other boys and girls. At dusk, it was time to come back in, kiss Granmaude on the cheek, and return home with his parents. As he re-entered her house, this time through the kitchen door, Ezra paused at the threshold and tapped on the doorframe as he had earlier.

"You're a Magee, all right." Granmaude's voice startled him. She was coming out of the pantry with a jar of peaches for Trudy. "You've got the Magee constitution." Ezra didn't know what she meant. He wanted to ask, but he was afraid.

"What are you saying about my son?" Trudy came in just then looking for Ezra.

"He's got something of his Uncle Nate in him," was all his grandmother would say.

❦

The things Ezra felt compelled to do in order to counter the sense of dread and foreboding that haunted him began to multiply: tapping door frames, counting steps (he found that three at a time worked best), staring at every corner of a room upon entering, whispering words or sentences three times in a row under his breath. It made him feel in control, if only temporarily.

Ezra was almost twelve years old, and before the fishing trip, his main ambition in life had been to pitch a no-hitter against Folly's bitter rival, the Huckabee Hornets. Unfortunately, the coach hadn't yet seen the wisdom of putting Ezra on the pitcher's mound during a game. He was usually sent out to right field where he saw little action. But still, Ezra considered himself a regular boy who did regular boy things. For instance, on a dare, he'd snuck a cigarette out of his mother's pack and ran into the woods to smoke it with Boyd and Floyd. By listening to his daddy, he'd acquired a considerable vocabulary of cusswords in preparation for manhood. And he'd even taken a look at some dirty pictures Boyd had stolen from his older brother.

So far, he could hide his new behaviors from the rest of the world. His dad—well, he was eccentric, himself, so he didn't seem to notice it in other people. His mom was working on a new book of paintings and spent most of her time poring over sketches and writing to her editor. Floyd and Boyd, who saw Ezra every day, hadn't noticed his odd behaviors because Ezra had, so far, only felt compelled to engage in them when he was indoors, and his mother didn't look favorably on inviting Floyd and Boyd into the house.

But Ezra felt something more than the usual dread in the pit of his stomach when the topic of school crossed his mind. It drew closer every day, like Napoleon's army marching on Moscow. His mom had gotten him a pretty good book on the Napoleonic wars, and he was just up to the part where the cold of winter was setting in as Napoleon was marching into Russia. It didn't look good for old Napoleon, and it didn't look good for Ezra, either.

In fact, Ezra would have gladly faced a Russian blizzard if it meant he didn't have to go to school. But unfortunately, it was a Folly summer like any other, with not so much as a chilly breeze in sight. In fact, Boyd had just demonstrated that you could fry an egg on the hood of Simp's car parked in the sun, and, at Simp's insistence, they'd been washing the car for the last hour as punishment.

After Ezra's cousins went home, his mom sent him to his grandmother's house to help with a few chores. On the way back home, he kicked a stone and practiced swearing.

"Jesus frickin' Christ!"

Maybe I shouldn't have said that one, he thought. God was listening all the time, even right now as he carried a sack of vegetables home from Granmaude's garden. The priests said so. It was a sin to take God's name in vain. Ezra guessed he wouldn't appreciate someone taking *his* name in vain either. Like if Floyd said, "Ezra dammit!" all the time, that would be right annoying.

Although Simpellion Magee was the most notorious atheist in the county, Ezra mostly believed in God. He went to Catholic school. Granmaude had insisted that Ezra and his cousins be baptized in the Catholic Church and attend Catholic school. Not even Simp was brave enough to defy his mother on that issue. The problem for Ezra was that his father's heresy was starting to rub off on him. Ezra sometimes had doubts about whether God was real. He'd spent many nights overhearing his father's debates with Reverend Hiram Johnson about the existence of God, their voices drifting up to his room through the heating vent.

"Jesus Christ, Johnson!" Simp would shout. "Just listen to what you're saying! Religion is nothing more than a fool making up a story to scare another fool, and then both of them believing it's true!" Or he'd say, "Jesus Christ, Johnson! Your Bible is a buncha baloney!" Trudy began referring to the minister as "Jesus Christ Johnson," an appellation that stuck.

It was hard for Ezra to know who to believe about religion: his dad, the priests and nuns at school, or the evangelical preachers who converged on nearby Buford every summer like a swarm of locusts with revival tents (the hot Alabama summers being a most convenient and appropriate time to talk about hell). When he asked his mom what she believed about God, she told him he should keep his ears and his mind open, think about what he learned, and when he was grown up, he could decide for himself what he believed. In other words, she was no help at all.

During the school year, Ezra was required to go to confession, where he regularly owned up to taking the Lord's name in vain and having sinful thoughts. After assigning some Hail Marys, Father Flanagan would advise him to think of wholesome things, like Jesus's words in the Sermon on the Mount or the Lord's Prayer, which was all right with Ezra.

As he shifted the bag of zucchinis and carrots to his other arm, he aimed a kick at a stone and then recited the Lord's Prayer. He made it all the way to the end but felt nothing. It didn't give him any relief from the feeling of impending doom traveling around in his gut. Not the way his tapping and counting did.

Was going crazy worse than being damned to hell? Or was it the same thing?

༶

The notion to go to a tent revival came a week later, with an invitation from Ezra's Great Uncle Homer Namey (a distant relation to Sissy Namey, because in Folly, nearly everyone was related to everyone else just a few generations back). Uncle Homer was Granmaude's diminutive brother. He was married to Great Aunt Eunice, an extra-large woman with blue hair piled high on her head in a complicated structure she fixed herself every morning. She worked as a dietician at the Buford Hospital. That always confused Ezra—weren't dieticians supposed to be skinny from always being on a diet? Floyd called her GargAuntua behind her back.

But Eunice was a person of fascination to Ezra, Floyd, and Boyd because of her sideline business as a hairdresser who coifed the locks of female corpses at funeral parlors. She made their hair look like they'd just come from the beauty parlor; an important part of the process of preparing bodies for the "final picture." Aunt Eunice was big on the "final picture."

"God don't want to see no uglies comin' through the pearly gates," she told Ezra once after describing a particularly difficult hairdo she'd just done on a corpse. Boyd and Floyd were always talking about Eunice's touching dead people and daring one another to shake her hand.

Homer and Granmaude had both been raised as Catholics, but when Homer married Eunice, he joined the Baptist Church where Eunice was a member. Homer was a simple man, content with his life. His wrinkled countenance still bore traces of the cheerful boy he'd once been. He always wore suspenders that pulled his pants up a little too high and exposed his white socks at the ankles. He worked as a bagger at the Piggly Wiggly grocery store over in Buford, which was a twenty-minute drive if Ezra's mom was behind the wheel, and fifteen minutes if his dad was driving. Homer had worked there since its opening day, thirty-three years earlier. He'd never missed a day, had always brought his lunch in a brown paper bag, and had always gone straight home when the store closed.

Ezra loved his great uncle Homer, but he thought the old man was a little weird. Homer took to heart the biblical injunction to "pray without ceasing." It was not uncommon to find him standing at the checkout counter stuffing groceries into bags while his lips moved a mile a minute in silent prayer. Ezra figured that the food Homer bagged had to be the holiest groceries in the state of Alabama.

Homer had taken to the Southern Baptist faith wholeheartedly. He was a True Believer. He believed the Old Testament and New Testament were literal and without error, and considered Heaven and Hell to be actual addresses. He believed God kept an eye on him at all times, even when he was just driving down the road in his green Chevy Nova hatchback. He believed God always guided his choices, from where to buy his checkered shirts and suspenders to whether or not to pick up a hitchhiker.

The hitchhikers he picked up may well have wished the Lord had guided Homer to drive on past, because Homer was a terrible driver. He drove consistently in second gear, and he used up a great portion of both sides of the road. Simp said that if God was in charge of Great Uncle Homer's driving, God must need some glasses. (In fairness, Simp allowed that there'd been a scarcity of Chevy Nova hatchbacks when Jesus last walked upon the earth.)

"How in the hell did he ever get a driver's license?" Simp's brother, Auggie, had once asked.

Simp had laughed. "He was persistent," Simp told him. "He took the driving exam fifteen times. Drove the state trooper examiner crazy. The guy finally gave him the license and told him not to come back."

A week before school started, Ezra accompanied his mother to the Piggly Wiggly. She let him choose his breakfast cereal, and he picked a new one called Count Chocula. Ezra had been itching for a box after being bombarded with countless commercials for it on the television. As Homer put the cereal in the bag, the old man paused to stare at the satanic-looking creature on the box, and his hands shook. He gave Trudy an alarmed look.

"It's a cartoon, Uncle Homer," she said gently.

The old man took a handkerchief out of his back pocket and wiped his forehead. "Say, Ezra," he started carefully, "if you're of a mind, Eunice and I would like to invite you to attend the revival meeting with us tonight."

"That's mighty kind, but—" Trudy began, but Ezra cut her off.

"Can I, Mom? Please?"

She looked at him in surprise. "Well, I suppose, if you really want to."

Ezra spent the rest of the afternoon helping his uncle carry grocery bags to customers' cars. Two customers tipped him a quarter each, and he used that to buy cherry popsicles for himself. At closing time, Uncle Homer hung up his apron, and he and Ezra walked five blocks home, where Aunt Eunice was waiting.

She made a big fuss over Ezra's desire to come to the revival and praised the Lord so many times that Ezra thought the Lord might be a little weary of hearing it before the tent meeting even began.

As a special treat, Uncle Homer took them out for hamburgers and fries, which they ate in the car. Then they drove slowly, amid a chorus of blasting car horns from frustrated drivers behind them, to Thrasher's field. Jim Thrasher owned a general store just south of Buford. He'd dug three ponds on the land behind the store where he raised minnows to sell as fish bait. He also had a big field, which he generously loaned to the evangelicals for their tent revivals.

Ezra felt self-conscious when he saw a few kids he knew from baseball dressed in their Sunday best. While the grown-ups greeted "Brother Homer" and "Sister Eunice," the kids shot him curious looks. They knew his daddy was Simpellion T. Dillon Magee, the dirty atheist and infamous letter-writer.

The August night was hot, and the crowd of more than a hundred stirred expectantly as they waited on hot metal folding chairs for the preacher to take the stage. Eunice handed around fans provided by the local funeral home and exchanged a few quiet words with neighbors and friends. Just when Ezra was about to burst with impatience, a tall man sporting a full head of silver hair strode onto the stage and raised his hands.

"Hallelujah!" he shouted in a booming voice.

"Hallelujah!" the congregation shouted back.

"It's a hot one, tonight," he said conversationally, unbuttoning his collar. "It's real hard to get comfortable in heat like this." He shed his light blue suit jacket and started to roll up his sleeves. "You feel like your skin is burning up. No matter what you do, you just can't get comfortable." People were nodding in agreement. "But we can stand a little discomfort. It's no big deal. Because we know that in a few minutes, or in a few hours or in a few days or in a few weeks," he paused dramatically, "it will rain! Or we'll get in front of a fan! Or we'll get in the car and drive up north where it's cool. We know this heat is not permanent. And that, my friends, makes it bearable. This heat WON'T LAST FOREVER!" he shouted. The congregation held its collective breath.

"But there is another heat that never ends," the preacher instructed them with quivering breath. "It *never* ends. For all eternity, it *never* ends. You know what I'm talkin' about, friends! I'm talkin' about Hellfire! I'm talking about Damnation!" he boomed.

A woman in the front row swooned and had to be fanned by her neighbors.

"Hell is real, like a monster with its jaws wide open, just waiting for unbelievers," the preacher promised, a finger pointing to the ground. "It's waiting for those who do not heed the word of the Lord. It's waiting for those who willfully ignore His truth!"

Ezra was mesmerized by the preacher. The boy silently compared this evangelical version of a truly terrifying hell to the one that the Catholic nuns taught in school. They were pretty close, except the preacher talked about weeping and wailing and the gnashing of teeth. Ezra didn't exactly know what the gnashing of teeth meant, but in the mouth of the evangelist it sounded like something you would want to avoid, especially when combined with weeping and wailing.

After a while, Ezra got bored with all the talk about hell, and he was ready to go home. But seeing as how he was squished between his great aunt and great uncle, there was no way out. He settled back to listen as the preacher started listing sins to avoid so as not to get sent to hell.

"Masturbation!" the preacher bellowed, "is an offense against almighty God!" Ezra blushed when Great Uncle Homer nudged him significantly (how did he know?!). The preacher warned about all kinds of evil things about sex: besides masturbation there was fornication, lewdness, carnality, lustfulness, and a lot of other things about which Ezra had no clue. It seemed that everything about sex made good paving material for the road to hell except the kind that was for married people to make a baby. Uncle Homer kept trying to catch Ezra's eye, so the boy didn't dare look away from the preacher, whose white shirt was glued to his body with sweat. The man paced back and forth across the stage, waving his hands and shaking his fists in the air. For a minute, Ezra thought he looked a little like his dad in high dudgeon shouting at Mabel.

Ezra was glad when the sex talk was over, but then the preacher moved on to warn them off game-playing, dancing (Ezra didn't think he'd miss that one much), and television. According to the evangelist, just about everything Ezra liked to do was going to land him in hell.

The preacher seemed to be winding down. His voice got really quiet, and he bowed his head. "We've all profaned Jesus's name. We've all sinned and come short of the glory of *God*!" The last word was aspirated as a harsh whisper that ricocheted through the evangelist's nasal and oral cavities. "You, and you, and you," he screamed, stabbing his finger at members of the congregation, "will condemn your eternal soul to hell if you don't get right with Jesus." One of the "yous" was hurled straight at Ezra, who sat transfixed as if a spotlight had him in its beam.

"You must be born again!" roared the evangelist. "Salvation is waiting right here," he said, pointing to the altar just beneath the pulpit.

Then suddenly he was chatting again like this was just a friendly conversation. He explained that when the literalist Nicodemus asked Jesus if he must again enter his mother's womb, Jesus had laughed at him. It seems that Nicodemus didn't understand, just as Ezra didn't understand. But, the preacher explained, it was simple: God's plan of salvation lay before sinful man in a manner that even a crazy person could understand.

Crazy person? Ezra's ears perked up. Was hell a place for crazy people? Was the dread he had been feeling the beginning of what the preacher was talking about? His stomach lurched from the tension and the hamburger and fries. Was salvation a cure from his misery?

All he had to do was walk down the aisle, under the gaze of fellow revival-goers, and profess his faith in Jesus?

The Catholic priests and nuns had never put it so simply. Ezra had swallowed the wine, eaten the wafer, and genuflected upon entry into the Catholic sanctuary. He'd dabbed himself with holy water and prayed under the watchful gaze of the brooding, saintly statues. But he'd never experienced the emotional angst this evangelist inspired in him; he'd never experienced the sweltering, hellacious heat of the revival tent. Ezra felt the swaying of the people being grilled over the fire and brimstone of hell, a picture of which the preacher was painting so eloquently. But he also had masturbation in his head now, from the earlier part of the sermon. The sense of danger and erotic tension made him dizzy. He longed to move, to stand up, to act.

"Stand up and give your heart to Jesus," the preacher's booming voice commanded. "Come and be saved!"

Ezra lurched to his feet and the congregation cheered. Homer shouted, "Amen!" and Eunice punctuated his amen with a "Thank you, Jesus! Praise God, thank you Jesus!"

An electric keyboard struck up the notes of the hymn "Just as I Am," and a sonorous voice began singing: "Just as I am / without one plea / but that thy blood / was shed for me . . ." Ezra found himself in a riptide of hands guiding him out into the aisle, where he lost his will to bolt out of the tent. Streams of people pressed up behind him and propelled him forward. When he arrived at the front of the tent, the pressure blessedly eased. Ezra stood in front of the stage and stared up at the preacher.

"Are you ready to accept the Lord Jesus Christ as your savior, son?"

Ezra blinked, and it was enough for the preacher. He and the others behind him were led outside to the minnow pool. When he realized what was about to happen, Ezra's fear of water kicked in, and he tried to turn away, but he was turned back around by the preacher's grasp. The preacher just laughed and said, "You watch how it goes, son. You can be second," and then he chose another boy and led him into the pond.

"I baptize thee, my brother, in the name of the Father," the minister intoned. Ezra saw the boy reach out and grab a minnow as it swam past and slip it into his pocket. When the preacher dunked the boy in the shallow pond, Ezra wondered if the minnow was now guaranteed a place in heaven too. When it was Ezra's turn, he strode into the pond looking for a minnow of his own. But before he realized what was happening, the preacher threw him back and dunked him in the mucky water. Ezra came out gasping and sneezing water out of his nose.

Ezra insisted on being driven home right after the baptism. He was soggy and smelled of pond water, and he was steamed. He thought things would change, that he'd feel different—being saved and all—but he didn't. The whole thing was probably just a big lie and he'd been dunked in Thrasher's pond for nothing. Eunice and Homer went on praising the Lord the whole ride, and Ezra was sick of the whole thing. When he finally got home, he sprinted from the car as soon as they were in the driveway.

Simp was over at Killian's at their weekly poker game, and Trudy was drinking coffee in the kitchen with a friend.

"How was it?" Trudy asked, but Ezra pounded up the stairs to his room.

"Fine!" he called back to her. He stripped off his wet clothes and rinsed his head and face under the tap. He still smelled like pond water, so he washed again and this time used soap. He threw on pajamas and went downstairs to watch television. *The Odd Couple* was just starting. Oscar and Felix weren't that interesting, especially not that night, but he thought he'd better try to enjoy the program more since he'd be going to hell for watching it.

CHAPTER 5

A few weeks after Ezra's marriage had begun its descent into a deep freeze, spring weather had begun to tickle the back of the West Virginia winter. It was spring break at the university where he taught. Since his break didn't line up with Dillon's, the family'd had no choice but to forgo a much-needed vacation. Ezra was home every day when Dillon got back from school.

On Tuesday, the weather beckoned him outside to wait for Dillon on the back steps. Sun warmed his skin with the optimistic hope that accompanies nice weather. Ezra basked in the warmth, eating an apple. It was the healthiest he'd felt in weeks.

"Hi, son. How was school?"

"Dad, are you mad at Mom?"

Ezra flung the apple core into the woods behind the house and watched it bounce and skitter before coming to a stop at the base of an old maple tree, giving himself time to form an answer. "It's normal stuff, Dillon. Husbands and wives go through times like this. It's just the way it is."

"You still love each other, right?"

"Don't you worry about us. We're fine," Ezra lied.

"I want to play soccer."

"You do?"

"Yeah. It's the first game tomorrow. Mr. Measley says I can play if I want. I'll do it, but only if you and Mom come."

The next day, Dillon played his first soccer game of the year. Celia and Ezra had been avoiding each other, but for Dillon's sake, they went to the game together. It was awkward at first, in the quiet pre-match bustle, but once the game began, the couple settled into their normal habits of cheering and high-fiving.

When it was over, Dillon surprised them again by asking if they could all go to the coach's house for the after-game pizza party. At the party, Ezra stared at Dillon. He didn't want to remove his eyes from the boy he once knew, acting like his old self; laughing with his friends as they spat watermelon seeds into a flowerpot. He and Celia exchanged tentative smiles when Dillon ran by with Wiley, laughing.

As they drove home that night, Ezra was lightly buzzed from the beers he'd had at the coach's house, but he felt good again. To finally feel some relief from the ubiquitous tension was a wonderful sensation. When Celia looked at him, her eyes were soft; not the hardened glare he'd grown accustomed to lately, just a warm, bright, emerald green that seemed to glisten in the moonlight. He remembered the warmth and joy that had permeated his home before the arrival of the tense, emotional tsunami.

As he walked up to Dillon's room to say goodnight, Celia intercepted him in the hallway and took him by the hand. She led him into their bedroom and closed the door. They undressed in the dark, not speaking, and moved onto the bed. Ezra ached to feel her in his arms. Celia moved to be on top of him. She kissed his fingers, one by one. He sighed with pleasure.

"Didn't you once tell me you were a real nail-biter?" Celia murmured.

"Aunt Lenore used to dip my hands in Tabasco sauce to make me stop."

"Have you noticed Dillon's hands?" Ezra froze, but Celia kept her tone light and stroked his chest. "Lately, he's taken to biting them so much his fingers bleed. When I beg him to stop, he says he'll try, and I can tell he wants to. But not a minute later, he's chewing them again."

The room went silent. He could tell Celia expected a response.

When he didn't offer one, she said gently, "It's time to tell me what's going on."

It seemed unfair. She was on top of him, her naked skin rubbing against the entire length of his body. Her fingers unleashed a kaleidoscope of urges, reminding him how much he needed her—how much he loved her. He said nothing, but his body's response was electric. He turned Celia onto her back, grabbing her wrists in his hands as he kissed her neck. Ezra eased himself inside her, slowly, and finally felt close to his wife again.

After they made love, Celia lay in the curve of his arm and stroked his cheek.

Celia stared at him. "I can wait as long as it takes," she said matter-of-factly.

He couldn't tell her. He couldn't tell her how he used to bite his own nails when he was a boy, even when it hurt, because it was one way to gnaw back at the anxiety.

"I can wait," Celia said again, tracing her finger across his lips and then pushing it into his mouth. Ezra instinctively sucked her finger as he felt himself stir again. "There is nothing you can tell me that will make me love you any less, Ezra Magee."

He wanted to believe her, but he didn't. But he also knew he couldn't dodge this moment any longer.

"I had what Dillon has, when I was a boy."

He couldn't see her face, but he realized she wasn't shocked at all. She'd figured it out. He realized now it had probably been obvious the whole time. Ezra tried to pull away, but she wrapped her arms around him, refusing to let go.

"What do you mean?"

Ezra took in a deep breath. "I had what is known as obsessive-compulsive disorder. It can be genetically transferred, and I gave it to Dillon. And I know I should have told you before I asked you to marry me. I just . . . it was all in the past when I met you. I didn't think it mattered."

Celia rolled away from him, curled up on her side, and burst into tears. "I thought you blamed *me* for what Dillon's going through," she said, sobbing. "I was so hurt."

Ezra felt a sharp stab of remorse. "I blamed myself, not you. I should have told you a long time ago I was defective."

"Yes, you should have told me," Celia said, reaching for a tissue and blowing her nose angrily. "But not because you're 'defective,' Ezra. You should have told me because married people share the important things about their pasts with each other."

It wasn't exactly as he'd predicted. She didn't hurl blame for Dillon's behavior at him, but she was just as angry and disappointed as he'd feared she would be. He sighed. "I know. I'm sorry."

"Sorry isn't enough. You need to grow up, you know?"

"I know."

"What did we tell Dillon when he used to throw tantrums? You need to use your fucking words. You punished me all this time because you thought I'd be mad at you. You thought the worst of me. You didn't trust me."

He was guilty on all counts. "I'm sorry I'm not a better man."

"So am I," she said, pulling the blankets up to her chin. "At least now it all makes sense—the drinking, the way you provoked me to keep me angry with you so you could shut me out." She turned back over to face him. "Honestly, did you really think I'd hold you accountable for Dillon's problems? If he gets skin cancer, will you blame me because it runs on my side of the family? If he needs glasses, is that my fault because I'm myopic?"

"Celia, this is different, and you know it. I gave my son a mental illness. I had it, I should have known our child might inherit the tendency from me, and I didn't warn you."

"I do not regret our son!"

"I'm not saying—"

"Yes, you are! You goddamn well are!" Celia paused, the volume of her voice echoing throughout the room. She lowered to a whisper.

"You are such an idiot! All the hope I need for Dillon is right here!" She jabbed him in the shoulder with her finger. "You!"

"Me?!"

"You're the proof that Dillon can be helped! You found a way to overcome it. And even though you turned out to be an idiot, at least you're an idiot with a hot wife, a good job, and an amazing, intelligent kid. Don't you get it? If you could do it, so can Dillon!"

Ezra was speechless, this time because he truly had nothing to say. He wrapped his arms around Celia's curves and pulled her close. "Hot wife, huh?"

She pushed him away and grabbed his face in her hands. His face was brushed in moonlight, and her eyes scanned it, took in every inch of him, studied his features. "Tell me what it was like," she whispered.

"Celia, I really don't want to talk about it."

"I don't care." Her frankness surprised him. "This is for Dillon. It's so hard to watch him suffer and not know what he's going through." Her eyes filled with tears again, but this time, here in their bed, her tears cracked the wall he'd built.

Ezra sighed. "It started when I was about the same age as Dillon."

"Before or after your parents died?"

"Before, I think. I think I had it by the time I went to live with my aunt."

Ezra's memories of life before age twelve were mostly a blank. When he tried to remember his childhood in Alabama, it seemed as if he came face to face with a wall. Even when he was twelve, just a few months after first arriving at his Aunt Lenore's home in West Virginia, it was already difficult to remember anything from before. And he quickly got to the point where he didn't really *want* to remember, because each time he tried to recall his past, or even just the events that had led to his relocation, a panic attack came and swallowed him up. The panic attacks were unbearable, the worst of all his symptoms, so eventually he had stopped trying to remember and instead repressed as much of his Alabama memories deep down inside of himself as he could. He shoved them into a limbo that, after a while, faded into a more livable, quasi-amnesic state.

"I went to live with Aunt Lenore after she came for me in Alabama. We flew on an airplane—I remember that. They'd given me a sedative, so I was kinda drowsy, but I wasn't scared. That surprised me. I remember thinking I ought to be freaking out, but I wasn't. I stayed home for a few weeks, reading books. I couldn't bring myself to go outside. Lenore didn't pressure me. One day, she told me I had to start school the next week or I'd have to redo the seventh grade. I got up that next Monday morning, got dressed, and ate breakfast, but I couldn't do it."

"Couldn't do what?"

"I couldn't leave the house. I tried to walk out the door and I had a panic attack. These panic attacks, they . . . the thing was, when it started, it brought on these crippling thoughts about . . . about dying, being abandoned, going crazy, that sort of thing. I really don't know if it started in Alabama or when I got to West Virginia." Ezra shook his head. "That probably doesn't matter. What's important is that part of my mind told me that if I did the sort of things Dillon's doing now—like the tapping on the table and the counting—my mind told me there was magic in those rituals that would ward off doom. It was weird, like waking up on a trip you didn't know you were taking. It didn't make any sense then, and it doesn't make any sense now. But that's just the way it was. When it happened on that first day of school in West Virginia, I knew that it had happened before, but I didn't have any memories about it."

"What happened in Alabama?" Celia whispered. "Can you remember why you had to come live with Lenore? You've never told me."

Ezra stared past Celia at the wall, his stomach muscles tensing. "For twenty-eight years I've been too afraid to remember what happened," he said finally. "And now I really *can't* remember. At least not much. I know that I was orphaned by a storm and my aunt came for me. That's it."

Ezra rolled onto his back and stared at the ceiling, feeling the memories converge into a river woven with pain and foreboding.

He took another deep breath. "Aunt Lenore found me a therapist over in Morgantown," Ezra said quietly, "and he put me on some medications. I hated the meds." He stopped for a moment, recapturing the pain the memories brought back. "Some of them made me feel tired and spaced out all the time. Some made the anxiety worse, and I couldn't sleep for days at a time. I did most of my schoolwork at home." Ezra stopped and looked at Celia. "Aunt Lenore arranged for me to take the tests after school. She was patient. The school was patient. It was hell for a while until my doctor found the right drugs. I improved every year, and by the time I graduated high school, the doctor told me I might not need the drugs or the therapy anymore. He seemed to be saying that I was cured. Well, that's how I took it, anyway. I went to college and never looked back."

Celia looked at her husband in silence for a moment. "College is the only part of your past you ever talk about," she said. She played with his fingers, lifting them one by one and letting them fall back against his chest. "I know all about how you broke one of the school's cross-country records your senior year. And the plays you were in." She smiled and looked down at his hands. "And, of course, all those girls you ran around with."

"Girls. Mmmmm," Ezra said. He moved his hands gently across Celia's lightly muscled shoulder. "I only fell in love with one. And she was crazy enough to marry me."

They made love again. It reinvigorated him, both of them, as if a summer rain had cooled down the hot spell that had tortured their bodies. Eventually, they ended up in a tangle of limbs. Celia burrowed into him and fell asleep, her lips curled into a peaceful smile.

Ezra luxuriated in their contentment. He remembered the first time he'd laid eyes on Celia. It was the second day of graduate school. He walked into his Russian history seminar and took a seat at the table. Celia walked into the room with an air of self-sufficiency and confidence, and for a moment he thought she might be the professor. She caught him staring and flashed a million-dollar smile before sitting down next to him and introducing herself. She was twenty-one years old, with long dark hair, a spray of tiny freckles across her nose, and wide, green eyes behind wire-rimmed glasses. She had the look of someone who'd been raised to know that she could do anything she wanted with her life. On their first date, he'd learned that Celia had been in love twice before. Ezra had been in a few relationships, but he'd never been in love, and he found himself irrationally jealous of her past. When they became intimate, she told Ezra he had the sexiest hands.

He loved the way she gave her full attention to him when they talked and when they made love. Even now, with his still-thick hair starting to show signs of gray, and faint age lines appearing at the corners of his eyes, Celia still seemed to find him desirable. It was a gift he'd never expected. He was sure he didn't deserve it.

☙

"Seems like Celia handled your big secret just fine."

Ezra stood in the doorway of the living room and observed as Hiram Johnson put his feet up on the coffee table. Ezra noted the worn soles of his cordovan shoes and wondered if the man owned anything other than blue suits, wide ties, and dirty brown shoes. His pounding head thrummed harder as he tried to picture Hiram in a track suit.

"So, things started falling apart after that?"

Ezra didn't answer.

"Instead of getting better, they got worse, didn't they?"

"Yes, goddamn it," Ezra admitted, feeling tears well up in his eyes.

"You're just like Sissy Namey after all, aren't you?" said Hiram.

Sissy Namey. Her apparition bubbled up from his cauldron of repressed memories as if he'd never forgotten her: the watery blue eyes that darted restlessly, her wispy blond hair and open-mouthed grin. Ezra remembered her long black skirt, frayed at the bottom, a purple sweater with tiny holes nibbled by moths. He couldn't remember ever having spoken to Sissy Namey. She was a generation older than he was and had been taken away in a strait jacket when he was just a boy—that memory, somehow, came back to him. But he knew they were alike. Sissy Namey was a loon. Certifiable. And he was . . .

Ezra stared at the reverend, in his blue suit and striped tie, looking exactly the same as Ezra remembered him, smiling at Ezra like it was the most natural thing in the world for him to be there after all this time.

"It's all coming back," Ezra said.

"What's coming back?" Hiram asked.

"The hell that's always been waiting for me."

Hiram suddenly jumped up from the couch and was pointing out of the front living room window. "Well, speak of the devil!" he shouted. He sounded almost giddy.

Ezra walked hurriedly to the window where Hiram was standing and saw a woman standing by the mailbox. She had yellow hair and seemed to be talking to the dead petunias. She wore a long black skirt with frayed edges, and a purple sweater with tiny holes eaten through. Ezra's mouth went dry. It was impossible.

"What do you think she wants?" asked Ezra, his voice quavering at the sight of her slight, eerie figure.

"Lord knows," said Hiram. "What did the poor thing ever want? Last time I saw her—" Hiram stopped mid-sentence.

Ezra turned to look at the reverend, but he was no longer at his side. He turned back to the window, and there was no one by the mailbox. "Where'd she go?" Ezra whispered, frantically searching the yard. "Reverend!" he shouted behind him. He turned and scanned the empty room at his back. He could see into the kitchen and stared at the bottle of bourbon he'd left on the counter. He needed some to wet his dry tongue.

Ezra returned his gaze to the window. He yelled and jumped back, dislodging a family picture from the wall, the frame breaking into pieces against the wooden floor.

Sissy was now standing on his front porch.

"Go ahead. Ask her what she wants." Hiram Johnson was once again leaning back in the chair, his feet up on the coffee table.

"You ask her," Ezra said nervously.

"It's you she's come for. Not me."

"Jesus Christ, Hiram, will you just ask her!?" Ezra's suddenly shrill voice made him realize how spooked he'd become. He looked across the road and saw the McCarthy's car pull into their driveway. Sally McCarthy hopped out to check her mailbox.

"Oh, God, I hope she doesn't see Sissy and decide to come over here," Ezra muttered.

The telephone rang. Ezra jumped again, this time without causing any damage. Despite his aching head, he ran into the den to answer it, praying it would be Celia. No such luck. It was only the Red Cross asking for blood. He replaced the phone without responding and returned to the window. Sissy was gone.

"She'll be back," Hiram prophesied. Now the old man was lying on the couch.

"God, I hope not." Ezra shuddered, scanning the street.

"You were telling me about you and Celia. You told her your deep, dark secret, and she forgave you. So why did she leave?"

Ezra didn't take his eyes away from the window. "It's a long story."

"S'okay," said Hiram, stacking throw pillows under his head to get more comfortable, "I've got a long attention span."

༄

He and Celia had enjoyed a kind of second honeymoon for the next three weeks after their intimate reconciliation. Celia's research for her book on Jane Addams was going well, and Ezra's paper on Lincoln was accepted for publication by the *Journal of American History*, provided he could revise the last section before the deadline. Dillon was over the moon because his great aunt Lenore had gotten him a belated birthday present: a six-year-old black lab named Izzy. A friend of Lenore's had given the animal up because she was moving into an assisted living facility, and Lenore promised to find the dog a good home. Seeing the delight on Dillon's face was enough for Celia and Ezra. Izzy was a perfectly trained, friendly dog. The whole family fell in love with her, in part because their house suddenly seemed loving again.

Izzy slept on Dillon's bed, and for a few weeks she guarded the boy against his nightmares. Ezra caught up on his sleep and began to take his morning runs again. He was still sneaking a cigarette once or twice a day, but he cut way back on the beer and bourbon.

He came home from work one afternoon to find Izzy moping on the back porch, her eyes drooping and head down, afraid to meet his gaze. "She was scratching, and I found ticks all over her," Celia explained. "I gave her a bath to kill the ticks, but we can't have her sleeping in Dillon's room until we know for sure she's not going to have another infestation."

"She's really good for him," Ezra began, then let it go. He didn't want to argue. He valued their rediscovered peace, so he let Celia do as she would do no matter how much he thought she was wrong.

Dillon was upset. He cried all through dinner and as he got ready for bed, but Celia was firm. "Deer ticks and Lyme disease can be dangerous. Wait until the tick season is over and we'll see," she said. She kissed her son on the forehead, turned off the lights, and left him to sleep on his own for the first time since Izzy had joined the family.

That night, Dillon's nightmares returned. Ezra stayed up with him, slipping back into the familiar routine as if the peaceful interval had never occurred. In the morning, Celia found Ezra asleep on the recliner in the den, reeking of bourbon.

"I go to sleep with a sober man, wake up alone, and find a drunk guy in the den." She smiled but she was only half-joking. Ezra knew he had to tell her about the nightmares their son was having so she wouldn't think of him only as a nighttime drunk.

When he did, she was livid.

"I wanted to spare you. Your insomnia, the pills . . . remember?"

"Maybe that wasn't your right. Maybe it's my decision."

"Celia, that makes no sense," he started to argue, but she stormed out of the room. Ezra audibly sighed, a rush of air forcing his frustrations out of his body, and he went after her. He found her in the kitchen, peeling an apple for no other reason than to occupy her restless hands. Ezra apologized three more times before she finally seemed to let it go. But they spent the rest of the night in silence.

Despite his promise to wake her if and when Dillon had another nightmare, Ezra went in alone when the whimpering started. He sat on the side of the bed and spoke softly, keeping the boy company even though he knew Dillon was lost in a private, hellish world, lying on his side with his back to Ezra.

"Four score and seven years ago, our forefathers brought forth . . ." Ezra recited the Gettysburg Address in its entirety from memory. When he finished, Dillon was blinking at him and trying to get his bearings. "You're back," Ezra said. "Good old Abe did the trick."

"Abe Lincoln?"

Hearing two normal words come out of Dillon's mouth loosened the knot of tension in Ezra's gut.

"That's right. You heard of him? Tall guy with a beard? I was thinking this summer we should take a family trip over to Washington, D.C. to visit the Lincoln Memorial."

"Yeah," Dillon said faintly. He rolled over, his back once again to Ezra.

Ezra rubbed his shoulders. "Want to tell me?" he asked softly.

"Just scared," Dillon answered, his voice hoarse from the moaning.

"Was it Voldemort? Darth Vader?"

"No."

If there was some way to make a bargain with the universe to spare Dillon this pain, Ezra was prepared to make it. He could still remember the hopelessness he'd felt at that age. He could remember his thoughts of ending his own life. Thoughts of Dillon and suicide turned his stomach, bile snaking its fingers up his esophagus and into his throat.

"Dillon, your mother and I love you, completely and forever, no matter what. You just remember that, okay? Whatever you're going through, we're here for you, okay?"

Dillon said nothing. He remained in bed, back to Ezra, gnawing on his decimated thumbnail. It was already chewed down to the quick. Ezra reached over and gently pried the hand away from his son's mouth.

"My advice? You've only got so much nail on each finger. Better save some in case you need to scratch. And you'll want to leave yourself a snack for later on."

Dillon wouldn't meet his eyes, and Ezra understood. The shame and confusion were terrible. He tried to think of something helpful to say to his son. Diversion, he suddenly remembered. When he had first gone to live with his aunt, she would sit up and watch movies with him late at night when he was having a bad episode.

And there was something else he could do, as painful as it was. "Dillion, look at me, son." Ezra demanded. Dillon turned to look at his dad. "When I was a boy about your age, I had the same thing as you. The world looked strange and scary to me just like it does to you. I had to do lots of unusual things, like tapping on door frames and shuffling my feet. I got over it. So can you."

Dillon stared at his dad for a moment with a questioning look. Then the boy lowered his eyes. *He doesn't believe me*, Ezra realized. *Have I really fucked things up so much that he can't believe me?* So, back to his Aunt Lenore's strategy: diversion.

"Hey, you want to watch an old movie on Flashback?" Ezra whispered conspiratorially. "Let's sneak downstairs and nuke a bowl of popcorn. What do you say?"

Dillon gave a little nod. Ezra wrapped him in his blanket and lifted him up easily, tossing the boy over his shoulder in a fireman's carry.

"Oof! I forgot you're part robot and weigh five tons because of your steel bone structure!" Ezra made a feeble robot sound and said in a whisper, "Puny human, take me to your popcorn." Dillon didn't respond, but that was all right. Ezra didn't expect him to.

They settled on the couch in the living room and watched some ridiculous black-and-white spy flick. On a good day, they would have laughed together at the bad makeup, cheesy special effects, and corny dialogue. But Dillon was exhausted, and within ten minutes he had fallen asleep, his head on his dad's lap, as the screen flashed shadows on his haunted face.

Ezra awoke sometime in the early morning hours, still sitting on the couch, Dillon's head still resting on his lap. The half-empty popcorn bowl lay on the carpet at Ezra's feet. Izzy was nestled against Dillon's back, a series of soft sighs puffing through her black muzzle. Ezra remembered letting Izzy into the house during the night. The boy's face looked serene now, and his left arm hung relaxed off the edge of the couch. Ezra tucked the blanket around Dillon and Izzy and started for his bedroom. As he passed by the kitchen, he hesitated for only a moment, and then went straight for the bottle. Just one drink, to help him sleep.

CHAPTER 6

"**H**ey! Some of us are trying to sleep up here!"

Ezra's complaint went unheard. The keys of his father's old Remington typewriter reverberated through the living room and up into the boy's bedroom, pounded with the emotional fervor Simp Magee felt when the muse hit him. Squinting at the pastel rays of dawn light pushing through the bottom of his window blinds, Ezra rolled over and tried to block out the sound with his pillow, but the percussive pounding penetrated it. He groped under the bed and found his baseball glove and jammed it over his ear, but he still heard the confounded noise.

Simp was a morning person, and lately he'd gotten it into his head to renew his one-way correspondence with Samuel Alger, editor of the *Sand Mountain Sentinel*. The readers of the *Sentinel* were well-acquainted with the political and religious views of Simpellion Magee, and his printed missives always provoked an outcry which, incidentally, also sold more newspapers. Trudy once suggested that Simp get himself hired as a columnist, but Simp laughed at her for suggesting that he would ever let himself work for "that man."

Simp drew a disability pension from a wartime injury incurred during his service in Korea. Ezra never learned what the injury was, but on rainy days his father complained of a painful, creaky hip. Simp spent his days hunting, fishing, and devising money-making schemes that nearly always ended up costing more than they made (like his fainting goat or the pair of emus he bought because they were somehow going to make him rich). It was Trudy who quietly supported the family by illustrating nature books and taking on magazine commissions. Occasionally, when income was low, Trudy would lease out their pasture to neighbors to make ends meet. Sometimes they sold vegetables in the local farmer's market in Buford. Ezra was aware that other boys' fathers were identified by their careers, like an electrician or a farmer. But his father was known simply as "eccentric."

"You awake, son?" Simp stood in his doorway clutching a sheet of paper. Ezra rolled over and pulled the covers over his head. He felt exhausted all the time since the fishing trip. All too often the wave came for him and caused him to jerk awake in the middle of the night in a cold sweat. Sometimes he'd awaken himself at the beginning of a scream and had to hope his parents hadn't heard.

He tried to hide his coping behaviors around them too. But he caught both his mom and dad sometimes watching him as he tapped and counted his way through a doorway, or up some steps. Thus far they hadn't commented about it, but their looks were enough to make him blush and run to his room.

When the terrors came, part of him wanted to run to his mother for comfort, but another part was ashamed to let his father know he was weak. Night after night he lay awake with his fists clenched until the tremors in his body subsided.

He told himself to stop being such a wimp. School would start soon. What was he going to do then? Sister Josefina taught the seventh grade, and she had a reputation for wielding a heavy ruler across the knuckles of boys who got up to any mischief. What if he started acting weird, tapping his feet and touching door frames like he'd been doing lately? Sister Josefina would see, and his classmates would make his life a living hell. Ezra wished he could stay in bed for the rest of his life.

Nothing seemed to make him happy anymore. Sometimes he wished he would just die.

The day before, Boyd had dared Ezra and Floyd to walk across the railroad trestle that spanned Cahill Creek. Ezra didn't hesitate. If he had fallen off the side and died or been hit by a train, it couldn't have been as bad as the way he was feeling. When they shot at cans with a BB gun, Ezra didn't even listen to Boyd's dirty jokes. He was imagining what it would be like to hold a gun to his head. Would he have the guts to pull the trigger? He'd heard that if you didn't shoot yourself in the right place, you could blow off part of your skull and still live. That would be awful—he'd have to go through life with half a skull. He'd be crazy *and* deformed.

"Ezra? Wake up, son. I gotta read this to you."

"Sissy Namey, Sissy Namey, Sissy Namey," Ezra muttered to himself three times, his head still under the covers. The mantra calmed him.

"This letter's gonna drive people crazy! Come on downstairs and eat your cereal while I read it to you."

The word "crazy" crashed through Ezra's brain like shattering glass. "Sissy Namey, Sissy Namey, Sissy Namey," he repeated under his breath nine times. His pulse finally slowed.

Ezra pulled on some clothes and trudged down the stairs. His father had a makeshift office in the living room consisting of a card table on which his old black typewriter rested. Crumpled pages littered the floor. Simp Magee had recently taken a hiatus from writing to the editor of the *Sand Mountain Sentinel*, mostly on account of the Presidential primary campaign and the Democratic National Convention taking up most of his energy. But when he'd heard through the grapevine that his boy had been to one of those wretched tent revivals and got himself baptized, Simp experienced a combustible mixture of emotions. It wasn't enough that his mother strong-armed him and Trudy into sending Ezra to that damnable Catholic school that Simp had attended as a boy (and that, he was sure, had messed him up aplenty). Now, those damned Baptists had lured his son into the circus they called a "spiritual revival." The nerve of them to dunk his boy in a minnow pond with the absurd claim of salvation and the washing away of nonexistent sins! Ezra was a boy, goddammit! You couldn't scare a boy with all that hellfire-and-damnation claptrap and expect the boy's father to sit by and do nothing. No sir! Not if that father was Simp Magee.

"You want coffee?" Simp asked, his back to the doorway.

"Not really," Ezra replied.

Simp spun around. "It's you!" he said, looking at his son. "Thought you was your mama. Cereal is on the table."

"Yeah, I see it," Ezra said, a hint of sarcasm in his voice.

There was an awkward silence.

"Well, alrighty then. Eat up."

Trudy saved father and son from more awkward silence as she joined them for breakfast. "I see the muse has got you again." She gave Simp a kiss on the cheek and laid her hand on Ezra's shoulder. Her blue-flowered bathrobe flowed behind her like the Nile, and the scent of her lilac powder momentarily distracted both Ezra and his father from their mutual irritation. "Am I in time for the dramatic reading?"

Simp seated her in a chair and poured her coffee. Then he took up his letter, cleared his throat, and read:

"'To the editor of the *Sand Mountain Sentinel*: We humans are a pretty sorry bunch. Monkeys are probably ashamed they're kin to us. We're born with the ability to think, and just look at the results. We send people to the moon with our knowledge of science, and yet we continue to believe in superstitious nonsense. We build monuments to this nonsense all over the world. Here, in Alabama, we've got a church on just about every corner of every town, and the countryside is fairly teeming with them.

"'The conjurers and frauds who profit from these monuments have made it their special mission to make people miserable when they want to enjoy life, and to scare the hell out of them the rest of the time too. Now, if an adult freely chooses to believe in their fables and fantasies, that is his or her right under the Constitution. But children are another story. Children should be protected from liars and conjurers; it's our job as adults to protect their young minds, and to teach them fact and truth, not lies and superstition.'" Simp paused and gave Ezra a long, significant look before continuing.

"'We send our young people to school to learn math and science, reading and history. Some parents have decided that they will expose their innocent, vulnerable children to the conjurers' theater: what they call revivals. And what do children learn? They learn about the dead being resurrected, and an ocean parting so people can walk across it, and a river turning to blood, and a place of eternal torment. The Bible is full of stories that should be read like a good work of fiction. But the conjurers want us to believe it's all literal, truthful fact. They are selling us *a pack of lies*.'" Simp stabbed the paper for emphasis on the last words.

"'It's no wonder humans are so messed up. We were doing all right, swinging around in trees and eating nuts and berries, when nature gave us a big brain, which was a terrible mistake. If our species is going to survive, we're going to have to wake up and run the magicians back into the forests, where maybe they and their disciples will do all of us a big favor and take up snake handling. Sincerely yours,' et cetera, et cetera."

Trudy clapped her hands. Ezra kept working on his cereal.

"Truth has its own sound!" Simp said energetically. "The ignorant are bound to hear it and see what I'm saying, don't you think, Trudy?"

"I hope that's what happens, dear."

"I think this is my best one yet!"

"It's certainly to the point," she agreed.

"Where are the stamps? I got to get this in the early mail."

"I'll find you one." She left the room and soon came back with stamps illustrated with wild, red spider lilies. Whenever the U.S. Postal Service published a new stamp displaying wildflowers, Trudy would buy a sheet of them. It was her secret ambition to have one of her paintings someday made into a stamp.

"Aw, you got to be kidding me!" Simp was of the oft-aired opinion that a flower-stamped envelope did not send the right message to the *Sand Mountain Sentinel*'s editor. "Those are ridiculous fucking stamps, Trudy." And they both burst out laughing.

⁂

Despite the effeminate stamp that conveyed it to the editor, Simp's letter was printed in the *Sentinel*'s Sunday edition.

"Go ahead and read it," he said to Trudy that Sunday morning. "Let's hear it aloud." But then he couldn't bear to let anyone else do it, so he took over and delivered another impassioned reading, including dramatic banging on the table. Ezra cringed, wondering how much teasing he'd get from his cousins for this latest rant.

Killian dropped by shortly after, carrying his copy of the *Sentinel*. "Saw your letter," he remarked. "Bold as clothes on a nude beach. The paper's circulation must be down, so they need to stir up the Christians."

"I hope to hell it does stir them up," Simp replied. "Those bastards start messing with my family, they're messing with me."

"Don't take it too hard," Killian advised Simp. "Kids go through phases. He'll get over it."

Simp lowered his voice. "The boy's been having problems since the fishing trip. He doesn't need a goddamn preacher making it worse."

"What sort of problems?"

"Started with nightmares," Simp said. "Now he's acting funny. Tapping on doors and shuffling his feet and such," he continued.

"Like Nate."

Simp gave Killian a stern look. "Maybe," he said. It was always dangerous to mention Nate around Simp.

"I recall Nate used to do a lot of oddball things: counting by threes, talking to himself, and such," Killian said calmly. Five years older than Simp, Killian had been close to the Magee family all his life, having grown up on the land adjacent to their place. He'd sold six acres of land to Simp the year Simp came back home with a wife. When Simp had introduced him to his bride, Killian Cagle had just shaken his head in amazement and got to work helping Simp build the house. Although the elder Magee sibling, Auggie, was closer to Killian in age, the two never got along. Auggie was interested in three things: football, beer, and himself. Simp, on the other hand, liked to read. He'd been in a war and gone away to college. For Folly, Alabama, that was a rarity. Killian liked to listen to his talk about philosophy, politics, and the nature of the universe. And despite his eccentric character, Simp Magee had integrity. Killian could always count on Simp to have his back, even when Simp was just a boy.

Killian drank a cup of coffee as Simp re-read his letter while pacing back and forth in the kitchen. "You think Ezra knows I wrote it for him?"

"He knows," Killian said, rolling his eyes. "All of Sand Mountain knows."

"You got to take this more seriously, Killian. The boy's at a delicate age."

"Maybe you ought to bring Hiram Johnson in to talk to Ezra. He's been sober for a week or more."

"Only because he's run out of money. Soon as he gets some more, he'll be back on the sauce."

Hiram Johnson was a defrocked Baptist minister who had latched onto Simp—quite literally—during an episode of delirium tremens outside Chauncey's bar in Buford. Simp had obligingly held him up until Johnson could pour enough whiskey down his gullet to recommence a cordial relationship with his own legs. The next time the shakes took the minister, Johnson wasn't lucky enough to find as sympathetic a bystander as Simp Magee, and he'd ended up in the county lock-up. Wade Cahela, a deputy sheriff and a practical jokester, provided Johnson with Simp's telephone number when

Johnson asked for a bail bondsman. Johnson promptly called Simp on the telephone, on Cahela's dime.

"Please, brudder Magee, in the name ah God, I beg yew. Please come get me outta this place!" the drunken voice wailed plaintively over the receiver.

Simp couldn't fathom why the preacher was calling him, of all people. "God, huh? Maybe you ought to ask God for bail money," Simp said, with some satisfaction.

"I have shinned, brudder Magee. Shinned turbly, come short ah the glory ah God. Turn His back on me." A wretched sob poured through the earpiece.

Simp bailed the drunken preacher out and brought him home, poured hot black coffee into him, and let him sleep it off on the living room sofa.

Trudy was suspicious of Simp's motives for being such a good Samaritan. "Hiram Johnson is a sad, broken man, Simpellion," she told him sternly. "He's got enough trouble without you giving him more. You leave him alone, now, you hear?"

"What?" Simp asked, assuming a look of pained incredulity. "Jesus Christ, Trudy. I thought you of all people would appreciate my effort to help my fellow man."

"Just as long as you really mean to help the poor bastard and not enjoy his humiliation so you can feel self-righteous about your atheistic beliefs," she said. Trudy didn't miss much.

Despite her suspicions, a genuine friendship developed between the atheist and the alcoholic preacher. Hiram Johnson, forty-three years old and the son of a Sand Mountain sharecropper, was one of the few Baptist ministers in the area with a college degree. Most of the ministers of rural churches were products of "the call"—God-fearing, God-talking souls who, like the apostle Saul, had experienced an epiphany on the road to their own Damascus and believed it to be divine revelation and a direct command from the Almighty to spread the Word, as defined in fundamentalist circles.

Reverend Hiram Johnson had come to religion through study and education. But, to his sorrow, his overactive mind never ceased concocting nagging questions. In the quiet of his study, he had wrestled with blasphemous thoughts until he couldn't handle it without a little help from Jim Beam. And when Jim Beam got too expensive, he'd settled for anything that had an alcohol content of at least eighty proof. Old American became his favorite brand.

Before his flock kicked him out, Hiram's sermons had become more and more outrageous. He challenged the Christian belief in monotheism, declaring that if God were a Father, Son, and Holy Ghost, then there was not one, but three gods. And if there were three, why could there not be more? He had read a tract published by the Oneness Pentecostalists positing a monotheistic deity rather than a triumvirate, which confirmed for Johnson the new direction his theological thought had taken.

"You're treading on dangerous ground," a fellow minister warned. "What you're sayin' is sheer blasphemy!"

Another thing that bothered Johnson was the proposition that the Bible was the literal word of God. If that were true, then it seemed to Johnson that the deity was terribly confused. The God of the Old Testament had advocated genocide, multiple marriages, murder, ethnic cleansing, and human sacrifice. It seemed to Johnson that the God of the Old Testament was a megalomaniac who surrounded himself with sycophants. During his last sermons, Johnson's congregation had sat in stunned silence as the bedeviled preacher strode before them in a paroxysm of confused and painful theological diatribes in his search for answers to imponderable questions. A few of them thought they even caught a whiff of alcohol emanating from the reverend's breath.

Hiram Johnson's Waterloo had come during a revival meeting. The visiting evangelist had called for members of the congregation to stand up and confess their sins and ask for God's forgiveness. In a moment that bode ill for Hiram Johnson, his church secretary—an attractive redhead who was also a church deacon's wife—stood up in an emotional frenzy. In front of God and everybody at the Riley First Baptist Church, Geraldine Hutto unburdened herself of her sin of adultery. Each word drove another nail into the coffin of his ecclesiastical career as she named the Reverend Johnson as her illicit lover.

After Hiram was thrown out of his church and the church association, and his wife had repeated that action in his own house, he had begun some really serious drinking in his search for philosophical understanding. But although theological conundrums kept tormenting his frayed brain, he couldn't abandon his most basic belief in a good and generous deity who had called the universe into existence. After his wife kicked him out of their home, Hiram settled into a rented room on the outskirts of Riley to pursue his reflections. When Johnson called on Simp to engage him in debate about religion, those conversations inevitably brought out Simpellion's worst nature.

"You want to talk to me about God?" Simp would storm at him. "Just look at yourself. Jesus Christ, Johnson, if there's a God, he's a miserable fucking failure." And it would go on like that for some minutes, the finer critique of theology getting lost in the profanity. The conversations invariably ended with Simp playing his trump card. "If that so-called Creator God of yours is so perfect, then explain why he created those good-for-nothing squirrels, and made it so they multiply like lice! Explain that, why dontcha!"

☙

Despite his agitation over Ezra's run-in with a revival baptism, Simp allowed that Killian might have a point: Ezra was clearly theologically confused. Simp decided that his son could be set straight if he heard Simp debate with Johnson.

It was a breezy Tuesday morning in July, and the sky was overcast with dark clouds. Distant thunder brought the promise that the dry, brittle fields might get some rain, and it also delivered Hiram Johnson to their door in Killian's truck. Killian dropped him off and waved goodbye before heading back to his place.

Simp was sitting on the back porch steps, just below Ezra's window, re-reading the dozen angry letters in the *Sentinel* responding to his Sunday missive. They were all variations on the same theme; namely, that Simpellion T. Dillon Magee was going straight to Hell.

"Good morning, Brother Magee," Johnson said. "Ain't it a lovely day that God has given us?"

Simp was glad to see the preacher, who always put him directly in an argumentative mood. "And which god is that?"

"The God of the universe, Simp," said the preacher.

"So, you've got it figured out this morning, have you?" Simp replied.

"Only God has it all figured out. It's our task to try and decipher God's will and divine purpose for our lives," Johnson intoned in his Sunday preaching voice. In a more normal tone, he added, "I've been reading your letter in the paper, Simp. I've got to admit, you made a few points I might even agree with."

Simp puffed up a bit. "Well, that's something, Hiram. This'll be the first time we're in agreement on theology."

Hiram removed his hat and combed the remaining strands of black hair on his balding head with his left hand. He wore a shiny, blue serge suit that had seen better days. His scruffy, cordovan shoes needed polish, and short stubby whiskers covered his puffy face.

"No one can deny your point that we humans are a mess," Hiram continued. "We all have sinned and come short of the glory of God. Yessir, I agree with you, but what you fail to see is the bigger picture: the universe as God's palette, and existence as his unfolding painting."

"Jesus Christ, Johnson, if God is painting this picture, he's made a terrible mess. Worse than Dali or Picasso, I'd say. Let's see: there's the war in Vietnam, starving millions, the war between the Arabs and Jews, there's a battle going on in Northern Ireland between the Catholics and Protestants, America and the Soviet Union are on the brink of a nuclear holocaust, and that's just for starters. Where's your God in the middle of all of that?"

Their voices drifted up to Ezra's room, where he and his mother were sorting out his clothes and figuring out what they'd need to buy at the department store in Buford before school started. His mom gave him a wink, and they leaned against the windowsill, listening to Simp's and the Reverend's exchanges floating up through Ezra's open window.

"Free will, Simp," the preacher said simply. "We are creatures with the freedom to do the right thing, or to mess things up."

"Like you and Geraldine Hutto?" Simp said.

Johnson sighed. "Yes, regretfully," he said. "Like the mess I made when I let carnal desire get the best of me. The Lord gave me a choice, and I made the wrong one. I could have turned to Him for comfort and guidance. Instead, I turned to the bottle and the flesh."

Simp looked at Johnson with both sympathy and disgust. "A man makes a choice and then he lives with it. Why bring God into it at all? You really think a being so powerful as to create everything is going to notice or care what you do with Geraldine Hutto? Ain't that just a big load of narcissistic, egotistical vanity?"

"Sometimes," Johnson said, with a faraway look in his eyes, "the questions that come into my brain are so troubling that I wish for death to come in that instant just so I can know the answers."

"You really ready to die?"

"Sometimes." Hiram's voice dropped and his shoulders slumped. He looked down at his hands. "Like Jesus on the cross, I sometimes feel like God has forsaken me, and in those moments, I reckon I would welcome the release of death."

Ezra was startled by that. He knew just what Hiram meant. He felt forsaken, too.

"Hiram," Simp said, his voice taking on a softer tone, "I believe this life is the only shot we've got, and we've got to make the best of it, here and now. You can talk about heaven and hell and all that other bullshit you preachers come up with, but there's no rational reason to suppose there's anything beyond this life."

"Sometimes I pity you, Simpellion Magee," said the preacher. "You have no feeling for the glory or the beauty of His creation! And there are questions we humans can't answer with our paltry brains. There are so many mysteries and imponderables. It's the height of arrogance for us to believe we have all the answers."

Ezra and Trudy didn't hear Simp's response, because a loud clap of thunder drowned it out. The men retreated inside as the first drops of rain pelted the roof. But Ezra wondered about it long afterward. If Reverend Johnson thought it was arrogant for people to assume they knew the answers, then why did they believe in anything at all? It made no sense.

That night, his father came into his room at bedtime. Simp looked like he wanted to say something, but at the last minute—to Ezra's relief—he chickened out. Instead, he ruffled Ezra's hair and told him, "Sleep tight, and don't let no preachy bedbugs bite."

CHAPTER 7

The weekend was warm and lovely. Some of Celia's peonies were beginning to bloom, joined by a multitude of daffodils. She clipped some azalea flowers and put them in a vase on the kitchen table. They took a trip to the hardware store and stocked up on fertilizer, and Ezra worked up a sweat digging in the garden.

"He needs professional help." Celia came outside and drew on her gardening gloves with a snap, a look of frustration once again making her look older than her age. "Dillon won't come outside. He's planted in front of the computer, playing a video game."

"Boys do that," Ezra said, but he knew it was wrong. Dillon loved working in the garden, and Izzy was already outside, rolling around in the grass, waiting to fetch tennis balls. Dillon should be outside with them.

"I don't know why you're so against taking him to Lance."

Ezra jabbed the hoe into the dark soil. "Lance Helman is an idiot."

Helman, a pediatric psychiatrist, was on the medical faculty at the West Virginia University medical center. Celia was a professor at WVU's history department. Ezra had met Helman several times over the years at various faculty events and believed the man to be an arrogant ass, the kind of pseudo-intellectual pissant who worked words like "gestalt" into every other sentence.

"He also happens to be brilliant, and I think Dillon would like him," Celia said. Helman had agreed to see them that afternoon, as a favor to Celia. "Unless you can offer a better alternative to an Ivy-League-trained pediatric psychiatrist who isn't two hundred miles away, then we're taking Dillon to Lance."

Later that afternoon, Ezra went upstairs and played a round of Warlocks and Wizards with Dillon. Dillon's face looked different. A pale, pinched look had replaced his carefree childishness.

"Hey, buddy. Mom and I are taking you to a special doctor later on today. He's going to help you with all the stuff that's been going on with you."

Dillon turned away and folded his arms.

"Hey, it's no big deal," Ezra said. "When I was your age, I saw a doctor just like Dr. Helman."

Dillon ran to his bed, jumped in, and turned his back to Ezra.

At 4:30 p.m., the three of them drove to Helman's office. The tall, tan, athletic psychiatrist greeted Celia with a hug that Ezra felt was just a little too warm, too familiar, two seconds too long. He shook Ezra's hand and flashed him a fake smile. Then he turned to Dillon and said, "Let's you and me talk without the 'rents." Dillon looked confused. "Parents," Helman clarified. Dillon glanced at Ezra and rolled his eyes, then followed the doctor into the office.

Thirty minutes later, Helman led Dillon back to the waiting room and shook his hand. Dillon looked miserable. "Celia, Ezra, let's have a talk just the three of us. Dillon won't mind."

Ezra resented that the doctor was talking for Dillon, but he took a deep breath and told himself to let it go. If Lance Helman could help Dillon, then he would put up with it.

Ezra and Celia sat side by side on a white leather sofa, another sign of Helman's pretentious inclinations. Their knees touched. Ezra wanted to take her hand but stopped himself. He looked around the room. There were framed abstract-expressionist art prints on the wall. A photograph of Sigmund Freud hung in the place of honor over Helman's desk. The coffee table in front of the sofa displayed what were probably unread books by obscure German authors. Ezra wondered if Helman could actually read German, or if the books were just props.

"I'm afraid your son has obsessive-compulsive disorder, or OCD," Lance announced with a flourish. Ezra couldn't help fuming as the doctor went on to spout a bunch of jargon from the Diagnostic and Statistical Manual. It was drivel that any idiot could look up online.

"When did you first notice changes in Dillon's behavior?" Helman asked.

"Ezra has a family history of OCD," Celia blurted out. She gave Ezra an apologetic look. "I just thought that might be relevant."

Ezra glared at her and then at the doctor. He wanted to wipe that superior smirk off Helman's face, to make him feel the pain he felt in that moment.

"I'm not surprised," Helman said. "OCD typically runs in families." He turned to Ezra. "Was it a parent? A sibling?"

"It was me," Ezra said, gritting his teeth.

"Ah." Helman's eyebrows shot up, and he scribbled something on his pad. "Ezra, I'll need your medical records and your full treatment history."

"My medical history?" Ezra knew he sounded belligerent, but what the hell? He felt belligerent and didn't have the energy to pretend otherwise.

"Ezra," Helman said patronizingly, "who are you working with?"

"Working with?"

"Your therapist."

"I don't see a therapist. I haven't had OCD since I was a teenager."

"But certainly, you are aware that what you have is a lifelong disease?" Helman turned to Celia. "We don't speak of a 'cure' with OCD patients; we hope for an amelioration of symptoms, but there are residual symptoms that never go away. It's important that you understand and come to accept the fact that Dillon will never lead a completely normal life. He has a disease. The sooner you eradicate your own denial, the sooner we can help him."

"That's bullshit," Ezra muttered. Celia shot him a warning look.

Helman bristled. "Did your mother or father suffer from OCD?"

"Let's leave them out of it. We're here for Dillon." Ezra folded his arms and stared at the therapist, who stared back.

"We'll get your family history next time," Helman finally said.

The interminably long fifty-minute hour finally ended. Ezra walked straight out of the office without a word and kept walking until he got to the car. They drove home in the silence to which they'd grown accustomed.

༄

"We are not taking Dillon back there," Ezra said later that night, sitting in a chair in the living room.

"Lance Helman went to Dartmouth," Celia argued.

"If credentials were curative, then I would give a damn."

"So, what do you suggest?" Celia demanded, throwing her hands up into the air.

"I suggest we take Dillon to a shrink who isn't a complete ass!"

"You're only upset because he asked about your parents."

Ezra was silent. He was upset about a lot of things when it came to Lance Helman, but Celia wasn't completely right. He hadn't refused to talk about his parents in the meeting because he was upset; he didn't talk about his parents because he had no memories of them.

When he was still a child and living with his Aunt Lenore, Ezra had been treated by a psychiatrist, Dr. Cadwallader, who said Ezra had something like post-traumatic stress disorder, and that it played a role in his memory loss. Dr. Cadwallader had told him a traumatic and painful event can cause the brain to push it out of consciousness to get some relief. That's just the way it was. He didn't need a jackass like Helman knowing that, especially in front of Celia.

Celia sighed. "Honey, I know you went through a terrible trauma when you lost your parents, but what about all those years before they died? Surely you want to remember your mother baking you a birthday cake or your father taking you fishing. There must be so many good memories you're missing out on. Lance believes that both your OCD and your amnesia are very treatable."

"You talked to Helman about me?" Ezra demanded.

"I think you need help, Ezra."

"You had no right!" Ezra stood up so fast his chair fell over. He walked down the hallway and shoved open the back door. He needed air. The house was closing in on him. Even the porch felt too confining. He stumbled down the steps and kept walking until he was across the backyard and among the trees that separated his land from his neighbors. When he was out of sight of his house, he leaned against an old oak and put his hands on his knees, taking deep breaths until he stopped shaking. He was angry with Helman, but he was angrier with Celia for going behind his back and telling his private business to that asshole.

Did she think he *wanted* to forget his parents? Did she really think that if only he tried, he could remember? How dare she? Forgetting wasn't a conscious choice he'd made. He wasn't a bad son who intentionally forgot the way his mother looked or the stories his father told him. Why couldn't Celia respect that? Why couldn't she understand?

The filmy image of his bottle of Wild Turkey formed in his mind. He needed a drink.

But when he neared his house again, he could see Celia framed in the light of the kitchen window, standing at the sink. Her face was in her hands. He knew she had meant no harm. She had only wanted to make things right in their family. Once again, he'd hurt the woman he loved. Once again, he'd failed her. But why did she have to push him? Why couldn't she leave well enough alone?

Ezra waited in the dark shadow of the trees until Celia turned off the kitchen light. A minute later, he saw the light come on in their bedroom. Only then did he slip back inside. He didn't bother putting ice in the glass because he didn't want to make any noise. He sat on the floor of the living room, his back against the couch, and polished off the bottle. That's where she found him in the morning, asleep on the floor.

※

The one thing Lance Helman did that Ezra admitted might be useful was to write Dillon a prescription for an antidepressant. The drug was called fluoxetine, and Celia and Ezra went online and read about it and agreed it was a good place to start. After Dillon counted his way downstairs in a whispery voice and plopped into his chair, Celia offered him a small capsule and a glass of orange juice.

Dillon made a face. "Do I have to?"

"Yes, honey," Celia said firmly.

"But I took it yesterday, and it's not working."

"The doctor said it could take up to six weeks to feel different."

Dillon slowly picked up the pill in one hand and his glass of orange juice in the other, all the while staring at the little green and white capsule on his palm.

"Bottoms up," Ezra said, toasting him with his coffee mug. "What doesn't kill us makes us stronger."

Dillon swallowed the pill.

"Good work, sunshine!" Celia said, mussing Dillon's curly hair.

"Mom!"

Celia and Ezra shared a smile. Ezra loved the soft look on Celia's face in the morning, before she did up her hair and put on her makeup. She caught him staring at her and blushed.

Ezra turned back to Dillon. "Doing anything special today?" he asked.

Dillon shrugged and stared off into the distance, chewing his cereal with a mechanical precision.

"Hmmm," Celia said. "You've got a bad case of the Sad Sack, my little man. Are you gonna just sit around in Gloomsville, West Virginia, all day? Or are you going to get out there, catch a tiger by the tail, smell the flowers, catch a falling star, or another of those other tried-and-true little sayings that make our lives a cornucopia of consolation and a credit to the continuing constancy of our characters?"

"Aw, Mom," Dillon moaned. "I've heard better babble from a fifth grader." Despite Celia's lame attempt to cheer up their son, he was at least looking up, and when his mother grinned at him, he rolled his eyes and half-smiled.

"Oh yeah? Let's see if you can top that," she said. "If you do, you'll win a million dollars."

It was one of their favorite games. Celia had always been able to cajole Dillon into doing things he didn't enjoy, like cleaning his room and taking a bath, by promising him a chance to win a million dollars.

"You'd better get going," Ezra said, glancing at his stainless-steel diver's watch, a wedding present from Celia's parents. He'd never been scuba diving, and the watch was a little too big and heavy for his taste, but he noticed Celia smile when she saw him wearing it. "Dillon, eat fast and go get your shoes."

"What's on your agenda today?" Celia asked Ezra. He didn't feel much like talking, but he decided it best to reply. He was grateful she was speaking to him.

"Just one lecture, and then I have office hours. I think there's a department meeting at four."

"Do your students even show up on the last day of class? Mine only come if it's a pre-exam review session, and then only if I hint that I might divulge a few of the questions that are going to be on the test."

"Mine are just as bad, but today isn't the last lecture. That's next week."

For a moment, Celia looked flustered. It was a sign of the strain on her that she was forgetting which week it was. She said lightly, "Being on sabbatical, I lose all sense of time."

Celia and Ezra both held doctorates in American history. Ezra was a tenured professor at Cunningham—a small, liberal arts college—and Celia was tenured at West Virginia University. They lived in a small town that was in between the two campuses, a rote fifteen-minute commute for each of them. Since Celia had been on sabbatical this year while working on her biography of Jane Addams, she chauffeured their son the four miles to middle school each day.

After Dillon finished putting on his shoes, he walked into the living room to sort out his backpack. Unexpectedly, Ezra felt his wife's arms surround him. He could never accurately describe her smell, but he breathed her in every chance he got.

"Be good," she whispered in his ear before breaking away.

"I'll try," he replied.

"You'd better!"

Ezra smiled to himself. The first time his Aunt Lenore had met Celia, Lenore had told him bluntly, "That one will always have to have the last word. Better get used to it." Coming from Lenore, that was high praise.

As soon as Celia and Dillon left for the day, Ezra dug into his pockets and found the cigarette he'd been aching to smoke since he'd woken up. He hated the adolescent feeling of hiding something he shouldn't be doing, but he couldn't bear to see the disappointment on Celia's face if she knew he was smoking again. He'd already given her cause enough to be disappointed in him.

"You're killing one of my two favorite people," she used to say every time he lit up. "I need you. Our baby needs you." She'd look at him with those beautiful green eyes, all serious and full of love. So, he'd quit. But that was before Dillon's OCD.

He knew smoking was bad for him. So was all the bourbon he'd been drinking. And he hadn't been running as much as he used to—he was the most out of shape he'd ever been in his life. He sat his coffee cup down in the sink, took a deep drag of air, and exhaled, mimicking the routine of smoking in hopes that his desire for a cigarette would disappear. But the nicotine craving was making him impatient. He walked to the back porch, closed the door, lit up, and walked down the steps into the backyard. He took a long drag of the real thing, and he felt the contentment, finally, as the smoke filled his lungs.

He surveyed his back yard. The grass needed trimming. Last year, Dillon had begged to take over the lawn mowing. Ezra had told him, "The job's yours, but not until next year, when you're twelve."

Would he still want to do it? Would he be able to, with his obsessive tics? Tears welled up in Ezra's eyes, and he knew it wasn't the smoke.

When it came down to it, maybe Celia was wrong. She didn't need him. Neither did Dillon. It was the other way around: he needed them. Celia was strong and self-sufficient. He was the one who'd fall apart if she ever left.

He took another drag, the smoke making him feel more substantial, filling and defining his empty spaces.

He was a good father and husband. He provided for his family. He loved his family.

He exhaled and watched the smoke drift off into the morning air. *But what if I can't handle it?* he thought. Lance Helman's comment about OCD being a lifetime affliction had stuck with him. *What if I wake up one morning acting like Dillon?* It was a thought that made him shudder. He was afraid of losing everything, because with few memories of his own childhood, *now* was the only thing in the world that he truly knew. *But what if the OCD came back? What would Celia do with two of us falling apart on her?*

Ezra sucked deeply on the cigarette and ordered himself to get a fucking grip. He hadn't had a panic attack in more than twenty years. He was a grown man, a college professor. He didn't have OCD anymore. Helman was just a pompous ass.

But what if he was right? What if . . . ?

Ezra felt an all-too-familiar pressure building inside his skull, a nervous roiling stampeding through his gut. The forgotten cigarette hung in his fingers as the old sensation of panic engulfed him. No matter how many years it had been since his last panic attack, its re-emergence was as familiar to him as his own face in the mirror. He knew exactly what was happening. His breathing became rapid and shallow.

For a moment, he tried to convince himself that maybe it wasn't panic. Maybe this time it really was a heart attack. "I'm going to have a heart attack and die," he said aloud, as if the fatal option was the better choice. His heart raced out of control, and he had trouble breathing. He couldn't stop the wave. It was coming, and there was nothing he could do now. It was out of his control. He would drown this time. It would pull him under and hold him there. He would—

A burning pain and the smell of seared flesh brought him back, out of the depths of his panic. The lit end of the cigarette was pressed against his thigh.

"Shit!" he yelled. Ezra slapped his trousers and dropped the cigarette on the ground. "Shit!" There was an unmistakable round burn in the fabric and a hairless red spot on his thigh. How would he explain this to Celia?

He hurried inside to change, forbidding himself to think about what had just happened to him for the first time in more than two decades.

༄

"So, you scared yourself silly," Hiram said, nodding as if he'd known it all along. "A grown man, and you nearly wet your pants."

"Hey!" Ezra frowned. "It wasn't like that. The panic attack was real."

"Real? Hmmm."

"What's that supposed to mean?"

"I reckon you know."

Ezra said nothing.

"So, after the panic attack," Hiram continued, "you told Celia?"

"I couldn't," he admitted.

"Ah," was all Hiram Johnson had to say.

☙

"Ezra, are you okay?" Celia asked.

"I wish everyone in this house would stop asking everyone else that question!" Ezra said, fuming, slamming every door and drawer in the kitchen, looking for nothing in particular.

"Are you?" Celia asked again, hands on her hips, eyes narrowed as if trying to decide whether to be angry or worried.

It was one thing to tell his wife about something that had happened when he was just a kid. It was very different to admit to her that the demons he thought were forever banished from his head were actually still there. Harder still to tell her they'd recently been rattling the bars of their cage. It had been a week since he'd had the panic attack and burned himself with the cigarette, and since then he'd felt like he was on the brink of spiraling out-of-control. It was a place he knew well. Ezra understood that the more he thought about it, the more he put words to it and gave it life, the more likely he would have another. Talking about it with Celia could be the opposite of helpful.

Ezra was clinging to normal, avoiding anything and everything that could push him into a downward spiral of anxiety, as best he could. His last lecture of the semester was scheduled for that morning. He just had to get through the day, and then there would be a short period of time in which he could sort himself out on his own—no therapist necessary.

He gave his wife a tight smile. "I'm finer than fine, okay? See you tonight." A perfunctory peck on the cheek for Celia, a real smile for Dillon, and a hurried exit out the door to keep himself as calm as possible.

In the car, Ezra took deep, centering breaths. "I'm fine. I'm okay. Everything is fine. Nothing bad is happening. Nothing bad will happen." He recited this litany three times to himself and then backed the car out of the driveway.

On his drive to work, he mentally rehearsed his day in an effort to steady himself. He would park in the faculty parking lot and walk across the campus to the history department, where he would get himself a cup of coffee from the fresh pot that Helen Grimes, the administrative assistant, brewed each morning. He would go to his office, turn on his computer, and organize his notes. At ten minutes before eleven, he would leave his office and exchange pleasantries with Helen on his way past her desk to the men's room.

Then he would go to the second-floor lecture hall. He would arrange his notes on the lectern, locate a piece of chalk, erase the blackboard, and count his students as they filed in and took their seats. After class, he would return to his office and drop off his papers, then meet his friend John Parker for lunch. They always ate lunch together on Thursdays. They would sit at their usual table in the faculty dining room, eat meatloaf because it was Thursday, and talk about baseball because it was springtime.

After lunch, Ezra would return to his office and hold office hours from two p.m. until four p.m. There was sure to be a line of students wanting to speak with him about the final exam and trying to find out what grades they were getting on their term papers so they could calculate how hard they'd have to study for the final. At four, he would pack up his briefcase, log off the computer, leave his office, and attend the department meeting. Afterward, he would exit the building, walk back across campus to the faculty parking lot, and drive home.

He had it all figured out, but he was still filled with foreboding.

Ezra eased his grip on the steering wheel and relaxed. "I'm forty years old," he reminded himself, "a respected historian with a loving wife, a wonderful son, a devoted dog, friends, and a nice house with a reasonable mortgage." He had plenty of things to look forward to: summer break and spending a week at the cabin by the lake, catching up on pleasure reading. Maybe he'd finally get around to painting the shed.

His life ticked to the clock of academia: two semesters and then a long, slow summer followed by two semesters and another long, slow summer. One semester of his course covered the colonial period, followed by a semester on the national era. He taught two courses on those subjects each semester, along with one interdepartmental course. This semester he was co-teaching a class on the history just preceding the American Civil War with a colleague from the political science department and another from sociology. Ezra was a popular professor; students filled his classes, and other faculty members thought well of him. He'd made himself a life he could be proud of. He reminded himself of this as he pulled into Cunningham College's faculty parking lot.

When he got to the lecture hall, Ezra noticed the cloudless, azure sky peeking through the windows, promising summer. Ezra could hardly blame the students who'd elected to skip this last lecture, but he was sorry they were going to miss it. It was his favorite one of the semester, and he saved it as a kind of reward for those who *did* show up. (And yes, he would be including questions about it on the final exam.)

At eleven a.m. on the dot, Ezra loosened his tie a bit and signaled the class to quiet down.

"Is it just me or is it warm in here?" he asked.

Several students replied affirmatively. A student in the back of the room opened a window, which drew a refreshing breeze through the lecture hall.

"For our last class, I want to talk about Abraham Lincoln." Ezra stared at a boy in the front who was slouched in his seat and doodling. The boy glanced up, saw he was being observed, and sat up straighter, flipping the hair out of his eyes. Ezra gave him a small nod and a smile.

"Our sixteenth president was a controversial figure, as you discovered if you did this week's readings. Many historians say he was our country's greatest president."

A young woman with a strong southern drawl interrupted. "That's not how they teach it at Robert E. Lee High School down in Norfolk!" There were titters around the room.

"Good point, Ms. Yardley," Ezra said, giving her a nod of approval. "History, as we've discussed, must be presented and interpreted, so it's about points of view as well as facts."

Class discussion evolved into a debate between a student from Connecticut and the young woman from Norfolk about the causes of the Civil War. Ezra memorized the home states of his students every year because he knew that their places of origin would affect their views of American history. He listened with pleasure as they referred back to previous class lectures.

See? I'm fine, he thought to himself, and felt a reassuring surge of satisfaction.

As soon as he had the thought, he began to doubt it. *Was* he okay? Why was his pulse still racing? What did it mean? Was he going to have a panic attack? Here? During class? It would be humiliating. He couldn't lose control in front of his students.

The pressure to avoid a panic attack grew in Ezra's mind until he knew it was inevitable. That was how it worked. It was a cycle that spiraled out of control—all of it starting from a single thought. His own mind would betray him. Again.

It's just the buzz from the nicotine, he told himself firmly. *Focus on the class.*

He tried, but he felt the familiar flutter in his chest. Standing in front of his desk, Ezra leaned back against it and took a deep breath.

The flutter flapped its wings faster. Maybe this time it really was a heart attack. Why not? He was under stress; he'd taken up smoking again. And then there was the bourbon. Blood rushed to his face. He told himself this was not a coronary thrombosis. This was not a myocardial infarction. He knew it was absurd—he wasn't having a heart attack. Yet the words poured through every channel of his brain, which only served to send him deeper into panic.

"What do you think, Professor Magee?" someone called out to him.

His attention swung back to the class discussion, and for a moment the panic was held at bay.

"Let's hear from someone else," he said, having lost the thread of the discussion.

"Lincoln is the American ideal," a senior from New Jersey spoke authoritatively. "He grew up poor and pulled himself up by his own bootstraps. He educated himself and became an inspiring speaker and a shrewd political leader. And he had a strong sense of right and wrong, something politicians today don't seem to have."

"I don't believe," Ezra said, giving her a brief smile, "that anyone ever pulled himself up by his own bootstraps. It's a myth—a popular one, but a myth, nonetheless. We were communal animals before we were even human. We are interdependent from birth, and we tend to remain so throughout life. But Lincoln was an extraordinary man and probably came as close to accomplishing that myth as anyone."

"He wasn't any different than politicians today," someone else countered. "It was all about money. The North wanted to control the cotton trade, and Lincoln went along with it."

"I never heard that, and I took AP American history in high school," a sophomore replied.

"But you grew up in the North, and Professor Magee keeps telling us that history is written by the victors."

Ezra concentrated on the flow of conversation, and his heartbeat slowed to a more normal rhythm. He posed more questions about

Lincoln's changing views on abolition: from his early belief that slaves should be freed gradually, that slave owners should be financially compensated for their loss, and the freed slaves returned to Africa; to his later action to free the slaves at once with no compensation to their owners and no plan for the former slaves.

"Here's something you might not know about President Lincoln," Ezra said, holding his students' attention. "What if I were to tell you that he suffered from a lifelong battle with depression?"

Murmurs of surprise filled the room.

"Some biographers have linked it back to the loss of his first love, Ann Rutledge, to Typhoid fever in 1835, when Lincoln was a young man of twenty-six. But others say he'd suffered from depression long before her death."

When Ezra had first learned about Lincoln's mental illness, he'd felt a deep bond with the man he already admired more than any other president. He'd read every biography written about Lincoln and discovered that melancholia had periodically enveloped the extraordinary man throughout his life. Often, when Lincoln descended into the depths of one of his funks, his friends feared he might commit suicide.

"How does knowing this new fact about Lincoln change your perception of his presidency?" Ezra asked.

Several students offered their opinions, but Ezra was distracted by movement at the back of the room. A sleek gray squirrel hopped onto the sill of the open window and nibbled an acorn. Ezra felt the hairs on the back of his neck stand up. He could have sworn the squirrel was staring at him, and he thought it looked irritable (Was that possible for a squirrel?). The squirrel gave a balletic leap onto the tree limb from which it had come and scampered away.

"It doesn't matter," the young woman from Norfolk was saying. "Even if he did win the Civil War, Lincoln can't be the greatest president; he was a mental case!"

Recovering from his staring contest with the squirrel, Ezra pointed to the student. "But Ms. Yardley, might his melancholia have had any collateral, positive effects on his presidency?"

"I don't think there's anything positive," she said confidently. "Depression makes people sad and miserable."

"But could his melancholia have made Lincoln a *better* president?" Ezra posed his question to the entire class.

"Maybe it made him better able to sympathize with people who were in hard circumstances," someone called out from the back.

"Yeah. Like the slaves," someone else said.

That stirred up the debate again, and Ezra sat back and let them work it out on their own, until they were at an impasse and turned to him for arbitration.

"There is no evidence that depression affects intelligence—" Ezra began, but then broke off as he saw the squirrel hop back onto the windowsill and stare at him. He shook his head. "Uh, I would need only to turn to Lincoln as proof," he ended weakly. His heart was beating erratically, and his palms were sweaty. "I think we'll leave it at that. I have to cancel office hours today, but you can schedule a time for tomorrow between two and four. Ms. Grimes has the sign-up sheet at the front desk."

A rustle of papers and an appreciative murmur at being dismissed half an hour early filled the room, almost mimicking the disarray inside of him. Ezra swept up his notes, his hands shaking to such a degree that he was almost unable to gather the stacks of papers. What the hell was wrong with him? First he thought he was having a heart attack; now he was being undone by a squirrel.

"Professor, are you going to have our papers graded before the final exam?" It was the student who always seemed to doze through class.

"Goddamn, mother-fucking squirrel!"

Not a shout, but it hovered at a nearby decibel. Everything in the room came to a halt, and complete silence prevailed. Everyone was looking at Ezra, who had rushed over to the window. The squirrel, which had just been on the windowsill, was nowhere to be seen. Ezra turned back to the room and saw their frozen faces.

※

At dinner that night, Ezra told Celia and Dillon a sanitized version of the story.

"A squirrel in your classroom?" Celia laughed. "Poor thing! It must have been so scared!"

"Or bored!" Dillon had a wide grin on his face. "Imagine having nothing better to do than sneak *into* school!"

His smile was a good sign, and Ezra managed a smile back. He hadn't told them about his swearing at the squirrel. Nor about having heart palpitations, or the panic attack in his car after class. Ezra had turned the whole nightmare into an amusing anecdote for the dinner table.

At least he'd made it to his car before the wave of panic fully engulfed him for the second time in only a few days. His senses had become hyper-aware, and then he'd felt the fear rushing in like a riptide, crashing into every corner of his mind with paralyzing force. When the panic was finished with him, after what seemed like an eternity adrift at sea, he had felt his body relax, his muscles unclenching as the riptide receded and he was able to breathe again. But he felt wrung out and defeated.

After Dillon went up to bed, Ezra cracked open a new bottle of bourbon. He felt self-conscious pouring himself a big glass of it while Celia watched, but his need for it was greater than his fear of her judgment.

"Want one?" he offered.

"Are you okay?" she countered.

"Sure," he said bitterly. "I'm okay, you're okay, we're okay. Okay?"

They sat on the back porch in their rocking chairs. Ezra sipped his drink and listened to the still night. Normally, this was his favorite time of day. He and Celia would share the little observations they'd saved up for each other about their colleagues or what they were reading or Dillon. And then they would sit together in contented silence. Ezra craved the intimacy of their silence, but as Celia fidgeted in her seat, staring at his half-empty glass, he knew there would be no silence tonight.

"That's your third drink."

"Is it?"

"This will not do, Ezra," she said, her voice surprisingly gentle. "I know the man I married. I know you are not fine. I also know you don't want to talk about it. But can you at least, for one goddamn minute, just admit that you are not fine?"

"I suppose I can do that."

"And?" She had to hear him say it. That was Celia.

"I'm not fine."

The truth didn't set him free, but he did feel a fraction better not having to pretend anymore.

"Do you want to talk about it?" Her tone was purposefully cautious. It was the same one he used when trying to help a troubled student open up, to confess the personal reasons that kept them from succeeding in his course. It sounded to Ezra as if it had a holier-than-thou intonation, wreaking of judgment.

"Not really."

"What a surprise," she said with uncharacteristic sarcasm. Celia stared at him, waiting for something she knew he wouldn't give up without a fight. A few moments later, she gave up on him, gave up waiting for an honest moment to bloom in the dark, and went inside.

Ezra sat alone in that darkness. The hum and tick of his house, the creak of the chair as he shifted his weight. He tried to take comfort in the familiar sounds of clocks and refrigerators and the night breeze in the trees. He closed his eyes and imagined Celia putting on her nightgown and climbing into bed. He imagined Dillon curled up under his blue comforter having peaceful dreams, dreams that wouldn't cause him to scream out, to cut the thick silence with panic. A wife and son, a house and job—these things were his life. They defined him and made him what he was. They were his niche in the universe. The past was done and gone. The future would never arrive. He had only the now, only this moment, sitting on the porch, inebriated and craving a cigarette.

Ezra half-wished Celia had stayed. She'd left him with his own thoughts, which were far more dangerous than hers. Today, the panic attack had made him acutely aware of his vulnerability. Today, he'd humiliated himself in front of his students. And the bourbon had only slightly dulled the waves of anxiety that lapped at the shore of his temporary calm, threatening to grow into a storm.

As a teenager, he'd learned how to manage the panic, negotiate with it. But back then he'd been in therapy and taking anti-anxiety drugs. On bad days, he had stayed home from school. Ezra was an adult now, though, and he couldn't afford a mental breakdown. His career wouldn't survive it. His marriage might, but even that wasn't a certainty.

It was amazing how fragile his whole life had become. One minute, he felt in control; the next minute, he was twelve years old again, wrestling his inner demons for control.

The night was getting chilly, even with the warmth of bourbon, and Ezra was exhausted from the day. Was Celia waiting for him to come to bed? He would let her down tonight, and he would let her down again tomorrow night. He would hate himself for doing it, but he would do it anyway. He was aware of the irony that a man who had written two books on the Lincoln administration was rendered mute when it came to talking to his wife.

Be a man. Go up there and tell her! he exhorted himself. *You know she'll be great about it.*

It was true—he did know that. But this wasn't about Celia, who was unfailingly supportive and loving. This was about his own damned pride. He didn't want Celia to know she'd married a loser.

The bourbon felt mellow on his tongue, and the cigarette left a bitter flavor in his mouth. It was the most satisfied he'd felt all day, and he wished he could drift off to sleep just like this. He was finally relaxed. No panic to ruin the moment.

Panic. The memory of the panic attack made his stomach lurch, and that in turn made his heart speed up and skip a few beats. He groaned as he put his bourbon glass down, the waves inside gathering strength. Like a sea captain watching a squall line approach, Ezra clutched the arms of his chair and braced for the agony.

It was short-lived this time. The aftermath of self-loathing—flotsam after the storm—was as depressing as ever. What if he really was cracking up this time?

"Fuck it!" he said aloud and swallowed the rest of his drink in one blazing gulp. He stumbled inside and headed for the couch. As he crossed the kitchen, his eyes fell on Dillon's medication bottle. He could imagine himself opening the lid and popping one or two into his mouth, chasing them down with a little bourbon. He felt small and weak. What kind of man considers stealing his child's medication? No, he was not that person. He would not be that person. If he was cracking up, at least he could be a man about it.

He flopped down on the couch and, within minutes, blacked out.

CHAPTER 8

Killian may have been right that the *Sentinel*'s readership was down when they decided to publish Simp's letter. In the days after, the letters to the editor swelled to four extra columns. The whole county seemed to be offended by Simp's atheistic rant. On a Friday afternoon, Simp taped his third death threat up on the refrigerator. If the writer had known Simp, he would have known the threat would not silence the man but inspire him. Simp sat at his typewriter and pounded out another letter—this one righteously indignant—for the *Sand Mountain Sentinel*.

> *Dear Sir,*
>
> *After sending my last letter to the editor, I got a spate of letters from local Christians who took offense at what I wrote. Three of them kindly offered to do me in so I could see for myself how wrong I am about heaven and hell. I don't reckon they've heard about Jesus telling them to "love thy neighbor as thyself" or "turn the other cheek." How about the golden rule? These folks who call themselves "good Christians" are downright nasty. Even the ones who didn't threaten to kill me still want me to go straight to hell, and Godspeed on my journey.*
>
> *Christians say theirs is a religion of love. That aspect is not evident in these death threats I've been getting from the saintly readers of the Sentinel. If these people ran our government, I'd be flayed, drawn, quartered, and burned at the stake. Just like back in the good old days when Christians had the Inquisition going.*
>
> *The Merriam Webster's Collegiate Dictionary defines the*

word "oxymoron" as "a phrase in which words of contradictory meaning are used together for special effect," like "wise fool." And like "Christian love."

I remain sincerely yours,
Simpellion T. Dillon Magee

Even if he hadn't been depressed, Ezra would have assumed a low profile to avoid being targeted by his peers for his father's ravings. He declined his mother's invitation to accompany her to the Piggly Wiggly on a shopping trip, which he always enjoyed because she let him pick out sugary cereal and candy. And he'd been waiting all summer for the new Western, *Jeremiah Johnson,* to come to the Roxy Theater in Buford, but then turned down an invitation to go with his cousins. He dreaded going out in public and hearing kids laugh and make fun of him because his dad was a fool. Ezra didn't know how his mama could stand it. She just smiled and nodded at the folks in town and went about her business. Simp rarely went into town, but these days when he did, Killian always found a reason to go along and keep an eye on him. There was no one to watch Ezra's back, and he didn't feel like getting into a fight, so he stayed home.

Ezra didn't understand why his father went out of his way to rile up people. It was like he needed attention all the time, even if it was the bad kind. Ezra was the exact opposite. He wished people wouldn't notice him at all. Not unless he was doing something heroic, like hitting a homerun with bases loaded in the bottom of the ninth when his team was down three runs. Or discovering dinosaur bones buried in the pasture. His dad was loud, he swore all the time, and he would say anything, even if it was totally outrageous, to get people to notice him. Ezra wished his father wasn't such a weirdo, and then felt guilty for being disloyal.

Ezra had only one day left before the school year started and he planned on spending it in bed. During the day, when there was no fear of falling asleep and having the nightmare, his bed was the safest place to be, as long as he lay on his back and kept both hands on the top of the sheet.

"Ezra!" His cousins stood under his window and shouted up. "Come on! We're building a teepee!"

Ezra imagined the poles falling on his head and crushing his skull (the whole skull, not just half of it). If that happened, then he wouldn't have to return to school. He yelled that he'd meet them in the woods. It took him five minutes to complete all his rituals to leave the house.

In fact, the teepee did collapse. But it was Floyd, not Ezra, who ended up with an impressive lump on his head.

Killian came to dinner that night bearing a gift for Ezra. It was a Crimson Tide baseball cap, and it instantly became Ezra's favorite possession. Killian also brought a bouquet of flowers from his garden for Trudy. And for Simp, he had a book on Buddhism.

"You tryin' to turn me into a hippie?" Simp asked, flipping eagerly through the book.

"Try it; you'll like it," Killian said mildly. Ezra laughed out loud, recognizing the slogan from a new TV commercial for Life cereal.

Simp stayed up all night reading his new book. It was all he talked about as he drove Ezra to school the next morning. Although Ezra couldn't keep up with all the various numbered parts of Buddhism (four noble truths, eight or nine other things you ought to do), the notion of karma appealed to him.

"It's a basic law of the universe, like gravity," Simp explained. "You get what's comin' to ya. Kill something, it comes back and kills you in another life. You're kind to people, they pay you back in kindness later, even in another life. Seems fair, don't it? You don't have to suck up to no god to get your just rewards. And the only things you're punished for are your own mistakes, and not eternally."

Ezra saw where he was going with that and nodded thoughtfully. The idea of fairness was appealing.

Fairness was not a concept spoken of much at Saint John's

School. As Simp dropped him off for his first day of the seventh grade, Ezra joined the flow of reluctant kids heading into the windowless ring of interlocked, pentagonal cells built around an open square at the center. A structural monstrosity, the building was conceived by a California architect who, Simp liked to say, must have been smoking opium when he came up with the design. Lacking windows to the outside and inner doors to the classrooms, it was reminiscent of a prison without bars. Worse still, the school had been built a quarter of a mile from a sewage treatment facility, and its malodorous emission hung over the school like a sour miasma. Ezra knew from past years' experience that after homeroom he would get used to the smell. Mostly.

꽈

After dropping Ezra off at school, Simp drove on until he got to the George Corley Wallace Bridge, a drawbridge that spanned the Tennessee River. He blew the car horn as he passed the control shack where Killian Cagle worked as the span lift operator. Killian, listening for radio traffic from tugboats plying the river, looked up and gave a salute.

When Simp arrived back home, the house had that too-empty feeling. Trudy was out in the pasture with her easel, painting wildflowers. She was working on a series on the goldenrod. "The goldenrod," she had told him just the night before, "was Alabama's state flower until it was replaced by the camellia. And this is interesting,"—she'd leaned in close like she was telling Simp a secret—"because the camellia is native to only Japan, Korea, China, and Taiwan. The goldenrod, wild though it may be, is like you, honey: native to Alabama."

Simp could see Mabel in the back pasture, fully upright and conscious. There wasn't a squirrel in sight, which was a shame since he'd cleaned his gun just yesterday. He stepped inside and picked up his Buddhism book from the kitchen table. He flipped to the chapter on meditation, and suddenly he had an idea.

Simp lit one of Trudy's scented bath candles, set it on the coffee table, and sat on the floor in front of it with his legs crossed. He stared at the flame for ten minutes, trying to clear his mind. Unfortunately, his mind was not inclined to cooperate. He kept ruminating on the death threats.

You are damned and going straight to hell, and I'm gonna help send you there, one writer had penned with a thick, black magic marker.

Don't bother repenting because it's about to be too late for you, another had written.

You will never see me coming, the third had said.

How the hell was he expected to attain a state of bliss or enlightenment when Christian Crusaders were out there right now plotting mischief against him?

After his unfruitful ten minutes were up, Simp decided he needed extra help getting into a proper meditative mood. The book said to try using a mantra. He'd read that the Hindus and Buddhists both liked the sound of "om." If the two religions could agree on that, then it was good enough for him. He took a deep breath, and on the exhale intoned, "Ommmmmmmm."

It went all right for a breath or two, but then he couldn't keep his mind from thinking about the similarity of that word with the English word "ohm," the term for electrical resistance. Seated in the lotus position with his thumbs and index fingers touching and his eyes closed, as per the book's instructions, he realized he was like a closed circuit. In fact, he couldn't stop thinking about electricity, and finally he lost the mood for meditation. He was about to open his eyes when he sensed someone standing in the living room. Simp subtly straightened his posture and let loose with a fine "Ommmmmmmm."

"You busy?" Killian asked, as if Simp was not deep in the throes of important mind-mastery work.

Simp opened his eyes. "I'm meditating."

"How's it going?"

Simp glared at him and then gave up and blew out the candle. "It's harder than it looks."

"Well, maybe this will help." From his overall bib, Killian produced a bag of dried green leaves.

"And just how's that supposed to help?" Simp hissed. "That stuff's illegal!"

"Relax. It's just green tea I got from the store. It's supposed to have a soothing effect on the brain."

"Says who?"

"I read it somewhere. Them Buddhist monks drink it all the time."

"I'll try it, but I'm not shaving my head," Simp grumbled.

Simp put a pot of water on the stove. When it boiled, they sprinkled the leaves in their mugs and poured the steaming water over them. "I think Trudy might like this," Killian said, taking a sip.

"Needs more sugar," Simp grunted, adding a fifth teaspoon to his cup. It tasted the way mown grass smelled. Not unpleasant, but not like something you'd want to drink.

They drank their tea in silence. "You feel anything?" Simp asked when their mugs were empty. "I can't tell a damn bit of difference."

"Give it time," Killian advised.

Trudy chose that moment to wander inside. "Are you boys having a tea party?" Simp scowled, but when he looked at his wife, her hair tumbling out of a kerchief and her top blouse button undone to reveal a bit of cleavage, his eyes sparkled.

"That tea is really something," she said, laughing as he pulled her onto his lap.

Killian decided his truck needed an oil change and diplomatically made his exit.

"We've got to stop, Simp," Trudy protested and pushed herself off his lap. "I'm on a deadline. The galleys for the new book are due tomorrow."

"Damn. Just when things were getting interesting," Simp said ruefully, and swatted her bottom. "At least you gave me something to meditate on."

༄

School had been in session for two weeks. For Ezra, it had been two weeks of misery. His anxiety peaked each morning before he left for school, and he had to wake up earlier and earlier to get through all of his rituals: counting his steps from the bed to his bathroom (stepping off with his right foot first and never touching the carpet); stopping at his bedroom threshold to tap on the door frame and count backward from thirty; chanting "Sissy Namey" nine times before he stepped into the bathroom. If he messed up any of it, he had to go back to the bed and start all over again. He just knew if he did it wrong—miscounted or missed a step—then something unspeakably awful would happen. He didn't know why, only that it was a terrible truth and that his life depended on it. But it was hard to get it right because he was always so tired. The nightmares were coming two or three times each night. The wave chased him down every time, and he knew he would drown in real life if it ever swamped him in his dream. So far, he'd managed to wake himself before that happened.

Small panic attacks kept him on edge during the school day, like when the bell rang, and everyone shot out of their seats. He had to wait for them all to leave so no one would see his tapping before he went through the doorway. But it was hard to come up with reasons to stay behind, and he was sure the sister was watching him, even though he did his best to hide his warding behaviors from the teachers. The other kids, well . . . they eventually spotted his tapping and talking to himself, and they started to tease him. It wasn't a surprise when it happened, but it stunk anyway. They started calling him "Happy Tappy." Even boys he'd been friends with his whole life gave him funny looks.

The third Monday was the crowning disaster. Miss Mini Maynard, his math teacher and one of the few teachers who wasn't a nun, had been drawing geometric figures on the blackboard and was talking about how arithmetic could lead to algebra, geometry, trigonometry, and calculus. She wasn't making a lot of sense to Ezra, but he sat at his desk and dutifully looked at the blackboard.

Miss Maynard brought to mind a bloated, frizzy-haired toad who favored polka dots. Her body jiggled and flapped to-and-fro as she drew circles, triangles, and squares. On the right side of the board, all by its lonesome, she drew a cube. Ezra stared at the cube and felt mesmerized by its three-dimensional shape. It was as if he were Spock on *Star Trek* and had gone into a mind-meld with the cube.

"I am you; you are me; we are one," the cube said to him, or he said to the cube. It was hard to tell who was doing what, but the cube grew deeper and wider with each blink of his eyes. At first it was just cool, but then Ezra began blinking faster and faster until the cube grew and became immense. Ezra wanted to stop blinking, but he couldn't. He sat in his seat feeling helpless and alarmed as the cube started to spin off the blackboard into the three-dimensional space of his classroom. He closed his eyes to make it stop, but the image was still there, behind his eyelids.

He wondered if he was hallucinating, because he was sure only lunatics hallucinated.

"Sissy Namey, Sissy Namey, Sissy Namey," he whispered to himself nine times. But even that didn't make the hallucination stop.

He'd been scared before by the near-drowning, by the nightmares, by his need to tap and chew his nails, and the whole list of new behaviors since the fishing trip. But this was a whole new level of terror. His scalp tingled with fear. His pulse shot up, and he began to hyperventilate.

"I'm gonna die!" his brain told him, over and over again. "Die! Die! Die!"

Simp collected him from the nurse's office forty-five minutes later. Ezra was sitting on the edge of the cot, his face a study in sheer wretchedness. He'd vomited all over his desk and on himself, and he was damp with sweat. Simp put his arm around his son's thin shoulders and walked him to the car.

"Rough day, huh?"

"Yeah," Ezra mumbled, trying to keep the tears at bay as he slumped into the front seat. The last thing he wanted to do was talk about how mortifying it had been to hear the other kids enjoying his misery.

Simp stood looking down at Ezra, one hand on the open passenger-side door and the other on the car roof. "You want to tell me about it?"

"It was a bitch," Ezra said, spitting the words through his teeth.

"Some days are like that."

"Today was the worst."

Simp squatted down on the ground beside his son. "Listen here, Ezra. I know something's not right with you. If you tell me what it is, I will fix it. I swear."

Ezra broke down and blurted it all out: the wave, the cube, Sissy Namey. When he finished, he felt miserable and weak. He waited to hear his father tell him he was a wimp, that he'd let the minor mishap on the fishing trip get to him.

"Damn, son. You been having a helluva time." Simp reached over and squeezed Ezra's knee. "I'm sorry you had to go through all that. I'm glad you told me, though. Real glad."

Ezra scrunched his eyes. *I'm not gonna cry*, he swore silently to himself. After a few seconds, he sat up and took a deep breath.

"You shoulda seen my desk," he said.

"A real gusher, huh?" asked Simp.

"Projectile," Ezra said, with a slight smile. He'd learned the word from a cartoon. "Dad, am I . . . " he couldn't say the word.

"Don't you worry, Ezra. There's not a thing wrong with you," Simp declared. "You can trust me on that. You are not . . ."

He couldn't say the word either. That did not reassure Ezra.

☙

They had to wait a week for a scheduled appointment with a psychiatrist. Ezra spent most of the time in bed, faking the flu. His dad knew the truth, but he just gave a broad wink and brought the television upstairs so Ezra could watch *Get Smart* reruns from bed. His mom, busy with her deadline, breezed in with tea and toast and cool washcloths for his forehead every now and then.

When he wasn't watching reruns, Ezra spent the week thinking up ways to end his life. Neither of his parents took sleeping pills, which definitely would have been the way to go. He'd heard it was quick and easy. He didn't think he was being melodramatic to consider his options; it was clear as day that he was a nutjob. When his parents took him to see the shrink, it would be confirmed, and he'd be locked away, just like Sissy Namey. Death seemed like a better fate.

On Friday morning, Simp shook Ezra awake at five. "Get a move on, son. Today's the day. Up and at 'em."

Ezra's appointment was scheduled for 10 a.m. at the Regional Mental Health Clinic, a state-owned facility in Huntsville. Although it was a separate agency, it was located adjacent to the state mental hospital, on the western edge of the city.

"The problem is there's too many crazy people in Alabama!" Simp complained to his wife. "That's why it took 'em a whole week to see our boy. It's them Christians! They're driving people nuts. I blame the Christians, all right." He stomped off to clean his shotgun and barely caught Trudy's mild reply that the hospital was probably just understaffed.

Trudy made Ezra shower and wash his hair, but she let him choose his own clothes. He thought about wearing overalls, imagining himself tucking his arms under the bib and acting as calm and collected as Killian. But they were none too clean, so he chose a just-washed pair of blue jeans and a plain white T-shirt. He jammed his Crimson Tide cap on his head. He planned on leaving it in the car when they got to the state hospital, so his mother could keep it to remember him by when they took him away in a straitjacket.

This was it. Today, it would all be over. Ezra Magee would go down in local history as the boy who went crazy and got himself locked up. The worst was about to happen. At least he wouldn't have to dread it anymore. He wouldn't have to pretend anymore that he was normal. He'd tried as hard as he could, but it was exhausting.

"Sissy Namey, Sissy Namey, Sissy Namey," he chanted to himself nine times, and then nine times again. He said a last goodbye to his bedroom, to his comic book collection and to his baseball glove, and he went downstairs to eat breakfast at his kitchen table for the last time.

As they drove away, Ezra looked hungrily out of the car window, trying to memorize the sight of his house and the front porch that needed painting and the tree house he'd built with Boyd and Floyd two years before. Trudy tuned the radio to "Beautiful 106," a station that played "golden oldies" nonstop.

"Well, they just told us that a minute ago, didn't they?" Simp pointed out after a news report. "Wife, why are we listening to this drivel?" He retrieved his recently acquired eight-track tape of Willie Nelson from the glove compartment and popped it in. Trudy didn't complain. They all liked Willie.

"I know I've done weird things," Willie sang. "I've told people I heard things / when silence was all around / Been days when it pleased me to be on my knees / following ants, as they crawl across the ground / Been insane on a train, but I'm still me again / and the place where I hold you is true / So I know I'm all right, 'cause I'd have to be crazy / to fall out of love with you."

Ezra loved the song. He'd heard it a hundred times. His mom sang along, off-key, which for her was the norm. She liked to describe herself as "singing-disabled," but she loved to sing just the same.

"Trudy, honey, Willie has a hard enough time as it is," Simp told her. "He really don't need your help."

"Simpellion Magee! If Willie Nelson can make a million dollars with that voice of his, I *reckon*"—she always emphasized the word "reckon" when she was pissed off—"you can listen to my squawks!" Trudy put a finger on the tape player's eject button and flashed her husband a challenging look.

"You ain't got the labia, woman!"

Simp didn't think his son would understand, and Ezra didn't. Trudy didn't go through with it, but she gave Simp a wicked smile.

Willie's melodious warble continued. "'It sure would be dingy to live in an envelope / waiting alone for a stamp,'" Trudy sang along defiantly. "'You'd swear I was loco, to rub for a genie, while burning my hand on the lamp / And I may not be normal, but nobody is / so I'd like to say before I'm through . . .'"

Simp joined in for the big finish: "'I'd have to be crazy, plumb out of my mind, to fall out of love with you.'"

Simp reached out and caressed his wife's cheek. Ezra just knew that his father's gesture and his parents' sing-along with Willie would constitute the very last happy moment he would ever experience on this earth. As they sped north on U.S. 35 to Scottsboro, then westward on U.S. 72 across "the great state of Alabama," in the words of George Wallace, Ezra counted the shotgun-peppered road signs and anxiously willed them to be divisible by three.

He was going to be locked away for life. How, he wondered, could his parents act so normal when he was going to be taken away from them forever? Maybe they wanted it that way. Maybe that's why they were singing a song about being crazy. Maybe they didn't want to be stuck with an insane kid. Maybe they'd go ahead and have another boy to replace him, and that kid would grow up to be an all-star pitcher and the perfect, un-crazy son.

His thoughts were spinning out of control. Locked up forever. *Sissy Namey Sissy Namey Sissy Namey.* Was this how she'd felt when they carted her away in a straitjacket? *Sissy Namey Sissy Namey Sissy Namey.* Ezra rhythmically banged his head against the back seat and chanted her name in his head in sets of three. He saw a look pass between his parents, but he didn't stop or lose count. When he reached thirty-three, he started over again.

A few miles later, Simp pulled onto the Joseph Wheeler Highway, which took them to State Road 20, where his mother had to stop to use the powder room.

"You want a cola, son?" Simp asked.

Ezra did, but he couldn't stop counting or banging his head.

"Alrighty then. I'll just duck inside and get us some," Simp said.

Ezra counted out three more sets of *Sissy Namey*s and then he was able to stop and drink his can of cola. That feeling he'd had when they set out, of being resigned to his fate, had burned away like a morning fog. Ezra gazed out the window at the overgrown tangle of woods and wondered how hard it would be to dive out of a moving car and survive. He'd seen James Bond do that in the movies. He drew a picture of the feat in his mind. He'd have to roll off his shoulder and get away from the road. It would probably hurt like hell. And then he'd have to run into the thicket and disappear before his parents knew he was gone. Ezra had some skills with a fishing rod and a BB gun. He could probably live all right on his own like a wild man in the woods. Most seasons, he could scrounge for nuts and berries, like in a Walt Disney movie. There'd be a stray dog that would find him and become his best friend, and they would walk across Alabama together having adventures and stealing pies off windowsills and finding loot stashed in a cave by bank robbers. That sure sounded a lot better than spending the rest of his life in a padded cell.

Bang bang bang, Sissy Namey Sissy Namey Sissy Namey. The panic rising in his chest calmed back down. His parents had been chatting when Ezra was drinking his cola, but they grew silent again, and Ezra heard himself moaning. He couldn't stop. *Bang bang bang, Sissy Namey, Sissy Namey, Sissy Namey.*

Soon, their beat-up Datsun was inching its way through downtown Huntsville. It was the biggest metropolis Ezra had ever visited. It had more cars than he'd ever seen gathered in one place. His father pointed off to the left, and Ezra was momentarily distracted from his counting by the towering vertical form rising up at the Space and Rocket Center. Like a giant phallus, the Saturn rocket jutted skyward into the hazy Alabama sky.

"That's the finest memorial to Nazi technical ingenuity to be found anywhere in the world," Simp declared sarcastically. "Werner Von Braun would have been proud of this display."

As Ezra was trying to process this information, his dad began singing.

"'Gather 'round while I sing you of Wernher Von Braun / A man whose allegiance / is ruled by expedience / Call him a Nazi, he won't even frown / "Ha, Nazi Schmazi," says Wernher Von Braun.'"

"I think I've heard you sing that song before," said Trudy.

"Yep," said Simp. "That was written and recorded by a Harvard mathematician by the name of Tom Lehrer—good man." He looked at Ezra in the rearview mirror. "That's what happened after World War II, son," Simp continued. "The Ruskies and Americans divided up the German scientists, no matter their background—like Von Braun, many of them were Nazis—and brought them home to build better weapons of mass destruction."

Ezra couldn't remember ever hearing the name Wernher Von Braun. He reached his thirty-third *Sissy Namey* and rolled down the window for a better view as his father drove past. The long, sleek fuselage of a decommissioned Blackbird Spy Plane sat out front of the Space and Rocket Center, where the Saturn I was moored. It had the look of a sinister bird of prey.

"Pretty cool, dontcha think, Ezra?" his mother said lightly.

"Yeah," Ezra mumbled, tugging his baseball cap down lower on his forehead. Concrete and steel buildings glided by, and men in business suits and women in bell bottoms hurried down sidewalks and across streets. There were advertisements and billboards everywhere. Seemed like every store was having some kind of sale. He didn't see any kids at all. Just a lot of buildings and sidewalks. Not even many trees.

"Thank God I'm a country boy," Ezra declared, remembering the John Denver song. For some reason, this made his father pound on the steering wheel in delight and his mother laugh.

They drove out of the downtown area and through a residential area, then over a small rise, through a copse of pine trees, and finally through an open gate with a faded sign on it: "Alabama State Hospital, Huntsville Campus." Ezra began to hyperventilate. Simp pulled the car over and hustled him into the bushes where Ezra vomited up his breakfast.

"Steady now, Ezra," Simp murmured, squeezing his shoulder gently. "It'll be okay. I've gotcher back, son. Steady now." Ezra felt like collapsing in his father's arms and bursting into tears. Instead, he climbed back into the car.

A tall fence followed the drive as they continued toward the administration building. Through the chain links they could see squat, red-brick buildings. Simp parked in a space marked "Visitor."

With deep foreboding, Ezra took off his Crimson Tide cap and laid it gently on the back seat. He gave it a last look of farewell.

"Come on, honey," Trudy coaxed. "I know it's tough, but the doctor here will know how to help you." His mother smoothed his hair and offered her hand. Ezra took it gratefully.

The closer they got to the squat, brick building, the more Ezra's feet dragged as if they knew what was coming. Four stories high, the hospital administration facility had a sad look of neglect; dead ivy, soot, and dirt coated its surface. There was a flight of stairs up to the front door. Ezra let go of his mother's hand and hopped up each step on his right leg, counting carefully. There were twelve, a number divisible by three, so that was all right. His mother and father waited patiently for him at the top. Ezra turned and saw a view of Big Springs Park splayed out behind them.

"Maybe we'll visit there afterward," Trudy suggested. "There's no need to rush home. We should see the sights!"

"That's a fine idea!" Simp enthused, overdoing it. "I read about it in the AAA book. They got some kinda artesian spring that spews up from the limestone caverns under the city. They got ducks, geese, and whatnot. What do you say, Ezra?"

Ezra grimaced. They were trying too hard, pretending they didn't know his real fate. He wished they wouldn't treat him like a baby. He let go of his mother's hand and pulled away.

"We'd best shake a leg," Trudy said lightly. "We don't want to be late."

But Ezra had to stop in the doorway and tap and shuffle and chant "Sissy Namey" in threes. He panicked when he thought he might have missed one, and he had to start the sequence all over again. His parents politely looked away and waited for him to finish.

There was no one behind the desk inside the entrance, and Simp was too impatient to wait. He hustled down one of the long hallways. Trudy and Ezra hurried to keep up.

"Simp! Wait!" Trudy was out of breath as they turned down another corridor identical to the last. "We'll never find it this way. We need to ask someone!"

Simp ignored her and kept up his mad rush down gray-walled hallway after gray-walled hallway. There were lots of doors with opaque glass windows, but no names or signs revealed whose offices they might be. The place was eerily quiet. Ezra thought there would be shrieking or crazy talk, but he reckoned they kept the patients drugged, or in another part of the building.

"Shh," Simp said, stopping suddenly and peering around a corner. Trudy fanned herself with her hat and leaned against the wall, grateful for the rest. But then Simp lunged out of sight.

Ezra heard a scuffle and then, "Hey! Get offa me!"

Ezra and Trudy turned the corner just in time to see Simp holding a white-jacketed orderly in a pretty good example of a half-nelson. The man's clipboard clattered to the floor with the staccato rattle of a sniper attack.

"Let me go!" the orderly said, indignantly. He was a slight man, completely bald and sporting a bushy moustache.

"I will, just as soon as you help us find the doctor's office."

"Help!" the orderly yelled.

Simp clamped his hand over the man's mouth. "We just need directions!"

Trudy intervened. "Honestly, Simpellion, you turn everything into such a ruckus! Let the nice man go."

Reluctantly, Simp released the orderly, who grabbed and shook Trudy's offered hand and reclaimed his clipboard from Ezra. "Sir, would you kindly direct us to the office of Dr. McClennon?" she asked sweetly.

Before the orderly could reply, Simp felt the need to justify his actions of a moment ago. "No offense intended, but how in the hell is anybody supposed to find anything around here!?"

The orderly held his clipboard in front of him like a shield. "If you just turn left up ahead—" he began.

Simp took off down the hallway and turned left, then paused. "Which door is it supposed to be?" he shouted back.

"Third door on the left after you turn the corner," the orderly explained, and Simp was off again. They followed quickly and got to the hallway just in time to see Simp open a door and shout, "Finally! Here it is!"

"Oh, no," the orderly said, speeding up. "You can't go in there now. He's got a—"

It was too late. By the time Ezra, Trudy, and the orderly arrived at the open door, Simp's hands were raised over his head and a gun was aimed at his heart.

"Honey, this here's the doctor," Simp said weakly.

The doctor, a relatively short man, stepped out from behind his desk, never lowering the gun. His close-cropped black hair grayed at the edges of his squarish face. The soles of his shoes were at least three inches thick, elevating the man to what he apparently perceived as a more desirable height. A tweed sports coat and khaki pants clothed a small but robust physical stature.

"Pleased to meet you," Trudy said coolly to the man still pointing a gun at her husband. "Is the gun really necessary?"

The doctor turned his head to look at Trudy, his hazel eyes taking her in. "You tell me," he said, lowering it. "Who are you people, and why did this man bust in here like he was runnin' from the law?"

"I was looking for a doctor," Simp explained.

"Well, you found one," the man said, lowering the revolver. "Matthew McClennon, M.D."

Simp stared at the doctor, giving the pearl-handled revolver an appreciative look.

"What in the hell is the meaning of this?" The doctor addressed the orderly. "Fritz, cain't y'all see I have a patient?" The doctor gestured to a wizened man in green pajamas, sitting at the side of his desk, grinning at them dopily.

"Sir, I apologize . . . they're—they're a little early," the orderly explained nervously.

"I see," Dr. McClennon said, squinting with interest at Simpellion, who returned McClennon's gaze with a look of equal interest. "Never mind, I'll take it from here," he told the orderly.

"Thank you ever so much," Trudy said politely as the orderly backed out of the room.

Ezra squeezed into the office of Matthew McClennon, M.D., behind his mother. It was a small rectangle with white walls on which hung a bank of framed diplomas. McClennon was a sharp-eyed, clean-shaven man of fifty or so. He didn't look like a doctor to Ezra. He looked slick and confident, like a car salesman.

A sudden, hyena-like laugh from the pajama-clad patient caused Ezra to shift closer to his mother. He noted a string of drool hanging from the corner of the man's mouth. The godawful laugh stopped abruptly, and the patient said, "Saw-right. I doan mind. Doan mind-a-tall. Y'all wan me ta leave?"

"I sure am sorry for bustin' in like that," Simp said, his eyes still locked on the doctor's. "The thing is, we come here to get some help."

"Obviously," McClennon said, not blinking. "But y'all need an appointment."

"We got one, for 10:30," Simp responded, then looked at the clock on the wall, which read ten minutes after ten o'clock.

McClennon looked at his schedule book and then at Simp Magee.

Simp looked at the doctor and smiled. Simp was suspicious of doctors in general—especially shrinks—but Ezra knew his father couldn't help but admire a man who kept a pearl-handled revolver in his desk.

"You workin' here at the insane asylum, must be nice for you to see some normal folks for a change, hey doc?"

And then Simpellion T. Dillon Magee winked at Matthew Mc-Clennon, M.D. He meant it to lighten the mood, but unfortunately Simp's winks made him look like an angry orangutan about to attack. The doctor grabbed again for his revolver. The blue metallic finish of the barrel gleamed in the fluorescent light. The adults in the room froze.

Suddenly, Ezra shrieked, and the hammer on the revolver slammed down on the firing pin. There was a loud click.

Simp smiled sanguinely and raised his eyebrows. "Helps if you load it, doc."

The drooling patient started giggling, at first haltingly, then uncontrollably.

But Ezra had shrieked for another reason: he'd just realized that he'd come across the threshold without performing the warding rituals. He was in danger. The floor—it was turning to quicksand. He would be sucked under! He'd never felt such sheer terror. He shrieked again while tapping his face and shuffling his feet frantically. In all the commotion, he was only dimly aware that someone was laughing at him.

Dr. McClennon reversed his grip on the revolver and used it like a gavel on the top of his desk. "Enough!" he shouted as he drove the butt of the pistol down on the bureau three times. The three taps soothed Ezra, who stopped shrieking and stood still. The drooling patient immediately stopped his giggling.

"Order in the court!" Simp said, unable to help himself.

Dr. McClennon shook his head.

Trudy pulled Ezra to her side. "Perhaps we might sit down?" she said into the sudden silence.

Matthew McClennon sighed and wiped sweat from his brow, then gestured Trudy toward the empty bench on the side of the room. "Wontcha please take a seat, ma'am?"

"That is very kind of you, sir," she said, putting her arm around Ezra and leading him to the bench. They sat, and she crossed her long legs demurely, holding Ezra close to her. He buried his head in her shoulder, humiliated and exhausted. Simpellion swung a chair around and sat on it cowboy-style, still smiling. He gave a nod to the patient, who had returned to the half-sleep of a Thorazine haze.

The doctor turned from Trudy back to Simp. "What-all is wrong with you?" he asked.

Simp blinked at the doctor for a moment, then cringed. "Not me!" he cried. "It's my son! Jesus Christ, doc, do I look like I'm crazy?

My boy needs help. Don't you have some kinda pills you can give him to make him stop having nightmares and tapping and counting and whatnot?"

"Peeyulls, yeah," the mental patient chimed in, his face breaking into a wide, dopey grin.

"Ezra's not one of your crazy-types," Simp hurried to say. "He's a bright boy; a good boy. He's a helluva baseball player." Ezra sat up a little straighter.

The doctor looked at Simp and then Ezra, sat down, and put the gun away in his top drawer. "Charley, how 'bout you and me finish up later?" he said to his patient, like it wasn't a question.

The man struggled out of the chair and gave a little bow to the doctor. "Ah'll see mahself out." He turned and nodded amiably to Ezra. "See ya later," he said. Ezra shuddered.

"I need y'all ta start from the beginnin'," McClennon said, addressing Trudy. He asked about Ezra's general health and then about his symptoms. He didn't address Ezra directly, much to the boy's relief.

"We'll start him on medication. It oughta help with the symptoms. Could take a coupla weeks to see a difference, so y'all make a follow-up appointment"—he gave Simp a pointed look—"for the thirtieth."

Ezra's head shot up. He wasn't going to have to stay there? A ray of hope pierced the fog of his misery.

"So, you can fix him!" Simp said happily.

"Ezra's got somethin' called obsessive-compulsive disorder. 'Smore common than you'd think. Usually shows up in kids his age. We cain't cure it, but we got medicine that'll help him control the symptoms."

No cure? He'd be like this forever? Trudy and Simp shared worried looks. Ezra's head was in his hands. He was trying not to cry.

"But science marches on, wouldn't you say, doctor?" Trudy

said. "Someone must be working on a cure, even as we speak!" She looked pointedly at McClennon and then gestured to Ezra.

"That's a fact, ma'am. Why, we can do things today we wouldn'ta dreamed of twenty years ago. No tellin' what kinda cures they'll have for your son in the next five, ten years."

McClennon wrote out the prescription and handed it to Trudy. "Make sure your boy takes his dose every night with supper, or every morning with breakfast," the doctor instructed. "Don't let him be skippin' none, ya hear?"

"How much do we owe you, doc?" A wad of cash appeared in Simp's hand.

"It don't work like that. Mah secretary'll send y'all a bill at the end of the month. You stop by the front desk and give her your information."

McClennon shook hands with Trudy, nodded to Simp, and gave Ezra a sideways look that made him cringe.

Ezra looked at the doorway in front of him. *Just walk on out*, he told himself. *Just this once. Just do it.*

It was no good. At the threshold, he was seized with panic. He couldn't cross over. He'd humiliate himself—again—in front of the doctor, but he had no choice.

His parents waited patiently in the hallway while he counted and tapped. Ezra didn't dare turn around to see if the doctor was watching him.

"Don't shoot him, doc," Simp said with a smirk. "He'll take his medicine."

After a stroll through the park—Ezra looked at each tree and stone with a new sense of freedom—they stopped at a pharmacy near the hospital and filled Ezra's prescription for a tricyclic antidepressant. Trudy let Ezra tell her which Good Humor ice cream bar and which new comic book he wanted for the ride back. He waited in the car while his parents went into the store. He jammed his Crimson Tide cap back on his head and let the feeling of relief wash over him.

He was really going home!

Simp said, "The sooner, the better," so that night, his parents watched as he swallowed the pill with a glass of water. Then Simp brewed him a cup of foul-tasting green tea and made him drink it afterward.

"It's like religion and horse racing, son. Always hedge your bets."

CHAPTER 9

"You know you can't solve your problems with alcohol," the reverend Hiram Johnson said pointedly. The sun was setting already, and Ezra wondered where the day had gone. He was still wearing his bathrobe. He hadn't brushed his teeth or combed his hair. Hiram was still hanging around in a most irritating manner, disappearing and reappearing without warning. Ezra looked around, trying to locate him by the sound of his voice. He found him leaning against the wall near the stove.

"I tried it, you know?" Hiram said, turning his head to stare out the back door.

"Tried what?" Ezra asked. He really didn't give a rat's ass, but something forced him to feign politeness to the reverend.

"Drinking my way out of my problems. Your daddy can attest to that. He scraped me off many a barroom floor back in the day."

"I'm not trying to drink my way out of my problems," Ezra said, aware of the irony given the bottle of bourbon in his hand. When had he given up on using a glass? "I was under a lot of stress, and the squirrel tipped me over the edge."

"Right. The squirrel." Hiram's face betrayed his skepticism.

"What's that supposed to mean?"

"Are you sure about the squirrel, Ezra?" Hiram had an infuriating smirk on his kisser. "Honestly now, was there really a squirrel in your classroom?"

"You don't believe me!?" Ezra almost shouted. "Of course there was really a squirrel! I was there! I saw it with my own eyes!"

"Didn't your study of history teach you anything about so-called eyewitness accounts?"

Ezra hated when someone answered his question with another question. He was growing tired of the irritating presence of Hiram Johnson.

"Maybe you oughta eat some food before you finish that bottle," Hiram said. It was the first helpful thing he'd said all day.

Ezra wasn't really hungry, but he also couldn't remember the last time he'd eaten. He was feeling buzzed—all right, more than buzzed. Half the bourbon was gone. He rummaged in the freezer and found a frozen pizza. As he tore away the wrapping, he remembered their last family dinner night at Tony's Pizza Palace. Had that only been three weeks ago? It felt like a lifetime.

❧

Ezra took a greedy bite. The slice of pepperoni had been hot, but not hot enough to burn the roof of his mouth. The crust was light, crispy, salty—just about perfect. He'd washed it down with a slug of Corona and looked around the restaurant at all the other parents out with their kids on a Friday night. Tony's Pizza Palace had long been the Magee family's end-of-the-week ritual, but for the past couple of months, Dillon hadn't wanted to go.

"I need a night out," Celia had declared.

"I don't want to go," Dillon had protested.

"Okay, but on the other hand, if you can eat four fully loaded slices of Tony's Meat Mania, I will owe you one million dollars." Dillon had hesitated for a moment, and then burst into a wide smile.

The whole family had been in good spirits on the way to the restaurant, with Dillon bragging about how he was going to spend his million bucks and trying to negotiate how many toppings each slice needed to have to in order to qualify for their deal. The three of them had walked arm-in-arm up to the entrance of the restaurant. Ezra held open the door for them and waited as Dillon tapped on the doorframe and shuffled his feet to the left and then to the right while counting. A family was heading toward the door, and Ezra offered up a silent prayer that Dillon would finish before they got close enough to see what his son was doing. He did.

The pizza was good, as always. Dillon was on his third slice and looking bloated, but cheerful. Ezra dabbed sauce off Celia's chin with his napkin, and she gave him a tentative, forced smile. He hadn't slept in their bed for a week.

Ezra slid another slice onto his plate and sprinkled it liberally with crushed red pepper. The fuzzy lines of a joke crept into his mind: *Question: What do pizza and pussy have in common? Answer: Some is better than others, but it's all delicious.*

He wondered where he'd heard such a crude joke. He paused with the pizza halfway to his mouth, trying to recall who had told it to him. He'd been a boy. Younger than Dillon. He'd been passing through a room when he'd overheard a man telling it to another man.

My father, he corrected himself. It was his father who'd told the joke to some man. Ezra could still hear his father's hearty laugh. The thought came that his father had always enjoyed his own jokes. Ezra was surprised, and a little rattled, by the memory.

"Dad? Earth to Dad!" Dillon waved his fourth slice of pizza in the air. "I'm about to win a million dollars!"

"Good luck, big guy," Ezra said, snapping out of his reverie. Dillon struck a dramatic pose, one arm flexed like a miniature weightlifter, and took a bite.

Celia lightly laid her hand on Ezra's arm and raised her eyebrows. "Where were you?" she asked.

"Some random memory of a godawful joke my father told someone when I was a boy."

Celia's eyes widened. "Your father? You remembered!"

"What's the joke?" Dillon asked with his mouth full.

"It's too raunchy to tell in mixed company."

"Your dad told dirty jokes?" Dillon looked pleased at the idea. "You never talk about him, or your mom."

"I don't remember much." Ezra shrugged, knowing how feeble that sounded.

"Don't I have cousins, aunts, uncles, and grandparents on the Magee side of the family?"

Ezra's heart squeezed painfully. "We're the last of the Magees, I'm told. And on my mother's side, there's just Aunt Lenore."

"Too bad," Dillon said. And then, "Mom, do I still get a million dollars if I finish it and then barf it back up?"

"No, you do not!" She grinned at him. "As the great General George Washington said, 'Better to live to try again another day than to go down in humiliating defeat!'"

"I'm so close!" he groaned dramatically. "But I don't think I can finish this." He'd made it two bites into the fourth slice.

"You gave it a good try," Ezra said. "With all those toppings, you probably ate about half a pig."

"Dad, do I look like your side of the family, or Mom's side of the family?"

"You look like me," Ezra grinned. "Lucky guy! We're handsome devils."

"Except you have my eyes," Celia added, fondly brushing the hair back from her son's face.

"Dad, who do you look like—your mom or your dad?" Dillon persisted.

"My dad, I guess."

"Can I see a picture?"

Before Ezra could tell him there weren't any pictures that he knew of, Dillon clutched his stomach.

"I need to go home," he demanded.

Celia and Ezra shot each other a look.

"You want to visit the bathroom?" Celia asked.

"Home," Dillon repeated, his face pinched and panicky.

"Sure thing, kiddo." Ezra stood and pulled out his wallet. He dropped some money on the table while Celia put her arm around Dillon's shoulders and walked him toward the door. The clatter and chatter of the restaurant grated on Ezra's nerves as they waited for Dillon to do his leaving ritual. A group of rowdy teenagers pushed past and gave Dillon a dirty look, but a glare from Ezra stopped any rude comments from coming out of their mouths.

Ezra leaned down and spoke low in Dillon's ear. "Don't worry, son. You just do what you have to do."

Dillon's shoulders slumped, and he commenced his shuffle and tapping ritual from the beginning.

When they got home, Dillon ran upstairs and slammed his door. Ezra walked out into the backyard and leaned against a tree, a wave of panic washing through him. Mercifully, it was a small one, and ten minutes later, he was back in the kitchen wiping sweat from his brow and pouring his nightly double shot of bourbon.

∽

Ezra held open the porch door as he and Celia went outside. He settled into his chair and sighed. "I don't really want to have this conversation, honey," he said proactively. "It always comes out the same. You get pissed off. I get depressed." He sipped the bourbon. "I don't talk about OCD because those were dark years, and I see no reason to look back now I'm past them."

"What about Alabama?" she asked softly. "Were those dark years too?"

"I told you, I don't remember my childhood. Aunt Lenore told me there was a storm and the doctors told her that I had a kind of post-traumatic amnesia. I moved up here to live with her, and she wasn't part of my old life. I put the past behind me and started fresh."

"But tonight you remembered something about your dad."

"Just a flash. Him telling this raunchy joke about pizza to some guy."

He told her the joke, and her grin was beautiful.

"And that's all you recalled?"

Ezra closed his eyes and summoned the fragment of memory. "Well, I could hear his voice in my head. He had a strong Alabama drawl, and he cussed a lot."

"What else can you remember about him?"

Ezra kept his eyes closed. "I don't know. Except," he took a slug of bourbon, "I recall he had a thing about squirrels. He hated them. I don't know why."

"Squirrels?"

"Yep."

"Can you remember your mother?"

He tried to imagine the woman who had been his mother, Trudy Magee. "I can't see her. I can't remember anything specific about her. But—" he hesitated.

"But?"

"But when I think about my parents, I feel . . . I feel affection." Ezra felt a lump in his throat. "Even though I was different, I know they loved me."

"Different like Dillon?"

"Yeah, like Dillon," he said, and a memory of an episode when he was a young boy at school flashed through his mind. Ezra winced. Celia took his hand.

"Ezra, is there something else you're not telling me?"

"Probably."

"Hmmm. Does it have anything to do with why you're drinking every night?"

"Yeah."

"Do you think you'll be ready to tell me about it soon?"

"I hope so."

"Do you want to put that bourbon away now and come to bed with me?"

"I'll be up soon," he said, knowing he wouldn't.

※

"So, you pushed her away again."

Hiram was perched on the edge of the green ottoman Ezra had dragged out of the shed. It was one of Ezra's favorite pieces of furniture, but Celia said it didn't fit the color scheme of the living room. In a mood of defiance, he had brought it back into the house after she left.

Again, Hiram had the semblance of a halo around his head. Ezra was momentarily startled, but then saw it was only an effect, the sunlight filtering through the light blue curtain in the den.

"Yeah," Ezra said after a long pause, "I never made it up to bed. Not that night, and not any of the nights after."

"You and the bourbon?"

"I didn't intend it that way."

"We never do."

"I can't believe she left."

"Really?" Hiram asked.

"No, not really."

CHAPTER 10

Ezra hated to think that Dillon was getting worse because his parents were fighting, but that's the way it looked. Despite his daily dose of antidepressant, Dillon's symptoms worsened. Celia had replaced Ezra as the one who woke up to hold the boy when he had night terrors, because Ezra was passed out in the den. He no longer heard Dillon's frightened noises. In the mornings, Dillon was exhausted and depressed. He dragged himself to school. Ezra dragged himself to his office to grade papers. His days were spent hungover, exhausted, and depressed.

It was May, almost the end of the school year, when the school counselor first called. Ezra and Celia drove in separate cars to the meeting.

"Dillon is having some difficulty," the counselor said as soon as they were seated. "We're aware that you're getting Dillon help for his OCD, but his teacher, Ms. Milligan, is concerned that Dillon's classmates are beginning to tease him because of some of his behaviors."

"Mr. Patterson," Celia began.

"Call me John," the counselor said, leaning in with a big smile, touching Celia's hand. Ezra wondered if John Patterson was trying to hit on his wife.

"John, is Dillon causing any problems in his classes?"

"In itself, Dillon's behavior is not a problem for his teacher, or even for his classmates," he said soothingly. "It's the reaction of the other children that's worrying us. At this age, any signs of difference become ammunition for teasing and bullying. We keep a close eye on the kids, but we can't monitor them one hundred percent of the time. Academically, Dillon's a high achiever, but socially, he's . . . he's already seen as someone on the outside of things. He's quieter than the other children and more cautious about joining in activities. There's nothing wrong with those traits, but Dillon has, on occasion, been a target of teasing by some of our more . . . aggressive students. And I'm afraid his OCD behaviors are drawing more negative attention. I'm worried that the stigma of being different will hurt his chances of having a healthy social experience in high school."

Ezra felt like punching the man in the face. How dare he call Dillon a social misfit? "So, what do you suggest, John?" Ezra said his name like a swear word.

"Well, with only three weeks left in the school year, his teachers believe it would be best for Dillon to complete the rest of his schoolwork at home."

Celia's face creased into a frown. "You want us to pull him out of school? He loves school! He'll think he's being punished."

"Celia, you should talk to him," the counselor said, reaching over to squeeze her hand again. Ezra glowered at him, but the counselor didn't notice. "You might be surprised by what Dillon has to say. From what his teacher reports, he's been pretty miserable these last few weeks. And it's not as if it's forever. You're getting him help, and I'm sure when he starts the eighth grade in September, he'll be right as rain."

That night at dinner, Celia told Dillon about their conversation with the school counselor. "Honey, would you rather stay home and finish your schoolwork here, with me?"

Dillon's face displayed a storm of emotions. He flung his fork down and ran up to his room in tears.

"He stays in school as long as he wants," Ezra said firmly. But in his heart of hearts, he wished Dillon would stay home with Celia. John Patterson was right: kids could be brutal.

"Dillon has an appointment with Dr. Stanhope, but she can't see him until July third," Celia said in a low, neutral voice as she and

Ezra cleared the supper dishes from the table. They were barely speaking. Ezra couldn't blame her.

"Did you hear me?" she demanded.

"I heard you," he muttered.

Victoria Stanhope, a psychiatrist and expert in OCD over in Wheeling, had agreed to see Dillon even though she normally worked only with adults. Ezra would be happy to drive any distance to take Dillon to see anyone who wasn't Lance Fucking Helman.

"She wants him to keep taking the medication, and she needs us to fill out some forms. One of them asks about family history." She slid a bundle of papers over to his side of the table. "Get it done by Monday," she added, and left him alone in the kitchen.

Izzy leaned on Ezra, reminding him that table scraps were a dog's responsibility. Ezra patted her head and scraped the leftover pasta into the dog's bowl. He masked his annoyance. The last thing he needed was to have the dog pissed at him too.

"Family history," he said to the dog. "Is this going to be multiple choice?"

He knew what Celia would say: "This is for Dillon." And she was right. Dillon needed him to step up. Maybe there were some clues in Ezra's history that could help his son. He thought of his Aunt Lenore. She might be able to fill in some of the gaping holes in his memory about his family.

"If she doesn't want to talk, she won't," Ezra told Izzy, who was double-checking the bowl for crumbs. "Not even the CIA could get her to open her mouth. I think she's part mule." He paused and sighed. "It's a trait that runs in the family, I guess."

☙

As he drove down State Road 7 to Aunt Lenore's house, Ezra felt a mix of relief and resentment. Celia had pushed him into dealing with his past, but he knew it was long overdue. He should have had this conversation with Lenore a long time ago.

It hadn't escaped his notice that once he'd agreed to go, his panic attacks had subsided. He didn't believe that was a coincidence, but the implications disturbed him.

"It's up to you to interpret your own thoughts and actions, and find meaning," his childhood therapist, Dr. Cadwallader, had told him. "Not even I, with my training and experience, can tell you what your mind is trying to communicate to you with these panic attacks. But I can help you learn to listen to yourself."

Ezra wished Dr. Cadwallader was still alive. He'd send Dillon to him. Hell, he'd go himself!

When Ezra was twelve, having just arrived in West Virginia, his OCD was so bad that he couldn't leave his aunt's house to go to school. After two weeks of patient worrying, Lenore had finally made an appointment for her nephew with a Morgantown psychiatrist, Dr. Cadwallader. Something had to be done.

"Ezra, I don't know how to help you, but this man does," she had told him. "If you keep missing school, they will come and take you from me and probably put you in a mental hospital. That is just unthinkable. So please find a way to leave this house and see this doctor."

Trembling, Ezra had thrown a blanket over his head, shuffled his feet while counting to thirty-three by threes, and held his breath as he sprinted out the door and right into his aunt's waiting Buick LeSabre. He kept the blanket over his head, hiding in the dark on the ride to Morgantown. Lenore kept a hand resting on his shoulder, and her steady presence had calmed him some.

She circled the block for ten minutes until a space opened up in front of the barber shop. Dr. Cadwallader's office was on the floor above.

"I can't do it!" Ezra wailed from under the blanket.

"You don't have to do a thing," Lenore said. Her voice was one of the most soothing sounds in the world. "You just stay under there, all nice and safe. I'll be right back, okay?"

She left him alone in the car. Ezra felt a panic attack threatening to grow. He counted by threes in the dark cave of his blanket and tapped his face, three times on the right side, three times on the left. He lost count when the car door opened. He had to start all over again.

When he finished his routine, Ezra heard a man clear his throat. He peeked out from under the blanket and saw a thin older man sitting in the driver's seat. Everything about him was narrow, from his nose to the hand he solemnly offered. Ezra thought he looked like an undertaker.

"Nathan Cadwallader," the doctor said.

"Ezra Magee," Ezra replied, extending his hand and letting the blanket slide halfway off his head.

Wisps of white hair gathered like cumulus clouds above the old man's ears, and a light snow of dandruff dusted the lapels of his well-pressed black suit jacket. The only things not black-and-white about Cadwallader were his piercing blue eyes.

"The Buick is a solid car, but I prefer the Cadillac," the man observed, running his hand across the dashboard. "But I suppose a young fellow like you would be more interested in the Camaro."

"Mustang convertible," Ezra said promptly. They talked about the merits of various makes and models of cars. The doctor was surprisingly easy to talk to, and he soon wound the conversation around to Ezra's predicament.

"So, first you have the thought that you might get a panic attack if you step outside your house?"

"Sort of. When it starts, I just feel like something real bad is gonna happen if I leave the house."

"And before it starts?"

"Before it starts—I guess I do have a thought, like you said."

"Hmmm." The doctor looked expectantly at Ezra.

"Uh, it's like I'm thinking, 'What if it happens when I'm not someplace safe? What'll I do?'"

"So, you worry?"

"Yeah. I worry."

"About having a panic attack?"

"And about bad things happening."

"Ah." Cadwallader looked at his watch and nodded. "Ezra, you've done excellent work today. Truly remarkable! I believe I can help you with this . . . if you'll allow me." He aimed his blue eyes at Ezra. "Will you allow me?"

Ezra took a deep breath, letting it out in a slow, steady hiss. "Yessir."

"Excellent!" He shook Ezra's hand again and got out of the car. He began to walk back toward the barber shop, but he abruptly stopped in his tracks, turned on a dime, and poked his head back into the open car window. "Say, would you like to pop upstairs and see my office? That way, you'll know what to expect when you come back on Thursday. It will give you one less unknown factor to worry about."

That made sense to Ezra. He quickly scooted out of the car, leaving the blanket behind. The office was small and cozy and slightly dusty, like the doctor himself. At Cadwallader's invitation, Ezra sat in the red leather wingback chair across from the big maple desk and agreed that he would be quite comfortable there for future sessions.

Ezra came back to the car by himself and found his aunt waiting for him, holding two fudge ripple ice cream cones. The look of relief on her face both pleased and embarrassed him, but he sat in the front seat on the way home, eating his ice cream and looking out the window with renewed interest at the West Virginia countryside.

From that day on, Ezra looked forward to his twice-weekly sessions with the doctor. Cadwallader gave the young boy his grave attention, clearing his throat politely before venturing a question or comment. He spoke to Ezra as an equal, explaining the various professional theories on obsessive compulsions and panic disorders, and soliciting Ezra's opinions as if he were the real expert. It was Cadwallader who helped Ezra find the right combination of medications that allowed him to go to school and live a mostly normal life.

He also taught Ezra techniques ("tricks of the trade," he called them) to help manage his panic attacks. For instance, before he started school, Lenore drove him to the building, where the guidance counselor met them at the door and walked Ezra through the whole building, showing him his locker, letting him practice the combination, and taking him around to where his classes would be held.

"One less thing to worry about," he told Cadwallader the next day.

"Exactly right," the doctor said approvingly.

The week before Ezra left for college, he had gone to see Dr. Cadwallader for a last session. The two men solemnly shook hands. "Ezra Magee, just remember: what does not kill us makes us stronger." It was not until two years later, in a philosophy class, that Ezra realized his therapist had been quoting Nietzsche.

Driving the stretch of road from Morgantown to Aunt Lenore's house, Ezra remembered with a pang how his aunt had driven him to Cadwallader's office twice a week for four years until he'd gotten his driver's license. Each time, she'd patiently wait for him in the car, reading Sherlock Holmes, Shakespeare, and John le Carré novels and drinking coffee from her thermos. He'd never wondered how she'd managed to pay for all those sessions. The psychiatrist's fee must have been a fortune for someone on a postal worker's salary.

As he pulled into the small town of Childersburg—he'd never quite thought of it as home, even though he lived there for seven years of his childhood—Ezra slowed the car to a veritable crawl. There'd always been a speed trap just past the market, and sure enough, the squad car was parked around the curve. Beyond it was the small strip of commerce: Huntley's Family Restaurant, Ridley's

Drugs, the supermarket, Duggan's Tavern, and the post office. Nothing seemed to have changed more than a coat of paint.

At the end of Main Street, Ezra turned left and drove past a small park, three churches, and an elementary school. He pulled up in front of a brown bungalow set back from the street on a small corner lot. Lenore's metallic blue, ten-year-old Buick LeSabre—she wouldn't buy any other brand or model—was parked in the driveway.

He walked up the cracked cement path and admired the blooming rhododendrons in the yard and the row of purple delphiniums in a bed along the walkway. Ezra noticed a shutter hanging loose on the second floor. One of the gutters was sagging. He felt guilty for not coming by more often to help his aunt. She shouldn't be climbing ladders at her age, but he knew she'd rather risk a broken neck than ask for help.

Lenore answered the door in gray sweats. "Just finishing my workout," she said by way of greeting. The Beatles' "Love Me Do" was blasting in the living room. She was pink-faced and breathing hard from exertion, but she smiled up at him and gave him a quick hug.

"I've got five minutes left on the treadmill. Get yourself some juice." She went back to the corner of the living room and hopped back on the still-moving belt, walking briskly, waving her arms in the air in time to the music.

Ezra walked into the kitchen and helped himself to a glass of orange juice. He studied the collage of pictures on Lenore's refrigerator, mostly of Dillon. Lenore came every few months to spend a weekend, and she always spent a week with them during Christmas holidays. Most years, she joined them at the cabin in the mountains during summer break. The summer before, she and Dillon had read the latest Harry Potter book together and caught night crawlers with a flashlight. Lenore and Celia had spent hours in the kitchen talking and whipping up complicated dishes, some of which were inedible, some that were sublime.

"Got to do my thirty minutes a day. Keeps the old ticker healthy!"

Lenore joined him in the kitchen and took a long drink of water. Ezra noted that her normally gray-streaked brown hair was now red. Her small, five-foot-three frame was looking trimmer than the last time he'd seen her.

"That treadmill is boring as hell, but at least I can listen to music or a book on tape."

"Are you listening to anything good?" Ezra asked, looking at a stack of tapes on the kitchen table.

"*Pride and Prejudice.*"

"Again? You've read that a dozen times already!"

"This book on tape is read by an actor with a sexy English accent. He makes Mr. Darcy sound heavenly."

"Aunt Lenore, Darcy was never real," Ezra teased. "Fiction, remember?"

"Oh, don't go and spoil it for me!" She smiled as she stepped close beside him. "You know," she said, lightly brushing his cheek with her palm, "it's always a shock to see you as a grown man, Ezra. Honestly, in my head, you're still a gangly kid no taller than I am." She gave him a proper hug, the smell of sweat and flowers making him feel the kid she remembered him to be. "It's nice to see you, honey."

"You too, Lenore. You look great."

"All compliments are welcome," she said with a grin.

They sat on the couch in the living room and chatted about his summer plans and her new job teaching English as a second language at the community center. "I'm not one to sit at home all day," she explained. "It was a relief to give up the route,"—she was referring to her daily mail delivery route, which she'd worked for thirty years—"but the boredom of sitting at home was killing me."

Ezra wasn't surprised Lenore had found retirement less than stimulating. She loved people and activity. When she was just twenty-seven years old, Lenore's husband had left her with no family to lean on, no money, no degree, and no job skills. The town's elderly postmaster, who knew everything about everyone in Childersburg, had had a soft spot for Lenore, and took her on as a mail carrier. The job suited her. She was privy to all the goings-on of the neighbors, their kids, and their dogs and cats. It had also given her plenty of time to think and read.

She'd been saving up to go back to college and finish her degree when she became, at age thirty-three, the sole guardian of her twelve-year-old nephew. She barely knew the boy, having spent only an hour with him when he was an infant and a day with him when he was three years old. But she was all the family he had left.

Lenore had arranged her work schedule so she could be home most afternoons by the time Ezra returned from school. Her small college savings fund went to provide for him. But Lenore had no regrets. She loved him as deeply as if he were her own child. And he'd turned out well—kind, thoughtful, and a good father and husband. Lenore was happy to tell anyone who'd listen that she counted Ezra's success and happiness as her greatest accomplishment.

When Ezra finished his master's degree, Lenore had started to save again, and eventually she'd enrolled as a part-time student at West Virginia State. Eight years later, she'd graduated with a bachelor's degree in speech, language, and communication. Ezra, Celia, and Dillon had been there to cheer as she walked across the stage to accept her diploma. Now Ezra saw it hanging in a heavy gold frame over the mantel, and he smiled.

It felt good to be sitting on the worn beige sofa. Lenore was curled up on her end with her feet tucked under her and her body turned to face Ezra. Ezra's feet were propped up on the coffee table, just like old times. He remembered so many evenings sitting just like this, his schoolbooks spread out on the cushions, and his aunt reading her novel and keeping him company in case he needed help with his homework. She never pushed, but she was always there, a comforting presence.

A few months after he'd come to live with her, Lenore bought Ezra a baseball glove and handed it to him after dinner. Ezra had stared at the glove for a moment, and instead of smiling, he'd quietly asked, "Why are you being so nice to me?" His intentions weren't rude. It simply mystified him as to why this strange person he had no recollection of ever meeting before had made up a room for him in her house and then bought him things like a baseball glove when it wasn't even his birthday.

"Because," she'd answered without hesitation, "I loved your mother. She loved you to pieces, and she would want me to take good care of you." She'd smiled at him, waiting for him to smile back.

But Ezra hadn't smiled. He'd stared down at his new baseball glove, and Lenore had watched as his brow creased instead into lines of puzzlement. "But . . . you don't even know me!" Ezra replied.

This time, Lenore had hesitated. Then she took a deep breath, stepped forward, put her arms around the boy, and held him with a mild awkwardness. "You're Ezra Magee," she'd said. "I loved you the first time I heard you were coming into this world, and I never stopped. I loved you when your mama wrote letters telling me about your first smile, and your first step, and when you learned how to read. I've loved you all along, even though you lived far away." Lenore had paused again. Ezra was still looking down at his glove and didn't see the tears in her eyes. "I know I'm not your mama, honey," she continued. "She'll always have a special place in your heart, just like she does in mine. You don't have to love me, Ezra. It won't hurt my feelings," she'd lied, "but I just know you and I are going to be great friends."

And from that day on, they had been.

"So, what do you think?" the red-headed Lenore asked Ezra, shaking him out of his reverie. She patted the back of the sofa. "Is it time to get rid of this old boat and buy myself a new sofa?"

"Maybe. But this one's all broken in," Ezra pointed out.

"Problem is: all the new sofas they're making these days are made out of leather. I can't abide leather. It sticks to your legs if you wear shorts, and you slide right off it in long pants. Oh, by the way, I've become a vegan. Did I tell you?"

"I believe you did," he said, grinning broadly. "And I believe you mentioned to Dillon the last time you called that you make certain exceptions, including ice cream, pork fried rice, and barbeque."

"Oh, hell! That is slander! Pure, unadulterated slander!"

They laughed, but Ezra jiggled his knee impatiently.

"And how's Celia's book coming along?"

"The book is coming along. She's working from a new set of authenticated letters by Jane Addams that were discovered in Salem last year, in someone's attic."

"Imagine that! A historical treasure forgotten in an attic," Lenore marveled.

"It was hidden beneath the floorboards," he added.

She shook her head. "Floorboards! My, my, my. And tell me, how's my favorite great-nephew, Dillon?"

There it was: his opening. Ezra cleared his throat and sat up straight. "Well, Dillon . . . he's actually . . . well, not great. That's why I'm here."

"Does he need a kidney? Because I've got a perfectly healthy spare." Lenore always joked when she was taken by surprise. "I take good care of it. Drink lots of fluids and do tai chi at the rec center on Thursdays."

"That's good to know, thanks, but his vital organs are fine. Except maybe for his brain." Ezra studied his hands. "It's looking like Dillon has what I used to have."

"Ah." Lenore looked away from Ezra while her hands gripped the waistband of her sweatpants, and then her left hand swept back some locks from her brow. She fiddled with the cross on her necklace before finally looking back at Ezra. "Poor thing!" she said.

Ezra didn't know if she was referring to Dillon or himself.

"So, Celia thought—well, we both thought—that maybe it would help Dillon, and me, to find out more about the family, since this seems to run in the family. I mean, it seems to at least have run from me to Dillon. I don't know if anyone else in the family had it."

Lenore studied her nephew's face. She'd always said he was one hundred percent Magee in the looks department: Irish to the core, with fair skin, curly dark hair, and a charming smile.

"I met your father once," she told Ezra. "He grinned like an idiot, laughed at his own raunchy jokes even when no one else did, and swore worse than a pirate. It was a wonder to me why your mother loved him, but she did."

Ezra digested this information. He could remember very few times his aunt had ever mentioned his parents. It was as if there had been an unspoken agreement between them not to talk about the past.

"From my side, the Clarks, you get your high cholesterol and a tendency to kick off early from heart attacks," Lenore continued. "The . . . *other stuff*—she cleared her throat before and after she said that—"must come from the Magees. I can't tell you much about them, and you and Dillon are the last of the line that I know of." Her voice drifted off as she looked out the window. Suddenly, she turned back to Ezra with a big smile and tapped his hand. "Speaking of which, did I tell you that some lady from Winston-Salem got in contact with me because she was doing genealogical research and thinks we might be fourth cousins?"

Ezra shook his head. "Lenore, about the Magees—there are things I need to know, for Dillon's sake."

Lenore's smile faded. She looked at the coffee table. "Well, you never wanted to talk about them, and I didn't want to push," she said, her voice tinted with a defensiveness that rarely speckled her inflection. "If you didn't want to do something, you always found a way out of it. Remember that time you faked a stomachache because you didn't want to see *The Nutcracker Suite* at the Baptist Church?"

"I didn't want to talk about my parents because it was too hard," Ezra said, trying to keep her on track. "But I'm grown up now, and I need to know."

"Not much to tell," she said curtly, frowning. She turned to look at the black screen of the television across from them, staring for a few minutes like the tape of her memory was playing on it. Her face softened into a small smile. "Trudy started college when she was twenty," she began. "Ole Miss. She and Mama fought all the time. Mama couldn't understand why Trudy wanted to study something as useless as art." Lenore rolled her eyes and smiled at Ezra. Then her eyes drifted back to the TV screen. "She met your father during her senior year, but we didn't know about him—she never brought anybody home. We didn't even know she had a boyfriend. He was older by five years. He'd been in Korea and was going to Ole Miss on the GI Bill. Trudy told me he'd been wounded in Korea and got some kind of disability payment from the Army. I can't recall what he was studying. Political science, maybe." She paused, took a small sip of water, and cleared her throat. She looked at Ezra. "Seven weeks before graduation, Trudy dropped out of school. She didn't say a word about it to Mama or Daddy, but she told me. She said she was moving away before Mama found out."

"Found out what? Why did she drop out?"

"You were born about three months later," Lenore said with a small shrug. "She dropped out because she was starting to show. Times were different back then, Ezra. People judged you more harshly for things like that. But the truth was, Trudy was done with college. She'd found her true love and wanted to start her life as a wife and mother. They eloped and moved to Alabama, where your daddy was from."

"So, I'm the reason my mother never graduated from college?" Ezra felt a tightness in his chest.

Lenore shook her head. "My grandma, bless her heart, used to say, 'Live trouble is worse than dead trouble.' Honey, in no way was

Trudy disappointed with her life. I know for a fact she loved her life with you and your father. I'm as sure of that as I am of anything in this godforsaken world."

Ezra stood up and walked to the window. "So, what happened after that?"

"She and Simp sent the wedding picture, and Mama took to her room for a month. Not even Daddy could make her come out. It sure made things tougher for me. After that, Mama watched me like a hawk."

"Did my mother ever go back to Mississippi?"

"Trudy wanted to come up after you were born and introduce you to your grandparents, but Mama flat-out refused to let Simpellion Magee in her home. I think Daddy would have liked to make peace with his new son-in-law, but Mama made it clear that if that happened, Daddy could find himself another place to live."

"So, they never saw my mom again?"

"When you were about a year old, Trudy came for a surprise visit and brought you along. Mama wouldn't look at you. I took you upstairs, and I could hear the two of them arguing. Then Trudy came up to get you. She packed up a few things she wanted to take with her from her childhood room. Then she took you out of my arms and left."

Ezra turned around and saw Lenore staring out of another window, as if her memories had moved from the TV screen to play across the sky. He didn't dare move from his spot across the room, for fear of waking her from the memories.

"She never came back," Lenore continued, "except for Daddy's funeral. He died about six months after Trudy's visit, and Mama followed less than a year later. I was twenty-three when Mama died, with a year of college and quite a little nest egg from Mama's and Daddy's life insurance. I begged Trudy to come home, but she was happy in Alabama. She invited me to come down there, and I might have, except then I met Henry Wheeler."

Ezra knew this part of the story. Lenore had told it to him many times. Henry Wheeler was the charming, handsome, smooth-talking insurance salesman who'd sold Lenore's father a hefty life insurance policy. Henry had started courting Lenore the week after she buried her mother. Three months later, he proposed marriage. After a short honeymoon, he'd quit his job, and they moved to Childersburg, West Virginia, where he'd heard real estate was cheap and the racetrack was less than an hour away. He bought them a sturdy brown bungalow in town and then proceeded to gamble away the rest of Lenore's inheritance. Lenore had once told Ezra that it was a relief to her when the money ran out, because then Henry'd had no more excuse to stay.

Ezra walked back over and sat on the couch again. "So, when did you meet my father?" he asked.

"After Henry and I moved up here to West Virginia, your mama and papa brought you up for a visit. Y'all could only stay one night. You were just a toddler. You probably don't remember."

Ezra quickly flipped through his catalog of memories and was surprised by a snapshot of recollection. "I remember a fire truck and a yellow dog."

Lenore laughed. "Henry got you that toy truck, and the neighbors had a cocker spaniel that chased you around the yard."

"But you never came down to see us in Alabama?"

"I only went to Alabama twice. The first time was to get you and bring you back. The second time was to bury your parents."

Ezra closed his eyes. "It was about a week after I came to live here. Mrs. Brown came and stayed with me."

She gave him a curious look. "That's right. I'm surprised you remember."

"I am too," Ezra admitted. He looked down at his hands.

Lenore shook her head. "The doctors said you'd experienced a trauma. They said time would heal you."

"I've had plenty of time," he grumbled.

"Seems to me there were things about that day you didn't want to remember. Maybe you needed to forget."

Ezra just stared out the window.

"Do you remember Granmaude?" she asked, her voice imbued with a caution that raised Ezra's blood pressure.

He closed his eyes. He could almost feel the past breaking through his chest as the hazy outline of an old woman's face reformed in his memory. "My dad's mom," he said. "She smelled like lilacs." He could almost smell the woman's faint, powdery odor. "I remember she made the best banana pudding in the world, but I can't remember ever eating it." He looked over at his aunt. "Did you tell me that—about the banana pudding?"

"No. I never heard it before."

"So, it must be a true memory," he said, almost to himself. "But it's like seeing it from far away, down a tunnel. I know these few facts about her, but it's not like the way I remember Dillon lying in his crib as a baby, or you dressing up as the bride of Frankenstein to scare trick-or-treaters on Halloween."

Lenore laughed again. "Keep trying, and more will come back to you," she suggested. "You're out of practice. That's all."

"What about my father? Can you tell me anything about him? Did he have any peculiarities?"

Lenore frowned. "'Peculiar' is a good word for your daddy. He was a handsome fellow, but strange."

"Strange in what way?"

"We only had that one visit . . ." Lenore stopped mid-sentence.

"Well, what do you remember?" Ezra prompted.

She sighed. "Simpellion was loud. He talked nonstop, but it was all nonsense to me. Things about the Soviets and religion, and robots taking over the teaching in our schools and brainwashing young people. I just stopped listening to the man. Also, he cussed a lot. Trudy laughed about it, but it didn't seem normal to me. But she adored him; that's a fact. Said he had her back no matter what, or something like that. Looking back, I guess that's no small thing."

Ezra took that in for a moment. Then his curiosity bent in another direction.

"Did he do odd things, like tap his face or count to himself?"

"Not that I noticed."

"Did he seem fearful or depressed?"

"Not a bit," Lenore said confidently. "Just the opposite. To me, he seemed foolish, and willing to play the fool, and not afraid of anyone's opinion of him. And he laughed like . . . like a court jester. Honestly, he was a strange one."

"Did my mother ever say anything to you about him having panic attacks?"

"Not in her letters." Lenore instantly sprang to her feet and made her way to the hall closet. She stood on her tiptoes, stretching to reach two decorative boxes sprinkled with small, indeterminate flower petals that looked like pink snowflakes. She took off the lid of the first box and began to dig through its contents. "I'll dig up those letters. You can look through them and see if they have any kind of information you're looking for. If I remember correctly, there were some photographs, too. Now which box did I put that in?"

Ezra felt as if the room had begun to spin. When Lenore brought him from Alabama to West Virginia, there was nothing left of his old life—even his clothes had been destroyed. He'd never even thought to ask if she had letters or pictures.

Lenore searched every closet in the house, but the box didn't turn up. Ezra was trying to be patient, but he felt unreasonably irritated with her. Why hadn't she told him there were pictures?

"You never wanted to talk about your past," she reminded him stubbornly, guessing what he was thinking. "And I didn't want to force you. The doctors said to wait until you were ready—"

"I guess I'm ready," Ezra snapped. He closed his eyes and shook his head. "I'm sorry." He looked back at her. "Lenore," he began, and his stomach lurched, "what really happened in Alabama? I know my mom and dad are gone, so they must have died in the storm, right? Why else would I have come to live with you?"

"You never wanted to talk about it, Ezra. A couple of times I almost *did* have that conversation with you, but—"

"I'm forty goddammed years old, Lenore."

"But you looked so scared whenever I started! I couldn't go on."

"I'm not scared now."

Lenore stared at her nephew. He stared back at her, unrelenting.

"They all died," she said finally. "All of them. Everyone who was in Folly at the time died. There was no one left. Only you."

Then Lenore told Ezra what she knew.

CHAPTER 11

All students at Saint John's were required to go to confession at least once monthly. In some respects, Ezra understood the logic of the confessional: people sinned, made mistakes, and needed to confess to someone who could tell them what rituals to do to make everything okay. But he never felt as if he'd accomplished anything good or positive when he left.

Ezra took a seat in the confessional. "In the name of the Father and of the Son and of the Holy Spirit. Uh, my last confession was a month ago."

Ezra could hear the rustling of the priest's cassock behind the screen. He prayed it was Father Flanagan, the youngest priest, who tended to be lenient.

As soon as he heard the man's voice begin to read the scripture, Ezra's heart sank. What rotten luck! He'd gotten Father "Go to Hell" O'Malley instead. Father O'Malley was the oldest and the strictest of all the priests. All the kids avoided him like the plague. When he walked down a hallway, O'Malley handed out detentions like they were holy wafers during communion. A few of the altar boys who served him and a few of the goody-two-shoes girls were left alone, but O'Malley gave the evil eye to just about everyone else. Ezra had learned to avoid him, ducking into the boys' room or the janitor's closet when he heard his voice chastising children on their way to class. A tardy slip was better than detention with Go to Hell O'Malley, where he'd make you copy hand-cramping verses from the Bible for an hour.

"'The fool hath said in his heart, there is no God. They are corrupt, they have done abominable works, there is none that doeth good.'" Ezra nearly rolled his eyes. O'Malley wasn't even trying to be subtle. Ezra knew he was referencing his father's latest letter in the *Sentinel*. He wanted to say it wasn't fair, to remind the priest that his father's sins weren't his own. But that wasn't the kind of thing you could say during confession, or to Father O'Malley.

After the scripture reading, Ezra confessed to lying to Ms. Maynard about losing his homework. He wanted to stop there, but O'Malley's scowl told him the priest wanted more. Ezra's mind raced through the list of sins. "I had impure thoughts about a girl, Father," he offered. It was all he could think of except masturbation, and he wasn't ready to have that conversation.

"Did you misbehave with the girl?" came the gruff question from the other side of the screen.

"No, Father."

"Go on."

The dreary litany continued: he'd taken the Lord's name in vain four—no, five—times and lied to his mother twice about having brushed his teeth when he hadn't.

"And that is all? You haven't left anything out?"

Ezra was about to say he hadn't, but then he realized the enormity of what he was about to do. Lying during confession was like double jeopardy. The nuns always said the priest wasn't the one you were confessing to. It was really Jesus who was listening.

"Um, I'm not sure," Ezra said.

"Not sure of what, my child?" O'Malley sounded stern and impatient.

Ezra wasn't sure about how to ask for a miracle. Those pills he was taking made him feel like a walking zombie, and, so far, they hadn't taken away the terrible feeling that something bad would happen if he didn't perform his counting and rituals. If the pills didn't help, nothing would. Dr. McClennon had said as much. Ezra's last hope was God.

"Does God hear your prayers, Father?"

O'Malley paused for a moment. "The Lord hears all of our prayers," he replied.

"But you're a priest. Your prayers must be worth a lot more than anyone else's." Ezra's own prayers had so far failed to bring down a miracle, but surely priests had a more direct line to the Almighty.

"Is your confession complete?" the priest prompted him.

"I . . . I . . ." He wasn't sure it was. (*Damn!* Ezra thought, and was immediately penitent.) "Father, I have doubts about God. He's not answering my prayers, and I pray all the time!" And then it all tumbled out, and Ezra found himself telling Father O'Malley about his nightmares, about the tapping and counting and head-banging that gave him temporary relief from anxiety. He even told the priest about getting saved and baptized at the revival meeting, but not finding God there, either, and wondering if his daddy was right and there was no God listening to his prayers, and then feeling guilty for doubting. "I need you to talk to God for me," he concluded breathlessly. "Please, Father! He'll listen to you!"

Father O'Malley was silent, and Ezra knew it was the bad kind of silence. His stomach flipped, kicking up a storm of anxiety. The enormity of what he'd just confessed filled him with horror. *Why, why, why?* he wondered. Why had he done it?! Ezra began to rock back and forth and mutter under his breath: "Sissy Namey, Sissy Namey, Sissy Namey."

"Will you make an act of contrition, Ezra?" the priest asked.

Ezra blanched when the priest said his name. And even though O'Malley had asked for his contrition, Ezra knew it was a command.

"Yes, Father. 'Oh my God, I am heartily sorry for having offended Thee, and I detest all my sins because I dread the loss of heaven and the pains of hell. . . .'" Ezra got through the recitation with only a few promptings from the priest, who then, without preamble, launched into a long recitation of Satan's temptations and of his legions of demons who plagued humanity with evil thoughts and deeds, entering into minds and bodies to do Satan's will. Then the priest recounted the story of Jesus casting out demons from swine.

"'And as his own killed Christ, those who would murder Jesus with hateful words, even as they would murder their own father, as did the sons of Sennacherib in the Bible slay their father, help us to stay their wickedness and defeat their evil designs, in the name of the Father . . .'"

Although Ezra had no idea what the priest was talking about, he made the sign of the cross and waited for absolution. Finally, Father O'Malley said sternly, "Go in peace, my son," and Ezra bolted out of the confessional.

Later, Ezra reckoned that God had already favored him with a small miracle: the priest had forgotten to assign him any penance. But all that sermonizing about the devil gave him new worries at night, when he lay in bed and waited for the nightmares to begin.

༄

Father Sean O'Malley contemplated his responsibilities as confessor, teacher, and guardian of young souls. The priest had known the Magee family for years. He was aware of recent changes in Ezra's behavior. There had been talk among the faculty, and he'd listened and remembered that Ezra wasn't the first Magee to suffer from these sorts of difficulties. Ezra's uncle, Nathan Magee, had manifested similar symptoms and then had died young. God worked in mysterious ways, because Nate's father, Moses Magee, had been a pillar of the community and the Church. Why God would choose to afflict the son of such man—a war hero and good Catholic—was a cipher. On the other hand, it was no surprise to O'Malley that the son of a godless atheist was being visited by Satan. He was surprised the boy had the wisdom to confess it. Clearly, Beelzebub hadn't entirely wormed his way inside Ezra Magee's soul, but it was only a matter of time.

Although he could not break the confidence of the confessional, it was not difficult for Father O'Malley to confirm with Sister Jean, the school counselor, that Ezra's strange behavior was marked by the Evil One. O'Malley prayed aloud that the evil influence invading the boy's soul would be mercifully cast out by God's Grace. Sister Jean was in complete accord with his diagnosis, which she punctuated with a loud "Amen."

"Will you do what needs to be done?" she asked.

"The boy's father will never give permission," he said in a low voice. "The man's evil nature created an opening for Satan to take hold of the boy's soul!"

The nun gripped her tea mug with both hands as if strangling it. Her stern features relayed no emotion, but she felt a tingling sensation in her body. To Sister Jean, a religious crisis, particularly one involving the Evil One, gave her a giddy feeling. "Satan has corrupted one of our own. We can't sit by and allow the evil to spread. We have a sacred duty to cast the demon from Ezra Magee. God is with us in this!" the counselor declared.

Father O'Malley agreed in principle, but he was thinking of all the red tape the Church required to authorize an exorcism. It would be even more difficult without the parents' consent. The bishop would have to be consulted, and his chief of staff was not overly fond of Father O'Malley. Just thinking about the bureaucratic nonsense he would have to go through was enough to give Father O'Malley second thoughts about getting involved in the Ezra Magee situation.

But the priest chided himself for being disloyal. Hadn't Ezra's grandfather, Moses Magee, been one of Father O'Malley's closest friends? He'd been dead for a long time, but O'Malley could still remember his towering presence. He owed it to Moses to save his grandson from eternal damnation.

☙

Josephine Frances Parker sat at her desk looking out of the window of the Saint John's School office. Having served as the school secretary for more than three decades, the cheerful spinster knew everything of importance that took place within its walls. She knew, for example, about the sixth-grade teacher's affair with the fourth-grade teacher's husband. She'd heard the rumors about Fathers Flanagan's secret stash of love letters from his childhood sweetheart and had heard about Father O'Malley's solitary drinking binges.

On this particular Friday afternoon, Jo was worrying over an item of gossip she'd just heard that would be of interest to her dear friend, Grandmaude Magee.

She and Grandmaude had been friends since Jo was a teenager, back when Granmaude was simply Maude Magee, before her grandchildren dubbed her "Granmaude" (and the town had followed suit). Jo's family and Grandmaude's family had gone to the same church, and although Granmaude was only a decade older than Jo, Granmaude had become a mother figure to her.

When Jo was fifteen, Granmaude had stopped by Jo's house on a Sunday morning with a homemade apple pie for Jo's family. Grandmaude found herself a witness to a violent domestic crisis involving Jo's mother and abusive stepfather and a piece of two-by-four lumber. Without a moment's hesitation, Granmaude had stepped in to defend Jo's mother. She chased the stepfather out of the house with the man's own shotgun and promised to finish him for good if he ever set foot in that house again. She had instantly become Jo's hero, and they later became great friends.

They still saw each other every week at the sewing circle, which met at the Buford VFW. The night after Jo had first heard the rumor involving Ezra Magee, she and two dozen other women sat on folding chairs, stitching quilts and chatting about politics, husbands, children, and recipes. Jo pulled Granmaude aside and told her what she'd heard.

"Are you absolutely sure about this?" Granmaude had the same look on her face that she'd had that famous day in Jo's living room. It gave the younger woman a thrill to know her friend was still undiminished in her rage.

"Sister Jean and Mini Maynard were talking about it in the ladies' room."

"O'Malley!" Granmaude spat out his name like a bite of a rotten peach.

⁂

Jo would have been surprised to learn that the priest had once been a regular visitor to Granmaude's home. In 1944, just out of seminary, Father Sean O'Malley was sent to the backwater town of Buford, Alabama. Trained by the Jesuits in Menlo Park, California, he believed fervently that the souls of young children were fertile soil for the teachings of the Church. Jesus had admonished his disciples to "suffer little children to come unto me," and it rang as a clarion call to young Sean O'Malley.

His missionary zeal carried him through the first three years at Saint John's, after which he had gradually come to the painful conclusion that he wasn't particularly fond of children. He'd barely been one himself. Growing up poor in a home with a violent, alcoholic father, O'Malley had gone to work at age seven doing odd jobs for the priests in his church. He was drawn to the Church, especially to the God described in the Old Testament—a figure not unlike his own violent father. He had spent his youth vainly striving to earn the love of a man who didn't know how to love. After O'Malley's ordination into the priesthood, he had transferred that yearning onto his vision of a deity who was perpetually disappointed with His creation.

When the troop ship brought Moses Magee home from the war,

Buford had given him a hero's welcome. He was the most decorated soldier in Alabama, having single-handedly staged a night raid on the enemy, freeing his captured squad and liberating a strategic town in southern France.

On his first Sunday home, Moses came to church accompanied by his wife, Maude, and their three sons. O'Malley knew the family well enough. The boys attended his school, and Maude came to confession every week. Father O'Malley had not yet met Moses, so he made a point of greeting him after the service. He was impressed by Moses's proud bearing, and when Moses invited him to supper that evening, O'Malley gladly accepted the invitation. That night was the beginning of a long and mutually satisfying friendship between the two men. Moses Magee's tyrannical presence in his home reminded O'Malley of the powerful Judeo-Christian God of the Old Testament, which imbued the relationship with a distorted, spiritual sheen.

A month later, when Maude came to confession in tears over the physical and emotional abuse Moses liberally meted out to her and her boys, Father O'Malley was unsympathetic. He told her they must have done something to set Moses off and admonished her to show more loyalty to the man who was, after all, a war hero. When rumors of Moses having a mistress and an illegitimate son reached his ears, Father O'Malley castigated the rumormonger and dismissed the story as a lie.

From that first invitation onward, Father O'Malley became an almost weekly guest at the Magee family's Sunday dinner. After dinner, when the mother and children had left the table, the two men would polish off a bottle of whiskey together and rail against disrespectful youth and women who abased themselves by working outside the home. For O'Malley, the Magee household was a home away from home.

That all ended when Moses disappeared. He'd gone hunting one Saturday and never returned. There was talk in the parish of the mistress again, but Father O'Malley knew better. There might have been a mistress, but O'Malley knew that wasn't the cause of Moses's disappearance. He waited as the sheriff's department dredged the river and searched the mountains for the missing man. Moses's body never surfaced. No sign of the man was ever found, and after two years of fruitless searching, the sheriff's office closed the investigation. But Sean O'Malley was sure his friend had been murdered, and that he knew the murderer's name.

CHAPTER 12

A loud, booming noise penetrated young Ezra's drug-numbed sleep, but his brain was wrapped in gauzy lethargy, and he merely rolled over onto his stomach. Seconds later, another loud boom forced him to drag his pillow over his head to once again secure silence, but not before he became aware of a pungent odor. Sulfur?

Hell? Am I in hell? he wondered. A collage of images trotted across his consciousness like a badly made movie: his father chased by demons, himself running through billowing columns of smoke, the sinister profile of a horned figure sporting a long tail, the shattered remains of Jesus lying on the ground.

"Jesus Christ!" The voice came as from a great distance.

Was that me? Ezra wondered, feeling as if he were floating in the air above his body, which would have been pleasant except for the nausea and general disorientation.

Something sounding like a cannon went off by Ezra's window, followed by a godawful shrieking wail that approximated the noise of a chorus of banshees going full tilt in his bedroom. Ezra had to open his eyes, but the light was too bright. He had to squint. Even staring straight at it, he couldn't make sense of what he was seeing. His father was in his room, crouched beside Ezra's window, a shotgun aimed out toward the hickory tree next to the house. A cloud of black smoke partially filled the room, and the wail of the smoke alarm continued unabated as Ezra listened to his father's curses pierce the pulsating waves of sound emitted by the noisy gadget.

"Goddamn bushy-tailed rats! I'll kill every last one o' ya sonsabitches if it's the last thing I do!"

The gun went off again, and another spurt of black smoke issued from the muzzle. "Goddamn black powder," Simp mumbled. "Son of a bitch sold me black powder again!"

Ezra stuffed his fingers in his ears. At least the mystery was solved.

Dr. McClennon's pills weren't working. After two weeks, all Ezra felt was sick to his stomach and stupid. His mother had assured him that he was tapping less, but that wasn't because his brain no longer wanted him to; he was simply too tired and too numb to move. His lethargy was so severe that he felt like he had to talk his neck into holding up his head.

Through Ezra's window, Simp fired off another shot and then howled with frustration. A clean shot, and he'd missed! "Damn squirrel musta jinxed me," he complained. He ejected the shell and put another one in the chamber. Aiming carefully, he pulled the trigger. This time, nothing happened.

"Damn it to hell!" he shouted.

Simp loaded his own shotgun shells. For squirrels, he used number six shot with an ounce of gun powder. For ducks, he used number four shot and one-and-a-half ounces. For chasing straying livestock from his yard, he loaded the shells with rock salt and three quarters of an ounce of gun powder. He'd had three misfires on the last batch of shells.

"Goddamn cheap caps they sold me, and black powder!" Simp sounded exasperated. Although his ears were ringing from the shotgun blasts, Ezra could hear every word.

"Simp," Trudy yelled up the stairs, "turn that darned fire alarm off! It's driving me crazy."

She isn't the only one going crazy, thought Ezra, who sat up in bed. But at least Ezra was, at long last, awake.

Simp shouted back down to Trudy to get some eggs going,

yanked the batteries out of the fire alarm, and then helped Ezra out of bed and into the bathroom. Simp hated the dull, deadened look in his son's eyes and his slurred speech. But what really got to him was the question he'd heard Ezra ask Trudy yesterday. Simp and Killian had been sitting in the kitchen sipping green tea (Simp had developed a taste for the mown-grass flavor) when he'd overheard Ezra in the living room ask: "Mama, why is God punishing me?"

Simp had choked on the tea, and Killian'd had to pound on his back. "Goddamn it to hell," Simp gasped, after catching his breath.

"Easy, Simp," Killian cautioned. "It's a natural question for the boy to ask. It's a legitimate question."

"There's nothing legitimate about religion," Simp had shot back.

"Didn't I hear you ask your mama the same thing one time when you were a little boy?" Killian said quietly, yet sternly. "There was a time you were a believer. Before your daddy came back from the war."

Simp had looked hard at his friend then. "You know I don't talk about that son of a bitch," he'd said flatly.

"I'm just saying, put yourself in Ezra's shoes. What's the boy supposed to think? His own brain went funny on him. Whose fault is that? Better to blame God, or to think there's some heavenly plan to it, than it is to blame himself."

"Sounds to me like you're defending religion," Simp said. He pulled a letter out of his back pocket and handed it to Killian. "The latest death threat came in the mail this morning from yet another holier-than-thou, self-righteous, religious bastard!" Simp glared accusingly at his friend.

"What Ezra's going through runs in your family," Killian said, ignoring the letter. "Nate had it. Now Ezra has it. That's just nature. Nothing to be done."

Nothing to be done. Simp hated those four words.

When Ezra was done with the bathroom, Simp took his boy by the arm and helped him down to the kitchen, where Trudy was burning the toast because she'd seen a robin on the back porch and had had to sketch it before it got away. Simp yanked the toaster cord from the wall just as the telephone jangled. Ezra was left alone at the table while Simp went off to the living room to answer the call. Ezra stared at his plate of scrambled eggs and had a sudden moment of clarity as he recalled breaking Jesus the night before.

It was a ceramic statue of Christ that had been given to him by Granmaude as a confirmation gift when he was eight. He didn't really like it—Jesus's face looked pinched and constantly disappointed—but it had been blessed by the bishop and lived in the place of honor on Ezra's dresser. Last night, he'd picked it up for some reason, and it had slipped from his hand and shattered to pieces on the floor. He'd gathered the pieces and looked at them for a long time before laying them gently in the garbage can. Was it, he wondered, a venal sin to break Jesus?

The lyrics from a song from *Oklahoma* ran through his mind like a wild creeper vine. His mother played the record all the time, so he knew the words to every song by heart. The corn was as high as an elephant's eye. He had a beautiful feeling everything was going his way. Except for Jesus of smithereens. Ezra's fork halted midway to his mouth. He dropped it and sat staring at nothing with his mouth half-open.

In the meantime, Simp was in the living room, yelling into the receiver: "Hiram? That you? Jesus Christ, Johnson, whadda you want? Are you drunk again? You're gonna do what? You're gonna kill yourself?! Why're you telling me?"

Simp listened for a minute and then snorted derisively. "Jesus Christ, Johnson. You think you're the only fuckin' human being with problems? We all got problems."

Just then, Simp saw a gray squirrel leap with acrobatic grace from the tree limb to the ground and scamper across the lawn toward the woods. It snubbed the peanut-loaded squirrel trap along the way. Simp dropped the phone and grabbed for his shotgun, but he remembered the failed shot. All he could do was shake the gun at the retreating squirrel.

"There goes another one of them sonsabitches," he shouted as he watched the squirrel run to safety. He picked up the receiver again. "No, not you, Hiram. It's them goddamn squirrels." Simp was quiet for a moment, then his tone changed. "Wait, Hiram. No! Wait, goddammit! Now listen, old buddy, suicide is a fool's mission. You're too good for that, and that's the truth. It's no kinda exit strategy. Listen, if you want out, I'll help you, but you gotta do it sober, otherwise it don't count. Lookee here, why don't I bring you on over? No, I'll come and get you—you're too drunk to drive." Simp listened for another minute. "Jesus Christ, Johnson! If you talk about suicide one more time, I'll kill you *myself!* Now stay right there. I'm on my way. And I don't care how much wine Jesus made. He didn't try to drink it all by himself."

Simp drove off in the old Datsun to rescue the reverend. Trudy was outside, working on a sketch of a robin, which was content for the moment to pose for her on a nearby branch. Ezra stared at nothing while a part of his mind noted that he was staring at nothing, and that was weird. But it wasn't really that strange, he told himself, because the drugs he was taking made everything bland. Nothing stood out. Nothing competed for his attention. Everything just rolled into a nondescript grayness. The panicky feelings were still there, but they were cordoned off in a corner of his brain with burly guards keeping them behind the rope.

Everything was farther away, even the teasing at school. But that didn't mean it wasn't still there. Ezra knew it was Dexter Blaxton who'd gotten all the kids to call him "Goofy Magee." Ezra thought about punching Dexter in the nose, but he was too spacey and lethargic to fight. Yesterday, Sister Agatha had handed him a tissue and told him to wipe the drool off his face. His classmates had whispered and snickered. It was happening too far away for him to care, mostly, although a tight corner of his mind watched in horror.

His mother stuck her head in the door. "Ezra, honey, try to eat those eggs before they get cold. I'll be right in to make you some fresh toast," she promised. And then, "Where did your daddy rush off to now?"

"Reverend Johnson's gonna kill himself," Ezra mumbled.

"That's nice, dear," Trudy replied, already back to sketching.

What if the preacher killed himself before his dad arrived? Why would the man want to die? Ezra knew that suicide was a terrible sin, maybe even a mortal one, but it did seem tempting. All the suffering would just stop. Thinking personally, Ezra wondered how he would do it. He wondered what would happen if he took all his pills at once. He'd probably need some of his father's whiskey to go with it. He'd go to sleep, and it would be done. No more waking up tired, nauseous, and headachy. No more crazy-brained life.

Ezra wandered outside and walked to the fence near the back field, thinking in a general way about suicide and concentrating so he wouldn't trip and fall over his own feet. The drugs made the ground swim away from him. He sat under a tree for a long while and didn't think about much. He heard his father return and watched as he helped a very drunk, emotional Hiram Johnson into the house.

Ezra got up and walked toward the barn. As he passed the corner of the fence, a lump caught his eye. Stepping in closer, he saw a large, gray rat lying on the ground near the corner fence post. It wasn't often that Ezra saw a rat, especially one as big as this one, and certainly not out in the open. It was lying on its side with its eyes open. It looked dead. Ezra groped around on the ground and found a stick. He poked the rat. It didn't move. Ezra reached down to grab its tail. The rat wasn't dead. It latched onto Ezra's finger and bit down hard.

Hearing the scream, Simp came running outside and saw Ezra cradling his right hand, holding his forehead with his left hand, and stomping on the head of a rat.

"Damn, son," Simp said after inspecting Ezra's finger and head, "that's sure a mean one. He'd been a little bigger, it would've been a helluva contest." Simp grinned happily. His boy had killed a rat. It was the first time Ezra had seemed really alive all week, and Simp was delighted.

"How'd you get the cut on your head?" Simp asked, noticing the blood dripping down into Ezra's eye.

"Rat bit me, and I fell against the post."

"Come on, let's get you fixed up." He led Ezra into the house. Hiram Johnson was slumped and snoring in a chair on the porch. On their way inside, Simp patted his head for luck.

"My Lord, Ezra," Trudy exclaimed, "you've got to get some stitches in that cut! And Simpellion, you go get that rat's body so we can have it checked for rabies. Poor thing musta got into the poison you set out last week."

The biggest logistical problem was waking Hiram Johnson and getting him into the car. Simp wasn't sure the suicide crisis had passed and couldn't risk leaving the preacher alone with Trudy. She was prone to wandering off to sketch some bird or other animal. And there were sharp knives in the kitchen; Simp hated to think what they might inspire the preacher to do.

"God loves me!" the preacher shouted when Simp shook him hard.

"Yes, Hiram, I know God loves you, but he wants you to get in the car right now."

"Where we goin'?"

"Buford General Hospital," Simp replied.

"Praise the Lord! I musta killed myself! And now you're taking me to the hospital! Jesus is Lord! Bless His name!"

"Jesus Christ, Johnson, you're a boring drunk," Simp told him affectionately.

☙

The emergency room was crowded, and most of the occupants were watching a football game on a television set on a table in the lobby. The Crimson Tide was beating up on Ole Miss, to the delight of everyone in the room, save one fellow sitting over in the corner with a bandaged arm, whose demeanor indicated that he was not happy with the way the game was going.

With his bloody shirt, a blood-soaked bandage tied around his forehead, and his glazed expression, Ezra was getting plenty of stares, as was Hiram Johnson, who lay stretched out across three plastic chairs, snoring lightly. (The nearby occupants had vacated their seats to get away from the pickled odor of the Reverend.) Simp paced nervously and visited the nurses' station every few minutes to see what the hold-up was. His boy, he kept telling them, needed a doctor before he bled to death.

"Sir, please sit down. We'll call you when it's your turn."

Fuming, Simp sat back down and wiped away the small ribbon of drool hanging from the corner of his son's mouth. If anyone stared at Ezra, Simp scowled fiercely at them until they looked away.

The football game's halftime show was just ending when a teenage boy hobbled into the waiting area, followed by a man who looked to be the boy's father. The youngster used a sturdy stick as a cane and cradled one arm in a makeshift sling. His face was a mess of cuts, and his shirt was torn across one shoulder. Most of the blood was coming from his nose, which looked to be skewed a little to the left.

"That your boy?" Simp asked the man.

"I reckon so," the man replied.

"What'd he do, piss off a bear?"

"Naw. It was a tree that got 'im."

Simp snorted and then started laughing and slapping his knee so that everyone in the room was listening. "No kiddin'! Do tell!"

"We was out huntin' rabbits," the man said, "but didn't have no luck. We was traipsin' back to the house when Luke here seen a possum crawlin' up a persimmon tree on the ridge. You know, the one right above Cahill Creek down there near Fenton?"

"I know it," said Simp, "but you don't see many possums in broad daylight."

"No sir!" The man was excited. "That's just what I says to Luke! And since we hadn't got no meat, Luke decides to climb up that persimmon tree and shake that possum out. Well, I reckon he shook a little too hard, 'cause they both come tumblin' down outta that tree and Luke here hit the ground real hard. Lordy! I thought he was a goner."

The man was silent for a moment, contemplating the story of the boy's misfortune. "But," he said, turning to Simp just as Simp stopped laughing and had settled back in his chair, "the good Lord was with us today and delivered my boy Luke from serious hurt." At the mention of the Lord's name, the man folded his hands before him in an attitude of prayer.

Simp studied the man for a minute, and said, "Is that a fact?"

"It is," the man replied.

"Hmmmm," Simp said, his tone rousing Ezra from his dreamy stupor just enough to feel a dose of dread in his gut. Even without looking, he knew there'd be a mischievous gleam in his father's eyes, which meant Ezra was about to be mortified.

"I 'spect that's your boy, there," the possum hunter was saying, pointing at Ezra. "What in heaven's name happened to him?"

Simp put his palms together, placing his hands under his chin in a prayerful pose. "Ezra here," he said to the room, "has been actin' strange lately, aintcha son?" Simp reached over and mussed Ezra's hair. Ezra kept his eyes closed. "You see," Simp continued, "a couple of nights ago Ezra went to church and got slain in the spirit. He started talking in tongues, fallin' down, that sorta thing. Know what I mean?"

The man's eyes widened. He looked at the drooling boy and swallowed hard.

"Well, I didn't mind so much at first," Simp went on, "but by the second night, I got worried."

"So, whaddija do?" the man asked, turning his wide eyes to Simp.

Ezra slumped down in his seat and wished he could disappear.

"Well, I prayed about it, of course," Simp answered. "And then," he paused for dramatic effect, "I heard a voice." He stared at the ceiling as if lost in thought.

"A voice," Simp's interlocutor repeated. "You heard a voice?"

"It was the voice of our blessed Lord and Savior, Jesus H. Christ."

The man gulped again. The whole room was silent, disrupted only by a commercial for Chevy trucks playing on the television.

The man looked at Simp. His right eyebrow was now raised, and he leaned his head back some, but he had to ask it: "What did He say?"

Simp smiled and raised a finger into the air. "He said: 'Get the demons OUT!'" His last word reverberated through the room.

The man pushed his chair away from Ezra. "See that hole in his head?" Simp continued, looking straight at the man. "Well, demons are hard to get at. Yessir, mighty hard. You have to be smart, 'specially when they get testy. Well, I didn't have no swine to run them into, and that woulda been a big help."

"I guess so," the man said.

"Well, I had to get them demons out, didn't I?" Simp declared. "The best way is to make a hole through the skull, 'cause we all know that's where they like to get into. I knew what I had to do." Simp lowered his voice, but it still carried to all corners of the waiting room. The only one not listening was Jesus Christ Johnson, who was sound asleep. "I had to follow our Lord's commandment. I went into the barn and got my ice pick." Ezra heard an audible gasp. "I walked back into the kitchen where my boy was rollin' around on the floor in the terrible grip of *deeeemons*." Simp let the word hiss out of his mouth. "There wasn't a hog in sight, but God always provides. I see this old yellow cur dog a-lyin' out on the porch. Well, I grabbed my boy and got his head under my arm. He was carryin' on like a herd of buffaloes, but I went ahead and drilled into his skull with the ice pick. I stopped when a little brain matter dribbled out." Simp pointed to the bloody clot on Ezra's forehead.

A woman sitting near the door gave a squeal and slumped over in a dead faint. A nurse rushed over and roused her with a sniff of smelling salts and gave Simp a severely disapproving glare.

The man had moved his chair as far from Simp as he could, which was only about a foot. Undeterred, Simp continued, "All of a sudden the demons come pourin' outta that hole! They flew through the screen door and took up in that old cur dog that was lyin' out there on the porch. The dog took off like he'd been struck by lightnin'." Simp straightened up in his chair and looked into the man's eyes. "I reckon he's still runnin', brother, since there ain't no cliffs around for him to jump off of, nor seas to rush into."

Simp gave the man a huge grin. The fellow got up quickly from his chair and led his son to the far corner of the room, as far away from Simp as he could get.

"Tha' was mean," Ezra slurred. "He was jus' bein' nice."

"I was just foolin' around."

"Why d'you have to be like that?" Ezra asked. "What's wrong with believin' in somethin'?"

Simp's smile disappeared, and he turned to look at his son. "You want to be an ignorant jackass who believes all that bullshit nonsense they call religion?"

"Maybe."

"Wake up, Ezra! It's mind control! The only demons we got are the ones we create ourselves."

"But that man wasn't doin' us no harm."

Simp looked, for a moment, like he felt a little bad for what he'd done. He gazed over at the man and his son across the room and then down at his hands. But then he threw his shoulders back defiantly.

"Son, in this life, you've got to choose, and I say: if you're gonna be a bear, might as well be a grizzly!"

At that moment, the disapproving nurse informed them that it was their turn to see the doctor.

They waited in the exam room for a few minutes until a young doctor knocked and came in. "What's wrong with the boy?" he asked, consulting a chart.

"Rat bite," Simp said. He held the plastic bag aloft. "Got the little pecker right here!"

The nurse narrowed her eyes and shook her head, but the doctor peered into the bag, grunted, and gave it to the nurse.

"It bit the boy's head?"

"His hand, but then he banged his head on a wooden post." The doctor checked hand and head and determined that the cut on his head needed stitches.

"You ever had stitches before?" the doctor asked Ezra.

"Sure," Ezra replied. He was lying passively on the examination table, blinking at the ceiling fan that kept going around and around and around.

"He always like this?" the doctor asked Simp.

"It's the medication the shrink gave him."

The doctor grunted again and then injected Ezra's forehead with Novocain. Ezra barely noticed. He closed his eyes and drifted away as the numbness crept over his forehead and eyebrow. He blocked out the noise of his father talking and concentrated on how nice it felt to float, to be removed from his numb, clumsy body and just float.

The doctor finished putting in the last stitch, then stood back and made a clucking sound with his tongue.

"Can't say I ever had a patient react to stitches that way before," the doctor said.

Ezra tilted his head to look at his father. Even in his dreamy state, he wondered why Simp had such a funny look on his face . . . until he looked down and noticed the tented rise in his own pants. He was as shocked as anyone to discover he had a boner. Ordinarily, the experience would have been humiliating for Ezra, but in his drugged state, he laughed.

Simp laughed too, then helped his son down from the table.

The only one who didn't find it amusing was the nurse. As soon as she got home that night, she prayed a long prayer, asking God to forgive her for the evil thoughts she'd had toward the man that day at the hospital. It was high time to see her confessor, Father O'Malley.

CHAPTER 13

Cordelia Lanier had been a nurse at Buford General Hospital for fifteen years, but nursing was her second career choice. All her life, she'd wanted to be a nun. She'd prayed to the Lord to send her the Calling, but Christ hadn't called her to be his bride. Some mornings when she tucked her hair under her nurse's cap, she imagined it was a wimple.

She had been filling in for an absent ER nurse when that horrid man came in with his bloodied boy and told everyone that absurd and blasphemous tale. She'd checked the boy's chart for his name and, with a chill, realized that the father was none other than Simpellion Magee, the letter-writing atheist. If she hadn't taken a vow to help the sick and injured, she would have kicked them out of her hospital right then and there. Instead, she got the boy seen quickly in the hopes of getting him and his father out of there as soon as possible. And then the boy's—well, she wasn't going to think about it, but it was wrong. She couldn't get it out of her head, nor could she forget the father's smiling, winking encouragement. It was horrible—and sinful!

Cordelia was full of ire and evil thoughts. She reckoned if she died in a car wreck in that state of mind, she would go straight to hell. A call to St. John's confirmed that Father O'Malley was hearing confessions that evening.

It was six p.m. when Cordelia entered the dark booth of the confessional. She collected her thoughts as Father O'Malley slid open the panel.

"Forgive me, Father, for I have sinned," she began. She started with the easy ones—thinking bad thoughts about a lazy coworker; lying to a friend to get out of attending her daughter's baby shower. Then she confessed her murderous thoughts toward Simpellion Magee.

"Magee?" Father O'Malley said, suddenly interested. "Do you know him?"

"No, Father, not really. I know about him, of course. Everyone in Sand Mountain knows his name. But he came to the hospital today with his son. The boy was bit while playing with rats. Rats! And I'm sorry, Father, but when I think of rats, I think of the devil's minions. And that man, his father . . ." She was too worked up to continue.

"Start at the beginning, my child," the priest recommended.

Cordelia related the blasphemous story Simp had told in the waiting room, emphasizing the way he had profaned the name of the Lord half a dozen times. "It was enough to make St. Peter gag," she said hoarsely.

"He spoke of demonic possession?" The priest was startled. "How did the boy seem?"

It speaks highly of the good priest to remember the true victim in all this, Cordelia thought, humbled. "Something about him . . . wasn't right," she said carefully. "His eyes were out of focus. His mouth hung open."

"Is that all?"

She hadn't planned on telling anyone the last part of the story, but Father O'Malley seemed genuinely concerned for the boy. She chose her words carefully. "When he was on the table getting stitched up, the boy was . . . I'm sorry, Father . . . sexually stimulated."

There was silence in the confessional as the subject of sexual stimulation settled awkwardly in the cubicle.

"A succubus!" the priest said, thinking aloud.

"A succubus, Father?" Cordelia was shocked. She had been fascinated to learn, in her medieval history class, about female demons—

succubi—who had sexual relations with sleeping men, causing them to sin against their will and without their knowledge or consent.

"Was the boy asleep?" O'Malley asked urgently.

Cordelia thought for a moment. "His eyes were closed. He might have been. Do you really think it was a succubus, Father?"

"It's possible." O'Malley had always found the idea of the sexual demon repugnant and stimulating at the same time. Theologians had debated whether God would condemn a man who had such an act perpetrated on him by a demon. But whatever God's judgment might be, in a good Catholic's mind, Ezra's behavior reeked of demonic possession. There was no doubt now that his soul was tainted.

O'Malley remembered where he was and who was speaking to him. He squinted at the confessional screen and could just barely make out Cordelia's face. His memory supplied the rest—red lips, well-formed breasts, curvaceous hips.

The intimacy of the confessional and subject matter sparked a moment of shared erotic tension. Father O'Malley dug his nails into his palm and his voice became stern.

"The evil in this boy can infect us all. We must be vigilant! Now, let us pray."

༄

Father Sean O'Malley was treading on thin ice. If Fathers Flanagan and Green found out, they would report him to the bishop. He could lose his position in the Church. He could even be defrocked! O'Malley balanced that reality against his conviction that an unauthorized exorcism was the only way to save Ezra Magee's soul, because only he, O'Malley, knew the depth of the evil well in which the boy lived. It surely was a test from God. O'Malley knew he had to do the selfless thing and help the boy despite the risks. Hadn't Jesus challenged his disciples and followers to do His will even in the face of death? And when it had to do with a child, well, that settled it.

O'Malley felt a surge of strength. He knew he was doing the right thing.

Although he had never performed an exorcism—it was a subject his professors had shied away from in the seminary—O'Malley had collected a number of books over the years that outlined the procedure. There was a prayer book written in the late nineteenth century by the archbishop of Baltimore that quite clearly laid out the entire exorcism ritual. He would need an assistant. Sister Jean would serve him well. He could count on her complete support and discretion.

Father O'Malley knelt in his room and prayed for guidance. After two hours, he sat down at his desk and, with trembling hands, pulled a manila folder from his file drawer. The label on the tab read: "Maimonides." Moses Maimonides was a Jewish philosopher born in Spain in the twelfth century. In truth, the information in the folder had nothing to do with Moses Maimonides. Instead, the file contained yellowed newspaper clippings, pages of notes, and a photograph. Perhaps O'Malley had been overly dramatic when he purposely misnamed the file, but at the time he'd felt compelled to keep some kind of record of his friend Moses Magee's death.

As he always did whenever he allowed himself to revisit the events of May 1, 1952, he took the photo out first. It was a picture of Moses Magee in an Army uniform, ruggedly handsome, with a rakish grin on his face. Magee had been forty-four years old when the photograph was taken, just home from the war.

O'Malley took out some of the newspaper clippings and read them. "Area Man Missing," headlined one article. "Disappearance on Sand Mountain," said another. The last clipping read: "Case of Missing Moses Magee Still Unsolved."

O'Malley could clearly recall the year after Moses returned from the war. Simpellion was a nine-year-old troublemaker, always picking fights. He was already tall and gangly and forever running off at the mouth. O'Malley disliked the boy, and he approved of Moses's harsh discipline.

Simpellion had two brothers: Auggie, two years older, and Nate, two years younger. Nate and Auggie treaded carefully around their father's wrath, but Simp routinely provoked his father into violent behavior. As the boy grew older and stronger, these discipline sessions with the belt sometimes turned into a near battle. O'Malley knew this from Maude, who appealed to him both in and out of the confessional to intercede with Moses. O'Malley had taken the high road and told her it was her God-given duty to honor and obey her husband in all things. He'd recommended she get her boys under better control and obey the admonition of St. John, who commanded women to "be submissive to your husbands." O'Malley was in complete agreement with Moses taking a firm hand with his recalcitrant son.

O'Malley replaced the clippings, notes, and photo in the file folder and put it back reverently in the file cabinet. Moses Magee had been his best friend. The man had served his country and fellow man honorably, attended church regularly, partook of the Eucharist, confessed his sins, and supported his family. What more could be asked of any man?

That he had just disappeared one day . . . it gave O'Malley chills to think of it. Although it was never proven, Father O'Malley knew in his heart of hearts that Moses Magee had been murdered, and that his killer was still at large. O'Malley had long suspected Simpellion of murdering his father, but he had no proof. The priest believed he could read a man's character by looking him in the eyes. He had looked into Simp Magee's eyes and knew the devil rode on the man's back.

And now Ezra was tainted by his father's sin. The sins of the father were visited on the boy, who was an innocent. O'Malley would fight the devil for Ezra's soul. The thought gave him pleasant shivers.

CHAPTER 14

On his way out of town from Lenore's, Ezra passed Duggan's Bar. He turned around, pulled to the curb, and turned off the engine. His hands were shaking, and his thirst for bourbon felt like an urgent burn in his stomach. It was just after six p.m. He was sure they were still celebrating happy hour.

☙

Six hours later, Celia grabbed the telephone, which was clanging like a carillon next to her ear. "Ezra! Is that you?" she yelled into the mouthpiece.

"Sorry, honey. It's just me." Lenore's voice was tired and scratchy.

It was the second time they'd talked that evening. Celia had called Lenore at nine p.m., two hours past the time she'd expected Ezra to be home.

"He said he'd be back by seven," she had told Lenore. "He's not answering his cell phone."

Lenore had reassured Celia that Ezra must have run into some traffic along the way, but when Celia hung up the phone at 9:03 p.m., she'd had a bad feeling. She had turned on the television to watch the news, but there was nothing about any accidents on the road near Morgantown. She'd sent Dillon to bed at ten o'clock and let Izzy out for her nightly needs, then sat in the den listening for the sound of her husband's car, trying not to imagine the worst. She'd almost drifted off to sleep when Lenore called.

"He isn't back yet," Celia said in a tight voice. She looked at the clock. It was after midnight.

"Ezra's all right, honey," Lenore assured her. "He just had a little accident. He ran off the road just outside of Childersburg, it turns out. He didn't do a lot of damage to the car, and he only got a split lip in the wreck. He wasn't wearing his seatbelt."

"How . . ." Celia began but couldn't continue.

Lenore heard the sound of Celia's soft sobs.

"He was drinking," Lenore said finally, unable to find an easy way to break the news. "But he had the sense to get Tom Drake down at the all-night service station to get the car out of the ditch and tow it to my house. I checked it. It's drivable, but he's not. I'm going to keep him here til morning."

☙

"You screwed up royally," Hiram Johnson opined. He was leaning back in the recliner, his hands folded comfortably over his stomach. For the first time that day, his gaze was stern and judgmental. "You really put Celia through the wringer."

Ezra sat opposite Hiram on the sofa, his feet up on the coffee table. He was working his way through a box of raspberry-filled Krispy Kreme donuts he'd found in the back of the freezer. They were still half-frozen and at least three weeks past edible. Ezra wouldn't have been able to place them as raspberry if they weren't labeled as such. They tasted like musty bites of fruity rubber, but he ate them anyway. The bottle of bourbon sitting on the coffee table was nearly empty.

"Did you think about Celia at all while you were sittin' at the bar, gettin' plastered?"

"Don't give me a hard time," Ezra said gruffly. "I know I messed up, okay?"

He looked up from his donut to glare at Hiram, but he wasn't there—again. Ezra swung his feet off the coffee table, turned his torso and head nearly a half-circle, and spotted him almost hidden behind the door of the dining room.

"That's all you got to say for yourself?"

Ezra growled at him and threw a half-eaten doughnut back into the box. "What do you want me to say?"

"I want you to say you understand," Reverend Hiram Johnson sermonized as he disappeared, his booming Sunday-morning pulpit voice starting in the kitchen but then coming from the living room. Ezra twisted his head back around to find Hiram once again in the recliner.

"I really *don't* understand," Ezra said. "It's like trying to unravel a tangled ball of string. Every time you find the end of the knot, you pull it, and it creates a new knot. That's my life: just one big friggin' tangle after another."

"You can tell me the truth, Ezra. I know why you swerved into the ditch that night."

Ezra squirmed. "You're wrong."

"Am I? You want to swear to me you didn't see her?"

Ezra's hands shook as he lit a cigarette. He dropped the spent match in his empty coffee cup. "Lay off," he muttered to Hiram. "I don't need this from you."

"There's no shame in—"

"I DID NOT SEE SISSY ON THE SIDE OF THE GODDAMN ROAD!" Ezra screamed across the coffee table.

"All right, all right," the reverend said gently, leaning forward in the recliner, arms out, with the palms of his hands upturned in front of him. "Take it easy. No judgment here. So just what did you tell Celia when you got home?"

Ezra calmed himself but then cringed immediately at the memory of seeing Celia's face as he'd walked through the door that next morning. "She was like ice. No yelling or crying; just cold and distant. She moved my clothes down to the den and told me not to bother coming upstairs again until I sobered up."

"And Dillon?"

"I lied. I told him I'd gotten dizzy and passed out from the flu, and that I'd had to stay at Lenore's overnight."

Dillon finally seemed to be improving, and Ezra was afraid his own breakdown would make things worse for his son. Maybe it was the medication, or maybe it was deciding to finish school at home, but the boy was noticeably happier.

"Celia and I bribed him with a new Xbox," Ezra remembered aloud. "His best friend, Wylie, was green with envy. I gave the boys chores to do around the house so they could save up for more Xbox games."

"What about you?" Hiram asked. He was standing at the window, his back to Ezra. "Did your situation improve after the accident?"

Ezra remembered Lenore's cold, straightforward retelling of the story of the deaths of his relatives, and small glimpses of the horror that had soured in his repressed memory had begun moving toward the surface.

Ezra had tried to shake it off and cut back on the booze and cigarettes after that night, and for a few days after the accident, he'd stayed sober. He took Izzy for long walks in the morning and thought about getting back to his daily run. But it was difficult—harder than it should have been. He felt irritable and tired every minute of every day, as though his mind was always pushing back at something waiting to rush in.

On a Saturday afternoon, Dillon and Ezra had been resting on the back porch steps together after a game of badminton. Izzy chewed on a stick in the shade. It wasn't yet summer, but it was hot enough to bead Ezra's glass of lemonade with moisture.

"I coulda beat you," Dillon said.

"Yeah, sure," Ezra teased. "Maybe if I had a broken leg and was blind in one eye."

"Hah! I was holding back because I felt sorry for you being old and all."

Ezra laughed. "Watch it, junior. This old geezer still has plenty of pep."

Ezra looked at his son. God, where had the time gone? The day Dillon was born, when the nurse had placed the wrapped bundle in Ezra's arms, he'd involuntarily exclaimed, "My son!" He'd felt an intense surge of pride and awe the likes of which he'd never experienced.

"He's perfect," he'd told Celia, who lay drenched with sweat on the delivery table.

A mottled face, a tuft of black hair, squirming limbs—suddenly they were responsible for a total stranger they'd named Dillon. And here he was, that same boy, now nearly as tall as Celia, full of ideas and questions and a quirky sense of humor that was all his own. Soon, his voice would change; he'd start to shave. He'd become a man. Time passed in the blink of an eye. In the intervals of passing time, Ezra discovered what it meant to wish that time would stand still.

"Look!" Dillon pointed at the sky. A hawk circled in the distance. Ezra admired its effortless glide. As a teenager, Ezra would take his binoculars and climb to the top of Old Rag to watch the hawks. He loved standing above the impenetrable horizon of trees that defined West Virginia. And he'd loved to watch the great raptors. Sometimes, he'd wish he had a younger brother or sister to take along.

"You ever wish you had a brother or sister?" he asked Dillon idly.

Dillon looked alarmed. "Is Mom—?"

"No! Your mother is not pregnant!" Ezra laughed at the look on his son's face. "I just wondered if you missed having siblings."

"I never really thought about it," Dillon said with a shrug. "A brother would probably be more fun, but Wylie always says his brother is a pest. You're an only child too, right?"

"Yep."

"Did *you* ever want a brother or sister?"

"Sometimes." Another forgotten memory jumped out of Ezra's past: sitting on a split-rail fence in a cow pasture having a spitting contest with two dark-haired boys.

"Dad? Earth to Dad! If you're going to space out, at least bring me back an ashtray from Mars!"

Ezra laughed and ruffled Dillon's hair. "Funny man. You must've heard that from Aunt Lenore. She said it to me all the time when I was a kid."

Dillon looked pleased. "She's coming to the cabin, right?"

"That's what she told me last week."

"Why couldn't I go with you to visit? I want to check out her new computer."

"I needed to talk to her. Grown-up talk."

The boy concentrated on tying knots in his shoelaces. "Did you tell her about me?"

"I did."

Dillon's head shot up. He gave his father an accusing look. "What did you say?"

"I said you have what I used to have."

Ezra could see his son absorb the information. "But you don't have it anymore?"

"That's right. I don't."

A look of relief crossed his face. "So, I won't have it forever either, right?"

"That's right," Ezra said, hoping he wasn't telling his son a giant fucking lie.

∽

On Monday night, Dillon and Wiley ate pepperoni pizza in front of the television in the living room. Celia was out at her book group meeting. For some reason, Ezra resented her being gone. He felt left out, as if she were letting him down, even though it was a relief to escape the tension that seemed to always be between them now. He nuked a burrito and ate it on the back porch. He allowed himself one beer, which turned into two. He remembered he hadn't brought in the mail yet. As he walked across the yard in the dim light of dusk, he smelled the fresh-cut grass, saw the warm light of his home spilling out through the living room window. He felt peaceful.

There were a few bills, some junk mail, and a large manila envelope from his aunt. He brought it into the kitchen and tossed it on the table. He popped open a third beer before he opened the envelope. Lenore had sent him four photographs. Ezra spread them out on the table, their sepia tones faded and their images unfamiliar. Three of the photos were of a young boy who looked so much like Dillon that Ezra did a double-take. He had never seen a picture of himself as a boy.

He picked up a picture of his younger self dressed in a cowboy costume and grinning at the camera. On the back of the photo, someone—surely his mother—had written, "My little man, age 3." There were two of his school pictures. His hair was neatly combed, and in both, his unmistakable gapped-toothed smile beamed. "Age 6" and "10 years old" were scrawled on the backs.

The last picture was of a tall, laughing man in a dark suit with his arm around a tall, smiling woman in a white dress. His parents on their wedding day. Ezra studied it, fascinated. He was the spitting image of his daddy. They had the same dark, curly hair, brown eyes that crinkled at the corners when they laughed, and strong chin. He looked to see if there was any evidence of his existence in the photo, but the picture was taken of the couple from the chest up. He wished the picture of his mother was clearer. He couldn't tell if he resembled her at all.

The loss of his parents instantly struck him—a full-body blow that made every inch of him ache and his stomach turn sour. Ezra struggled to catch his breath. He wished he could remember more—the sound of her voice, the way they looked at each other and at him. But those memories had not returned.

A letter from Aunt Lenore accompanied the photos, penned in her distinctively crabbed cursive.

"It was that Sunday after Thanksgiving, about eight o'clock at night, when I got the telephone call," Lenore wrote. "A sheriff down in Alabama said there had been a storm, and my sister, her husband, and her husband's whole family had been killed. The only survivor was my twelve-year-old nephew, and could I come and get him? The next morning, I got on a plane and flew down to Huntsville. The sheriff's deputy picked me up and brought me to the hospital. You were lying in a hospital bed. The right side of your face was bandaged." Ezra traced a finger along the faint scar on his right cheek. "The doctor told me you had been unconscious when the ambulance brought you in, but when I saw you, your eyes were wide open and staring at the wall. I said your name, but you didn't respond. He said you were in shock."

Ezra tried to remember, but the thoughts that came were muddled and confusing. His first clear memories started on the airplane. He was holding someone's hand. He was aware that he had an Aunt Lenore and that she was taking him back to her home in West Virginia. He didn't say a word, but he didn't let go of her hand. His next memory was in an unfamiliar house being given a tour of an unfamiliar room that was now his. He had crawled under the covers with all his clothes on and stayed there, save for bathroom breaks, for days—was it three days? He remembered lying in that bed, hoping that it had been a bad dream and if only he could get back to sleep and find that dream again, he could get back home.

Ezra went to the cupboard and found the bourbon. He took a long pull from the bottle, gasping at the burn in the back of his throat.

"A week later," wrote Lenore, "I got a call from the sheriff. Bodies had been found, and they needed me to come down and identify them. I asked a neighbor to come and stay with you while I flew back to Alabama. The only Magees I knew were Trudy and Simp. A man who said he was a friend of the family came and identified the other bodies. He was weeping so hard I couldn't make out his name. Everyone who died was a Magee or a Magee relative. The house you grew up in had been severely damaged. Everything was in ruins. There was a lawyer who produced a will. They left everything to you, and they left you to me. The judge signed the papers, and I became your legal guardian."

Ezra remembered. When she returned from Alabama, it had been late at night, and Lenore had come straight to his room. She had asked him how he was doing. He'd said he was fine because he didn't know how to put words to his paralyzing fear. She said she'd been to his home, and she was sorry to say it had been destroyed. She said his mother and father were buried in the family cemetery, and he could go back whenever he wanted and lay flowers on their graves. Ezra had remained dry-eyed and numb as she walked him through the facts of his parents' deaths. Then she'd told him he'd be living with her from now on, and that she loved him and she'd take good care of him.

"Okay," was all he could muster. Then he'd rolled over and closed his eyes. A few minutes later, he heard her tiptoe out of his room, and he fell asleep and slept for twenty-four hours.

☙

"And did you show the letter and pictures to Celia?" Reverend Hiram Johnson asked.

"I was going to," Ezra said defensively.

"You were going to?"

"No, I didn't show them to her."

"Why not?"

He'd been good and drunk when Celia returned home from her book group. She shooed the boys up to bed while Ezra sat smoking on the back porch.

"What's wrong with your dad?" he'd heard Wylie ask.

"Nothing," Dillon had replied. "He's just like that sometimes."

The words had burned in Ezra's brain. His own son thought he was a loser. He was a loser who had panic attacks. He sat on the porch and cried, his tears constructed of self-pity and disgust. Even Izzy hadn't wanted to stay outside with him; she'd pushed her way through the dog door and went up to find the boys.

Celia didn't come outside to yell at him or say how disappointed she was. She ignored him and went up to bed. Ezra drank until the bottle was empty, and then he stumbled to the den and fell onto the recliner.

He slept late and woke up hung-over and ashamed. He'd fully intended to apologize to his wife first thing, but when he got downstairs, he'd found her note on the kitchen table.

"So, she left, and now you've got me," Hiram said.

Ezra nodded. "It's a miserable trade."

The preacher was now perched on the edge of the green ottoman, kitty-corner to the couch, looking at Ezra with what could only be called disgust with a hint of compassion. "She left, even though she could see you were suffering." Ezra cringed at the sound of pity in Hiram's voice.

Ezra wanted to feel the clean certainty of self-righteousness, but he couldn't. Celia was right to leave.

"She left, but I abandoned her first," he admitted to an empty room.

Hiram Johnson was nowhere to be seen.

CHAPTER 15

"Granmaude? It's me," Josephine Parker whispered into the telephone. The faculty was busy with third period classes, and Jo was alone in the empty teacher's lounge, but she still felt the need to whisper. "Father O'Malley will call Ezra out of his last period class and take him to his office in the rectory. That'll be right at 2:30."

"Jo, I owe you," the old woman said.

"No, you don't," Jo replied fiercely. "There's no talk of owing between us."

In her kitchen in Folly, Granmaude hung up the phone and started hunting for her purse. It was Friday the thirteenth. Nothing good ever happened on Friday the thirteenth.

After a lifetime of praying and following the blessed sacraments, Granmaude still lacked faith that the Almighty had His eye on things down here. There was plenty of evidence that He was busy elsewhere. Unfortunately, He had left His underlings in charge, and one of them was that bad apple, Sean O'Malley.

She spoke to the dark and heavy rainclouds that blotted the sky. "Don't you go and make things worse, now. It's already bad enough."

Poor Ezra had been born with the Magee curse. She remembered how it had afflicted her son, Nate. But she couldn't dwell on it, because thoughts of Nate inevitably led to memories of the day he died, and whenever she thought about it too long, sorrow and rage would send her to her bed for a week.

Granmaude drove an old Ford Fairlane with a finicky starter.

After trying to get the engine to turn over and flooding the carburetor, she went back inside and called Killian for a ride.

☙

Dexter Blaxton had done it again. He'd called Ezra "Goofy Magee" during lunch, and Ezra finally took a swing at him. Ezra missed, tripped over his own feet, and fell flat on his belly on the cafeteria's sticky linoleum floor while the whole school—especially Dexter Blaxton—pointed and laughed. It was like a bad dream. Then the bell rang.

"Everybody back to class!" Miss Maynard ordered. "No running!" Ezra's classmates scattered. He struggled to his feet and discovered that he'd managed to fall on the remnants of a sloppy joe someone had dropped on the floor. He went to the boy's room to wash it off his pants and was only partially successful.

"Check out Goofy Magee!" Dexter stage-whispered while the teacher wrote a math problem on the board. All the kids turned to stare at Ezra, and some could see the wet, brown stain on his tan pants. Ezra pretended to be copying the problem into his notebook. The meaty tomato smell made him slightly nauseous.

After math, there wouldn't be much left to the day except study hall. Luckily, Dexter wasn't in Ezra's study hall. Ezra heartily wished his fist had connected with the red-headed boy's jaw.

☙

A loud clap of thunder rattled the windows and rain lashed the building in blinding sheets. Was it an omen? That thought ran through Father O'Malley's mind as he stood in the lobby of the school and shook rain off his cassock. The down spouts began their regurgitation into the drainage spillways. It was a cleansing rain, the priest decided. It was sent by the Lord to remind Sean O'Malley that evil could be washed away. Sin would be removed when he cast the demons out of young, innocent Ezra Magee.

He'd spent a good portion of the previous night reading and re-reading Church history and documentation on exorcism. He knew what had to be done. But why, he wondered, did he have a troubling sense of foreboding? For courage, he turned his thoughts to Daniel in the lion's den, Saul on the road to Damascus, and Jesus in the garden of Gethsemane.

O'Malley asked a school aide for the day's attendance sheet and scanned it for a particular name. Yes, the boy was indeed present and accounted for. He asked the woman to tell the study hall monitor to send Ezra up to the school office right away.

☙

When Ezra got the summons to the office, he couldn't believe he'd gotten into trouble when he hadn't even touched Dexter! Father O'Malley was waiting for him by the front door of the school. The priest didn't say a word—just opened his umbrella and escorted Ezra to the rectory, which meant he was in some real trouble. The rectory was where serious punishments were meted out. There'd be no simple detention for this. The drugs Ezra was on dulled his feelings, but he still experienced a wave of dread.

Go to Hell O'Malley took Ezra right into his office and pointed to a straight-backed wooden chair. Ezra sat. The priest towered over and scrutinized him.

"How are you, Ezra?" the priest wanted to know.

Ezra was taken aback. "Uh, okay, Father."

"That's good, very good."

Ezra was getting the creeps. Go to Hell O'Malley was never nice.

"There is a special prayer we can say together. It will help make you feel better. What do you say?"

"Sure, Father." Saying a prayer wasn't so bad. O'Malley was going easy on him for some reason. Maybe he didn't like Dexter Blaxton, either. Maybe he was glad someone had tried to punch his weaselly face.

"You just sit there, and I'll be back in a minute." O'Malley closed the door behind him.

Ezra slumped in the chair and wondered if this would take long and how many Hail Mary's he'd have to say. He never saw the point, but he said them just the same, in case there really was a God. But they sure took up a lot of time. Was the point to bore a person so his soul would become obedient? If so, the bored part was working. He wasn't so sure about the obedience.

Father O'Malley came back into the room clothed in a chasuble draped over a glowing white alb. The priest was followed by Sister Jean. Ezra reactively sat up straighter. She was famous for swatting boys on the head for slouching.

"He's consented?" Sister Jean asked, her mouth a tight, disapproving slash as usual. She was tall and bony. Some of the kids referred to her as "Sister Skeleton," but Ezra'd never had the guts to utter the name. He was sure the one time he did she would overhear him, and then he'd spend the rest of his life—and his entire afterlife—in detention.

"All is ready," Father O'Malley announced, lighting the censer. "Bring the tools."

༄

Traffic was slowing as the rain began. The harder the storm pelted down, the slower everyone drove. Granmaude grumbled in frustration at the long line of cars and trucks ahead.

"We cain't be late!" Granmaude pounded the dashboard.

"We won't be," Killian said from the driver's seat. "They got some construction started a quarter mile down the road. We'll be past it soon enough."

Granmaude fretted. It was a quarter past two. According to Jo, the exorcism was scheduled to start at half past the hour. They were still twenty minutes away, and now this.

"Ain't there some other way to git there?"

Killian considered the problem and made a sudden U-turn. Even though they were going the wrong way, Granmaude was glad to be moving again. He cut across the line of stopped traffic and onto a rutted dirt road. They bumped along into Buford the back way, splashing through deep puddles and jouncing over rocks. Killian made it to the rectory parking lot by 2:35 p.m., and Granmaude was out of the truck before he put it in park. Killian had to run to catch up with her. She was still spry in her old age. Granmaude marched straight to Father Sean O'Malley's office and burst in without knocking.

The interior of the room was suffused in shadows cast by a single, low-wattage lamp perched on the front of O'Malley's desk. The blinds were closed. Ezra lay on the floor with a silver cross clasped to his chest. Sister Jean and the priest circled the prostrate form of the boy, chanting in unison in Latin and casting censers over him. The room was thick with the fragrance of incense.

When the door flew open, all movement in the room ceased except for the swinging censers. The shadows of the priest and nun loomed ghost-like on the walls.

"What foolishness is this?" Granmaude shouted. "What in the name of the Lord do you think you two are doing?" Granmaude advanced on the priest, whose face displayed the frozen shock of a culprit caught red-handed. He dropped the bottle of Holy Water he'd intended to sprinkle over the prone figure of Ezra, smacking the boy on the chest.

Ezra emitted a muffled cry and sat up. It was an unfortunate move, because at that moment, Sister Jean's censer nailed him right on the forehead. He fell back again, blood gushing from the same wound that had recently been stitched.

"You ridiculous old man!" Granmaude jabbed O'Malley in the chest with her finger and drove him back toward the window. "There will be a reckoning!"

Father O'Malley was appalled. How had she found out? Was she also in league with the devil?

"You oughta be ashamed of yourself," she continued. The priest stood with his mouth open, but no words came out.

Sister Jean moved toward Granmaude. "We are doing the Lord's work!" she shrieked. "The boy has the devil in him!"

Granmaude rounded on the nun. "Pah!" She spat on the floor between them in disgust. "Don't you tell me my grandson is possessed by the devil! The only one who's got evil in his heart is this one here." She jabbed the priest in the chest again. By this time, O'Malley was sputtering incoherently. While Granmaude railed at the priest, Killian scooped the bleeding boy off the floor.

"We'd best get him to the hospital," he told Granmaude before turning toward the door. Blood was now trailing down Ezra's face from the reopened wound.

Granmaude glowered at O'Malley. "I do believe we'll be paying a visit to Bishop Strauss," she hissed. "Let him see what you've done to my grandson." She narrowed her eyes at the priest. "I'd like to hear from his mouth why he authorized you to perform an exorcism without the family's permission."

Sean O'Malley blanched. It was his worst nightmare come true, and she saw it in his eyes. Granmaude's blood stirred. "I knew it! You had no business doing what you were doing here today. No business at all! And all those years when you coulda helped my family, you refused, you self-righteous bastid! Now I tell you: you will stay out of our business from here on in!" She gave one last spit in Sister Jean's direction for good measure. Then Granmaude allowed herself a dramatic exit, spinning on her heel and slamming the door behind her.

☙

Ezra remembered being carried to the truck in Killian's strong arms, and his grandmother's powdery lilac smell as she dabbed the blood off his face with her lace-edged handkerchief.

"Don't you worry, my boy," she cackled. "We sure got him good!"

"Don't tell Daddy," Ezra mumbled. "He'll kill Father O'Malley."

Killian and Granmaude exchanged a look. "I already called him to say I'd be giving you a lift home from school," Killian admitted.

"Simpellion never could control that temper," Granmaude said. "No tellin' what he'll do if he hears."

"O'Malley crossed the line," Killian growled. Ezra was surprised. Killian never got angry, not even when Boyd and Floyd imitated his limp.

"I mean, I was bored, but he didn't hurt me or nothing," Ezra said.

"O'Malley knew Nate. He shoulda known you've got the same."

"As soon as we get to the hospital, I'm callin' Bishop Strauss," Granmaude said. "That man's been a cancer in our parish for long enough."

"Then again, you got him by the balls," Killian said. He and Granmaude both grinned. "Yep, he'll be worryin' about whether you're gonna make that call."

"You got a good point there, Killian. God forgive me, but I like the thought of him stewing in his own juice!" She slapped her thigh and laughed.

Ezra had to have six more stitches. "I cain't promise you won't be scarred," the doctor said, cheering Ezra right up. Boyd and Floyd would be so jealous.

Killian dropped him off at home, and Ezra told his parents he'd taken a fall at school. Trudy sent him up to bed with ice for his head and a plate of cookies. Exhausted, he lay down and closed his eyes. But something tickled at the back of his mind.

There was that name again: *Nate*.

CHAPTER 16

Father O'Malley's knees ached after he'd spent the night in the chapel praying for deliverance from the wrath of Maude Magee. He imagined her marching into the bishop's office and spilling the beans. O'Malley couldn't believe this was happening—and just when he was beginning to think about enjoying a comfortable retirement! He'd given everything to the Church, and he would be cast out over a momentary lapse in judgment—if it could even be called a lapse. There had been a moment, just before that dreadful woman burst into his office, when O'Malley had felt an unwholesome presence in the room that surely was the spirit possessing the boy.

O'Malley stayed in his room for the rest of the day, brooding over his future and waiting for the fateful phone call. If the bishop decided to take pity on him and let him stay in the Church, O'Malley knew he could still be sent to some godforsaken place filled with genuine heathens, dust, and flies. But that wasn't the biggest worry in the old priest's mind. It was only a matter of time before Simpellion Magee found out. The man was unstable. Heaven only knew what that heathen would do.

༄

Amazingly, in a place where gossip was faster than electronic media, it took five days for the rumor to reach Simpellion's ears. Trudy called Killian and alerted him. Five minutes later, Killian drove into Simp's yard. Simp was standing on the front porch in full voice, demanding of Trudy where she'd hidden his shotgun.

"Tell me it's just a rumor," Simp demanded of his best friend. "Tell me that sonofabitch didn't go and do what I heard he did. And don't tell me you don't know what I'm talkin' about, 'cause I know goddamn well you do."

Killian wished he'd thought to bring a rope. "You look upset," he observed.

"Don't you use that psychobabble bullshit on me! You're goddamn right I'm upset! I just heard that sonofabitchin' spy from Rome tried to exorcise demons outta my boy! And I want to know if it's true so I can go kill the bastard!"

"Now just take it easy for a minute, Simp," Killian cautioned, as a splotchy red stain spread up Simp's neck. It was a sure sign that Simpellion T. Dillon Magee was on the verge of an apoplectic fit. "You want to be careful. You could have a heart attack if you don't calm down."

"Don't tell me to calm down!"

Killian really regretted the absence of a length of rope. Hog-tying Simp seemed the only sensible option. He followed Simp into the house where Trudy stood glowering at her husband.

"No," she said firmly. "You cannot have that shotgun, because I will not allow you to kill a man in cold blood. Not even an obnoxious, self-righteous ass like O'Malley. I love you too much. Ezra and I need you. What will we do when they put you prison for life? I will not have it, Simpellion. The answer is no!"

"Woman, now is not the time. I need my gun!"

"No!" she said forcefully, crossing her arms across her chest. "I draw the line at being married to a murderer."

"Trudy, come on!" Simp whined. "He's got it comin'!"

As she opened her mouth to refuse him again, Simp saw her eyes dart to the broom closet. Quick as a weasel, he lunged for the closet door and yanked it open. Simp found his shotgun under an old coat, grabbed it, and howled triumphantly. Then he took off out the door. Trudy screamed for him to stop.

Simp's keys were not on the dashboard where he always left them. He eyed Killian's truck and jumped in the driver's seat. Killian always left the key in the ignition, and he'd barely got into the passenger seat before Simp roared away toward Buford. Simp cradled the shotgun in his left arm (far from Killian's reach) with the barrel sticking out of the window, changing gears and steering with his right hand.

"You got any shells for that?" Killian asked neutrally.

Simp patted his pocket. "Got enough," he said. "Trudy hid the gun, not the ammo. I'm loaded for bear." He skidded around a corner, and Killian grimaced. Those were newish tires he'd just put on the truck.

"You really gonna do this?"

Simp glared down the road, a wild smile growing on his sweating face. "You betcher ass I am," he said.

∽

Ezra had been working on a school assignment in his room when the shouting and arguing started. He heard his parents arguing about the gun.

"But Simp, what about us?" he heard his mother plead. "What about me and Ezra? You're not thinking straight. You could go to prison! They could give you the electric chair!"

Ezra saw Killian pull up in his truck and disappear into the house. More yelling, then moments later, he saw his father leap into Killian's truck with his shotgun. A part of him admired his father for being a man of action, even though most of the time his actions were misguided.

"Is Daddy gonna kill Father O'Malley?" Ezra called down to his mother.

"Oh, honey, I sure hope not." She was crying. She almost never cried. Ezra blamed himself. It would be his fault if the priest was killed. It was because of him that his daddy was on his way to commit first-degree murder.

"Don't let him do it, God," he prayed. Ezra even got down on his knees by the side of the bed, which he hadn't done since he was really young, and squeezed his eyes closed tight. "Don't let my daddy kill anybody. I'll be good, I swear it. Just don't let him kill anybody, especially Father O'Malley."

Trudy turned on both the radio and the television in case there was any breaking news from Buford. She sat by the phone waiting for the sheriff's department to call.

An hour later, Killian's truck pulled into the yard. Trudy and Ezra ran out to the front porch and saw Simp hop out, swinging the shotgun in his left hand. Killian pulled away without tooting his horn or calling out a goodnight.

"Didja do it?" Ezra asked.

"Yep," Simp replied with a smug look on his face. "Trudy, we got any of that potato salad left? I'm famished!"

CHAPTER 17

The ringing phone woke Ezra from an uncomfortable sleep. He stumbled across the living room looking for the phone, but he reached it too late. The number was blocked, and the caller left no message.

Celia hadn't contacted him since she'd left thirteen days ago. What would he say to her if she did? He was a disgrace. Ezra's nose wrinkled at the smell of his own body odor, his breath like fallen, rotting apples decomposing in the sun. He hauled himself upstairs and stripped off his robe in the bathroom. When the water was good and hot, he plunged into the shower and scrubbed himself. His hands were trembling too much to risk shaving in the shower, but when he got out, he lathered up his face and slowly scraped off his beard. Despite his caution, several blood trails dripped down the face in the mirror.

He stared into his own bloodshot eyes and yellowed, rough skin. He was clean on the outside, but he still looked like hell. His hair was almost down to his shoulders. He brushed his teeth vigorously, then attempted to floss, though his unsteady hands made it nearly impossible. He had never had the shakes before. It was nothing like chattering from the cold. It was his body begging him to have just a sip, just a taste. Two days before, when he'd gotten the package from his aunt Lenore, he'd finished the bottle of bourbon and had fought the urge to replace it.

Ezra drew a glass of water from the bathroom sink. He swallowed a small pile of aspirin that filled his palm. The phone rang again, and he decided to let it go to voicemail. If it was Celia, he couldn't imagine what he'd say to her anyway. When the message light blinked, he hit the play button.

"Ezra, call me." It was Lenore. "There's something else I'd plumb forgot about until last night. About a month after you came to live with me, a box came in the mail from Alabama. It was sealed with duct tape." He wondered why that random detail stuck in her mind. "It was addressed to you."

Ezra called her right back. "This box—what was in it?"

"I never opened it!" She sounded offended at the idea. "It was addressed to you; that would have been a federal offense." As a former postal worker, she followed the mail code religiously. Ezra would have smiled if he hadn't been so irritated. "I figured you'd open it when the time came," she was saying. "I must have stored it up in the attic. Thinking about Jane Addams's letters under the attic floorboards made me recall it. Did you know the brain's neurons can fire off trillions of connections in an instant?"

He wanted to hop in the car and go right over to Lenore's, but he was in no shape to drive. "I can't come today, Lenore. I'll try to get there tomorrow." He lied when she asked about Celia and Dillon. He told her they were out at a soccer game.

☙

He laid off the booze all day and had one of the worst nights he'd ever experienced. Somewhere around 1 a.m., he took a sleeping pill and fell into medicinal sleep. In the morning, he still felt crummy, but not quite as bad as the day before. More water and aspirin helped, and finally his brain was ready to think about the box. Like a washed-up, alcoholic Pandora, he had to know what was in it, even if it meant unleashing a mess of evils on his world. Nothing he found in that box could destroy him worse than he'd already destroyed himself.

"Where do you think Celia is right now?" Hiram Johnson had

joined him on the back porch and declined the offer of a cigarette. It was morning, and the sunlight felt like a million-watt light bulb shining directly into Ezra's eyes.

"Her mother's house, probably working in the garden." Gretchen Talbot lived an hour east in Harper's Ferry. Dillon loved visiting his grandmother in the quaint town with all the touristy fudge and souvenir shops, and he especially loved to wade in the creek that ran behind her house. Or he used to love it. He was probably sitting in Gretchen's living room playing his video games and refusing to go outside.

Celia and her mother were close in a certain way, but Gretchen could be critical, and eventually it would get on Celia's nerves. What had his wife said about him to his mother-in-law? He felt a flush of shame. What did Dillon think about Ezra being so far away and not even calling?

"Isn't this what you wanted?" Hiram asked. "You pushed 'em both away, and now they're gone."

"Hiram, what in the hell are you doing here?"

"You invited me. Remember?"

No, he did not remember, but it was useless asking the man to explain himself. He'd never get a sensible answer.

"I've got to go over to Childersburg, to my Aunt Lenore's house."

"I'm coming with you."

"No reason for you to come," Ezra insisted.

Around noon, he called Lenore and told her he was on his way. "Bring Celia and Dillon," she said. "I haven't seen them in a month."

"I'll see if Celia can tear herself away from her writing," he lied.

When he got in his car, Hiram was already settled in the back seat with his eyes closed.

It was after 1 p.m. when Ezra pulled into Lenore's driveway. He found her in the garage knocking down cobwebs from the rafters with a broom. Her hair was covered with a blue bandana, and her pink sweatsuit was streaked with dirt.

"I haven't cleaned this place in decades."

She stood on her toes and tried to reach a cobweb in the corner. Ezra took the broom from her and brushed it down. Then he went around to the side of the house and retrieved the ladder. What Lenore called her "attic" was really a crawlspace above the garage. It was packed with detritus collected over the past thirty years. Ezra remembered making annual sorties into its cramped quarters to pull down Christmas lights and Halloween decorations.

"I always meant to clean it out," she said as Ezra climbed the ladder and pushed open the trap door. He had to turn his head away from the puff of dust that drifted down. He sat on top of the ladder and pulled items out, one by one, and carefully handed them down to Lenore. She cheerfully went through the boxes, making give-away and throw-away piles. Old plastic Christmas wreaths, out-of-style (and now badly moth-eaten) clothes, boxes of *National Geographic* magazines, and a collection of warped jazz records all went into the throw-away pile. There were boxes belonging to Ezra up there too: his high school notebooks that went into the throw-away pile, yearbooks he thought he might keep, and a box of old comic books that he put aside for Dillon.

Occasionally, Ezra stuck his head down out of the attic to make sure Lenore didn't wander out to his car. He didn't want to have to explain Hiram dozing in the back seat.

The heat was stifling, and Ezra was relieved when he finally saw the last of the boxes.

He wiped sweat from his face with an already wet sleeve and looked at his aunt. "Are you sure it's up here?" he asked. "We're pretty much done clearing this out."

Lenore frowned. "I was sure I'd stuck it in the attic," she said. "Would've bet money on it."

"Must be it's in the other attic," Ezra joked.

Lenore thought for a moment and then beamed at him. "Of course! That's exactly right!"

"What are you talking about?"

She marched right into the house and upstairs to her bedroom. Ezra followed, and when she opened her closet door, he looked up and saw a trapdoor.

"I never store anything up there anymore because it's so damned inconvenient," she explained as she pushed hangers out of the way and moved her shoes to the side. Ezra went back outside and dragged the ladder upstairs. After some maneuvering, he was able to fit the ladder in her closet.

He pushed the trapdoor aside and stuck his head through the opening. The place obviously hadn't been disturbed for a very long time. He hauled himself up and was instantly covered with powdery dust. Cobwebs hung like grimy lace from the rafters.

The box sat alone in the middle of the half-finished floor. It had to be the one: a cardboard box with dull gray tape wrapped around it, as if the person who sent it wasn't used to mailing packages and didn't trust that a stranger wouldn't try to open it. Scrawled in badly faded magic marker in the upper left-hand corner was a return address to a post office box in Buford, Alabama. There was no sender's name. The box was addressed to Ezra.

He hesitated, feeling as if he had come into possession of a magic lamp, which, if he rubbed it, might call forth an evil genie—the kind that would grant your three wishes, but make sure you regretted every single one.

CHAPTER 18

After Trudy finally stopped telling him what a fool he was and how he'd ruined all their lives, Simp told them what happened.

They had been about a mile down the road when Killian spoke up. "You realize, Simp,"—Killian had kept his voice low and calm—"that if you do what you're talking about doing, you'll destroy not only your own life, but Trudy's, Ezra's, and Granmaude's as well? And that'd be a terrible thing to do, don't you think?"

When Simp didn't respond, Killian had continued. "Not only that, but you'd make me an accessory to murder. I'm not saying you should let those things stand in your way, old buddy, but it's somethin' to think about."

"You know I can't just let that sonofabitch get away with it!" Simp protested.

"There was no harm done," Killian reminded him.

"No harm done, hell!" Simp gesticulated wildly, and the butt of his gun tangled in the steering wheel and caused him to veer into the oncoming traffic lane, which luckily was empty. "What about Ezra's reputation? That bastard made everyone think my boy's possessed by a demon! And there's no tellin' what he's done to the boy's head with all that mumbo jumbo bullshit."

"Ezra's fine," Killian reasoned. "Did you even talk to him?

"He's not fine."

"Did you even talk to the boy about it?" Killian repeated.

Simp didn't respond.

"You know that Alabama's got only one method of execution,

Simp." Simp was still silent. "Yessir," Killian continued, "that's the electric chair they call 'Old Yellow Mama' down in Holman Prison. It's been a while since the last execution, and she's just sittin' there, waitin' for fresh meat. A priest killer—that'd sure make you famous. No jury would find you innocent. So he mumbled some Latin over your boy. Big deal. You're going to put buckshot into a holy man."

"He ain't holy!" Simp raged. Suddenly his expression changed to one of grim amusement. "At least not yet, he ain't," he muttered.

"Come on, Simp. Give this up and let's go get ourselves some beers," Killian said. They were in downtown Buford now, and it was locked up tight for the night, but across the railroad tracks there was a bar with a Budweiser sign lit up in red neon.

Simp ignored him and took a left toward the river and Ezra's school. Killian sighed and cursed himself a third time for forgetting the rope.

The darkened edifice of the church loomed ahead as they drove onto the church and school grounds. Lights from two windows in the staff living quarters shone like Halloween eyes carved in a giant pumpkin. Simp pulled right up to the walkway leading to the rectory. He disentangled his gun from the car window and dropped a cartridge in. It made a satisfying click as it fell into the chamber.

Killian leapt from the car and ran around in front of the hood. "I'm beggin' you, don't do this," he said. But his best friend breezed right past him and was already knocking on the rectory door.

It took a minute, and it was Father O'Malley who answered the knock. When he opened the door and saw Simpellion Magee holding a shotgun, he tried to slam it shut. But Simp was too fast—he jammed his foot in the doorway. The priest took off at a run, and Simp pushed the door wide open. Killian saw the old man scurry toward the back of the hall as Simp raised the gun. The blast reverberated through the building. Killian heard a scream, and a light on the second floor came on. Simp was already pounding up the stairs after Father O'Malley. Another gun flash burned through an upstairs window, followed by an echoing explosion and another scream. Killian leaned against the side of the truck and shook his head.

For a couple of minutes, Killian could hear little movement until the front door of the rectory burst open, and the priest made a break for the sanctuary next door, his slippered feet beating a staccato rhythm on the sidewalk.

Simp was a dozen steps behind when he raised his gun. He had a clear shot. He took aim and pulled the trigger, and Killian heard another scream.

☙

"And that's all that happened," Simp concluded. He took two steps toward Trudy, who was standing in front of the fridge, her eyes and mouth wide open. He put his hands on her shoulders. "I told you, honey," Simp cooed, slowly moving her body out of the way. "Everything's all right. Now let me get to that potato salad." Simp opened the refrigerator and peered inside.

Trudy grabbed Simp by his shoulders and spun him around. "Just tell me O'Malley is alive."

"He's fine, I swear it. Although," he grinned, "I think he'll have a sore ass."

"Simp!"

"I swear it on my ACLU membership," he said. "The holy father might walk funny for a few weeks and have a hell of a time sittin' down, but O'Malley is still alive and kickin'."

The sheriff's deputy showed up just before ten p.m. Ezra perched at the top of the stairs to eavesdrop.

Deputy Cahela accepted Trudy's offer of a cup of coffee. "If you can't beat 'em, shoot 'em, huh, Simp?" He gave Simp a broad wink.

After a second cup of coffee and a long conversation about the chances of the Crimson Tide in the Iron Bowl, the deputy confiscated Simp's shotgun and arrested him for reckless endangerment with a firearm.

"Y'all can pick him up in the morning," Cahela said, tipping his hat to Trudy. "Thank you kindly for the coffee, ma'am." Simp rode away in the front seat with a grin on his face.

In the morning, Killian gave Trudy a ride into Scottsboro, and they picked Simp up from the jail where he'd been booked, photographed, and released on his own recognizance.

"You can't go 'round shootin' priests, Simp," Sheriff Stanley McCullough told him sternly on their way out, although there was a faint smile on his face.

Simp rolled his eyes. "I didn't kill him, Stan. I just gave him a sore ass."

"It wasn't him that complained," McCullough admitted. "One of the sisters called it in. She said you were trying to kill him. O'Malley doesn't want to press charges, but the D.A.'s probably gonna have to do something. The election's only two years off."

"Yeah, I know," said Simp, "and all the local Christians are gonna be calling for my head. 'Specially the Catholics. I been thinkin' I'll take up a new sideline: priest killer for hire. Run an ad in the *Sentinel*."

"Don't joke about it when you come to court," the sheriff advised.

"He won't, Sheriff," Trudy said, clamping her hand over Simp's mouth. "I'll make sure of it."

"Those nuns are going to be pretty convincing witnesses," McCullough continued. "They're going to say Simp here was shootin' with murderous intent."

"That's not a very Christian thing to say about me," Simp protested, wiggling free of Trudy's hands. "O'Malley and I were just foolin' around. Everyone knows if I'd wanted him dead, I'da killed him. Besides," he said, holding back a snicker, "the Father's got a big fat ass, and I was just tryin' to help him preserve it. I used rock salt, you know."

Sheriff McCullough shook his head, and Killian helped Trudy

drag Simp outside before he made things worse for himself.

"It was worth it," Simp told them with a smirk. "I don't regret a single shot fired."

Back at home, Trudy made breakfast and slapped it down in front of her husband.

"If you ever scare me again like you did last night," she said, "you'd better hide that shotgun from *me*!"

She left the room, and suddenly Simpellion found himself alone with his son. He and Ezra stared at each other. Then the boy said, "Thanks a lot, Daddy."

Simp's heart swelled with love. "I always got'cher back, son. Don't you ever forget it."

CHAPTER 19

Lenore insisted on feeding Ezra supper before he drove home. He drank only water with the meal. He hoped his aunt noticed that he was staying sober. One day at a time. Day Three was almost conquered.

"Well?" Hiram asked on the ride back. "What did you find?"

"A box."

"From who?"

"Don't know. Haven't opened it yet."

"Why not?"

"Why don't you go back to sleep?"

"Haven't been asleep."

The rest of the ride was silent.

Once he got home, Ezra took a long, hot shower to wash away the attic grunge. Then he dressed and walked slowly into the living room. The box was sitting on the couch.

"You gonna open it?" Hiram was sitting on the ottoman and toying with a loose button on his jacket.

"Eventually."

"It's just a box, boy. It's not gonna bite."

"Sure. That's just what Pandora said." Ezra burned for a drink of bourbon. Instinctively, he looked toward the kitchen.

"Liquid courage?" Hiram had stood up and was standing in front of the bookcase, studying the book titles.

"Shut up, please," said Ezra. The preacher was getting on Ezra's last nerve. He badly needed a drink.

CHAPTER 20

But he didn't drink any alcohol—mostly because he hadn't replenished his supply. Instead, he cut through the duct tape with a pocketknife. The first thing he saw was a woman's blouse. It looked familiar. The robin's-egg blue fabric evoked a fuzzy memory of his mother standing in Granmaude's kitchen holding a bowl of potato salad. He pressed the cloth to his face and inhaled, but there was nothing left of her scent. He felt like a fool sniffing a musty old shirt and trying to remember a woman he hadn't seen in twenty-eight years. But he couldn't escape the feeling that had begun spreading over his body.

"Steady there, old son," Hiram said, sitting in the recliner. "One step at a time."

Underneath the blouse was a sealed envelope with his name written on the front. He opened the letter with his knife. A date was scribbled at the top: December 26, 1972.

Ezra,

It is with a heavy heart that I write this, but I figure you'll want these things I'm sending. We're all still in shock over what happened. All the Magees—it's just hard to fathom. Your daddy and your mama and uncles and cousins, Granmaude—they were closer than family to me. I miss them, and I already miss you, boy. I hope you're not letting any crickets get in your bed.

Just remember, your ma and pa thought the sun rose and set in you. They loved you with everything they had, and I know they would want you to be happy, to live your life without worrying about what could have been. It was a miracle that you survived. Your pa would give me a hard time for believing in miracles, but I'd give him a hard time right back, because it truly was a miracle. Here you are, a real survivor, and I can't tell you how glad I am. It's the one good thing I can think of right now. I hope you will come back to visit. Tell your aunt you can stay with me, and I'll teach you to fish the proper way.

I hate to be the one to tell you, but I went by your place, and everything is gone. I found that photograph I'm sending. Its condition is not too bad. I didn't know whether to send the blouse. It was your mama's, and it was in the mix. I didn't want to throw it away. Most of the books were your daddy's. He'd loaned them to me, which is why they survived. I thought you'd like to have them.

I should have been in Granmaude's house that day, watching the game with all of them. I had planned to be there, just like every year. My knee gave out on me the day before, as it still does sometimes, and I could hardly walk. Of course, if I had, I wouldn't be here right now, writing this letter. I still can't believe what happened.

I've got more to say, but it's better said face to face, so I'll just sign off now. Never forget you got a friend here in Folly.

Sincerely,
Killian Cagle

A telephone number was written underneath the signature.

Who the hell is Killian Cagle? There was a slight tickle in Ezra's skull as he read the name, but the man remained a mystery.

Ezra laid the letter aside and picked up his mother's jewelry box. It had once sat on her white vanity, beside her hairbrush, jar of cold cream, and packets of bobby pins. The memory came back like a piece of a jigsaw puzzle locking into place, linking to another.

The jewelry box gave rise to memories of things he had forgotten since he was a young boy: his mother sitting at her dressing table, the bottles of perfume she kept there but rarely used. He opened her jewelry box and found a simple garnet bracelet, the string of pearls she used to wear when she went shopping in Buford, a slim gold watch that he couldn't recall her ever wearing, and her gold wedding band.

Ezra held the ring in his hand and closed his eyes. He remembered that she would take it off whenever she painted or washed dishes, so she was forever misplacing it. His father would tease, "You lose that ring and I swear our vows are off, Trudy!" All three of them would drop what they were doing and retrace her steps until the ring was recovered.

Ezra clutched her ring and fought back tears, grateful for that piece of memory. After a time, he took the next bundle out of the box. It was his father's black leather wallet, worn shiny and brittle from the attic heat. Ezra opened the wallet and pulled out three one-dollar bills, an ACLU membership card, and a receipt from the Piggly Wiggly for $4.53. He also found his father's driver's license, yellow and faded.

Ezra squinted at it. Simpellion T. *Dillon* Magee? When Ezra had suggested the name Dillon for his son—with its unusual spelling—he had forgotten that it was his father's middle name. He'd thought he just liked the sound of it: Dillon Magee. It turns out he'd named his son after his father. This time his tears came like a waterfall. After a few moments of silent weeping, Ezra tucked the license back into his father's wallet.

Next, Ezra drew a rectangular picture frame out of the box. It held a black-and-white photo that may have been damaged by water, but Ezra could still make out a short, severe-looking young woman in a black dress. She was posed on a chair on the front porch of a house, surrounded by three young boys. Ezra recognized his father squatting in front. He looked just like Dillon. According to writing on the back of the frame, the oldest boy was Auggie and the youngest was Nate. So, this was Nate. Ezra stared at the picture for a moment, his eyes scrunched in concentration. In the middle was his daddy, Simpellion. The brothers all bore a close resemblance to one another. The woman was his grandmother, Maude Magee, whom everyone called Granmaude. Ezra studied her face. He'd known her when she was decades older, gray-haired and wrinkled. He remembered that she was kind and she had loved him. He laid the picture down gently.

The next layer of the box held books. There was a paperback on yoga, Mark Twain's *Letters from the Earth*, and Robert M. Pirsig's *Zen and the Art of Motorcycle Maintenance*. Inside the front covers, his dad had written, "Property of Simp Magee, Folly, Alabama."

He read the inscription again: Folly, Alabama. The name went through him like electric current. That was where he was from. That was his home.

The final book was a hardcover with a painting of a brilliant cardinal on the cover. *Wildlife in Its Habitat*. Ezra stared at it and remembered. The day it had come in the mail, his father had whooped and hollered, and his mother'd hugged the book to her chest while spinning in circles. Ezra flipped it open to the back flap. There was a photograph of his mother, smiling demurely, her hair done up in a wave.

Born in Oxford, Mississippi, the short bio read, *Trudy Magee studied art at Ole Miss. Her nature studies have been published widely in magazines and books.*

Ezra spent half an hour leafing through the book, looking at his mother's artwork. He marveled at the vivid colors and the lifelike precision of her craft. He suddenly recalled how he used to hunt for bird feathers and proudly bring them home to her. She could always identify the birds they came from.

Ezra thought of his own book on the American Civil War, published two years prior. He felt a rush of despair that his parents would never hold it in their hands. They would never know the man he'd become.

After all these years, Ezra was glad for the returning memories, but he felt cheated; cheated that he was forty years old before he ever felt the sorrow associated with losing his parents. For a moment he wished he had some belief system that placed them in a radiant heaven, forever beaming down at him. But he didn't believe it worked like that. His parents had been complex people with interesting lives who had walked on the earth, made love, and created his very existence. And then they had departed, and that was the end of them. Except for what remained in this box and in his sorry memory and genetic makeup. And in Dillon. That last thought, finally, was a comfort.

Ezra gazed at the meager artifacts of his parents' lives: small things they'd held, works made by their hands. He was grateful to Killian Cagle, whoever he was.

Ezra sighed and closed his eyes, thinking of this box languishing in the space between his bedroom ceiling and roof all these years, filled with answers, with treasures from his life before Childersburg.

༄

Hiram gave him a recriminating look as Ezra helped himself to a beer out of the fridge.

"It's just a beer," Ezra said.

"Uh huh," Hiram said, rolling his eyes. "Who do you think you're talking to, boy? You know how many times I tried to sell myself that lie?"

Ezra drank half of it down and belched. "I needed it."

"You opened the box."

"It was from Killian Cagle."

"Good ol' Killian," Hiram said with affection. "Simpellion's shadow, we called him. He'd be pretty old, if he's still alive."

"Tell me about Killian. Apparently he was close to my family," said Ezra.

Hiram nodded. "He was practically part of the family. He was your daddy's best friend and confidant. He must have been something like an uncle to you, because you seemed very fond of him. And he of you. He was a good fellow, the kind you want to be your friend." Hiram smiled and shook his head. "And I never saw him wearing anything but overalls."

"How old was he?" asked Ezra.

"Oh, about your daddy's age, I'd guess, maybe a little older."

"Say, Hiram, how old are you?" Ezra asked, the hint of a smile on his lips.

"Old enough to know better. And so are you." He nodded toward the second beer Ezra held in his hand.

CHAPTER 21

Ezra's first day back at school after his father's ruckus with O'Malley was the worst day of his life. His teachers, his classmates, and even the lunch ladies looked at him funny, backing away from him as if he were a leper. They didn't even tease him about the exorcism. It was as if they all believed he really was the devil's spawn.

"Sissy Namey, Sissy Namey, Sissy Namey," he whispered to himself thirty-three times after homeroom.

Delilah Carlisle pointed at him. "He's talking like a serpent," she told the others. The girls ran shrieking from him in the halls. Even Boyd and Floyd, who were a year ahead of him, made the sign of the cross with their index fingers when they walked past.

When the school day was finally over, Ezra made his way outside to the parking lot. "Ezra, over here!" his father shouted and waved from the car window. Ezra put his head down and rushed toward the car.

"Yer dad's a pussy," Dexter Blaxton said as Ezra hurried past him. "He shot at a priest, and he couldn't even hit him."

Simp only heard part of the comment. He thought Dexter was insulting Ezra, and he shot out of the car and towered over Dexter. "You little twerp!" Simp sneered. "Don't you ever talk like that to my boy again."

Dexter just smirked and said, "Yessir."

Ezra burned with shame the whole ride home. His father had made a fool of himself in front of Dexter Blaxton and the whole seventh grade. Simpellion Magee was the laughingstock of Folly, Alabama; Buford, Alabama; and all of Sand Mountain—with his fainting goats, his obsession with squirrels, his loud atheism, and his bombastic letters to the *Sentinel*. How could Ezra ever hope to have a happy childhood with a father who never let up being an oddball?

Ezra stayed in bed for the next three days. He couldn't face school or his father. He turned and stared at the wall whenever Simp came into his room to try to cheer him up. He didn't respond, even when his dad offered to teach him how to pitch a curve ball. Ezra couldn't even bear to sit at the dinner table with his father. The man chewed too loudly and talked with his mouth full. For the life of him, Ezra could not understand what his mother saw in this man.

On the day before Thanksgiving, and Ezra's fourth day in bed, Killian stopped by after supper. He and Simp sat out on the front porch chewing tobacco and talking about the upcoming Iron Bowl, which fell on the Saturday after Thanksgiving. Ezra cracked his window open to listen. The Iron Bowl was the last game of the regular football season for the Alabama Crimson Tide, and they always played their rivals, the Auburn Tigers, in that game. Ranked number two nationally, the University of Alabama was strutting toward a perfect season and a shot at the number-one ranking and a post-season bowl game. Coach Bear Bryant's houndstooth attire had become a nationally recognized symbol of the school's prowess on the gridiron. Ezra, who knew the names, hometowns, and statistics of every Crimson Tide player, was eager to hear what Killian thought of their chances.

"Maybe them commies have it right," Simp suddenly interjected just when Killian was getting started on the Tide's defense. "We act out these little wars on the football field and send our sons in there to get knocked around. Instead, we should send 'em over to Mexico and Canada and grab us up some more land. This football is just misdirected aggression."

Ezra nearly choked with rage. Leave it to his dad to be the one man in the whole South who was indifferent about football.

"So, does that mean you're not plannin' on watchin' the game?" Killian spat a wad of tobacco juice onto the lawn. Most of the time he was a smoker; today he was a chewer.

"Course I am," Simp said, spitting one of his own. "It's a family tradition. I'm just sayin', folks in Alabama seem to care more about football than they do about who runs our government. And that's the way the government likes it, dontcha see? Keeps their minds off o' important things like politics. You comin over to Ma's to watch it with the family, aintcha?" he asked Killian.

"Sure thing," Killian answered.

Ezra couldn't bear to listen anymore.

The next day, Ezra, his parents, and most of the extended family—Uncle Auggie and Aunt Peg and their six kids; Boyd and Floyd; Granmaude's brother, Homer; her sister-in-law, Eunice; their daughter, Sarah; and Sarah's husband, Gustavus—gathered at Granmaude's for the Thanksgiving feast. Boyd and Floyd's mom and dad couldn't come; they were both on assignment for a maintenance shutdown at a local industrial plant. Their dad was an electrician, and their mom was his helper, and when the union called, they had to go, even on Thanksgiving. As always, Killian had been invited and was in attendance.

The Iron Bowl was the general topic of conversation. Ezra was relieved that they weren't talking about the Father O'Malley incident. But when he walked into the kitchen after supper with a load of plates, he interrupted their gossip. "That Simpellion, up to his tricks again . . . coulda killed someone . . . so typical . . . always been crazy as a loon." Ezra could have died from embarrassment when Sarah noticed him and shushed the others. He turned red and fled to the back yard, where he threw rocks at the back fence until he heard his mother calling him for dessert.

"Alabama's first in football and last in just about everything else, like education, civil rights, and brains in the state legislature," Simpellion observed as Granmaude spooned out generous portions of banana pudding. The comment earned a loud protest and several oaths from the gallery. Granmaude stopped the arguments by threatening to withhold dessert.

Ezra's appetite was gone. Once again, his father was ruining everything. Boyd and Floyd gave each other knowing looks and whispered, "Your old man's a commie, atheist nutcase," in Ezra's ears. Then they hissed in his ear and called him serpent boy and made the sign of the cross when Granmaude wasn't looking. They even grabbed up his bowl of pudding before he was finished eating.

"I'll make a fresh batch of banana pudding for the game Saturday!" Granmaude promised as they took their leave after dinner. It was a tradition that the family gathered again at her house to watch the Iron Bowl and finish the Thanksgiving leftovers.

As soon as he was excused from the table, Ezra mumbled to his mom that he was walking home and, before she could answer, wiggled out of the crowded room and made his escape.

"Son! Hey, Ezra!" His father came to the door. "Hold on a sec and I'll go with you! I just have to find my jacket."

Ezra didn't wait. He took off at a trot for home.

There was no school on Friday, so Ezra slept late and then moped around his room until Trudy sent him out to restack the woodpile. He worked on it for an hour, but it was slow going. He was sleepy and irritable from the drugs. They were having more of an effect now. He didn't do nearly as much tapping as he had done, but he didn't feel right, either. His head throbbed where the stitches were healing. He lay down on his bed and pulled the blanket up. When his father started firing off the shotgun at a squirrel, Ezra covered his head with a pillow to muffle the blasts.

"Simp, run down to the Piggly Wiggly and pick up a few groceries, would you?" Trudy called outside. "Everyone finished the sweet potatoes, and I'll have to make more for the game."

His father stomped into the house and put his gun away.

"Ezra?" he called upstairs. "You wanna come along?" Ezra ignored him. "Ezra? You sleepin'?"

What an idiot, thought Ezra. *If I'm sleeping, then you're just waking me up!*

"Leave him be," he heard his mother say. "He'll be all right. Just give him time."

Simp snorted, but he took the list and stomped out to the Datsun. Ezra heard the front door creak open and then slam shut. But before the engine turned over, he heard a panicked scream: "Holy fuckin' Christ!"

Ezra ran to his window and saw his father tumble out of the car, clawing at his face. A squirrel bounded out, ran over Simpellion's foot, and shot away up into an oak tree.

"Goddamn squirrel! Somebody put a goddamn squirrel in my car!" Simp was screaming bloody murder. Ezra scanned the area and saw his cousins Boyd and Floyd sprinting over the rise toward Granmaude's house. A part of him was furious with them for terrorizing his father, and another part of Ezra felt angry with his father. Maybe Dexter was right—maybe his dad was a pussy: afraid of a little old squirrel. Ezra felt thoroughly disgusted.

At noon on Friday, Ezra went over to help Granmaude get ready for the Iron Bowl gathering the next day. Some of his relatives were there. He avoided the women cooking in the kitchen in case they started talking about him or his father. His Uncle Auggie waved to him from the living room, where he was rearranging furniture so everyone would be able to see the color television set. Ezra helped his uncle for a while, then slipped outside and wandered around back, where he found Granmaude picking up trash.

"The possums been knockin' over the trash can agin," she said, shaking her head.

"Here, I'll do that," Ezra offered.

She gave him a pat on the shoulder and went inside to supervise the preparations.

It might not have been possums. It might have been the wind, Ezra thought to himself as he chased a sandwich wrapper into the azaleas. The sky was dark gray and looked like it was getting ready to drop a big storm on them. As he reached for an empty Miller can in the bushes, he saw a ratty old baseball, which he retrieved.

"Here, LBJ!" he called a few times. Granmaude's old dog ambled over from where she'd been dozing beside the shed. Ezra was fascinated by how one dog could look a little like so many different breeds. LBJ had the nose of a hound, the hair of a lab, the ears of a spaniel, and paws that looked just like a German shepherd's. He threw the ball, and LBJ bounded after it and brought it right back to him. Ezra didn't even mind the slobber. He rubbed her ears and threw it again.

༼༽

A gray dawn greeted the hamlet of Folly on Saturday morning. It was overly warm for that time of year, but with the Iron Bowl just a few hours away, nobody seemed to notice. All the Magee clan and their assorted in-laws and cousins were at Granmaude's by lunch, chatting and eating in front of the television long before the game started. There was a thrill of excitement in the air.

Granmaude was a devoted fan of Coach Bear Bryant and his team, but she was always too agitated to sit during the games, so she'd stand in the doorway and leave the room when the score got too close, or some gridiron crisis occurred. Ezra always enjoyed Granmaude's running commentary during the game and her admonitions and excitement when the Crimson Tide scored.

Before the game started, Ezra headed into the kitchen to see if anyone had saved him a bowl of banana pudding.

Granmaude had. She let him eat it with the last of the whipped cream, and he enjoyed the grumbling of Floyd and Boyd as Granmaude told them off for skipping out on chores the day before.

When Ezra made his way back into the crowded living room, he realized one person was missing. "Where's Killian?" he asked his dad.

"Couldn't make it," Simp replied, his eyes glued to the television. "Trouble with his knee again. Said he can't walk."

Ezra waved to his mother, who was perched on the arm of a chair talking to her sister-in-law. She was wearing a robin's-egg blue blouse, and Ezra thought she was by far the prettiest woman in the room.

Uncle Auggie roared at everyone to be quiet; the pre-game show was on. They all cheered when Alabama's million-dollar marching band entered the field and cheered again when the Crimson Tide's cheerleading squad made a human pyramid.

But then the show cut to a special weather report, and his relatives started gabbing again. Ezra wriggled closer to the television to look at the meteorologist's map. There was a large mass of warm, moist air moving up from the Gulf of Mexico on a collision course with a cold, dry air mass moving down from Canada. "Storm warnings are in effect for most areas of North Alabama," the meteorologist reported.

"It'd better not interfere with the game!" Uncle Auggie yelled, and everyone cheered as the football stadium once again appeared on the screen and the players ran out on the field to the wild frenzy of their fans.

For Alabama fans, it was an exciting game, since the Crimson Tide were leading the first half. Ezra was barely aware of the wind picking up outside. It was too loud in the living room to hear the raucous ringing of Granmaude's wind chimes in the blowing gale.

During halftime, the women got up to serve second plates of turkey and potatoes. Ezra, Boyd, and Floyd went out to the front yard and watched the wind strip the last leaves from the trees. Ezra took the old baseball he'd found the day before out of his pocket and threw it as hard as he could into the yard. LBJ bounded after it, and when she brought it back, Boyd and the Floyd wanted a turn.

"You boys come in here!" someone yelled out the door at them. "There's a tornado comin'."

The boys grinned at each other with delight. They had never seen a tornado, although there were tornado watches every year.

Granmaude stood in the doorway with her hands on her hips. "Boys! Your mother told you to git inside!" she scolded. "They're talkin' about flash floods and tornadoes headed this way, so y'all keep safe inside."

Simp walked out into the front yard next to Ezra, right past his mother and her warnings. He shook his fist and yelled up at the sky, "Go on! Give us yer worst! We can take it!"

Boyd and Floyd waved their fists in imitation, which cracked both of them up. Ezra was mortified, but Simp just laughed and pulled him inside.

Ezra was torn between watching the sky through the windows and watching the game. He couldn't help but stare at the ominous, roiling bank of black clouds moving in from the west.

"For Alabamians, every month is tornado appreciation month," his father said, appearing at his side again.

Ezra ignored him.

"What say we make a bet on this here storm?" his father tried again. "I'll give you ten-to-one odds it don't even rain a drop on us."

Ezra gritted his teeth and looked away.

"Alrighty then, twenty-to-one odds on a tornado taking out the Piggly Wiggly. Come on, that's easy money." His father was trying too hard. It was pitiful. Ezra pushed through his relatives to find a seat on the floor, away from Simp.

The game had settled into a defensive battle, and the fans were getting restless. Granmaude's phone rang.

"Thank you, Wade. Come on over," she said into the receiver.

"I just remembered," Simp bellowed, loud enough to get everyone's attention. "I've got to call Killian. Gimme the phone, Mama! I'm worried about my yacht!" Ezra flinched. Simp had left his canoe at Killian's. "Cap'n Killian, tie the yacht up real good, we got a squall comin' in!" Simp yelled into the phone without dialing. His uncles, aunts, and cousins all guffawed, and Ezra blushed with shame as his father preened at the attention.

A few minutes into the third quarter, hail started to beat down on the roof. It wasn't even five p.m., but it was as dark as night outside. The wind blew the kitchen door open, and Trudy went out to secure the latch. Flashes of lightning were visible to the west, and the game was interrupted again by the weatherman saying that a tornado had touched down on the Alabama-Mississippi border and was headed east toward Folly.

An atmosphere of eerie quiet descended on the congregation. The men got up and checked the windows upstairs. After some argument, Uncle Auggie went outside and shut off the gas line.

"Simp, should we go home and wait this out?" Trudy asked, worried.

"Don't you worry, Trudy," Uncle Auggie said, grinning. "God knows not to bother an Alabama man when his team is playing."

Ezra pressed his nose to the glass pane of the front door and looked outside. The sky was pickle-green with dark clouds scurrying across the firmament as if in some kind of hellish race.

"Jesus Christ," Simp uttered as hailstones large enough to dent metal fell on the house. Ezra wished he'd stop taking the Lord's name in vain. In a situation like this, it couldn't help.

"Granmaude, is the storm shelter still stocked with candles and blankets?" Aunt Liza asked, her voice shaking just a bit.

"It was, last I checked," Granmaude replied. Ezra shot a guilty look at his cousins. The three of them knew for a fact that there were no candles down there; they'd burned them all up last summer.

A car came puttering into the driveway, and Simp and Uncle Auggie ran out to help Homer and Eunice into the house.

"We hope you got room for us in your shelter, Maude," Eunice said, huffing up the porch steps.

Ezra wrestled LBJ off of Uncle Homer. "Ezra, put the dog in the kitchen," his mother said.

Instead of the kitchen, which was a dangerous place to leave a turkey-eating hound like LBJ, Ezra took her upstairs. "Be good and I'll come get you soon," he promised, then raced back downstairs to see what he'd missed.

The game was still on, but all the women had moved into the kitchen to listen to storm reports on the radio. Even the men displayed only a half-hearted interest in the game. The Tigers had pulled ahead, and things didn't look good for the Tide anyway.

"Heavy rain and flash floods pose a serious risk, so stay off the roads, y'all," said the announcer. "Locate your flashlights, candles, matches, and extra batteries, and don't forget your radios." The aunts started making sandwiches even though no one was hungry. Ezra suspected they just needed something to do. He knew he felt that way.

A sheriff's cruiser pulled into Granmaude's driveway, and Sheriff's Deputy Wade Cahela dashed up to the front porch. The hail crashing onto the metal roof sounded like gunshots.

"You folks get ready to move to your storm shelter," he said, shaking off the rain in the front hallway. "Phone lines are down. There's a tornado on the ground southwest of Riley and heading in your direction."

Moses Magee had built the shelter in an embankment behind the house decades earlier, after a particularly destructive tornado had touched down near Folly. It was constructed of cement blocks with large poles laid across the top. A mound of dirt had been piled on top of the poles for a roof. Crude seats had been built of cement blocks and wooden planks. Periodically, the uncles repaired the roof and removed nests of critters.

Everyone suddenly became aware of the eerie silence: the wind had hushed, and the rain and hail had stopped.

"Son?" Granmaude addressed herself to Auggie, her eldest.

"Should we go to the shelter now?"

"We won't all fit," Ezra heard himself pipe up. He tried not to look at Great Aunt Eunice when he said it.

"How about the culvert?" Great Uncle Homer suggested.

"That ought to shelter us from the tornado, but what about flash floods?" Simp said, frowning.

"Cahill Creek?" Uncle Auggie's booming laugh was echoed by others. "That ol' puddle? Simp, grow yourself a pair. That little piss stream is about as likely to flood as my can of beer!"

Ezra couldn't agree more. His father was a pussy. He was scared of a little creek. He was scared of squirrels.

They wrapped themselves in coats and blankets and carried flashlights and candles. The uncles formed a chain and helped everyone through the dark. Howling winds lashed them as they made their way to the culvert. Lightning flashes stabbed through the sky like a crazed strobe light gone mad, and the cacophony of roaring thunder made it impossible to talk. They crossed the road and went down into the culvert, which was sheltered from the rain and hail, but was already swirling ankle-deep in cold water.

"Just until the tornado danger passes," Uncle Homer shouted to his wife when she complained about standing in the cold water.

Trudy grabbed Ezra's hand and held on tightly. Simp held her other hand. Ezra held onto LBJ's collar.

In the culvert, the family huddled in the dark and waited. Ezra was shivering from the cold air whistling like a roaring jet engine through the culvert, but he wasn't scared. It was exciting to have an adventure in the storm, like in one of his books. He could hear the waters of Cahill Creek rushing downstream a few yards away.

Just then a bolt of lightning lit up the sky, followed immediately by the deafening roar of thunder. "I'll not stay here a minute longer," Granmaude declared. "Lightning will kill us all with our feet in the water," and she marched out of the culvert back into the roaring storm toward the house.

A few minutes later, they were all standing in her living room, soaked to the skin. LBJ's wet-dog smell contributed much to the ambience, and Ezra tried to muffle it with a blanket.

The electricity was out, but candles cast a warm glow and giant shadows around the room. Ezra stood as close to the windows as his mother would allow so he could watch the brilliant and stunning display of lightning strikes. Eunice's voice pierced the gloom as she began wailing a prayer to Lord Jesus to save them all. Homer joined in, and soon the room reverberated with a chorus of prayerful supplications. A loud clap of thunder made Aunt Eunice shriek, causing Uncle Homer to instinctively fan her as if they she had been overcome by the Holy Spirit.

"We're all gonna die!" a raspy voice (that was either Boyd or Floyd fooling around) whispered from a darkened corner.

"Are Homer's prayers not getting through?" Simp asked sarcastically.

"Don't start, Simpellion," Trudy scolded.

Another grumbled, "Thinks he's so smart, Mr. Atheist. Let's see how he feels when the lightning strikes his car and no one else's!"

Several of them laughed. "Y'all hush up," Granmaude's voice broke through harshly. "Now's not the time."

Ezra gritted his teeth in frustration. Why was his father so rude? Everyone thought he was a fool—even his own family. Ezra was ashamed to be related to Simpellion Magee. He imagined what it would be like to have a normal father who was respected.

Simp found Ezra and Trudy and put his arms around them. Ezra squirmed away.

Cousin Doyle was moving through the living room when he tripped over a foot and fell into Simp.

"Jesus fucking Christ!" Simp bellowed.

"Watch your mouth!" Aunt Eunice replied.

"I will say whatever I goddamn well please!" Simp yelled at

everyone in the room. "If you believe in God so much, then why are you sittin' here scared to death and worryin' about a goddamn tornado!?"

"Simpellion!" Granmaude's voice cracked as sharp as a lightning bolt. "I will not have you speak that way in my house!"

"Fine! If that's the way you feel, we're leavin'! Trudy, Ezra, let's go."

"I hate you!"

The scream leapt out of Ezra's mouth as the next shock of lightning lit up the room.

"Ezra!" Trudy's voice was cut off by a clap of thunder.

"I hate him!" Ezra said again, though not so loudly, as he wrestled the door open and ran out into the storm. LBJ, in a panic from the loud thunder, dashed outside with him.

For a moment, even in the dark and rain and wind, it was a relief to get away from everyone—especially his father—and to run. Lighting flashed so constantly that he could see his way toward home. Adrenaline carried him halfway up the steep hill that lay between his house and his grandmother's. He paused at the top of the hill to catch his breath, and just then a bolt of lightning struck the giant oak near him. Ezra was deafened by the blast. He threw himself on the ground and trembled. Rain pelted his back and the wind roared around him. His relief had quickly turned to regret and fear. What was he doing out here? Fingers of panic rose up his spine as he realized what a stupid mistake he'd made.

He thought he heard his mother scream and lifted his head to look for her. She was standing on Granmaude's porch, illuminated only by flashes of lightning, her arm wrapped around a post and the other waving at him to come back. He saw his father step out onto the porch next to her, wrapping one arm around Trudy and cupping his mouth to shout with the other.

But it wasn't the sight of his parents that grabbed his attention. It was the wall of water in the distance, roaring down Cahill Creek, charging toward the back of Granmaude's house. Ezra gasped in horror. It was his nightmare come true, only the wave wasn't coming for him; it was headed for Grandmaude's house and everyone he loved.

There was no time to warn anyone; no time to save them. And yet it all seemed to happen in slow motion. Ezra stared at the bright blue speck of his mother on the front porch, and his father with an arm around her as they were calling out to him through the storm.

"Run!" he shrieked. "Get outta there! Run!" The wind tore the words from his throat and scattered them uselessly as the massive wave reached the house. Trunks of trees, pieces of lumber, a mattress, and what looked like the flailing body of a horse tumbled in and out of the crest. Then the wave crashed over Granmaude's house and shattered it as easily as if it had been made of cardboard. Everything was pulled under the roiling mass of water and debris. The shed, the cars, the apple and peach trees—they all vanished under the raging waves in seconds that felt like an agonizing eternity for Ezra, who stood atop the hill and bore witness.

He saw Cahill Creek fill the plain and submerge the little village of Folly like it was no more than an inconvenience. Ezra's mind couldn't fully comprehend what he was seeing. He gaped at the new landscape. There was a lake where his hometown had been just a minute ago. The Namey store, Uncle Auggie's house, everything—gone.

The water slowed as it digested Folly. The rain kept pelting down, or maybe it was hail. Ezra didn't feel anything. He was numb. Thunder boomed like a giant kettle drum in his ears, and he trembled, not knowing where to go. The wave was still coming, picking up steam again, sliding up the hill toward him, its foaming waves racing toward him like evil hands reaching out for another victim.

He was twelve years old. He didn't want to die. Ezra Magee turned and ran down the road toward his home, ahead of the wave, not daring to look back.

CHAPTER 22

Ezra regretted the beer, but not until the following morning. He felt like an idiot for falling off the wagon when he'd barely gotten on board.

And somehow, he'd ended up sleeping in Dillon's bed. It was too small for him, and his legs had hung over the end. Soon it would be too small for Dillon. Ezra pulled the blue comforter over his head and sighed, wondering if he could just hide there until his life sorted itself out.

"You can run, but you cannot hide!" Hiram Johnson stood at the foot of the bed.

"Go away," Ezra muttered. It took him a few minutes to get up, and by the time he did, Hiram had disappeared.

Ezra forced himself to shower, shave, and dress. He stripped the sheets from the beds and started a load of laundry. He methodically went through the downstairs rooms with a garbage bag, filling it with empty doughnut boxes, beer cans, bourbon bottles, pizza boxes, and cigarette butts. His home smelled like a frat house. Ezra opened all the windows and doors to air the place out. He took out the trash, then gassed up the mower and cut the grass. He even trimmed the edges of the lawn. Celia's flowers were all dead. He pulled them up and made a list of what he needed to replace.

By the afternoon, he was exhausted. He realized he hadn't eaten anything, so he went inside to scrounge for what little there was: macaroni and cheese, wilted celery, and half a jar of green olives. It tasted terrible on one plate together, but it was the first time he'd sat down and eaten a complete meal in days. He eyed the six-pack of beer in the fridge. He thought about pouring each can down the drain, but he couldn't bring himself to do it.

"Later," he told himself, feeling weak.

"Toss 'em now." Hiram was waiting for Ezra on the porch. "You drink 'em later, you'll hate yourself."

Ezra shot him a dirty look and sat down on the rocker. When he woke up four hours later, the sky was dark. Hiram was watching the trees, rocking silently in his chair. At the moment, Ezra was glad for the company.

"So, now what?" the preacher asked.

"I'm going to call Killian."

He went into the kitchen to find the phone, and on the way back out to the porch he grabbed a beer and drank it down. Liquid courage.

"You coulda done without it," Hiram said matter-of-factly.

Ezra's mouth tightened, but he didn't respond. He punched in the phone number and waited. He heard a computer message announce that it was no longer a working number. Ezra called information for Huntsville, Alabama and the surrounding area and asked for anyone by the name of Cagle.

Nothing came up.

"Well, thirty years or so is a long time," said Hiram as Ezra replaced the telephone. "Killian may well be in the arms of our Maker by now."

That was what Ezra was afraid of. Killian was his last connection to the past he'd mostly forgotten. What if he was dead?

The memory of bourbon beckoned him. Ezra needed a distraction. He knew the grocery store would be open for another hour. As he searched for his car keys, he passed the refrigerator, and a second beer somehow found its way into his hands. He went to open it and then stopped himself and put it back. The last thing he needed was a DUI.

"I'll be back," he called out as he left the house. There was no reply. Where, he wondered, had Hiram wandered off to?

He was sitting in the back seat of the car, waiting for Ezra.

"Don't you want to ride shotgun?" he asked the old man. Hiram didn't answer, just folded his arms and stared out the window. "I don't need a damn chaperone," Ezra muttered.

The preacher stayed in the car while Ezra shopped. He wandered slowly through the aisles, filling a cart with eggs, bread, milk, apples, coffee, a bag of peanuts, a half-gallon of ice cream, and a pile of frozen dinners. He stopped in the liquor store for a bottle of bourbon and hid it at the bottom of a grocery bag.

By midnight, he was plastered.

"I see the devil has you in his grip," Johnson said, appearing in the den where Ezra was watching Letterman.

"Fuck you, and fuck your devil, Hiram." He closed his eyes. When he opened them again, he was alone.

Ezra stumbled upstairs and managed to make it to the bathroom before he threw up his supper. He splashed water on his face and rinsed out his mouth. The face that stared back at him in the mirror was a mask of defeat.

"Goddamn you, Celia!" he whispered. Hot tears burned his eyes.

"You think you got any lower to go before you hit bottom, Ezra?" Hiram leaned against the bathroom doorframe.

"Why won't you go away?!" Ezra flung a can of shaving cream at him. It hit the door. "I don't need you here!"

"You sure that's what you want?"

"Yes, goddammit!" Ezra shouted.

When he looked again, Hiram was gone. Ezra placed his hands on either side of the mirror and banged his head against it, hard.

☙

It took all the willpower he had to stay sober for a week. The morning after Hiram left, (he'd looked everywhere for the old man, meaning to apologize for his outburst) Ezra had ruthlessly poured all the alcohol in the house down the drain. As an afterthought, he'd thrown away his cigarettes, too. He walked from room to room in his empty house and wrote up a long list of things that needed fixing. He needed distraction. He needed purpose.

At the hardware store, he bought paint, paintbrushes, sandpaper, plastic tarps, and a scraper. On the way home, he broke into a sweat as he drove past the convenience store. Instead, he pulled into a fast-food drive-through and got himself a burger and a cola. He had no appetite, but he made himself eat.

He spent the afternoon prepping Dillon's room for a new coat of paint. He spread tarps, moved furniture, and wiped down the walls. He spackled cracks and old nail holes. While it dried, he put on his running clothes.

The first quarter mile was hell. He was winded and his legs felt like lead. At the one-mile mark—a weeping willow by the river—he had to stop to work out a stitch in his side. He decided to walk along the river path while he caught his breath.

It was a Saturday, and families were picnicking on the grass. A teenage girl played Frisbee with her friend while her yellow dog ran between them, attempting to catch the disk. The sight of happy people doing happy things made him feel funny inside. Had he ever really been like them? Or had it all been a façade? Who was Ezra Magee? What kind of person could forget his past as thoroughly as he had done? Why had he not shown the least curiosity about his own parents?

He stopped in his tracks. This was what Celia had been saying to him all along, and she was right. She was absolutely right. He'd been playing the game of life without having all the pieces. He was a screwed up human being, no doubt about it.

He turned up a path that led to the main avenue of his town. It would take him past the convenience store. He carried a credit card in his pocket.

"A few beers. You're not an alcoholic. You can handle it." The little voice in his head sounded so reasonable.

Just then, he heard a horn honk. Ezra turned to see Dillon's friend, Wiley, leaning out of a car window. "Hey, Mister Magee! When's Dillon coming back?"

Ezra waved to Wiley and his parents and called out, "Soon!"

They drove off, and Ezra turned away from the convenience store. He ran the mile back home.

※

After he'd experienced sobriety for two weeks, Ezra called Celia at her mother's house. Gretchen told him Celia didn't want to speak to him.

"I understand," Ezra said. "Please tell her I've been sober for two weeks, and I intend to stay that way."

There was a long silence while his mother-in-law covered the receiver and conveyed the information. Then, "If you can stay sober for a month, I think she'll talk to you, but not a day sooner. You really screwed up, Ezra."

"I know, Gretchen. And I'm sorry—I really am. Please tell Dillon I love him and miss him, and I'll see him soon." Ezra fought back tears. "Tell Celia . . . tell her I'll talk to her in two weeks."

He hung up before he lost it.

Three days later, he found a letter in the mailbox from Celia. "I am coming by the house on Tuesday at three p.m. to pick up some of our things. Please don't be there. I'm just not ready to see you."

Ezra called Gretchen. "Tell Celia I got her note and I understand. She doesn't have to worry. I won't be here."

"That's the right thing to do, Ezra," she said, thawing a little. "You still sober?"

"Yes, ma'am. And I quit smoking."

"Well, that's something."

☙

He spent Monday planting new flowers in Celia's flower beds. He gave the lawn another trim. The whole inside of the house had been freshly painted, and he'd rented a steam cleaner from the hardware store to do the carpets and upholstery. He hoped the stale cigarette odor was masked by the paint smell.

In case she was checking up on him, he stocked the refrigerator with vegetables, fruit, and yogurt, and he put a vase of flowers on the kitchen table. He also left a few wrapped presents for Dillon on the table, including an Xbox game, two science-fiction books, and the box of comic books he'd found at Lenore's. He tried to write a note to Celia, but nothing came out right, so he left the flowers and gifts to speak for themselves.

At two p.m., he drove to his office on campus and spent the afternoon cleaning out old files and checking over his class notes for the next semester. It made him feel substantial to be in his office, to see the spines of the books he'd written, to turn on his computer and read the usual summer memos about policy and meeting schedules.

He returned home at six p.m. The presents were gone. So were Dillon's summer clothes, his bicycle, and his skateboard. Izzy's food bowls and kibble were gone too. Ezra didn't have the heart to see what Celia had taken from her closet. He lay down on the clean carpet, closed his eyes, and pictured his wife slowly dismantling their lives, one hanger at a time.

A week later—three weeks and two days sober—he returned from a four-mile run and heard the phone ringing. His hopes soared as he sprinted into the kitchen.

"Hello!"

"Ezra? It's Lenore."

"Oh. Hi, Aunt Lenore. I'm sorry I've been out of touch."

"I talked to Celia. I know what's going on." She sounded hurt. "Why didn't you tell me?"

"Because I'm a fool."

Lenore laughed. "Well, I'm glad we settled that!"

Ezra laughed weakly. His aunt was a wonder. If he ever confessed to being a mass murderer, she would find a way to forgive him.

"How have you been?" Ezra asked, ashamed that he hadn't called since his visit.

"I'm taking a tango class at the rec center. And I'm thinking about signing up for a cruise next spring."

They chatted until Ezra had built up the courage to ask, "So, what did Celia have to say?"

Lenore was quiet for a moment. "She said a lot. You have a lot to answer for, son."

He could barely breathe. "Is she—will she give me another chance, do you think?"

"Depends," Lenore said.

"I'll do anything."

"I know you will, Ezra. I believe in you."

The kindness of her words overwhelmed him. He could feel the tears coming. *Jesus*, he thought, *I'm turning into a goddamn crybaby.*

"I don't believe in me, Lenore. Celia deserves better. And Dillon. What kind of a father am I?"

Lenore didn't jump in with words. She just listened, a solid, steady presence of love on the other end as Ezra poured it all out, item by item, until he felt drained and empty.

"When Dillon started having trouble with OCD, I could have gotten him help, but I was a damned coward. I didn't want to tell Celia about my own problems with it. I didn't give her credit for being the person I know she is. I should have told her before were married. I was a coward. I made my son suffer. I made my wife suffer. I made their lives miserable while I became a stupid drunk.

What kind of stupid idiot does that to his family?" His voice broke, and he stopped.

His aunt sighed. "Honey, you and I know Celia is a stubborn woman, but she loved you once, and I believe she still does. But you can't hide from the past anymore. You know what I mean."

He did. "I've got to go back, don't I?"

She didn't answer the question. She just told him she loved him and that she'd call him again in a few days.

It had been a while since Ezra had been up in the Piper Cherokee 140 that he rented at Jake's Airfield, a small airport not far from his home. Until recently, he'd flown a few hours each month to keep his pilot's skills up-to-date and his license current.

"I don't know what possessed Lenore to give you flying lessons for your seventeenth birthday," Celia once complained. His wife was fearful of flying and had refused most invitations to go up with him.

Celia'd had a good point. How could someone with an anxiety problem fly an airplane? Flying required concentration and a steady hand. Yet, instead of adding to his anxiety, there was something about flying that had produced a calming effect in Ezra.

He remembered his first airplane ride at an event at the local airport where he had gone with Lenore. "Plane Rides - $10," a sign announced, and Ezra had begged his aunt to let him take an airplane ride.

"Are you sure?" she asked, her face troubled by thoughts of her sixteen-year-old nephew riding in an aircraft with his problems (even if he was doing well at the time).

Ezra was completely sure, and the look on his face showed it. Lenore paid the pilot.

When they returned from the flight, both the pilot and Ezra had big smiles on their faces.

"You got a natural born pilot," the man told Lenore. "I let the boy fly the plane for a little bit, and he was as steady as a rock."

Ezra knew the pilot's comment wasn't completely honest, because he'd done a few bobbles when he'd first taken the yoke, but he'd straightened it out and the aircraft had flown smoothly until the pilot took over again. It had been the most gratifying thing he could remember doing in years. And he hadn't been frightened. Just the opposite. When the pilot went through his takeoff and landing checklists, Ezra had found the ritualized structure soothing.

When Lenore bought him flying lessons at seventeen, Ezra took to it like a fish to water.

She told him later it had been an act of faith buying all ten lessons at once. "You might've hated it." They both knew she meant he might have had a panic attack and refused to go. But for Ezra, flying was pure pleasure. Lifting off the ground and soaring through the air gave him a feeling of release, of freedom from the demons that pursued him. He earned his private pilot's license when he was nineteen. Over the years, he'd accumulated more than a thousand hours in his pilot's log.

"When I'm up there, it's another world," he'd explained to Celia when they first started dating. "It's hard to explain, but I feel calm and focused, like when I'm doing a crossword puzzle." It was the way he felt the fifth mile into a good run, only more so. The wide horizon, the sense of endless possibility—in those moments, Ezra came close to understanding religion. He felt a part of the larger flow of life.

The day after his talk with Lenore, Ezra drove out to Jake's to see about renting the Piper.

"I'm planning a trip down to Alabama next Thursday," Ezra told Jake Jr., who had taken over the business from his father.

"Down to Dixie," Jake said with a grin.

"Yep! The heart o' Dixie," Ezra twanged back.

"How long you need it?"

"Not more than a week. I don't know for sure."

It was the last of June, and it was hot, and the Thursday morning on which he had chosen to begin his journey dawned overcast and muggy. The FAA weather service predicted possible rain along his route. Without an instrument rating, Ezra thought he might have to abandon his plans. But by the time he arrived at the airfield, breaks had appeared in the clouds, and a new forecast promised only scattered cloud cover. Ezra had a few changes of clothes in a duffel bag. His flight bag contained sectional maps and a radio headset.

"Not a bad day to fly," Jake Jr. observed as Ezra went through his aircraft inspection checklist of the Cherokee.

"Looks that way," Ezra agreed.

Everything checked out fine. Ezra went in to use the men's room one last time and, on his way back, glanced past the fuel pumps and stopped short. Was that Hiram Johnson? Ezra hadn't seen him for nearly a month. But then the man turned, and Ezra saw it was only Jake Sr. Like Hiram, Jake Sr. was almost bald. They gave each other a wave. Ezra finished his pre-flight check, tipped his cap to Jake Jr., and climbed into the aircraft.

He taxied out and prepared for takeoff. After checking the gauges and announcing his intentions on the airport frequency, he pulled onto the runway, eased the throttle forward, and felt the little aircraft shudder and gradually pick up speed. Rotating at sixty miles per hour, the tires lifted slowly off the runway, and Ezra experienced the pleasant rush that came whenever he left the ground. He wondered if birds experienced the same joy when they felt the wind beneath their wings.

With the drone of the engine penetrating the buffer of his headset, Ezra checked the communication frequencies and scanned his gauges. Damn, it felt good to be flying! For the next few hours, he kept busy communicating with air traffic controllers for flight following, checking VOR frequencies, and watching out the windows for other aircraft.

He stopped to refuel at a little airport in London, Kentucky, and stretched his legs. He ate a surprisingly good turkey sandwich from the airport cafeteria, then he was back in the air, and it wasn't long before he was crossing over the invisible state line into Alabama. Over the nose of the aircraft, Ezra saw the checkerboard pattern of farmland carved out of the sea-green forests. He pushed the control yoke forward to drop the nose slightly and get a better look at the countryside. Sweet home, Alabama. He had little feeling of allegiance to the place of his birth, but he hummed the song as he flew.

When the distance indicator showed he was thirty miles from Clayton Airport, Ezra scrutinized the countryside below. Most of the hardwoods had been cut down and replaced with the ubiquitous green of pines, planted by the owners of paper mills who owned large sections of the state. But from the sky he could see a scattering of the older growth, native trees missed by loggers. They broke up the tedious lines of evergreens.

As he took in the scenery, Ezra was suddenly glad he'd come. He'd look for Killian Cagle, visit his parents' graves, and put some of his ghosts to rest. Then he'd go home and make it right with Celia. He'd been sober for nearly a month, and he hadn't had a cigarette in all that time either. He was back on track.

The serpentine channel of Cahill Creek eased into view off the port wing. Cahill Creek provided baptismal waters for exotic congregations of Christians who lived in the area. Ezra suddenly remembered a boy in Buford bragging that the water moccasins didn't dare bite Christians because the preacher could kill them on the spot with the word of God. Sweet home, Alabama: buckle of the Bible Belt.

He followed the coil of the stream as it flowed toward the distant Tennessee River, and found the road running parallel. He banked left and looked down at his native soil.

"This has to be it," he decided, looking down at the remnants of what had once been Folly, Alabama. He didn't recognize it, but he knew it was south of Buford, on Cahill Creek, thirty miles from Clayton Airport. Ezra suddenly recalled his mother laughingly saying that Folly "languished in the eddy of progress."

He looked down on the skeletons of houses, the rusting hulks of pick-up trucks and overgrown fields smothered by the ubiquitous kudzu vines. Ezra's throat tightened, sadness choking him at the sight of his home. He nosed the small plane back up into the sky. His fuel gauges were running low, so he turned back toward Clayton. Before Folly was out of his sights, he glanced down one last time. There, in the corner of a pasture, stood a small black goat.

"Mabel?" Ezra said, astonished that he remembered.

CHAPTER 23

The squirrel-shaped clock on the wall said it was nine p.m., but the old man was certain it was running slow. He'd watched the second hand make its lazy circuits for the last hour. You couldn't tell him it wasn't slowing down just for spite. The clock knew he was waiting for closing time so he could go home and put his feet up. Clocks and men—surely, the two had never had an easy association. A man wearing a watch was under the illusion that he was master of time, but that was bullshit. The watch owned *him*. *Tick tock*—it was waiting—*tick tock*—to finish him off.

"Daddy, you're scowling."

Josie came by with a rag to wipe down the counter where sweating beer bottles had left rings of moisture on the dark varnished wood. He looked at his daughter. Josie was the bright light of his existence. Just last week she'd thrown him a birthday bash. He hadn't been expecting it. Who makes a big deal outta turning seventy-eight? Josie, that's who.

"Seventy-eight's a wonderful age, and a lucky one at that," she'd told him. She read her horoscope every day, but other than that she was a down-to-earth child. (*Woman*, he corrected himself. She was twenty-seven years old already. It was hard to reckon. Time had its way with everything.) Josie had tried to throw him a big party when he reached his seventy-seventh year, but he'd been in the hospital on that day, and the doc wouldn't let her bring a crowd into his room. So, she had saved it all up for the next year.

She'd planned the surprise so well he hadn't suspected a thing. Near the end of his birthday, he thought he'd gotten by without anyone noticing. But when the noisy cheers erupted from the back room, and the balloons fell from a bag on the ceiling above the bar, he'd laughed in surprise. For one thing, how did he know so many people? He'd always been a solitary sort. But there were his regulars, his neighbors, friends, and a few ex-boyfriends of Josie's. He smiled at the memory.

Josie was his only child, and he was happy that she'd consented to take over the business after college. It was a special pride he felt that he could leave her something tangible, something that would shelter and feed her and see to her future. Fatherhood had been the singularly most rewarding and bewildering experience of his life, and he was grateful Josie had turned out so well, despite his blunders.

He didn't tell her—and never would—that he had started to prepare for what came next. He knew she wouldn't understand, not until she was in her old age. This was not something the young needed to know. Young people could talk about it, write songs about it, but death was only an intellectual exercise for them while they ran around in their healthy bodies. He'd seen the picture of his rotted-out lungs at the doctor's office—the result of many years of faithfulness to unfiltered Camels. He'd felt the shadow of his own death hovering about. It was waiting for him to let go and move on.

Dying was a complicated business. No one really knew much about it. It would have been nice to have a friend his age to talk about it with. The thought made him wistful.

"Last call!"

Josie's shout caused some good-natured groans from the regulars. The old man was fond of the denizens who frequented his bar and felt sorry for them in equal measure. Many of them had no one waiting for them at home; some of them did and they were wasting their lives sitting in his bar, cracking stale jokes and making up lies. Josie had already called a cab for Elmer Hood, and now she closed out tabs and poured the last drafts and shots of the night. When the horn outside tooted, Elmer eased off his stool, touched his head in salute, and tottered toward the door. His blood-alcohol level would peg the meter, but Elmer never forgot his manners.

"Good evenin', y'all," he called out.

As soon as the door closed behind Elmer, it was suddenly thrust open again by a somewhat disheveled man who made a beeline for the bar and ordered a bourbon straight up. Josie poured the drink and told him the bar was closing in fifteen minutes.

"Better set me up with another, then," the fellow said, although he hadn't yet touched the first one. Josie poured another and watched the man look around the bar. His eyes seemed to take in every detail: the bottles lined up against the mirror behind the bar, the pool tables in the corner, the green vinyl booths and dark wood tables. She saw his eyes widen when he took in the clock, and she smiled.

Josie gave him a curious look as she set the second shot of bourbon next to the first. "Your first time here?" she asked.

"Actually," he said, "I'm not sure."

He looked at her intently, as if trying to recognize her. What he saw was thick, dark hair, almond-shaped eyes that were startlingly blue, and a half-smile that reminded him of someone. But no, he was sure he'd never seen her before. She had to be at least fifteen years his junior, so they never would have met.

"Are you the owner of this bar?"

"I am," she replied.

"Are you the one who came up with the name for this place?"

"No," she said. "That's my father's doing."

"Where can I find him?"

"Right here." The old man eased out of his chair and hobbled up to the bar. The two men stared at each other.

"Do I know you?" The younger man's voice was strained.

"I reckon you should. I named the bar after your daddy." Killian Cagle offered Ezra his hand. "It's good to finally see you again, boy. You look just like him."

☙

Ezra and Killian stared at each other for a while, too full of emotion to speak. Ezra's shots of bourbon sat untouched in front of him. He'd found Killian Cagle in Buford, Alabama, in a bar named Simp Magee's.

Killian Cagle. As soon as Ezra shook his hand, he saw an image of the Killian he'd known as a kid. Ezra was somewhat disappointed to find the man wearing jeans instead of overalls. He'd gotten old, and he'd shrunk some. His gray pallor and wheezing breath were stark reminders to Ezra of the sheer number of years that had gone by since the last time he'd seen him. Ezra was overwhelmed. He felt twelve years old all over again. Everyone he knew and loved from childhood was gone—except Killian. Regret and sadness flooded Ezra's body, his hands trembling as he tried to steady his breath. He pushed the whiskey away and reached over and clasped the old man's arm, just to be sure he was real.

Killian's eyes shined, and he covered Ezra's hand with his own. "It's good to see you, Ezra," he said finally, with a slight tremor in his voice. "It's been a long time." The two of them stood like this for a moment, letting the silence say all that needed to be said.

The booming chimes of a clock reverberating outside broke the silence and marked the hour at eleven p.m. The men let go of each other and sat down at the bar together. "That's Buford's very own 'Big Bill,'" Killian said, nodding his head in the direction of the chiming clock outside. Ezra loved to hear him talk. The soft lilt of Killian's Alabama accent was the closest he'd felt to home in decades. Tears came to Ezra's eyes, and his heart pounded so loudly that he could barely hear the story Killian was telling him.

"Years back, the mayor—everybody called him Big Bill—he just had to have the clock. Put it up right over Buford City Hall, and it disturbed the hell out of everybody. It's way too loud for this little town." Killian smiled and shook his head. "But Big Bill wouldn't hear any of it. Thought it was the best thing to happen around here since ESPN. I reckon most of us have got used to it by now. Big Bill's been dead for ten years, but the damn clock is still up there, clangin' away every hour of the day."

Josie turned off the "Open" sign on the front door, then busied herself clearing tables, but Killian knew she was listening. He'd told her some about Ezra Magee and his daddy, of course, but everyone in Sand Mountain County knew the story of the Magee family and its sole survivor who had disappeared into the mountains of West Virginia and was never heard from again. She continued to glance at Ezra as she tidied up, as if she were afraid he'd turn to dust when she looked away.

Looking at Ezra, Killian suddenly wondered if he had named the bar for Simp Magee not just for sentimental reasons, but also with the hope that Ezra would come home one day and find it. He thought of the framed picture of himself and Simp by his bedside and smiled at the similarity between Simp and his son.

"Your daddy and I had our first drinks here when we were just boys," Killian said. "Used to be called 'The Tavern' back then. Wasn't as fancy as this," he gestured toward the pool tables and the stained-glass fixtures over the booths. "Buford men didn't complain so long as there was beer, and it was lukewarm or better."

"My dad didn't like beer," Ezra said, remembering. "He drank bourbon. Any kinda whiskey."

"That's right," Killian agreed. "And he'd get piss drunk on one shot and start swearing and speechifying." Killian started laughing. "I'd make him drink three more just to get him to pass out and shut up!"

Killian's laugh turned into a cough. Josie hurried over with a glass of water. He drank it down and caught his breath, assuring her with a look that he was fine.

"Many a night I carried your daddy home while he cussed me

and all the gods in the sky. I'd be ready to dump him on the side of the road, and then he'd suddenly start talkin' about the purpose or meaning of life, or predictions about the future of agriculture on Mars, or why the South was lucky to lose the Civil War, and I'd change my mind."

Killian's words were like an elixir. And it seemed like Killian needed to talk about Simpellion Magee and the old days in Folly just as much as Ezra needed to hear it. He let Killian's reminiscences lead the way to memories he'd shoved in the dark places of his mental attic.

"Remember how he'd get when one of his letters was published in the *Sand Mountain Sentinel*?" Ezra asked.

Killian laughed. "When it came to writing letters to that newspaper, he was a man obsessed."

Ezra smiled and nodded.

"And that treehouse you and your cousins built—or thought you did. . . ." Killian stopped to catch his breath. He knew he was talking too much, something he almost never did, even before the lung trouble, but he was excited now. Ezra had come home, and Killian had so much to tell him.

Ezra frowned. "What do you mean 'thought you did'?"

"I'll tell you about it in a little while. Just let me get my breath," Killian said, looking down at the floor to concentrate on his breathing.

Ezra closed his eyes and let returning memories caress him. He could see his mother's frown of concentration when she was painting. He could picture the way she'd look up from sketching and not recognize Ezra for a moment, because she still had a feather or a flower petal emblazoned in her vision. Ezra could see her hanging wash on the line on a bright summer day, stopping suddenly to study a bee that had landed on the basket, then abandoning the laundry to rush inside to get her sketch pad to capture it in that perfect light. He remembered the smell of cigarettes and murmur of conversation drifting up to his window on soft summer nights, when his parents sat out on the porch after he'd gone to bed. Ezra remembered being small and sitting in his mother's lap, feeling perfectly safe. His chest tightened, and each breath labored as the images of his mother sprung up, one by one, from the once-empty garden of his memory.

"You've been missed, Ezra," Killian said. "I wish you'd come sooner."

The unasked question hung in the air: Why had it taken so long for Ezra to return to Folly?

"Dad, we gotta get you home." Josie was standing by the door with keys dangling from her hands.

"I'm tired," Killian admitted. He needed to take his medication and maybe suck some oxygen out of the tank by his bed. But he didn't want to leave Ezra—not when he'd just gotten Simp's boy back.

Killian put his hand on Ezra's shoulder and smiled. "You look like a horse that's been rode hard and put up wet," he said. "I can't let you stay at the Hidey Hole. It's a dump. You'll stay with me and Josie."

Ezra was grateful for the invitation. He went across the road to the town's only motel and checked out, then followed Josie's truck back to Folly. Even in the dark, Ezra knew the roads. It was as if he could feel them in his brain.

Killian's cabin had been replaced by a real house now. Inside, there was a modern kitchen and signs that a woman lived there: a vase of wild daisies on the table, curtains on the windows. Ezra wondered where Josie's mother was.

They gave him a spare room upstairs with a pull-out sofa. Killian had a bedroom set up on the first floor so he wouldn't have to negotiate the stairs. Ezra was still wide awake when he heard Josie come upstairs and get ready for bed. Her room was right next to his. He felt guilty, listening to her rustle around, probably taking clothes off. He tried not to imagine her unbuttoning her blouse and removing her bra. It had been months since he'd slept with his wife, and he felt the familiar ache. He reminded himself that he was a married man, and this was Killian's daughter.

He was exhausted, but he felt far from sleep. He crept downstairs to get a glass of water and found Killian wide awake in his recliner.

"Old men don't sleep much," Killian explained. "And your bein' here gives me plenty to think about."

"Me, too," Ezra said. "I was just remembering the time I got saved at a revival."

"I remember that," Killian said. "Your daddy went nuts. He got drunk a few nights later and got into a fistfight with old Hiram Johnson."

Ezra felt the hairs on his arms stand up. "Hiram Johnson. Whatever happened to him?"

"Cirrhosis of the liver got him back in 1976. Didn't tell nobody he was sick. Just faded away and died in his motel room one day."

CHAPTER 24

In his dream, Ezra tried to tell Celia something important, but she couldn't hear him. He was getting ready to shout when he woke up.

The sun was already up in the sky. Erza rolled back the blanket, swung his legs off the side of the bed, and sat for a moment. Aromas of coffee and bacon were coming from the kitchen downstairs, and his stomach growled in response. As he pushed up off the bed and stood up, he luxuriated in the feeling of sobriety. It had been three and a half weeks since he'd last had a drink. His body was free of the craving, but his mind still wanted to reach for the bottle. He was truly grateful not to have one at hand.

He put on his running clothes and went downstairs, self-conscious about the possibility of seeing Josie after his thoughts of her the night before. Thankfully, she was gone. Killian was awake, sitting in a chair in his kitchen wearing a baseball cap and reading a newspaper. When Ezra walked in, Killian got a big grin on his face. He told Ezra he'd prepare more breakfast when Ezra returned from his run.

Ezra went outside and limbered up. Running wasn't easy at first, but his muscles remembered and warmed, and he soon settled into a good rhythm.

The morning was sticky with humidity, and the temperature was rising. Ezra found his pace and watched the undulations in the road to make sure he didn't twist an ankle. Every so often he looked up to marvel at the tall beech trees and the dripping kudzu vine. Black-eyed Susan and Queen Anne's lace lined the sides of the road. Flies followed him for a few steps and then gave up. Ezra purposely avoided the road to Granmaude's house and the one leading to his old place. He ran on a back road that skirted overgrown pastures and woods. When he judged he'd gone about three miles, he turned back and considered his own cowardice. After everything, he still wasn't ready to face Folly.

When Ezra got back to the house, Killian had already eaten and let Ezra serve himself. The old man sat in a padded chair in the kitchen, a plastic tube snaking back to his oxygen tank in the living room.

"You smoke?" he asked Ezra.

"Not anymore," Ezra said honestly.

"You miss it?"

"Like the mischief."

Killian smiled. "I'd know you were lying if you said you didn't. I miss it every day. Hardest thing I ever did was to give it up. It was back in 1988. Josie had asthma. Doc said the smoke was hurting her. But I got lung disease anyway." He gestured to the oxygen.

Ezra had a thousand questions waiting at the tip of his tongue, but he let Killian take the lead. Killian told him about Josie's mother. He'd met her right after the disaster. She was a nurse in Buford, and she stitched up a bad cut Killian had gotten while clearing timber off the road after the storm. Somehow, he had found himself telling her the story of the loss of his friends, and she'd comforted him in his grief.

"Her name was Desirée," Killian told him. Her mama had been part Chinese, a product of the importation of Chinese workers to build the first transcontinental railroad. Her great grandfather had been one of those workers.

She was a Chinese-American with a French name. "A beautiful woman with a beautiful name," Killian said. She'd soon made her way into his heart and into his bed, and that was the beginning of Josie. "Best thing that ever happened to me," Killian admitted, smiling and showing Ezra a picture of himself and a pretty young woman who looked a lot like Josie, holding a baby.

"We were happy," Killian said. He took a labored breath in and sighed it back out. "Then Josie came, and money was tight. Desirée may have regretted marrying a man with so few prospects. She left me twice, came back both times." He shook his head sadly. "And then she got cancer when Josie was nine years old. It all happened fast. Desirée died four months after surgery. It had already spread to her liver." Killian frowned at the picture. "After that, it was just me and Josie."

It was strange to think of Killian as a father. "I used to think you were an old man, when I was a boy," Ezra blurted out.

Killian nodded. "Probably was. Forties are old to a young boy."

"Were you older than my father by much?"

"By five years, I reckon. But I was old enough to remember when he was born. Your daddy . . . he was somethin'." Killian smiled at Ezra. "He used to try to follow me around, and when he got to be big enough, I let him. He always had plenty to say, and he was smart as a whip. Before he went off to war, we did just about everything together. Then he came back with Trudy. I asked her what was wrong with her, fallin' for a rake like Simp. She just laughed. Your mama was a fine woman. Simp always said she was the best thing that ever happened to him. And I reckon she was."

"I remember," Ezra said softly. "He called her his good luck charm."

"I miss him, the old fool. Him and his speechifying."

"I remember thinking of you as being really quiet," Ezra said, quickly adding, "but wise."

Killian laughed, and it turned into a cough. When he caught his breath again, he looked out the window and smiled. "'Course, anyone who spent time around Simp would seem real quiet," he said. "He never gave a body a chance to get a word in edgewise!" Killian turned his gaze on Ezra. His smile faded. "I thought you'd come sooner."

It sounded like an accusation. Ezra nearly crumbled under the weight of his guilt. He looked at the ground, away from the old man's stare. "I'm sorry I didn't, Killian. You know, I just opened that box you sent. Five days ago." Then he told Killian everything—about the box, about his son's behavior that had led him to it.

"I'm real sorry 'bout your boy," Killian said when Ezra was finished. "I'm sorry you've been so hard on yourself. But you gotta know: what happened to your parents, that . . . that wasn't your fault. There was nothin' you did, and nothin' you coulda done to stop that storm. Runnin' out of Granmaude's house like that . . . it saved your life." Ezra remembered his run from Grandmaude's house, stopping at the top of the hill and seeing the wall of water rage toward her house. He knew Killian was right; there was nothing he could have done to save them. The sorrow that he felt anew was softened by this awareness.

The conversation continued until Ezra became aware that the sun had begun its descent toward the western horizon. He fixed Killian lunch and ate a sandwich himself, even though he wasn't hungry.

"I tried to call you before I came down, you know," Ezra said between bites, "at that telephone number you wrote in your letter. But it wasn't in service, and there were no Cagles listed anywhere. That's why I decided to fly down and look. Why no telephone number?"

"We have a private number," Killian answered, "it's not given out. Anybody wants to call us calls the bar. Too many junk calls."

Ezra nodded.

"So, what about you and Celia?" Killian asked.

"I don't know," Ezra answered bleakly. "I hope she'll have me back, but this thing with Dillon—"

"Not your fault," Killian interrupted firmly.

"But—"

"They never wanted you to know about your Uncle Nate," Killian said.

That name again. Ezra felt goosebumps on his arms. "Why didn't anyone talk about him?"

"It upset your grandmother too much, so no one could bring him up. Then it got to be a habit. We just didn't talk about poor ol' Nate. But it's time you heard." He set his sandwich plate on the side table and sat up straighter. He took a shaky breath in and out. "There's a lotta secrets I been keepin' 'bout the Magee clan. You're the last one I know. Guess I was keepin' 'em for you."

Ezra settled back in his chair and sipped a soda as Killian took a long breath from his oxygen tank.

"Nate was small and quiet," Killian began. "He tried to please everyone, especially his father. He wasn't like most boys. Didn't like to fight or hunt. Granmaude wanted him to become a priest. When Nate was eleven or twelve years old, he started acting real strange. Wouldn't leave the house, or if he did, he'd do all kinda odd things like counting and stamping his feet a certain way."

Ezra caught his breath. The Magee Curse. It suddenly dawned upon him that he'd heard that phrase before, when he was just a boy. It all came rushing back: Ezra was at her house, walking up on the porch. Grandmaude had said it. He remembered the sad, inquisitive look on her face, as if she'd been trying to revive blocked memories. "He had it, too," she had said.

Killian was quiet for a time, a distant, unfocused look in his eye, and he almost shuddered when Ezra spoke.

"Killian, tell me about my Uncle Nate."

CHAPTER 25

Maude tried to intervene whenever Moses yelled at Nate for his odd behavior. "He can't help it!"

"The hell you say!" Moses Magee harrumphed. "No son of mine is gonna act like a goddamn sissy."

Nate cowered in his room, paralyzed by fear of some invisible terror. Even his father's threats wouldn't make him budge.

The only way Moses Magee knew how to handle a problem was to attack, just like he'd done in the war. He'd sighted down the barrel of his weapon at many an enemy soldier during the American military's campaign through Europe. He remembered the satisfaction of squeezing the trigger and watching his targets drop. Those were good times. There had been a mission to perform and a sense of accomplishment at the end of the day. No time for fear or pussyfooting around, looking for places to hide. Nate's enemy was his fear. He needed to hunt it down and kill it. Moses would see to it that he did.

One day, Moses found a baby squirrel and brought it into the house. He couldn't say whether he was going to make a pet or a meal out of that squirrel, but he put it in a small birdcage in the meantime. One day, the squirrel got out of its cage, and Nate picked it up to put it back. Just when they got to the cage, the squirrel bit Nate, who screamed. Simp and Killian came running and found Nate with a squirrel dangling from his hand and Nate's blood pouring out of its mouth.

From that time on, Nate developed an obsessive fear of squirrels. Moses dragged Nate into the woods with a shotgun and tried to make him shoot as many squirrels as he could.

"That's what you do when you got a problem!" Moses told him. "You shoot the goddamn thing and get rid of it!"

But it didn't work for Nate. Day after day, Moses dragged him out into the woods, and day after day, Nate missed every shot. Nate hated hunting. He loved the story of St. Francis, who was kind to animals. Moses saw only weakness. He taunted his youngest son mercilessly, desperate to make a "real man" out of him.

One day, when Nate was thirteen, Moses caught three squirrels in a wire cage and kept them hidden in the barn. On a Saturday afternoon, while Maude was in town with Auggie, and Simp and Killian were off fishing, Moses dragged Nate into the barn and threw him into one of the seed bins. It was a small, four-by-six-foot crib. Then he threw the three squirrels into the bin with Nate and locked them all in together. The only light that seeped into the box came through two small cracks in the door.

Nate thrashed and screamed wildly. The terrified squirrels bit him over and over and over again. When Simp and Killian returned from fishing, they heard a noise in the barn. When they opened the door to the seed bin, three squirrels came whipping out, and Nate was passed out and covered in his own blood.

Simp lifted Nate from the bin and headed toward the barn doors, where Moses stood with his arms crossed and his wide body blocking the opening. Moses shouted at Simp to quit babying Nate and let him learn to be a man. Simp pushed past Moses and carried his brother to Killian's truck.

"You mind me, goddammit!" Moses yelled after them. "I told you to leave him be!"

Simp handed Nate to Killian and marched back to his father. Simp was as tall as Moses, but much scrawnier. As soon as Simp was in front of his father, Moses backhanded Simp, the force of his strike slamming him up against the side of the barn.

Simp stood up straight, wiped the blood from his mouth, and

got right up in his daddy's face. "You ever do anything like that again to my brother, old man, I'll kill you."

Moses just laughed, spat on the ground, and walked back into the house.

॰ॐ

A few weeks later, Simp came home to find his mother collapsed on the front porch, sobbing hysterically. A dark crimson stain trailed up the steps and across the porch to the front door.

"Mama, what in the hell is goin' on?"

"He's dead! He's dead! Oh, God, he's dead!"

Simp ran into the living room and stumbled over his father's feet. Moses was on his knees, turned away from Simp. The right shoulder of Moses's hunting jacket was a deep crimson. Nate lay face up on the floor in front of him, eyes open in a fixed, vacant stare. Moses was kneeling over the boy, his hand pressed against Nate's stomach. Blood was caked and drying between Moses's fingers.

Simp jerked his father away from Nate's body. "Get off him, you bastard! What did you do?"

Moses stared up at Simp, his eyes wide and red. "The gun," his father said. "It was an accident, I swear it!"

"You killed him, you son of a bitch!" Simp could smell the whiskey sweating through his father's pores.

His father moaned. "An accident . . . he fell . . . I didn't mean . . . God help me, it was an accident!" He tried to put his hand on Nate again, but Simp kicked him away.

Simp knelt down and cradled his brother's limp form in his arms and cried. Killian ran in a few minutes later, took in the sight, and called the sheriff.

When he finally arrived, the sheriff's deputy tried to pry Nate from Simp's arms, but finally gave up and let Simp carry his brother out to the ambulance on his own. Once the ambulance drove off,

Simp couldn't comfort himself, let alone his mother. He headed away down the road, walked into the woods that followed Cahill Creek toward the river, and disappeared.

Killian went out every day searching for him. He finally found Simpellion a week later, in one of their old hunting camps. He was curled up on the ground, starving and hollow with grief. Killian took him back to his cabin, cleaned him up and fed him, and then drove him to Nate's funeral.

"Where have you been, boy?" Moses demanded when Simp walked into the house. Simp ignored his father and walked into the kitchen, hugged his mother, and nodded to his brother Auggie.

"Don't walk away from me like that!" Moses shouted after his son.

"Don't you dare, Moses!" Maude gave him a look of thunder, and Moses seemed to deflate, the anger flushing out of him like air from a punctured tire.

CHAPTER 26

The hunting season was almost over, and the weather forecast was cold and sunny—perfect for hunting. Although it didn't really matter to Simp what the weather was. Ever since the funeral, he'd taken off every few days with his gun and a sleeping bag and disappeared into the woods. He never came back with any game. Whenever he came back, he was silent and withdrawn, keeping to his room or, more often than not, staying with Killian in his cabin.

Simp would have left home after Nate died, but he worried about his mother. Auggie was useless. He worked at the auto body shop and stayed out all night with his friends. Moses stayed out three or four nights a week too, showing up at home with no explanation and no apology for disappearing. Simp knew the rumors that his father had a mistress in Buford, and he despised his father even more for disrespecting his mother. When Moses did come home, his sweat always reeked of whiskey. His job as a construction foreman at a nuclear power plant site kept him sober for four days each week, but he used his three-day weekend to catch up on a week's worth of drinking.

Simp and Moses were like two bull elephants taking the measure of each other. They knew they were eventually going to charge each other; they just didn't know when.

The day Simp came home and announced that he'd transferred from Saint John's to Buford Public High School, Moses went ballistic. It was his mother who stopped that fight. She asked Simp why he didn't want to go to Catholic school, and he said he'd read Bertrand Russell's *Why I Am Not a Christian* and had thought the man made a lot of sense.

"Besides," he told his mama, his voice quieter now, "why would anyone want to worship a god who let Nate die like he did?"

Maude cried, but she left Simp alone.

That night, Moses came home drunk and took a swing at Simp with a fire poker. Granmaude called Killian to come and take Simp out of the house before more violence was done.

Since Nate's death, hunting for squirrels had become an obsession for Simpellion. The morning after the fire poker incident, Simp and Killian stopped back home to pick up his gun. Moses intercepted them as they were leaving through the front door.

"Where you goin'?" Moses stood on the front porch, between the doorway and the front steps. His eyes were bloodshot, and his hands were clenched into fists. Killian edged between the two Magees and pushed Simp past Moses and down the porch steps.

But once he was out on the front lawn, Simp turned back toward his daddy, dropped a shell into his gun, and snapped it shut. "What's it matter to you?" he asked. He held the gun down, but all of them were aware that it was loaded. "Where you been the past three nights?"

"Whas'it matter to you?" Moses asked, mocking Simp.

"It don't," Simp said flatly. "You already done enough damage. It'd be better for everyone if you stayed gone."

Moses glowered at him. "Why'nt you go ahead and say it then, you little shithead."

"You're drunk, as usual," Simp told him. "And you and me both know what you did to Nate. Someday, you'll get yours, old man."

༄

Simp and Killian got to their favorite hunting spot at about ten that morning. It was where Cahill Creek emptied into the Tennessee River. It had an abundance of hickory trees and therefore an abundance of squirrels and other small game. They were cooking a fresh-caught catfish over some coals when a shotgun blast shattered the calm.

Moses strode out from behind a bush with his twelve-gauge shotgun slung over his shoulder and a dead squirrel dangling by its tail from his hand. He said nothing as he approached, twirling the dead squirrel in his right hand.

"You got nothin' better to do than follow us around?" Simp asked him, disgusted.

Moses stopped a few feet away from them and dropped the squirrel to the ground. He took the gun off his shoulder and nestled it in the crook of his left arm, the barrel pointing in Simp's general direction. He stared at his son.

"You're a smartass," Moses said to Simp. "A goddamn smartass boy who's got no respect!"

Simp folded his arms and glared at his father.

"Down here with this goddamn queer," Moses gestured to Killian. "You boys are huntin'? I don't think so! Suckin' dicks is more like it. Goddamn queers!"

In one swift movement Simp jumped up and lunged at his daddy, and Killian made a grab for Simp to try to stop him. Moses dropped the barrel of his gun into his left hand, but Simp got his hand on it just in time to push it away as Moses fired.

The pellets struck Killian in his left knee, and he tumbled backward on the ground, screaming. Then he fell silent, succumbing to the darkness of unconsciousness from the pain.

When Killian came to, his leg was wrapped in Simp's bandana. Simpellion was holding his own shotgun and standing on the shore, looking out over the river. Moses was floating downriver on his back, bobbing along away from shore. Simp stood peacefully and watched him go.

The air was warm and the humidity rising, but Ezra and Killian had settled comfortably into a couple of rocking chairs on the front porch.

"Did my daddy kill his father?"

The old man took a deep breath of oxygen from his tank. "He might have, but I didn't see it. When I blacked out, they were both still standing. I believe Moses woulda killed Simp if Simp hadn't gotten his hands on the gun. The man was drunk and mean, and he and Simp together were a death waitin' to happen."

Killian shifted his weight in the rocker, and Ezra noted the look of pain on the man's face. "So that's what happened to your leg! Moses shot you."

"Funny, ain't it," Killian said, "how some things never seem to go away? This here," he said, pointing to his knee, "is something I'll carry with me to my grave."

"Do you think Moses killed Nate?"

Killian was silent for a moment, gazing up to the left as he considered the question. "I reckon he might have done it accidentally. He was a violent man. Settled things with his fists. And he couldn't change Nate by beatin' him up. That frustrated him bad and made him meaner than he already was. Sober, I don't think he had it in him to kill Nate. Drunk, I don't know. I think maybe he could have done it."

Ezra let that sink in. He couldn't imagine the horror of killing his own son.

"What happened after Moses floated away?"

"Your daddy took me to the hospital where I got patched up, and we never said nothin' to nobody 'bout what happened. You are the very first person I've ever told this to, and I doubt your daddy told anyone, either. Granmaude seemed more relieved than worried when Moses didn't come home. The sheriff found Moses's shotgun in the river, but he gave up lookin' for the body after a couple of months. Everybody figured Moses got drunk one too many times and drowned. Granmaude held a memorial for Moses that fall. I remember your daddy refused to go. I went, to support your grandmother. Father O'Malley said some things during the service. It was clear he assumed the worst of Simp."

Hearing the name of Father O'Malley after so many years caused a shiver to pass through Ezra.

"Father O'Malley," Ezra said slowly. "I remember that guy. The students called him 'Go to Hell O'Malley.' He once said my OCD had something to do with the sins of my father, and I had no idea what he meant."

"After Moses disappeared, O'Malley seemed to get older and meaner overnight," Killian said. "He and Moses had been good friends—best friends, I'd say, as much as either of them could be friendly. The two of them would get piss-drunk every Sunday after O'Malley ate supper with your family, and they would rant about communists and atheists, especially after Hoover and McCarthy started their crusade."

Ezra laughed, not at what Killian had just said, but at what it made him realize. "So, my dad grew up to be the infamous commie-sympathizing atheist of Sand Mountain," Ezra said.

"Now you get it," Killian said, nodding.

The afternoon passed quietly as Ezra and Killian sat out on the porch and watched gray clouds move in and blot out the sun.

Squirrels and atheists. Ezra thought about his father. He'd been a complicated man. Fiercely loyal, angry, unafraid, foolish. But he also remembered his father's strong arms holding him at night when he'd had nightmares. He remembered his father's confidence in him, telling Ezra that one day he'd overcome his OCD and play ball for the Crimson Tide if that's what he wanted to do. Whatever he'd done, whoever he'd been, Ezra knew that

Simpellion T. Dillon Magee had loved him unconditionally.

"Whatever became of Father O'Malley?" Ezra asked.

"He died a long time back," Killian said. "It was a few years after the storm. Somebody found his body in a motel room in Huntsville, where he was attending a conference. The police said he was beat to death. I never liked the man, but that was surely a rough way to go. The police snooped around for a long time, but never came up with a suspect."

Ezra nodded thoughtfully, but he had one more question. "I'm pretty sure my dad got some sort of military pension. For disability, right? What the heck was his injury?"

Killian sighed. "It wasn't no injury," he said. Then he smiled. "At least not a physical one."

Ezra waited on him to explain.

"You see, things went a bit sideways for your daddy in Korea. No surprise, that. Not much room in the military for an anarchist. But at the time he needed an out, and the Army obliged him." Killian massaged his knee and shifted a bit in his seat. "Anyways, he and his unit were ordered to do something downright nasty and bloody with a lot of civilians involved, but Simp would have none of it. He led a mutiny that saved quite a few lives, friendlies and not-so-friendlies. And one of those friendlies was a general's son." Killian paused. "In the end, your daddy had to make a choice between a Section 8 or a court martial. He chose the court martial, but they gave him the Section 8. That's the Army for you. Now, that should have prevented him getting a VA disability pension, but someone put in a fix—that general whose son your daddy had saved. Still, I'm not for sure what they said his disability was. The best I can figure is he gave a damn."

# CHAPTER 27

Ezra woke up early the next morning and let himself out of Killian's house quietly. No one stirred. The day was dawning hot and humid, with a strong, southwesterly wind that pushed young saplings over into a stooped attitude of supplication. Ezra took off running, watching the clouds scud across the sky. By the time he got back from his run—winded, but high on endorphins—Killian was up and dressed. He suggested that Ezra might like to sample the world-famous biscuits and gravy at Aunt Edna's Diner, just outside of Buford.

After a feast of eggs, country ham, and cat head biscuits with gravy, Ezra went up to the register to pay the bill. He couldn't remember the place from his childhood and asked the counter man if Aunt Edna was still around. Fixing Ezra with a cross-eyed stare, the fellow replied: "Hell, she's been dead fo' years, I reckon."

Dead. The word made Ezra's skin crawl. They were all dead, all of his kin, every single Magee except himself and Dillon. Even the owner of this nice diner. The weight of all that loss left Ezra breathless for a moment.

After breakfast, Killian and Ezra headed toward Folly. Ezra figured he was as ready as he would ever be to see it up close again.

"The flood left a terrible mess," Killian told Ezra. "The National Guard was called down to help. Folly was a disaster. They had to widen Route 11 to get a crane in here to lift the cars and whatnot onto flatbed trucks to carry most everything to the dump. I went up to your place. It was still standin' after the storm, but barely. The roof was pulled off and everything inside got washed away. I dug around in the mud some, but I couldn't find nothin' to salvage. Then I looked up in a tree. That picture I sent you, your mama's jewelry box—I found that in the old magnolia at the side of the house. The books of hers I had at my place."

Approaching the juncture where the main road circumvented Folly, Killian pointed out the rotting hulk of a cotton gin where the "Welcome to Folly, Pop. 35" sign used to be.

"Remember right over the Folly sign, high up on that tree, someone stuck a big sign that said, 'Jesus is coming'?" Killian laughed. "It always stuck in your daddy's craw."

"Maybe that's why it was always full of bullet holes," Ezra replied, and was rewarded with another laugh.

Ezra crossed into Folly with laughter in his ears and an old friend at his side. He surveyed the desolate landscape with sadness, but not grief. The throw of the cosmic dice had made this bedraggled village on the outer fringes of civilization his native soil. Kudzu vines had taken over the structures that had been his Uncle Auggie's place. They created giant topiaries in their aggressive climb over the trees, remnants of fences, barns, and sheds—anything providing a scaffold on which to climb. Ezra noticed the hood of a rusted truck peeking out from under the strangling green vines near the foundation where a house once stood.

☙

When Killian pointed out the roadway leading down to Granmaude's homestead, Ezra stopped the car and got out. He looked down the road at the remnants of the devastation. He could see a rectangle of foundation stones covered over with weeds and bushes, and off to the side he recognized the old well casing and a large oak tree that had survived the flood. Everything else was gone.

"Not much left," said Killian, climbing out of the car and looking out across the yard. "I could barely walk, but when I got here, there was nothin' left. Water was everywhere. I couldn't believe it. I started searchin', callin' people's names. I couldn't go down there," he said, pointing to what remained of the foundation of Granmaude's house, "because the water was still too high. I knew no one coulda survived, but I had to look. When I turned around to leave, my flashlight caught something white up yonder in that tree up there." He pointed to a giant double-boled oak in a copse of woods near to the top of the hill. "It was your white shirt. You were in the tree. Somehow . . ." He shook his head at the memory and looked over at Ezra. "That tree saved your life. You woulda been washed away in the flood."

Ezra crossed his arms and stared at the ground. "That's a memory I don't have. Not sure I want it, really." Then he surveyed the overgrown skeleton of Granmaude's home and it hit him. "This is where they all died."

"It's all right, boy." Killian put an arm around his best friend's son. "It'll be all right. This is where they died," he said softly. "And this is where you *lived*. This is where your life was spared."

Memories came back to Ezra, hazy but charged with emotion. The blue of his mother's blouse; the far-away images of his mom and dad standing on the porch looking for him in the storm; his father gathering his wife into his arms as the wave towered over them . . . and Ezra running from the house screaming, "I hate you!"

Even in the heat, Ezra shivered. "I told my dad I hated him," he said. "Twice I said it—yelled it at him. Just before he died."

"Aw, don't you worry 'bout that, Ezra." Killian's sad eyes crinkled into the semblance of a smile. "You was just a kid. Plenty of times when she was a girl, Josie told me she hated me. I didn't take it serious. Your daddy knew you loved him. Hell, Simp had a skin thicker'n a crocodile! What you said wouldn'a bothered him at all."

There was no atonement, but Killian's words of forgiveness pushed him over the edge. Ezra put his face in his hands and wept.

☙

"It's time to go home," he told Killian about half an hour later, after he'd recovered some. "I need to see it."

They turned off the road and drove up a graveled driveway that meandered through an overgrown field. Clumps of dead and dying bitter weeds and crabgrass clawed at the tires. He stopped in front of the old house, and they sat for a moment, observing the ravages of weather and time. The house sat in the middle of a thirty-five-acre plot of land, with two crepe myrtle bushes, grown to the size of scrubby trees, leaning against each side of the porch. Branches from a sweetbay magnolia raked against the side of the house.

It was just the husk of a house. The doors, roof, and windows were long gone. Weeds had grown up around the foundation. Crushed beer cans and used condoms were scattered about. A tattered sleeping bag had been tossed into the bushes. Ezra felt sad. This was the place where his parents had loved him and loved each other. Some of the memories that had come flooding back about his family and home were happy ones.

The realization was bittersweet and startling. It was a new perspective on his past that had eluded him all of these years, yet he knew it was true. Until the OCD and the storm, he'd been happy, but he hadn't appreciated that.

Ezra spent thirty minutes walking around the back pasture. It still smelled like home—a certain green and humid tang. He recognized some of the wildflowers along the roadway that his mother used to sketch: the prairie foxglove, the lemon bee balm, and the goldenseal. The contours of the hills were as familiar to him as his own face. It surprised him. He'd never felt he was from somewhere, but he'd been wrong. He was from right here.

Killian was sitting in the car looking like a man at peace with the world and in no hurry. Ezra joined him but made no move to start the engine.

"There's a name I recall," Ezra said, and hesitated before speaking it: "Sissy Namey?"

"You remember her?" Killian asked, genuinely surprised.

"Yes, I remember her," Ezra said thoughtfully.

"I spent some time around her. I liked her. If I'd gotten ahold of a nerve, I might have asked her out on a date," Killian admitted.

Ezra was dumbfounded. "Sissy *Namey*? The crazy lady?"

"She did okay most of the time, when she took her pills," Killian explained, "but her mother used to hide 'em from her, and once she got off 'em, Sissy was no good to herself or anyone else."

"Wait—her mother hid her medicine?"

"She was a nasty piece a work, that woman. Didn't want her baby leavin' home. Needed someone to pick on and harass all the time, and Sissy obliged. I guess dysfunction has its own peculiar logic."

Ezra shook his head. Sometimes, nothing was as it seemed. Sissy Namey had been a girl, a woman, not just the hagridden creature burned in his memory. He thought of what might have happened had his parents and Aunt Lenore not been there for him when he most needed them.

"You ready to head back?" Killian asked.

"Hey," Ezra said, gesturing toward a large oak standing back from the house, "there's my old treehouse!" A few timbers of the structure poked through the foliage. "My God, Killian, I built that with Boyd and Floyd! I can't believe it's still here."

Killian chuckled. "After you boys built it, yer daddy and I rebuilt it for you in the dead of night. Didn't want to hurt your pride, but you boys put it together with six nails and some chewing gum! We reinforced it with steel brackets. I reckon we did a pretty good job. I'll bet you never knew your daddy fell through the floor of that thing while we were workin' on it and nearly broke his neck!"

"I'm going to climb up and take a look," Ezra said, delighted.

"You be careful, now," Killian warned.

"I will," Ezra called back.

At the base of the tree, he gazed up at the wonder of the boy-sized tree fort that was still perched there after all these years. It looked to be about fifteen feet above the ground, and he recalled his mother complaining to her husband, "Simpellion, those boys are going to fall and break something that can't be fixed!" and his father laughing and telling her it was a boy's prerogative to do foolish things. The ladder he and his cousins had built to climb up was gone, and after assessing his options, Ezra reckoned he could grab onto a lower branch and swing himself up. Fortunately, the water oak sprouted a multitude of limbs, and with considerable effort, some swearing, and quite a few nicks in the palms of his hands, Ezra slowly climbed his way up the tree.

When he got to the treehouse, he looked down and waved at Killian, just in case the old man was watching. He caught his breath for a moment and then carefully pulled himself up through the opening. He was halfway through when he heard a timber split with a loud crack and felt the floor of the tree house lurch to the left.

He was trying to determine if the scream he heard was his own when he hit the ground.

CHAPTER 28

His nose itched. His whole head felt like it needed scratching. And what was that horrible smell? Chair legs scraped and the sound of feet on the tiled floor echoed across the room.

"He'll be comin' 'round pretty soon. The stuff's wearin' off." The voice came to him soft and fuzzy, as if through a long tunnel.

"Ezra?"

"Daddy? Can you hear me?"

"Where am I?" He struggled through the fog and opened his eyes. Celia was looking down at him. Her eyes were moist and beautiful, and words failed him.

"You're all right," she said, looking relieved.

He raised his hand to his head and felt a bandage encircling his forehead. A pain in his shoulder made him wince.

"You're in the hospital, Daddy."

"Dillon?"

"You fell out of a treehouse!"

"A treehouse?"

"You're going to be just fine," Celia assured him. He loved the sound of her voice and tried to ask a question to keep her talking, but his eyes kept closing.

He woke up for real the next day, alone in his hospital room. There were bandages on his shoulder and head, an ache in his ankle, and some scratches on his arms and face. He wondered if he'd only dreamed Celia and Dillon had been there.

"You're free to go," the doctor told him. "With a little TLC, you'll be as good as new."

Just as he was wondering if he had clothes or a car, Dillon flew in the door and threw his arms around Ezra's uninjured shoulder. "Dad, can we go see the treehouse?"

Ezra glanced at Celia. She looked drawn and anxious. She shook her head no.

"Absolutely not!" Ezra told his son, who groaned good-naturedly.

He didn't feel as good as new, but he was glad to get out of the hospital and away from the smell of alcohol and cleaning fluids and death. Dillon held his hand all the way to the parking lot and only released it, reluctantly, when they got into the car. To Ezra, the hot and humid Alabama air smelled welcoming and wonderful.

"Dillon, honey, run back in and get me a soft drink from the machine," Celia said, handing him a dollar.

As their son ran off, Celia turned to Ezra. "Ezra, whatever possessed you to climb up into that tree? Were you out of your mind?"

Ezra winced. She was talking about his drinking.

"Celia, it was an accident. I haven't had a drink in a month, I swear it."

"Haven't you put us through enough?" She crossed her arms and looked away.

"I'm glad you came down," Ezra said. "This isn't something I planned. But now that you're here, I hope we can talk."

"You want to talk?"

Ezra winced at the sarcasm in her voice. He knew he deserved it. "I have a lot to tell you, if you'll hear me," he said.

She didn't answer. Dillon came back with the soda, and his chatter filled the air while Celia drove back to Killian's house.

Josie insisted they all stay with her and Killian until Ezra was able to travel. Josie assumed Ezra and Celia would share a room, and neither wanted to apprise her of the situation. That night, Ezra offered to sleep on the floor.

"You've had a severe concussion, and you almost broke your shoulder," she told him. "Just get in."

She turned her back and went to sleep. Ezra stayed up for hours trying to think of the rights words to say to fix his dilemma. The woman he loved had hardened her heart toward him, and it was his fault.

The next day, Ezra was feeling better, and Dillon was eager to see the Magee family land. Killian took them in his truck, with Dillon ecstatic about getting to ride in the truck bed over the bumpy roads. Celia made pleasant conversation with Killian while Ezra stared at his hands.

The truck pulled up in front of the ruins of Granmaude's house. Dillon hopped down first and opened the door for his father. When Ezra got out, Dillon took his hand and tugged him toward the stone foundation.

Ezra squeezed Dillon's hand. "This was your great-grandmother's house."

Killian hobbled along behind them. He crouched down and pointed to what remained of the stone casing surrounding the old well. "That there was a well. Your great-granddaddy dug it himself, with a pick and shovel."

Dillon looked at Ezra to see if the old man was pulling his leg. Ezra smiled.

"What happened to everything?" Dillon asked.

"There was a big flood," Ezra said, sitting down heavily on the foundation. Dillon joined him, and Celia and Killian sat on a fallen log facing them.

"Where did all the water come from?" Dillon asked.

"There was a big lake just up that creek yonder," Killian said, pointing to Cahill Creek. "They called it Masterson Mill Lake. 'Bout three miles or so south of here. A man named Masterson dammed the creek and built a grist mill over a hundred years ago. Some fifty years later, the county built the dam higher, a lot higher. Made a big lake for fishin' and swimmin'. Even built a campground for campers. It was real popular. Your granddaddy and I used to go up there every once in a while during the summer to look at all the pretty girls." He smiled and patted Dillon on the shoulder when the boy made a face at the mention of girls. "The dam was nothin' but dirt. The lake was already full from a lotta rain upstream when the storm came. That storm dropped six more inches of rain in an hour. It was too much, and the dam broke."

"Did you see it?" Dillon asked enthusiastically.

"I saw it," Ezra said in a small voice. The others grew still. "I was up there on the hill. I'd run out of the house because . . . because I was mad at my daddy. I said some mean things to him and then I ran out into the biggest storm in Alabama history. And when I turned to look back, I . . . I saw my mama and daddy standing on the front porch, calling me to come back." He paused for a moment.

"What happened?" Dillon whispered, holding Ezra's hand.

"I saw a wave—a big wave, like a tsunami—heading for them. It was taller than the house. I tried to say—" The words caught in Ezra's throat. "I tried to warn them, but I was too far away, and the thunder and lightning and rain were too loud." Tears ran down his face. "I saw my daddy look up just as the wave hit the back of the house. He pulled my mama into his arms. And then they were gone. Everyone was gone. I ran toward my house because the water was coming for me, and then it hit me and I started to drown, and then something caught me, and I—" Ezra gasped at the memory. "I started to climb." His jumbled emotions took over, and he turned away to hide the tears.

"Shhh, shhh," Celia murmured and sat next to him to put her arms around him. "It's okay, honey. It's okay."

*

Later, they walked up the hill to see the tree that saved Ezra's life.

Killian stayed below in the shade. Ezra and Celia walked side by side, their hands almost touching.

"Tell me about my grandpa," Dillon demanded. "Did he like soccer?"

"Tell me about your mom and dad," Celia pleaded, sounding just like Dillon. They sat near a patch of wild foxglove.

"I had a good family," he said, thoughtfully. "My mother and father loved me. They loved each other too. We were happy." His voice had a touch of wonderment in it, and Celia watched him with her steady gaze. "My father was unconventional, loud, and obnoxious. I don't think he played soccer, but he liked to swear."

"Cool!" Dillon said approvingly, and Celia gave him a playful swat on the head.

"But he was also kind and loyal, and he gave a damn. My mother—she was an extraordinary woman and an artist. She had her own work, and she didn't hover over me. Kind of like how you are with Dillon," he said to Celia. "Our family is a lot like the family I grew up in, I guess."

He faltered here, and Celia just nodded that she understood. He took a deep breath and continued. "Right before the storm, I was starting to become a teenager, and I was embarrassed by my parents. Especially my father—he was such an oddball. I couldn't see that he was special, even courageous. He wasn't perfect, but he thought about things. He cared about things. The world didn't quite fit him, but in Folly, he was just a local character. But as a boy . . . you know what I mean? I wanted someone normal. And on the day of the storm, I . . . I said some things I regret."

"What did you say?" Dillon asked, plucking a blade of grass.

"I told my dad I hated him."

Dillon furrowed his brow and tilted his head, thinking. "I betcha he knew you really loved him," he said. "He was your daddy. He just knew, right?"

Ezra smiled. "You're probably right," he said. "But for a long,

long time I felt so guilty about it that I didn't let myself remember." He didn't feel ashamed when the tears started up again. He wiped them away with the back of his hand. He knew that it was just feelings, just tears, just regret, and they all came from love.

In a quiet voice, he told them what he'd lost that day: the people who knew and accepted him; the love his family had for him; his whole world, all gone in a moment that he'd had the life-saving misfortune to witness. By the time he finished, they were all wiping away tears.

"There's more," Ezra said after he could speak again. "It's about how I've been acting the last few months." He turned to Dillon, who turned away and put his head down, pretending to retie his sneaker lace. "I owe you both an apology for the way I behaved. I am ashamed of myself."

"It's because of me," Dillon mumbled.

"No!" Ezra took Dillon's face in his hands and made him look in his eyes. "It was not because of you. It was only because of me, okay?"

Dillon nodded, and Ezra let go of him. Dillon continued to watch his father. "Son, I told you I had OCD when I was a boy your age, you remember?" Dillon nodded. "Well, at first I felt like it was my fault when you started getting the symptoms, because you inherited it from me. Your mom set me straight about that," he looked at Celia, who was watching him closely. "But right after you started taking the medicine, something happened to me. My own symptoms started to come back. I started having panic attacks. And I didn't want you or your mom to know, because I was ashamed."

Quiet followed his confession. He heard crickets in the grass and the sound of Dillon breaking a twig into little pieces.

"You said I shouldn't be ashamed," Dillon said in a small voice, "when it happened to me."

"That's right. And I shouldn't have been ashamed either, except for not telling your mom. But I was ashamed. I felt out of control and scared, and I should have talked about it and gotten help. Instead, I drank booze. And it was the wrong choice. And I am sorry for the pain I've caused you and your mom."

"Do you still have the panic attacks?" Celia asked. It was the first time she'd spoken in a long while.

"Not since I made the decision to come back to Folly," he said, turning to her, "and I called a counselor at a mental health clinic in Morgantown. I'm scheduled for an appointment with a clinician whose specialty is OCD."

She smiled at him, a bright, open smile that he remembered from times past, like the first rays of sun following a dark storm.

"Dad, I forgive you," Dillon said, putting his hand out for a manly handshake. Ezra and Celia laughed, and they shook on it.

"I suppose I forgive you too," Celia said lightly. Ezra stuck his hand out, and she shook it, and then she held on firmly. The gesture gave him pause, and he looked into her eyes. He squeezed her hand, and she returned the pressure. Ezra felt a lightness of spirit he had thought he'd never feel again.

They walked higher up the hill to the oak tree, and Ezra told them Killian's story of his rescue. Dillon put his hand on the trunk and said, "Thanks, old son," and Ezra and Celia had another good laugh. Dillon tucked a lucky penny in its roots.

Over the crest of the hill, they came to the cluster of gravestones marking the Magee family cemetery. As they drew near, a squirrel leapt off a headstone and scaled a hickory sapling. The headstone read "Simpellion T. Dillon Magee 1934-1972." Ezra chuckled to himself and wondered if the squirrels were getting even with Simp even now.

The grave beside his dad's read "Trudy Clark Magee 1939-1972." Ezra, Celia, and Dillon picked wild daisies and laid them on the graves. Ezra paused at each gravestone and said the name out loud, and he told Dillon and Celia a little about what he remembered of each of his relatives. When he came to Floyd and Boyd's gravestones, Ezra had lots of stories about the two rapscallions and all the trouble they used to get him into.

As the sun moved overhead, they sat in the shade by his parents' graves, and Ezra talked. He told his wife and son about Aunt Lenore coming to get him after his parents' deaths, and about his painful teenage years in West Virginia, struggling with OCD and anxiety and not remembering his childhood or the trauma of losing everyone he loved. He described his joy flying airplanes and falling in love with Celia, and how exultant he'd felt the day Dillon was born.

"You've had a good life," Dillon said.

"Why, yes, I have," Ezra agreed.

"I mean, it had hard stuff, but if you hadn't gone through that, you wouldn't be you."

Ezra put his good arm around his son. "When did you get so wise?"

Before they headed back down, Ezra, Celia, and Dillon stood for another moment in front of his parents' graves.

"Mom, Dad, I'd like you to meet the most wonderful woman in the world. This is my wife, Celia, and I know you would love her as much as I do."

Celia gave him a kiss on the cheek.

"And this is Dillon. He's a true Magee," he said proudly. "You'd be proud of him. I know I am."

Ezra put his hand on each headstone and rubbed the back of his fingers across the top of the smooth granite. "Thanks, Mama. Thanks, Daddy. I love you. I couldn't have made it without you," he whispered.

They walked back over the hill, and Ezra felt the peace of Folly in his bones. Dillon looked thoughtful. "So, we're really the last Magees?"

"Yep! The future lies with us."

༼༽

It was already hot the next morning as they loaded the rental car in preparation to leave. Ezra took out his handkerchief, mopped his brow, and looked up into the morning sky. It was tinted a vaporous cerulean blue, a color more common in cooler weather. Maybe a cool front was on its way. He hoped the weather would hold until they landed in West Virginia; he knew Celia would hate it if the ride was rough. She had consented to fly back with them in the small plane, something she almost never did. It was a good sign.

Killian took Ezra aside and said, "I've got something to show you." Dillon tagged along as they walked behind the house, passed the barn, and finally came to a small corral near the woods. Standing in the center was a small, black goat. Its coat was shiny, and its eyes were large, amber orbs.

"This here's Tiberius," Killian said. "Tiberius, say hello to the folks."

The goat responded with a rude snort and a fake charge.

Dillon grinned and crawled up on the wooden structure of the corral, partially blocking Ezra's view.

"Tiberius?" Ezra asked.

"Your daddy's other middle name, the 'T' in Simpellion T. Dillon Magee," Killian replied.

"Funny, I never knew what the T stood for," Ezra said.

Killian laughed. "Not terribly surprising. It was a name he shared with his own daddy, Moses Tiberius Magee."

"If I have a little brother, you can name him Tiberius," Dillon suggested.

The goat snorted again and pawed the ground with a front hoof. "Watch this," Killian said, and stepped up on the bottom board of the corral and put his arms over the top rail. The intemperate goat stared back at him. Killian clapped his hands loudly. The goat's body became rigid, its eyes glazed over, and it promptly fell over on its side.

Ezra's smile was as wide as Alabama.

About the Authors

Daniel "Seth" Holliday is an attorney in Dalton, Georgia. Most people who meet Seth come to know him as a father of two daughters, a prolific reader, a non-profit and charity supporter, and a former partaker in triathlons and marathons. Seth grew up on a small farm in Hillsboro, Alabama. Before going to law school, he was a hunting guide in Idaho and a simulations director and kid counselor for the U.S. Space & Rocket Center in Huntsville, Alabama. Working with mules and small children prepared him for the vagaries of law.

Daniel "Wayne" Holliday, Seth's father and coauthor of this book, is a retired jack-of-all-trades who lives in Decatur, Alabama. Wayne grew up in Lawrence County, Alabama, in a log cabin (no kiddin'). He left Alabama for the Air Force, which took him to Alaska, where he stared at green radar screens waiting for the Ruskies. Since no Ruskies showed up, Wayne then went to the University of West Virginia and became a history professor before eventually returning to Alabama to become a quality control inspector for the Unemployment Compensation Bureau of the State of Alabama. As a child, Seth was always frightened of the question, "What does your dad do?" He still doesn't quite know.

The Daniels like to go fishing on warm, sunny days and discuss the latest political inanity. The fish don't seem to mind.

CPSIA information can be obtained
at www.ICGtesting.com
Printed in the USA
LVHW111246101122
732762LV00005B/112